A DEATH IN
AND A REIGN OF TERROR.

The Camerons had little chance to dwell upon the tragedy, however, for within twenty-four hours, the terrorists began attacking other Europeans, exclusively those in outlying districts . . . On the morning of June 16, on a rubber estate a few miles east of Sungei Siput in the state of Perak, terrorists executed an estate manager named Walker, shooting him in the head and heart. Half an hour later, a dozen miles away, a manager called Allison and his young European assistant were bound to chairs and shot. In both instances cash in safes was left untouched and Malayan workers told:

"Our war is not with you unless you make it so. We're only out to kill the running dogs."

Strictly speaking money was not the purpose of the mutilation . . . Discipline was the object. Obey, or else.

POINT OF HONOR
by the bestselling author of
Circle of Deceit and
Seven Minutes Past Midnight

WALTER WINWARD

Walter Winward Books
From The Berkley Publishing Group

POINT OF HONOR

WALTER WINWARD

Previously published in hardcover as
Music of a Distant Drum

BERKLEY BOOKS, NEW YORK

Previously published in hardcover as *Music of a Distant Drum*.

This Berkley book contains the complete text
of the original hardcover edition. It has been
completely reset in a typeface designed for easy
reading and was printed from new film.

POINT OF HONOR

A Berkley Book / published by arrangement with
Hamish Hamilton Ltd.

PRINTING HISTORY
Hamish Hamilton Ltd. edition published 1987
Berkley edition / June 1991

ISBN: 0-425-12820-2

A BERKLEY BOOK ® TM 757,375
Berkley Books are published by The Berkley Publishing Group,
200 Madison Avenue, New York, New York 10016.
The name "BERKLEY" and the "B" logo
are trademarks belonging to Berkley Publishing Corporation.

PRINTED IN THE UNITED STATES OF AMERICA

10   9   8   7   6   5   4   3   2   1

Paselabilan is a fictional state. The people who inhabit it are fictional too. However, their way of life, and all too often death, throughout the period of this story was experienced by nearly everyone who lived in what was once Malaya.

ACKNOWLEDGMENTS

The author wishes to thank the following organizations and individuals for their help during his research for this book.

M. Rajadurai, Esq., Society of Planters, Kuala Lumpur.

Ismail Ibrahim, Esq., RGA (Malaysia) Berhad, Kuala Lumpur.

K. H. Watson, Esq., Singapore International Chamber of Commerce Rubber Association.

The Rubber Growers' Association, London.

W. Newall, Esq., Kuala Lumpur.

R. A. S. Shotter, OBE, PJK, AISP, Somerset.

H. R. Crawford, Esq., Edinburgh.

Goodyear International Corporation, Akron, Ohio, USA.

Royal Geographical Society, London.

. . . Oh, the brave music of a distant drum.
Omar Khayyam

Prologue

Paselabilan State, Malaya
1948

The house slept.

The area of lawn in front of the verandah was well illuminated by spotlights and a moon in its third quarter, but away from the lawn there was only darkness and jungle, where the trees, densely packed, soared to heights of one hundred and fifty feet and more. The sun never penetrated the canopy of foliage, though its heat did. Even at this late hour the temperature was seventy degrees Fahrenheit and the air heavy with humidity.

The watching youth was unaware of any discomfort. His skin was a different color to that of the house's occupants.

He sniffed the air like a hunter, his brain subconsciously identifying the different night scents. Bamboo, fern, orchids, bougainvillaea, frangipani, rubber. Somewhere in the distance a leopard roared, and a troop of monkeys chattered with alarm. Nearby frogs croaked and nightjars churred.

The youth gave it another hour before slipping quietly out of the shadows and padding noiselessly toward the house. In his right hand he carried a parang whose blade gleamed in the moonlight. Pausing, he counted the windows until he found the one he wanted. Seconds later he was inside a groundfloor bedroom.

In the moonlight, the moment he pulled back the mosquito net the youth realized that the naked woman, asleep on top of the sheets, was not his intended victim. Briefly he was confused, undecided. This was not how it had been planned. Then he recognized her and saw how he could turn the situation to his advantage. He had never possessed a European woman. When he thought about it he was almost beside himself with excitement.

Still clutching the parang, he quickly disrobed and climbed on to the bed beside her. She stirred and moaned but did not sense danger. He knelt over her and parted her legs. At this she opened her eyes, which widened in disbelief and horror. Before she could scream he hit her across the temple with the flat of the parang. Her body went limp.

He plunged into her, whimpering deliriously, shuddering from head to foot and burying his face into her shoulder to stifle animal noises.

Empty, he lay across her until his breathing returned to normal.

Then he took the parang and cut her throat.

Part One

1932–1945

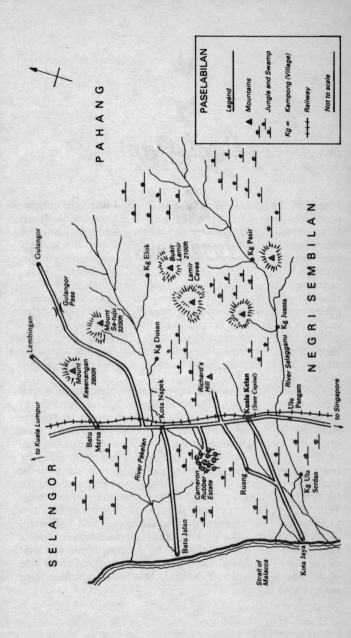

1

In spite of the heat, Jessica Cameron shivered when she contemplated the apparent fragility of the Imperial Airways de Havilland Hercules biplane due shortly to take her two sons on the first leg of their seven-day flight from Karachi to England. It looked scarcely larger than the single-engine fighters that had campaigned over the Western Front during the World War, and as vulnerable. Mike, of course, was oblivious to any danger. With the natural enthusiasm of an eight year-old embarking on an adventure, he was poring over the Imperial publicity literature with his father, trying to absorb the technical information on the aircraft and the details of their 5,000-mile route. Six years older, Jeff was sitting on his hand baggage feigning indifference, as though he were a seasoned air traveller. In truth he had never flown and had only even seen an airplane twice before.

There was some talk that Imperial were planning to extend their India service to Calcutta and Rangoon, and thereafter to Singapore, but that was generally reckoned not to be feasible until 1933 at the earliest. For the U.K. bound air traveller from Malaya, for now, it meant a ship from Penang across the Bay of Bengal to the Indian city of Madras, and then either by rail to Karachi or continuing by sea, which was the way the Camerons had come and the way they would return aboard the SS *Southern Pride*, an Australian trading vessel of 7,000 tons. Total time at sea, one month; fourteen days each way plus two to three days' unloading and offloading cargo, and bunkering. And they'd been lucky there inasmuch as the *Southern Pride*'s skipper had been making directly for Madras as his first port of call after Penang and had not been coast-hugging either side of the Bay of Bengal, which would have added a further three weeks to the voyage.

In actuality Harry Cameron could not really afford to spend so much time off the plantation, but it was not every day that his two sons finally left the nest to attend boarding school, and he would not be seeing them again for a year at least; longer, possibly, if the extended air routes did not open on schedule. On the other hand, if he had not agreed to make the trip he doubted if Jessica could have been persuaded that the time had come for the boys to start a more formal education than was obtainable in Malaya. As it was, they'd left it more than a little late for Jeff, but Jessica had insisted they go together or not at all, and she would not allow Mike to leave until he was eight. He wondered how the pair of them would fare in England. They had never been outside Malaya.

"It's powered by three 420 h.p. Bristol Jupiter VI engines," he recited to Mike, "and carries eight passengers at a cruising speed of 110 m.p.h. Your range is about 400 miles."

"And the route. Show me the route again."

"Well, here's Karachi, and from there you fly Gwadar—Jask—Lingeh—Bushire—Basrah—Baghdad—Ruthbah Wells—Galilee . . ."

"Where we change airplanes to the Calcutta flying boat . . ."

" . . . where you change to the Calcutta, which takes you to Castel Rosso—Athens—Brindisi."

"Where we have to take the train to Paris," said Mike, pulling a long face. "Why is that?"

"Because the Italians and the French aren't getting along too well with each other at present. The Italians, especially, won't permit aircraft to overfly Italy coming from France or enter French air space from Italy, and it's too dangerous to try to go over the Alps. Still, from Paris to Croydon, the last leg, will be by air. Do you realize that you'll be in school before your mother and sister and I are out of Indian waters? You'll be well settled in before we're back home."

"It's a long way, isn't it," said Mike thoughtfully.

"Not changing your mind about going, are you?"

"Noo-oh."

"That's the spirit. Here, you study the route so that you'll know where you are at any given moment while I have a word with your mother."

Harry Cameron walked over to Jessica.

"Okay?"

"I suppose so. How much longer do we have?"

"Not long."

Jessica slipped her hand into her husband's.

"Oh, Harry, I'm going to miss them."

"Of course you are. So am I."

"A whole year, perhaps more. Easters, Christmases."

"They'll be going to your sister."

"It won't be the same."

"Well, if it gets unbearable you can always take a few weeks in England yourself."

"No," said Jessica firmly, "we agreed that wasn't a good idea. It won't be doing them a favor if I keep popping up. But—Mike's so small."

"Mike's a damned sight tougher than Jeff and far more capable of looking after himself."

"For God's sake, he's eight years old."

"You know what I mean."

"Yes. I think Jenny will miss them too."

Jessica made a slight gesture in the direction of their eldest child, and only daughter, two years older than Jeff, who was talking to a handsome, suntanned ground representative of Imperial Airways. Harry wondered if Jessica was right. Jenny was sixteen now and blossoming rapidly into womanhood. She was going to be a beauty, tall and slender, with a natural, easy grace and a ready wit, sometimes caustic. It seemed no time at all since she was a little girl. She'd grown up almost overnight.

"I'm not sure you're right there," he grinned.

Jessica caught his meaning.

"She's still only a child," she said severely.

"And I don't know about that, either," Harry teased, trying to keep her mind off Mike and Jeff. "She looks very adult to me. Besides, sixteen is hardly a child. Now when I was in France during the war, girls of sixteen . . . "

"You can spare me the details."

"She looks a lot like you, you know," said Harry, after a moment.

"When I was sixteen? You didn't know me when I was sixteen."

"Which is my loss. But no, I meant now."

"Don't be absurd. There are twenty-four years between us."

"Even so."

He meant the compliment, too, Harry was a little surprised to discover, as he was not usually given to flattery. There was a striking similarity between the two that could only mean mother and daughter. At forty, even though she'd lived the last thirteen or fourteen years in a climate that frequently wasted European women, Jess had kept her looks. Not quite as tall as Jenny at five feet seven, she was still almost as slim even after bearing three children and doing more than her share on the estate, and both women had the same thick black hair and greenish-blue eyes. Harry sometimes felt guilty that he found it necessary to seek female company elsewhere on occasion, in Kuala Kelan or, rarer, in KL or Singapore. None of his casual affairs did much for him. Still, that was how he was. Indeed, that was how *life* was in Malaya, with some European women—European meaning White, whether they came from the Continent or the U.K. or, as in many instances, the United States—indulging in illicit relationships almost as much as their husbands. He didn't think Jess had. In fact, he'd have staked his life on it. Nor, of course, had Jenny—yet. She would have to be watched, however, for her own sake, because with her looks and youth she was an obvious mark, and an older man, say, could well turn her head. Physically she might resemble her mother. In temperament she was like him. It was something that had to be considered regardless of what Jess thought, and it was a pity, in many respects, that girls were not also sent to school in England. No doubt the time would come when they were, but for the present girls remained with their parents—not that Jenny had ever expressed a desire to do otherwise—until they found a husband in the Civil Service or among the sons of other planters. Then they settled down in Malaya, which was home to this new, postwar generation, who knew nothing of England—peasoupers, Ascot, Goodwood, Lord's—apart from what they heard from newcomers or read in the *The Times*, generally six weeks out of date.

Maybe not for much longer, though, thought Harry, if the airlines succeeded in reaching Singapore. And, after Singapore, Australia. Within a few years people might accept airplanes as a means of travel as easily as they now accepted ships.

A flurry of activity near the Hercules seemed to indicate that the aircraft was ready for boarding. This was confirmed a moment later by a uniformed official with a megaphone asking all passengers to make their way to the port hatch. Harry beckoned his daughter. She came over to her parents, her eyes shining mischievously at her easy conquest of the ground attendant, who followed her departure wistfully.

Jessica held on to Mike longer than was strictly necessary before he boarded, until her younger son protested by trying to wriggle out of her grasp. She was wise enough not to do the same with Jeff, simply pecking him on the cheek, as Jenny did with both her brothers. Harry shook hands formally. Then the boys were aboard and the hatch was closed. The ground attendant with eyes for Jenny asked them, politely, to stand behind the barrier, where they joined others who had come to see their loved ones depart.

The aircraft taxied to the end of the runway and turned into what little breeze there was. The pitch of the engines increased. Then the aircraft was moving, gathering speed. Finally it lumbered into the air, skimming the 'drome at a height of only a few feet for what seemed for ever. Excited natives chattered and pointed, and fled in terror as it headed for the perimeter fence. Gradually it gained altitude, banked, and turned due west for Gwadar, the first refuelling stop before it entered Persia. The Camerons watched in silence until it was lost in the afternoon heat haze.

They were twenty-four hours out of Karachi aboard the SS *Southern Pride*, making for Bombay, before Jessica felt composed enough to consider joining her husband and daughter for meals. She was missing her sons more than she would have thought possible, and would probably have continued to eat in her cabin had Jenny not come up with a solution to her mother's misery.

Since they were the only passengers on what was essentially a freighter, they ate with the captain—Peter Ross, a widower—and his ten-year-old daughter Lucasta, who had made it quite clear on the voyage out from Penang that she hated her given name; who had insisted upon being called Luke. As her father, a grizzled forty-five-year-old life-long mariner and native-born Australian explained, Luke had been christened by his late wife, an English-woman, while he was at sea. Lucasta had been her mother's name and she hadn't stopped to think that an Aussie child growing up with such a handle was likely to be ribbed mercilessly.

While she loved sailing with her father when school permitted, and occasionally when it didn't, Jenny soon spotted that the little girl was frequently either in someone's way and being sent packing, or sitting by herself. Steaming to Karachi it hadn't mattered so much. She'd had Mike to either cosset or bully as the mood took her.

Without informing Harry or Captain Ross, Jenny took Luke to see her mother the second afternoon out of Karachi, after telling the child that Jessica Cameron was missing her two sons and needed some company. She left the pair together. The same evening Luke led Jess in to dinner. Thereafter the two were inseparable.

Two hundred miles south of Madras, at Pondicherry, the ship picked up an extra passenger. The first the Camerons knew about him was when he arrived at the lunch table wearing faded ducks and a short-sleeve shirt that had seen better days. Jenny took a shine to him immediately. He was an inch taller than her father at six-one, bronzed and obviously very fit. His fair hair had been bleached even lighter by the sun. Harry guessed his age at twenty-five, which proved to be a year out on the low side.

Captain Ross introduced him as Dan Holden, American citizen, making for Singapore.

"Sorry about the clothes," Holden apologized, smiling pleasantly. "I've been travelling by train and I lost my bags, or they were stolen, somewhere between here and Bangalore. I was lucky I had my money in a belt or I'd be working my passage to Singapore. Not that it would be the first time."

"You're a sailor, Mr. Holden?" asked Jessica.

"I've done some sailing, but I'm a little bit of everything, I guess. I like to travel, earn my keep when I can and spend it when I can't. I'm hoping to pick up a ship in Singapore that will take me to Borneo or the Philippines, maybe China. Captain Ross offered me a berth aboard the *Pride*, but I've been to Australia."

"You sound a little footloose," said Jessica, the comment in no way a criticism.

Holden shrugged.

"I guess that's me. But with good reason, Mrs. Cameron. You see, back home I have a business waiting for me which is likely to tie me to a desk for the rest of my life. Office supplies. When I graduated college I was expected to go straight in and join my father, me being an only son and all." He seemed appalled by the notion. "Can you imagine it? Forty years of selling stationery and typewriters, joining the country club, martinis at five? It's been a family business for two generations, and it's big enough not to need me for a year or two. So I made a deal with my father. I wouldn't ask him for any money and I'd come back as soon as he felt it was time to hand over the reins, but until then I wanted to travel the world." He grinned ruefully. "I haven't got that far. I went west from the States instead of east so I've seen nothing of Europe. But I have cruised the Pacific and been to Japan, Australia, New Zealand, India and Malaya."

"Where in Malaya?" asked Harry.

"Perak state, up near Ipoh. Tin mining. No—that sounds more highfalutin than it was. The Chinese did the mining. I guess I sort of supervised, not that the Chinese need much supervising. Anyway, it wasn't much fun. Maybe it's just that I prefer the sea."

"So why work on land?"

"In the first place there wasn't a ship with a vacant berth heading the way I wanted to go. In the second place, I love Malaya. I suppose that sounds crazy. I mean, Americans are supposed to love America first and America last, and nothing in between. We don't have a history of colonizing the way the British do. Or the Dutch or French. Not colonizing other countries, I mean. Our antecedents came from Europe and their descendants spent the next two hundred and fifty years opening the frontiers of America, which I guess was big enough to keep them occupied. Anyway, I like India and some of the Pacific islands, but there's something special about Malaya. I know it's hotter than midsummer's day in hell—excuse me—and the humidity can poleaxe you until you're used to it, but . . . I can't explain it."

"You don't have to. Tell me," said Harry, "are you really dead set on hopping a freighter to China?"

Before Madras Harry had offered Dan Holden a job. He'd liked the young American on sight and talking to him at length did nothing to alter his opinion. There was room for another "European" on the estate now that Jeff was on his way to England. Even though Jeff was only fourteen he had helped, when out of school, to keep the wheels of the estate turning smoothly. It would not be a permanent post. Naturally Dan would be leaving sooner or later for the United States.

Jenny approved wholeheartedly of the offer, quite certain that she would enjoy having such a good-looking, vaguely piratical man around the bungalow. Jessica reserved judgement, though she could see Harry's interest in Dan. In many respects he was the same breed as Grandfather Richard Cameron.

For himself, Dan wanted to know a great deal more about Cameron Rubber and what he would be expected to do.

The Cameron plantation (explained Harry) covered two thousand acres of prime land in Paselabilan, midway between Kuala

Kelan, the state capital, and Kota Napek on the highway that ran through the state from Kuala Lumpur to Singapore.

The family always referred to the main house as the "bungalow" although nowadays the living space was a far cry from the two and a bit rooms and primitive plumbing that Great-Grandfather Richard Cameron had hacked out of an uncompromising jungle before the turn of the century. With his bare hands and precious little help, he had often boasted in his twilight years. A legendary romancer, he had frequently claimed, among other things, that the Cameron Highlands in the neighboring state of Pahang were named after him, which everyone knew to be untrue. Still, he'd made some mark on the map of Malaya before he died by constructing a small hill station east of the highway connecting KL to Singapore, a place to escape to when the heat lower down became unbearable. He'd wanted to call it Cameron Hill but the government cartographer wasn't having that. A compromise was reached with Richard's Hill, sometimes referred to, on older maps, as Bukit Sedikit, Little Hill.

Let alone the six bedrooms, two bathrooms, living rooms, work rooms, other offices and a library, strictly speaking the bungalow wasn't a bungalow at all, inasmuch as it had more than one storey, albeit that the upper level was no more than two single rooms, each fifteen by fifteen. One was used for storage; the other, with huge windows running much of the length of each wall, had been tacked on by Richard's son, Edward, an amateur astronomer, with the idea of turning it into an observatory by adding a dome and a large telescope. Until overseeing a rubber estate interfered with his hobby, which, in any event, would have been stillborn since observatories need clean, dry air to function effectively, and there was none of that in Malaya.

Richard Cameron had arrived in Malaya with his wife Amanda and Harry's father Edward, then a youngster of fifteen, in 1882, soon after the first rubber plants were imported from Brazil by way of Kew Gardens and Ceylon. Richard was forty-two at the time, his wife two years younger, and he had spent most of his adult life with the Colonial Service in India, resenting practically every moment of it. The possessor of a fierce temper and a reputation as a gambler and womanizer, he saw himself, in his heart, as an adventurer who had married too soon and who had been forced, through lack of accessible finance, into the wrong career. Being transferred from India to the Straits Settlement of Malacca was a move that did not please him and caused him to quarrel with his immediate superiors, who informed him he could either like it or resign the Service. Reading between the lines, Richard suspected that the India Office had sanctioned his transfer as a means of easing him out. Nevertheless, he contained his rage and waited a year before exercising his option to resign, a decision made easier by his father dying and leaving him a fairly generous legacy. With this in his London bank he had to decide whether to return to England and live the life of a relatively impoverished country squire—his elder brother having inherited the manor house and the surrounding land—or remain in the Far East, where his money went further, and try to make his fortune. He elected to stay.

His wife and child, he soon found, were an encumbrance. In his own way he loved them both, but he could not expect, in what he saw as his middle years, to make his mark while burdened with the responsibility of being a good husband and father. With calculated sangfroid, therefore, he more or less abandoned them. Thereafter, until and if he chose to return, they were on their own.

He spent several months in Colombo, Ceylon, contemplating what to do with his inheritance while exploring various possibilities—and doing his fair share of drinking and gambling.

The rubber business was not exactly new, of course, but until the 1820s the product had been of comparatively limited value commercially, being used mostly as an eraser for draftsmen's errors, from which it took its name, and in surgical catheters. Then, by accident, a Scotsman in the cloth trade found that naphtha would dissolve rubber, and that the resultant liquid, when rolled and dried between two sheets of cotton, possessed waterproofing qualities. Mr. Macintosh had made himself a rich man. So too had Thomas Hancock, who eventually formed a company with Macintosh, and who discovered that when the latex imported from South America was cut into strips and heated, the strips stuck together, enabling them to be shaped and made into gloves, shoes, soles, hoses, bicycle tyres. Now rubber was starting to be needed for motorcar tires, though motoring was in its infancy.

Still, motoring notwithstanding, rubber was in great demand worldwide and the cost of importing it from a foreign power prohibitive. Until Sir Henry Wickham brought seeds out of Brazil, the plant had not been cultivated elsewhere. For Great Britain to have her own source was obviously desirable, and the first planters would undoubtedly become wealthy men.

In Colombo, Richard set out to discover all he could about the plant. The merchants to whom he spoke and with whom he drank and gambled seemed of the opinion that the Malayan climate was ideal. Some already had acres under growth; others were exporting seedlings to estates they had bought on the Malayan Peninsula. But it was still a risky business. For a man to succeed he would need a combination of good luck and a strong nerve.

"As you will have gathered by now," said Harry to Dan Holden, "my grandfather was not what you would call a nice man. There again, Malaya in the last century wasn't a country for nice men. If the jungle or the swamp or the snakes or malaria didn't get you, chances were you'd find yourself in the middle of a local war. Either that or on the wrong side of freebooting bandits, who'd kill you because they hadn't anything better to do that day. You had to be tough to succeed, which my grandfather was, and ruthless, which he certainly was. A lot of what I'm telling you came from his lips or my father's, and some of it you may think you have to take with a large pinch of salt. I did when I first heard the stories, though nowadays I'm not so sure. However, to hear Richard Cameron tell it, he more or less founded Malaya." Harry smiled in fond remembrance. "He told a hell of a good story, whatever else.

"It wasn't quite as simple as he thought, naturally, starting up a rubber plantation. Some of the merchants he spoke to in Colombo were more than willing to take him on as an equal partner, providing he would put up half the capital and do all of the work while they remained in Ceylon and counted the profits, if any. Richard wasn't interested in such a deal, but he could not find anyone to sell him seedlings. Malayan acres he could find in plenty, and at a price he could afford, but no one would sell him plants. Not enough, anyway. In any case, he calculated how long it would be before the trees were mature enough to tap for latex and estimated that he'd be in his fifties before making a profit. What he needed, he concluded, was a few hundred acres that were already under growth. He found those in a card game with a down-on-his-luck English baronet by the name of Carfax, who owned 800 acres in Paselabilan. The game was draw poker, which as an American you'll understand. So did my grandfather, or so he thought."

Richard Cameron did not realize until much later that he had been the victim of a confidence trick. He had spent weeks stalking Sir William Carfax, aware that the baronet was in financial difficulties due to his habit of believing that drawing to an inside straight had merit; aware equally that the titled Englishman's ready money was running out and that all he had to offer, if cornered in a high stakes card game, were the 800 Malayan acres, where the rubber trees, it was generally conceded, were close to maturity. Even if the dirt roads to the west coast ports of the middle Peninsula, to Batu Jalan and Kota Jaya, were impassible more often than not, a dozen streams and minor rivers led off the estate to the major rivers Pakelan and Selagganu, which emptied into the Malacca Strait, where Richard would have little trouble getting the bales of solidified latex to a ship or a broker.

But Carfax seemed to possess the devil's own luck. Twice, when the stakes were at the table limit and the only players left were Richard, Carfax and one other, the baronet had folded his cards before he could be enticed into making a foolish bet. On another occasion Carfax raised the stakes but Richard did not have a good enough hand to compete.

Then came the fourth time.

Richard was dealt, without drawing, a heart flush. He knew his arithmetic. The odds against such a hand were slightly over 500 to one. His highest cards were an ace-king, making the flush virtually unbeatable by another flush. Carfax kept four cards and drew one. Against his original cards being four of a kind, the odds were over 4,000 to one; thus the likelihood was that he had two pair, making him already beaten by the heart flush. The odds against improving his hand to a full house were about 11 to one, and Richard suspected he hadn't made it.

The other players gradually dropped out as Richard forced the betting higher, higher than it had ever been before, gambling that he had the winning hand. For, if he did not, most of his legacy was lost. All he'd have left would be the money he had deposited for the upkeep of Amanda and their son.

Carfax stayed with the wagers until he had no more ready cash or available credit. He then asked Richard if he would accept an IOU on his rubber acres, valuing them at £4,000, an amount that would not only cover the last raise but was double it. Richard agreed and promptly re-raised Carfax to the limit of the promissory note. Carfax hesitated before taking the challenge—and lost, his two pair being beaten by Richard's flush.

The following morning Carfax passed over the deed of transfer, duly notarized, and Richard became the owner of 800 Malayan acres in the state of Paselabilan, as well as inheriting, according to Carfax, an Irish overseer by the name of McFee and two Indian clerks.

It was three days before he could arrange a passage on a ship sailing for Malaya, and the crossing from Ceylon took a further eight days. The third leg of the journey was made by fishing smack and started in the port of Batu Jalan and thereafter up the River Pakelan to Kota Napek. This took ten miserable days. When he was not being drenched by the tropical rain or eaten alive by mosquitoes and leeches, Richard cat-napped with his rifle close to hand. It was not unknown for a traveller beginning an upriver trip never to see his destination, especially if the traveller was white and looked as if he had money or other valuables. The last leg was made by canoe, which he bought and risked paddling himself rather than chance, in his exhausted state, hiring native boatmen who might well decide that his rifle and ammunition alone were good enough reasons for slitting his throat.

There were no signs to tell him he had reached the estate, but the map that had come with the deeds and his own instincts convinced him he had. His spirits sank. It was little more than jungle and swamp, a green nightmare where it was almost impossible to discern where the jungle ended and the plantation began; impossible, too, to calculate whether he had 800 acres or 200. That he had rubber trees was undeniable, but they were three years from maturity. Carfax had cheated him. The estate was worth closer to £400 than £4,000.

But there was no use crying about it. Even if he decided to return to Colombo and have it out with Carfax, at the point of a gun if necessary, the baronet, he suspected, would no longer be in Ceylon, would have headed for Australia or some such faraway destination aboard the first steamer. He'd been had, and that was all there was to it. He would now have to see if anything could be salvaged. He still had plenty of money, that was one plus, and in the kampongs, the Malay villages, along the river he had seen many families. The labor force was available if he knew how to harness it, and what he wanted it to do.

Further upriver he came upon a clearing and in it a basha, a small hut constructed of atap and bamboo. As far as Richard could see this was the only building, if building it could be called, on the estate—if estate it could be called.

Of the two Indian clerks there was no sign. Of McFee there was, a huge red-haired hulk of a man but one whose age it was impossible to determine since he evidently hadn't shaved for weeks. He was lying inside the basha on a makeshift charpoy, dead drunk judging by his posture and his snores. A gourd of some evil-smelling liquor was at his side, as was a Malay girl who seemed no more than fifteen, and who fled in terror when she opened her eyes and saw the newcomer. There were ants everywhere, some huge, swarming over unwashed dishes and over McFee himself. The smell of rotting vegetation and stale human sweat was overpowering. Richard felt his gorge rise.

McFee hardly stirred when the girl left his cot, and Richard, his anger at being swindled aggravated by fatigue, debated whether to blow the overseer's head off with the rifle or carry him to the nearest sungei, and throw him in. Then he thought about it in greater depth while squatting on his hunkers and studying the Irishman. If McFee—and who else could it be?—had native liquor at his disposal and a Malay girl as a bed companion, the chances were that he was more than familiar with the nearby kampongs and on nodding terms with their inhabitants. Which could prove important. Besides, if Carfax had been, until now, his employer, the poor bastard probably hadn't been paid ever and could be excused for taking any pleasure, alcoholic or female, where he found it.

Still, it would be as well to let the Irishman know, from the word go, who was the new boss.

Richard lifted the charpoy and tipped McFee on to the floor. With the instincts of the animal he had so nearly become, McFee scrambled to his feet roaring, a parang Richard hadn't seen in his hand.

"Take it easy," said Richard, pointing the rifle.

McFee swayed drunkenly. "Who the hell are you?"

"No friend of Sir William Carfax."

"That bastard."

"Seconded. Why don't you put the knife down?"

"Why don't *you* put the rifle down?"

"Okay." Richard grounded the weapon and reached for his pack. He produced a bottle of whisky, two-thirds full. McFee licked his lips greedily. "Now if you can provide the receptacles . . ."

McFee found two empty coconut shells. Richard poured a generous measure into each.

"Your health, Mr. McFee."

McFee finished his drink in one gulp and held out the shell for a refill. Richard obliged him.

"How is it you know my name?" asked McFee between sips, taking the whisky more slowly on this occasion.

"From Carfax. How long since you last saw him?"

"A year, maybe more. I don't remember."

"And the two clerks who are supposed to be here, the Indians?"

"Christ, they ran off almost as soon as Carfax left. What wa
to keep them? The bastard left them no wages and there was n
clerical work to be done even if he had. I'd have gone with them
but there was nowhere for me to go."

"How's that?"

"My business."

"Maybe mine too." Richard handed over the deed of sale
McFee scrutinized it.

"God help you, though maybe now I get paid. Carfax owe
me. Or you do, I don't care which."

"We'll talk about that later. Tell me why you didn't leave whe
the Indians left."

"I had some trouble in Batu Jalan awhile back, killed a Portu
guese sailor who thought I was drunk enough to rob. I was tryin
to get a berth on a ship when Carfax found me and offered me
job overseeing his rubber." McFee laughed bitterly. "*His* rubber
when I planted every tree more or less with my own hands."

"Impossible. That's too big a job for one man. Don't try i
on, McFee. I didn't inherit Carfax's debts along with everythin
else, but you'll get what's coming to you, maybe more, if you'r
straight with me."

"All right, so I had some help from the local Malays and som
Chinese families. The fact remains that all Carfax did was ship th
seedlings upriver from Batu Jalan. The Malays and the Chines
and I spent months clearing the jungle and getting the trees int
the ground. Then Sir William bloody Carfax ups and leaves."

"You mean he stayed here—here—for months?"

"Not him. He stayed in Batu or, more often than not, in Malac
ca. He'd put in an appearance every few weeks, just to see wha
was happening, bring wages for the natives, whisky and tinne
food for me."

"He didn't pay you?"

"What was the point? There's nothing to spend money on here
But I was promised a share of the profits from the first consign
ment. That and a ticket out, a new identity, if I wanted to leave."

"How did he pay the Malays and the Chinese?"

"Tools, cloth, mirrors. Anything he could lay his hands on tha
didn't cost a lot. They were happy enough with the arrangemen
until, about a year ago, more than the usual number of week

went by without him putting in an appearance. It was then that
the Malays decided they'd had enough and went back to fishing.
The Chinese followed them. If they were not going to be paid they
were not going to work. Nobody needs to here. There's fruit on
the trees, fish in the rivers, game in the jungle. It was a bloody
tragedy. We'd got it all organized by then, everything cleared,
planted and thriving. You wouldn't know it to look at it now."

Richard thought he could guess at the reason for Carfax's non-
appearance. He'd got into financial difficulties, probably at a gam-
ing table, and he'd gambled on McFee, not being able to go elsewhere due to the killing of the Portuguese, looking after things
until his finances improved. Which they never did.

"How bad are things?" asked Richard.

"They're not bad at all if we had some labor. The jungle's
a bastard, as always, but we could save most of the trees with
a lot of hard work."

"How many acres have we got? Carfax told me eight hundred,
but in view of everything else it wouldn't surprise me to find out
he'd lied."

"No, eight hundred would be about right." McFee frowned.
"You said 'we.' How many acres have 'we' got?"

"And that's what I meant. You've got nowhere to go and I can't
handle this by myself. If you want to stay and help put this place
on its feet, you'll get whatever Carfax promised you and a bonus
besides."

"You've got money?"

"I've got enough to see us through a few years in whisky, medicines, canned food, weapons, tools and mirrors. After that we'll
have to start making a profit."

"Is there a market for rubber out there?" McFee gestured vaguely in the general direction of the rest of the world.

"There is and it's growing. It'll take time but it'll be big. What
do you say, is it a deal?"

McFee hesitated. "I'll need to think it over. This isn't exactly
God's own country, you know, not for someone brought up in
Killarney and accustomed to getting back there every few years.
Hell, thirty minutes ago . . . " He seemed suddenly to realize that
his bedmate had gone.

"She left in a hurry," said Richard. "Didn't like the look of
me, I suppose. Come on, what is there to think about? Whatever
happened half an hour ago, yesterday you had nothing to look forward to, certainly not Killarney. I'm not guaranteeing you'll ever

see Ireland again, but trying it my way you stand a chance."

"You're right." McFee nodded slowly. "You're absolutely right. However, I wouldn't want you to get hold of the wrong idea just because Carfax hired me. I'm pushing forty, an Irish sailor with a mate's ticket who's got little experience of anything apart from ships. What I know of rubber and planting I've picked up since I was here, and it isn't much. What I mean is . . . "

"What you mean is that you don't want me, in a couple of months or a couple of years, to decide that you're not pulling your weight or that you've outlived your usefulness. And then mention to somebody in Batu Jalan that I know the whereabouts of a fugitive killer."

"Something like that."

"Forget it, it won't happen. But if it'll make you feel any more secure I'll have proper papers drawn up. You'll have a contract for as long as you want it."

"No, don't do that. I don't want my name anywhere on a piece of paper. I'll accept your word. Is there any of that whisky left?"

"There is, and one more bottle in my pack. After that's gone we're either going to have to go without or drink some of that foul-smelling stuff you seem to like. Until I make a trip for stores, which won't be yet. I'll pick up an extra razor as well. You look like a derelict. Don't you ever bother to clean yourself up?"

"What for? In any case, have you taken a look at yourself?"

Richard rubbed his chin bristles, and grinned. After the journey from Batu Jalan he realized that he, too, must seem and smell less than wholesome.

"The first thing we do," he said a little later, leaving the basha and pacing the length of the clearing, "is build somewhere a bit more substantial than this to live in. If we're going to make a success of this enterprise, we might as well start off the way we mean to continue."

"I've never found I've needed more than this," called McFee, offended.

"*I'll* need it. If things work out, the Camerons are going to be in this part of the world for some time."

"Camerons? Plural? You're going to get married and raise children?"

"I'm already married with a young son. They're in Singapore."

"Which is where they should stay. This is no place for them."

"It's going to have to be when we're organized. Look at it this way. There are just the two of us. A lot of the time I'm going to be away, arranging stores, talking to agents and brokers, ship owners, setting things up for the future. We've got eight hundred acres and you'll be here by yourself. You're going to need help. My son can give it. We might get ill and need nursing. My wife can handle that. She can also cook. The days are going to be long and back-breaking, and we can't live on fruit and fish and canned food all the time. I don't know about you, but I don't want to have to go out and shoot something, skin it, and then make a meal of it. Besides, I want to start something here and see it grow. I want it to go on, generation after generation. In a hundred years' time I'd like someone in England to look at a map of Malaya or at least the state of Paselabilan and think, 'Oh, yes, that's Cameron country.' I don't want to build something and have no one to pass it on to, Mr. McFee. Look, I can't keep on calling you Mr. McFee."

"The name's Michael."

"Michael McFee. I'll remember that. I'll name a grandson after you. And there's another thing to remember, Michael McFee. The world's growing smaller. It's not impossible we'll meet up with Carfax again one of these bright days. That's another reason for building proper accommodation—to show him what we made of the estate. We'll rub his nose in it, just before we feed him to the fishes."

McFee was well into the second bottle of whisky by now. Richard, too, was feeling light-headed due to tiredness and alcohol. Returning to the basha, he took the bottle from McFee and held it up.

"Dear God, Michael, I can see I'm going to have to ration you and your thirst."

McFee chuckled drunkenly. "Tell me," he said, "how soon are you planning to send for this wife of yours?"

"Haven't you heard a word I've said? As soon as we're organized. As soon as I've got somewhere decent for her and the boy to live."

"That's likely to take some time, isn't it, what with persuading the Malays and the Chinese to go back to work?"

"It's not going to happen overnight, but I'll have plenty of business in Singapore. I'll be seeing them again long before I bring them here to live."

"And what do you plan on doing for female companionship until then?"

"I was going to talk to you about that."

"You've come to the right man."

* * *

"It was not until 1896 that my grandfather brought his wife and 'child' up from Singapore," said Harry, "though he visited them regularly once he considered himself established—if not yet making any real money—and on several occasions he ferried them up to the plantation so that they could see how his work was progressing. But by 1896 my father was almost thirty years of age and set in his ways, working for a small shipping company. He'd also been married to my mother, Alice Cameron, the daughter of the chief clerk in the company, for five years. I was four years old and had a sister who was born the year after me but who died when she was two."

"Why did it take him so long to bring them into the business?" asked Dan Holden. "I can maybe understand why he wouldn't want your grandmother there until he was satisfied everything was as it should be, but your father, his only son?"

"You might well ask. One family tradition has it that my father had inherited some of Richard Cameron's bloody-mindedness and refused to go when first asked, when he was twenty. Another theory—and much more probable in my view—is that Richard was enjoying himself too much during the construction years. That rings true to me. He was fulfilling his dream after decades of frustration.

"Rubber was not due to begin making really handsome profits for another ten years, in about 1906, but even before then my grandfather and Michael McFee were earning a living of one sort or another, and building up the plantation, expanding, starting a primitive factory where the latex could be taken by the tappers and dried and compressed into bales for shipping. He'd also founded what was a rudimentary Planters' Association whereby other estate owners and managers could get together and exchange ideas, making bulk deals for shipping, import machinery in bulk and buy seedlings from Ceylon as a kind of cooperative. Roads within Paselabilan and connecting with other states, bridges, schools, hospitals—my grandfather was in on the ground floor, either getting the planters to part with their own capital or, more often than not, persuading a reluctant Colonial Office and very occasionally the Sultan that it was all an investment in the future.

"Not that the future always looked so assured. There continued to be periodic wars between rival chieftains, which didn't bother my grandfather too much until they spilled over into kampongs from which he drew his labor. Then he and McFee strapped on pistols and rifles and set out to do something about it. Eventually the chiefs would realize that it wasn't such a good notion to offend Richard Cameron, and take their wars elsewhere. By the time the soldiers arrived, if they ever did, there was nothing for them to do. 'War? What war?' Richard would ask innocently.

"But the wars had their uses, and before the end of the century Richard concluded that estate workers living in their own kampongs was inefficient. Those who wanted employment with him had to live within the estate, where he could keep an eye on them and protect them. Many Chinese saw the sense in that, and accepted. Many Malays did not like the restrictions or leaving their kampongs, and did not accept. There were other reasons of course—one being that the Chinese are naturally industrious and the Malays happy-go-lucky—but it was the curbs on freedom which means, today, that you'll find ten Chinese families working as rubber tappers to each Malay.

"The biggest problem my grandfather had in 1896, however, was not with warring chieftains or casual bandits. It was with Amanda Cameron directly and, indirectly, with Edward Cameron and Alice Cameron, my father and mother. They told him bluntly they did not want to leave Singapore and live on the estate, no matter that the bungalow now had several bedrooms and entertaining rooms and that Michael McFee was no longer in residence but had built a smaller bungalow of his own away from the main compound. She was fifty-four, Amanda argued, and too old to uproot herself. Edward was secure in his job and had prospects, and Alice's health had been delicate since the death of her daughter, my sister. And taking a four-year-old child—me—into what was more or less jungle, with dangerous rivers, snakes and wild animals, was nothing less than irresponsible.

"Richard Cameron tried persuasion, which didn't work. Then he lost his temper, which didn't work either. Finally he used his head and all the ruthlessness for which he was well known. He didn't, sad to say, really give a damn about my father who, I suppose, was something of an intellectual, more interested in books, mathematics, astronomy than in running a rubber plantation. But Richard hadn't built up the estate to see it sold when he died. If Edward was hopeless, he'd see to it that I wasn't, that I'd grow up in situ, learn to love the plantation as he did, and one day inherit.

"So he did two things. He had a quiet word with the shipping line owner who employed both Alice's father and Edward. He had done some business with the line in the past, as had other planters of his acquaintance, and would doubtless do so again. But not if the line continued to employ Edward Cameron. Secondly, he cut off my grandmother's source of income. Instantly. He pleaded that he needed the capital for reinvestment and could not afford to support two homes. Thus my father was in danger of losing his job and my grandmother had nothing to live on. Naturally he told them that what he was doing was for their own good, that he knew what was best for his family."

"So they went with him. He sounds like a hell of a character."

"He was and they did, and to do my grandmother and my father justice they tried to adapt to the new life. My mother, Alice Cameron, couldn't adjust. She genuinely was suffering from ill health, and the rigors of plantation life, especially the climate, killed her within four years. She died in 1900, aged thirty-two, when I was eight. I don't remember an awful lot about it. One day she complained of a headache and shivering, and took to her bed. Within forty-eight hours she was dead. My father didn't go to pieces, that wasn't his style, but he scarcely spoke to my grandfather ever again. Nor did my grandmother. I don't know whether or not Richard Cameron felt guilty, but he moved out of the bungalow and in with McFee, where they lived the life of Riley. There was a lot of carousing and noise late at night, I do recall that, and young women, not always Malays, came and went, but whenever I asked my grandmother what was going on she told me it was none of my business.

"Sometimes my grandfather would come back to the bungalow after dark, mostly drunk, and then there'd be rows where he'd break things. I suppose most young boys would either have hated him or feared him, but I saw him as a sort of hero. I realize now that I was the son he'd wanted Edward to be. He'd take me hunting with him, exploring the hills and jungle in the eastern part of the state. Or fishing. Or by boat or raft upriver or down to Batu and Kota Jaya. Very often we'd be away for weeks, sometimes staying in the hill station he'd had built.

"I don't presume ever to have got to know him. Although he appeared to outsiders to be an extrovert, in many ways he was a very secretive man who kept his innermost feelings to himself. Until McFee died, which was the only occasion I saw him close to tears. Guilt again, I expect. The estate was making a substantial profit by 1906 and McFee was all for retiring and taking a trip to

Killarney. Although he and my grandfather had never had a contract that said they were partners, it was an unwritten convention that they were, in proportions of four to one. My grandfather could easily have afforded to buy McFee's share, which is what McFee suggested. They were both getting on in years, both in their middle sixties. McFee swore that the trip was to be a long vacation, nothing more, but with his customary selfishness my grandfather persuaded him to stay a little longer, suspecting, probably rightly, that if McFee returned to Europe the two would not see each other again."

"Look, Michael, you'll never survive a long sea voyage alone at your age. I know you. You'll get into bad company and drink too much. You'll be dead before Suez or, worse, you'll fall under the influence of the first widow on board who finds out you've got some money and who flutters her eyelashes at you. Leave it another year and I'll come with you. Better still, leave it two and we'll make a real trip of it, stay away as long as you like. Live it up."

"What difference will another two years make?"

"Harry will be almost seventeen then. He'll be old enough to hold the fort and make sure his father doesn't do anything idiotic while we're away."

"I don't know I'll see another two years out."

"Don't be a fool. I'm older than you and I've no intention of dying yet."

"I'm tired," said McFee.

Richard could see that he was, this only true friend he had. For a big man he seemed to have shrunk in stature in the last twelve months, loose flesh now where once there was hardened muscle. Neither of them did any real work any longer, admittedly, but the climate had finally taken its toll of Michael McFee, as it did of most Europeans sooner or later. But he could not let McFee leave. If he did, what, then, would he have to look forward to?

"Well, if you want to go I suppose I can't really stop you, but I have to say that you've come to me at a bad time to buy out your twenty percent."

"What rubbish is this? We're making more money than we know what to do with, you've said so yourself."

"Agreed, but I've also been plowing it back into the estate rather than leave it with the banks. If you paid a bit more attention to the accounts you'd be aware of that."

"Figures have never been my strong suit. I've always left that to you."

"And you've not done badly out of it."

"I'm not complaining. Anyway, I wouldn't need it all, just enough." McFee smiled cynically. "If I don't come back you can take it out of my share. That goes to you in any case, you know that, seeing as I have no family."

"We're your family, Michael, and this estate is your home. Killarney belongs to another time, perhaps another Michael McFee. Look, let's compromise. Never mind two years, make it one. We'll book our passages next time we're in Batu. What do you say? Twelve months from today we sail."

"McFee agreed, of course," said Harry, "because my grandfather could be very plausible. But he never lived to make the voyage. He died before the year was out. Not of anything in particular, just old age and a lifetime of hard work. I stood next to my grandfather when we buried McFee. It was pouring with rain, and it was hard to tell whether it was that or whether he had tears in his eyes. He said something very strange to me. 'Be your own man. Never get to like anyone too much, Harry, it all ends in failure and disappointment.'

"I was with him at the will reading in Kuala Kelan also. Just the two of us. McFee had left his holdings in the estate to my grandfather as expected, and to me he left his guns and a few personal mementoes. There were also a couple of lines about William Carfax which seemed to affect my grandfather more than they should have done, and which I didn't understand until several years later. They read: 'If in God's good time you ever come across Carfax again, kick him in the backside for me and tell him I hope he rots.'"

"Yes, I was going to ask about Carfax," said Dan. "Did he ever put in another appearance?"

"No, no one ever heard from him again. You have to remember that he'd have been getting on in years too. Assuming he was still alive. Judging by the way he did business, the odds were against him reaching old age. But there is a sting in the tail of this story."

The sudden wail of the ship's siren warned them that they were entering Madras. Harry realized that he had been talking for hours without a break, and that he'd lost Jessica, who'd heard it all before anyway, to Luke Ross. His wife and the skipper's young daughter were leaning over the taffrail, exchanging banter with the occupants of the bum-boats. Jenny was in the wheelhouse, chatting to the pilot, who was allowing her to hold the wheel.

"You'll recall," said Henry, "that McFee took the job with Carfax because he'd killed a Portuguese sailor in a fight and had to get out of Batu in a hurry. Well, the sailor didn't die. He recovered, and the chances are that Carfax knew it. Richard Cameron certainly did. I went through his papers after he died in 1909, his diaries. He evidently made some enquiries concerning McFee shortly after they first met and he established that the Portuguese pulled through. It was written down there in his own hand. But he kept the information to himself for almost a quarter of a century, worried, I suppose, that if ever McFee found out that he wasn't a murderer he wouldn't stay—not, certainly, in the early years when my grandfather needed him. So poor old McFee went to his grave with a crime on his conscience he never committed."

"Christ," said Holden. "He'd have made a great politician in the States, your grandfather. What about your grandmother?"

"She outlived Richard, dying in 1912. Which is ironic when you consider that she was the one who'd said she was too old to uproot herself. Her son, my father, died two years ago, in 1930. Once I was old enough to take over the reins he lost what little interest he'd had in the estate and spent most of his time travelling and reading. There's a theory about travellers, you know, which I expect you're familiar with. They go from place to place because they can't settle anywhere. I loved him, naturally, my father, but he was essentially a weak man. He should have stood up to Richard Cameron, though I suppose, if he had, there wouldn't be a Cameron rubber estate now. It takes all sorts."

Luke Ross squealed from the taffrail for everyone to come and see what "Aunt" Jessica was bargaining for with the bum-boats. Harry got to his feet.

"There you have it," he said, "the story of the Cameron clan. What do you think—do you want to join this lunatic breed?"

"It beats the hell out of selling typewriters." Dan held out his hand. "Looks like I'm in the rubber business."

"I'm delighted to hear it. Who knows, you may get to like us."

"I'll cable my father from Madras, tell him what ship I'm sailing on and where I'm bound. I've been out of touch for a couple of months."

Five days east of Madras, the radio operator aboard the *Southern Pride* delivered a signal to Dan Holden's cabin. After reading it, Holden went to find Harry Cameron.

"Bad news, I'm afraid. It looks like I won't be joining you." He waved the radiogram. "From my mother. My father had a heart attack two weeks ago and is in intensive care. They need me at home." Holden looked out over the Indian Ocean. "Well, it couldn't last. Seems I'm in the stationery business after all."

"Perhaps we'll meet again some day."

"I hope so."

The Camerons left the *Southern Pride* at Penang after saying goodbye to Captain Ross and Luke, the little girl weeping when she realized she would not be seeing Jessica again. Dan was sailing to Singapore, where he hoped to pick up a trans-pacific liner or cargo boat.

On the quayside Harry bought a copy of the *Straits Times*. A leading news item said that Japanese forces, having subdued Manchuria, were now pushing on into China. At the time it didn't seem to mean much.

2

Stretching in her stirrups astride Spartan, the six-year-old chestnut gelding her father had given her for her sixteenth birthday, Jenny had a perfect view of the bathers in the sungei sixty feet below; all were boys and all were naked, and their ages ranged from the very tiny, three or four, to the near adult, seventeen and eighteen. She envied them their freedom. She would have loved to slip out of her dress and cool down herself, but that of course was out of the question. For that matter she should not have been where she was at all; this was a part of the Cameron estate reserved for the Malay workers to take recreation in. But it was only natural, she told herself, that she should be curious about the opposite sex's bodies. Especially Malay bodies. The Chinese, who had their own stretch of water elsewhere, so that if they wanted to roast a wild pig they could do so without offending the Muslim Malays, were not nearly so interesting. But Malay bodies seemed much more— well—beautiful than the bodies of the European boys she swam and played tennis with. And much more well endowed. She shuddered with delicious guilt at the prurient image.

Not that, apart from her brothers, who didn't count, she had ever seen a European boy naked. Well no, that was not strictly true. At a swimming party on the Harrison plantation, Jamie Harrison, who was only sixteen himself, had drunk too much Tiger beer and proceeded to strip off his swimming trunks, waving them above his head. The other girls had shrieked in mock horror and fled. She hadn't, not even when Jamie advanced on her, leering. She had stood her ground, stared him down, dared him with her eyes to do something. He hadn't of course. His nerve had given out as she continued to inspect, unmoving, his shrivelled genitalia, so pink and wormlike. Finally he covered his embarrassment by diving into the river. A little later she saw him being sick.

31

Spartan snorted nervously and pawed the ground, aware of something that Jenny could neither scent nor hear. "Easy, boy, easy," she soothed, patting the horse's neck, concerned that the bathers would look up. They did not.

She wheeled the horse carefully on the narrow path, where one side led down to the sungei and the other to impenetrable jungle. But, cautious as she was, Spartan's off fore hoof missed its footing and slid off the path toward the sungei. Panicking, the gelding reared. Jenny hurled her weight forward, to rebalance the horse. To no avail. A moment later she was thrown. Instinct caused her to hang on to the bridle, but she was no match for half a ton of horseflesh. As the gelding regained the path it kicked its heels and galloped off. Jenny was dragged thirty or forty yards before she had the wisdom to let go. Then her bare head struck a jutting rock and she passed out.

When she came to a young Malay was bending over her, peering at her anxiously. She struggled to a sitting position.

"Where's the horse?"

"Over there."

Spartan was standing calmly a few feet away.

"Did I faint?"

"You hit your head. The skin isn't broken."

She recognized her rescuer, the son of one of her father's rubber tappers, doubtless a tapper in his own right by now. She also prided herself, as her father did, on knowing every one of the estate workers by their first names. But she had to think very hard in this instance. Then she had it. Rashid.

"Help me up, please."

"I think you should sit there for a few more minutes." Like most Malays brought up as second or third generation tappers, Rashid spoke excellent English.

"No, please help me up."

He pulled her to her feet by the wrists. She stumbled against him, her head spinning. When working he wore European dress, a cotton shirt and cotton trousers. Today he had on a batik sari from the waist down. From the waist up he was naked, and she could smell the freshness of the sungei on his chest.

Feeling uncomfortable at their proximity, he pushed her away gently, holding her at arm's length so that she did not fall. After a moment her head cleared, but she would have a duck egg of a bump on it before the day was out. Already there was a swelling.

"*Terima kasih*, thank you," she said, adding: "Stupid horse," as though that explained everything. "Were you close by when he bucked?"

"No, I was down there. But I heard him and saw what happened."

"I must have been day-dreaming. I'm miles away from my usual route."

"Yes. Will you be all right to ride back?"

"Of course." Now that the dizzy spell had passed Jenny was embarrassed and wanted to get as far away from Rashid as she could, as quickly as she could. "Thank you again. *Selamat tinggal*."

Rashid watched her until she was out of sight, wondering at the habits of Europeans. It was common knowledge among the Malays, especially among the seventeen- and eighteen-year-olds, his own age group, that the mem's daughter came to spy on them at least once a week. They all thought it a great joke.

During the following fortnight Jenny found herself going more regularly to the sungei bathing area, though on these later occasions she made no secret of her presence, taking Spartan into the sungei downstream and allowing him his head to wander up. She took care not to get too close in case she frightened the Malays off, but she always let them know she was there, a hundred yards away, round a bend, by singing or whistling or talking unnecessarily loudly at the gelding. At first she was reluctant to admit to herself that her object was to see Rashid again. He was very handsome, of course, with the sort of fairish skin that indicated some European blood in his lineage, but . . . No, there were no buts, she finally conceded. She wanted to get to know him better, and that was that.

The only fly in the ointment was Jamie Harrison, who had ridden over from his parents' place one afternoon and, quite by accident, though he admitted he'd been looking for her, found her. He'd made it clear before the incident when he removed his bathing trunks that he was interested in her and now he had something extra to prove, seeing as how he'd made a fool of himself that day. But she was in no way attracted to him, and she had to be quite sharp when he seemed reluctant to take the hint and leave, which he eventually did, only with bad grace. Thereafter she sometimes sensed that he was nearby, watching her. But she never saw him and she soon dismissed the notion as a figment of her imagination.

For the first few days after she sent Jamie packing, Rashid didn't approach her, although she knew he was there, bathing with the others. It didn't bother her that she was ignored. She felt strangely contented, sitting there astride Spartan or on the stream bank, dangling her legs in the cool water. Malays could be abnormally shy away from their own kind.

Then one evening he appeared clutching two bunches of rambutans. Without a word he handed one bunch to her, sat down on the bank and started to eat the other. In between mouthfuls he asked her how her head was. It was completely better, she told him, and he nodded, satisfied. When he finished his own fruit he said *selamat tinggal*, goodbye, and left to rejoin his companions. A gift of fruit became a regular evening ritual from thereon.

Jessica was part pleased, part perplexed, at the change that had come over her daughter. For the first month of the two months that had passed since the boys flew to England, Jenny had not taken much interest in anything, had simply moped around the bungalow or read alone in her room; or had gone for long solitary rides on her horse. Whenever asked whether she was all right, the reply was invariably a polite monosyllable. "Yes." Or: "Of course, don't fuss." She was missing her brothers, in Jess's view, finding life lonely now that they had gone, although she probably would not have admitted that even to herself. She was also growing up very fast, making that sudden transition from girlhood to womanhood and becoming slightly bewildered by it all. She still played tennis and went to parties on other estates, but usually, Jess was told when not there to see for herself, she could be found sitting by herself in a corner, apparently not in the least interested in what was going on around her or in making more than the most perfunctory of conversations.

Now that had changed. She still went out on Spartan each afternoon or evening, but she did so with an eagerness not evident hitherto.

Jessica discussed it with Harry, who, typically engrossed as he was in running the estate, had not noticed anything out of the ordinary.

"She probably meets friends," Harry conjectured, only half listening.

"That's not the impression she gives me. And she certainly doesn't mention them. Who are these friends that she's reluctant to talk about?"

"How do I know? Could be anyone, anywhere."

"No, not anywhere. She doesn't go far, I can tell that by Spartan's condition when she stables him. In any case, why doesn't she invite them home? She used to."

"Hell, Jess, I don't know. We're old fogies, don't forget, as far as she's concerned. All of her contemporaries have horses. They probably meet somewhere and chat. Or tether their horses and go for a drive. Some of the older boys have use of their father's cars. I've seen Peter Bryant's Buick on many occasions. Young girls are a mystery to me, but you were one once. What did you do at sixteen?"

"When I was sixteen Edward the Seventh was on the throne and life was very different."

"He was on the throne when I was sixteen too."

"But you were out here. I was in the U.K."

Harry put down his pen, leaned back from the accounts book he was working on, and picked up his stengah glass. He took a sip of the whisky. "If that's supposed to mean something I'm afraid I don't understand it."

"It means that in 1908 young girls behaved in a certain manner. For all I know they do so in 1932, in England."

"You've been in Malaya long enough to know it's different here. Not better or worse, just different." It was the wrong thing to say. The boys were in England and Jess was pining for them, though she never said as much. However, for Jess, for now, England represented everything that was gracious and civilized, whereas Malaya might just as well have been Mars. "Would you like me to have a word with her?"

Jess considered the offer. Harry Cameron was a splendid man, a strong man hewn from the same teak as his grandfather; a husband she loved. But, as he'd admitted himself, he knew nothing of sixteen-year-old girls.

"No," she said. "No, it's probably nothing, a phase she's going through. Let's leave it."

They dropped the subject. Harry put it to the back of his mind, where it would have remained had he not received an anonymous letter in his pigeonhole at the state Planters' Club in Kuala Kelan a week later. The words were handwritten in capitals. Judging by the style the unknown author wasn't very old.

IF YOU WANT TO KNOW WHAT YOUR DAUGHTER GETS UP TO EACH EVENING SUGGEST YOU RIDE OUT TO THE SUNGEI WHERE YOUR MALAYS BATHE.

DOWNSTREAM OF THERE YOU'LL FIND OUT WHY
JENNY PAYS NO ATTENTION TO EUROPEAN BOYS
HER OWN AGE.

The notepaper and envelope were cheap, and Harry's immediate
reaction was to treat the letter with the contempt it deserved and
toss it on the fire. But he didn't. He put it in his pocket and worried
about it while drinking whisky in the bar with his friends. He left
before his usual time, unable to concentrate on a conversation
concerning what Goodyear and Dunlop were up to in the next-door
state of Negri Sembilan.

The letter continued to nag him while driving back to the estate.
It was all nonsense, of course, the innuendo that Jenny was up to
something she would not want her parents to know about. One
of Jenny's schoolfriends was jealous of her for some reason and
had taken the coward's way out to get her into trouble. Or under
suspicion.

He considered, and rejected, showing the letter to Jess. She
would want to tackle Jenny, ask their daughter what it all meant.
That was not the way to go about it. By the same token he didn't
know how to talk to Jenny on a personal basis. He would find out
what was what for himself.

Only in one respect did the note bother him. Whether innocently or not, Jenny shouldn't be riding in an area set aside for
the Malays' bathing. They wouldn't like it and neither did he. If
it were true, he'd have to put a stop to it. However, he'd sleep
on the problem for a couple of days, see what his subconscious
came up with.

It was Sunday. After a late lunch Jenny excused herself and went
to saddle Spartan. Jessica was running a slight temperature and
retired to her room to lie down. Harry sat in the shade of the
verandah cradling a long gin and tonic. Jenny waved to him as
she left.

Harry gave her half an hour. There was no hurry. If the poison-
pen letter was right, he knew where she'd be. If she wasn't there,
it was highly likely that the nameless writer was acting more out
of malice than fact.

He took his time saddling his own horse, an eight-year-old mare
called Sapphire who seemed both puzzled and pleased to be taken
out at this unusual hour, and who whinnied with delight on seeing him.

From the bungalow to the sungei bathing area was almost exactly two miles. He kept Sapphire down to a walk, as though reluctant to face whatever might be ahead. He also felt ashamed of his actions, which were those of a snooper, and once almost turned for home. But he didn't. He pressed on. Having come this far he might as well find out once and for all if Jenny was breaking estate rules. He couldn't contemplate her doing anything more sinister than that.

When he saw Spartan tied to a tree but no sign of Jenny, he experienced acute disappointment. When he heard Jenny's voice, or rather her whimpers—and there could be no doubt why she was whimpering—his stomach turned over. What he saw when Sapphire had taken a few more strides his mind refused to accept.

Harry Cameron was not the sort of man to witness his daughter being made love to by anyone, be that person white or even her husband, without suffering a severe psychological jolt. But to see her beneath a Malay—his arms around her, his loins buried in hers, her legs around him—caused Harry to go temporarily insane. For a split second he froze. He could not have moved had his life depended upon it. And within that heartbeat he experienced a whole range of violent emotions, each one crowding in on the next. Panic—bewilderment—despair—rage. And finally hate, for Jenny was not, could not possibly be, a willing partner. Specks of foam appeared around his mouth. Although his eyes told him Jenny was not struggling, his reason dismissed the evidence. His daughter was being raped.

The howl that left his lungs was a terrible sound, the cry of someone who had looked into hell. When questioned later, the Malays swimming five hundred yards upstream all confessed that they had never heard anything like it, and that they were terrified into immobility.

Then Harry was upon Rashid, hurling him with a madman's strength from Jenny's body—Jenny who lay there on Rashid's sari, lay there naked, her eyes wide with terror. Harry would never forget that image of his daughter, her tiny breasts, her tuft of pubic hair, the wetness on the inside of her thighs. It was a sight no father should have to look upon.

Harry went after Rashid, who tried to scramble away, attempted to run along the path, toward his friends. To safety. Harry caught him and battered him to the ground with a huge fist, blows that would have felled an ox. Behind him Jenny screamed and screamed. Harry didn't hear her words, or heard only a few. That it wasn't Rashid's fault. That he'd done nothing wrong. That he wasn't attacking her. That her father must leave him alone. That she would explain.

Rashid's face was a mask of blood where Harry's boot connected with it again and again. After the first few seconds he was barely conscious, but, feebly, he kept trying to crawl away. His nose was broken, his teeth were smashed, and several ribs were fractured. Harry didn't let up, continued kicking him, torn between wanting to exact revenge there and then and running back to Sapphire for his rifle, whereupon he would have shot Rashid.

Finally Rashid was still, but Harry hadn't finished. His rage was unabated, his craving for retribution unsatisfied. With one mighty movement he picked up the Malay and hurled him down into the sungei, down sixty or more feet, where his body struck a boulder that broke his neck and split open his chest like a rotten apple.

Jenny let out a wail of anguish and started to run away. Harry sprinted after her, tried to cover her with the sari before realizing what the garment was and heaving it away. He stripped off his shirt and placed it around her shoulders. She pounded her father's face with her fists. He pinioned her arms to her side.

"It's all right, it's all right."

"But it was me!" she wept. "It was me! I wanted him to do it. It was ME."

"You don't know what you're saying."

"She doesn't know what she's saying."

Four hours had passed since Harry brought Jenny home, where Jessica, after listening to no more than the briefest details, had put her to bed, fed her brandy and comforted her until the police arrived.

Harry radioed for them. He saw no reason not to. In his mind he had committed no crime. He had stumbled across his daughter being violated and had killed her assailant.

The sergeant in the sub-station at Ruang quickly decided that this was too big for him to handle and wirelessed Kuala Kelan, telling them what had happened as far as he knew it and asking for a senior officer and a police doctor. Together with two uniformed constables, they had arrived two hours ago. One hour ago Rashid's body was brought up from the sungei, strapped across Spartan's back, and taken to the stables, where it now lay under guard. It could not stay there long. In Malaya it paid to get a corpse interred as soon as possible. An autopsy would not be necessary. No one disputed the cause of death, least of all Harry. But, whereas he said he'd killed a rapist, Jenny argued otherwise; she had gone with Rashid of her own free will. She had made that statement to the chief inspector—Bill Hyde, an old friend of Harry's—before the police doctor, Alan Fielding, another friend, had given her a sedative and put her under.

It was Jenny's statement, admittedly unsigned yet and therefore unofficial, that was causing all the problems.

The servants had been dismissed. Harry, Hyde, Fielding and Jessica were sitting around the huge dining table. Harry was drinking whisky, Jessica brandy. The policeman and the doctor were sipping cool beers. Hyde wasn't sure he should be letting Harry drink, but concluded there was little he could do about it without causing unpleasantness. Besides, Harry wasn't getting drunk.

"She won't be shaken, Harry," said Hyde. "Jess was present, so was Alan. I put it to her half a dozen times in several different ways. She was a willing party to what, er, transpired."

"Balls. She's had a terrible time. She's not responsible for her words. Christ, you weren't there!"

"I know. And there's the rub. No one was except you and Jenny and the Malay. The Malay can't testify so it's your word against Jenny's and you're both giving me different versions."

Bill Hyde scratched his graying head. A medium-sized, thickset man with the face of a boxer, he had been a policeman in Malaya since the early Twenties and a chief inspector in the state capital for two years. He had seen the police force grow from little more than a ragbag of misfits to its present level of efficiency. A decade ago, a European planter killing a Malay worker wouldn't have raised more than the odd eyebrow. Now it was different. It wasn't going to be easy to shovel this under the carpet; possible, with some fancy footwork and fast string pulling, but not easy, not with an hysterical girl saying that she was a willing partner. What the hell had got into her? Of course, if she could be persuaded to change her testimony, agree that she was raped, that would be a different matter. It wouldn't even come to trial. A word with the Malay's parents, perhaps some compensation for the loss of an extra bread-winner, and that would be that. But, as of now, it was a bad business. He wasn't going to tell Harry as much, not yet, but Alan Fielding's examination went along with the girl's story. There were none of the usual signs that a rape had occurred. For that matter, it was Fielding's professional opinion that Jenny had lost her virginity before today. If that were so, it made the rape theory even more unlikely. What a bloody mess.

"A bad business," he said aloud.

"I don't believe what I'm hearing," said Harry. "You're telling me that Jenny went voluntarily with that animal. You're as good as calling her a whore."

"Not me, Harry. I'm not saying anything. I'm just listening. Jenny's the one who's saying she went of her own volition." Hyde threw a sidelong glance at Fielding. "And if she continues saying it I'm afraid you've landed yourself in a lot of trouble."

"You can't mean what I think you mean," said Jessica quietly. She too believed Jenny's version of events, but it was up to her to save her husband and daughter from humiliation at best. "If I understand you correctly, the chief witness in a murder trial involving Harry would be Jenny. My God, you can't be serious."

"That's why I'm saying it's a bad business, Jess," said Hyde. "Jenny's old enough to know her own mind. If she persists with her story, it'll cause a sensation. The newspapers will have a field day. Harry's not exactly unknown in these parts."

"Jenny will come to her senses," said Jessica. "I'll talk to her."

"Christ, Jess, you're siding with them," protested Harry.

"She's siding with you if you did but know it," interrupted Fielding. "Look, this is not my area of competence and perhaps I'm talking out of turn, but we're all old friends in this room and it won't do the European community any good if this goes to trial. It could ruin you and Jess even if you're acquitted, which I'm sure you would be. We're a long way from convicting Europeans for killing Malays under these circumstances, but in order to get an acquittal your counsel would have to give Jenny a hard time. A *very* hard time, for a court would want to know what sort of daughter it is who calls her father a liar. No family could survive it. The Malay's dead, and good riddance. *He* should have known better. Nothing's going to bring him back."

"Be careful," cautioned Hyde, suspecting what was coming.

"The way I see it we have two alternatives," went on Fielding. He was a tiny man, thin as a stick, but with a very sharp mind and a reputation as an expert bridge player. In three years he was due to retire; he wanted to coast along in neutral until then. He certainly didn't want to be called upon to give medical evidence under oath against Harry Cameron. He was confident Jenny was telling the truth, but she should not have done what she had. Neither should the damned Malay, of course, whose wisest course would have been to turn tail and flee when he perceived Jenny's interest. If only everything were that simple! The case wasn't unique. In his professional capacity he had come across several European women with Malay lovers, though they had been much older than Jenny. And a hell of a sight more discreet. "Either Jenny changes her testimony and makes a formal statement that she was raped, or she holds to her current story and starts something we may not be able to control. Whatever *really* happened out there—shut up, please, Harry—Jenny must be apprised of the probable consequences."

"You'll be able to discuss this more freely if I wasn't present," said Hyde, standing up.

"Go with him, Harry," said Fielding.

"To hell with that. This concerns me more than anyone."

"Bill?" Fielding jerked his head in the direction of the door.

"Technically I could arrest you," said Hyde. "I don't want to do that. Let's sit outside, leave this to Alan and Jess."

"Please, Harry," said Jessica.

Harry took his whisky, Hyde his glass of beer. They sat on the verandah, listening to the night sounds.

"Children," said Harry bitterly, taking a long swallow of whisky. He knew they were right now, all of them—Bill, Alan, Jess. And Jenny. Not that it would have made any difference. The Malay deserved his fate.

"I'm sometimes glad Molly and I didn't have any," said Hyde. "Molly's not, of course."

"What's going to happen?"

"I'd rather not anticipate events. We've first of all got to hear what Jenny has to say. Officially. However, I think Alan and Jess between them can persuade her that she made a mistake with her first statement. Shock or something. This is off the record, you understand, but she'll probably say something to the effect that she was out riding when she was attacked. You came along, just a little too late, saw what was happening and fought off her assailant. In the struggle he fell to his death. It won't be pleasant for Jenny, but it's better than the alternative. You never said how you happened to be on the spot, by the way."

"No." Harry hesitated before producing the anonymous letter and passing it across.

"Jesus."

"Bad?"

"Not good," said Hyde, "for two reasons. One, if this were produced in court, at your trial if it came to that, the implications are that it wasn't the first time Jenny and the Malay—sorry, old boy—had got together. Which almost certainly disposes of the rape angle, though I suppose it could be argued that you weren't to know Jenny wasn't being attacked before you sailed in. Two, somebody has been spying on Jenny, and that somebody could cause us trouble. Any idea who wrote this?"

"None."

"Unfortunate. I'll hang on to it, if you don't mind, make a few discreet enquiries. I suppose Jenny might know who the writer is?"

"It's possible."

"Has anyone else seen it?"

"No."

"Let's keep it that way. Don't mention it at all, not even to Jess and certainly not to Jenny. If anyone has to talk to Jenny about it, that'll be me."

Alan Fielding appeared on the verandah, alone.

"Jess has gone to sit with Jenny. I told her she'll be unconscious until tomorrow morning, but Jess wanted to do it anyway."

He took a pull at his beer.

"This is what we've decided. You can hear it, Bill, it won't compromise you. Jessica will talk to Jenny when she wakes up. Now that's important, Harry. Let Jess do the talking. It's highly likely that Jenny will agree she made a mistake in her original statement, and admit that she was raped. Once she's done so, Bill will come out to take a formal testimony. My report will confirm that a rape took place. Thereafter there shouldn't be any trouble regarding the Malay's death. Right, Bill?"

"If Jenny testifies as you've indicated and your examination confirms a rape, right, there'll be no problem. I'll need a statement from Harry, of course, though he can tell it as he saw it, his original story. Then I'll kick the whole file upstairs to the superintendent, but he'll rubber-stamp my recommendations. What about the Malay's parents?"

"In my view Harry should keep away from them for now, until you've seen them. Tomorrow morning, maybe. Later, in a few days, Harry can have a word with them, let them know that in no way does he blame them for their son's actions, confirm that they still have jobs. Okay, Harry?"

"Whatever you say," said Harry dully. Everything was moving too fast for him.

"There's one other matter," said Fielding. "Not only as a medical practitioner but as a friend also, I'd advise that Jenny go away for a while. Up country, perhaps, or even out of the state. Jess agrees. The child's been through a lot and she needs rest, lots of it. Besides, some of this is bound to leak out. It'll be healthier for her if she's not around to be questioned by the nosy parkers."

Harry accepted Fielding's reasoning. Jenny would be telling a lie in her statement, not only to save her father's skin but to protect her own reputation. It was unlikely that she'd want to be anywhere near the estate until the horrors of the day were forgotten.

After Fielding and Hyde departed with Rashid's body, Harry returned to the dining-room. He didn't recall pouring another whisky, but there was one at his elbow when Jess came in. She stood behind him, massaging his neck with her fingers.

"I heard them drive off," she said. "Is everything settled?"

"It seems to be. Not that I had much say in matters. How's Jenny?"

"Asleep. It'll be best for everyone if we do as Alan and I agreed." She sat beside him, holding his hand. "Are you all right?"

"A bit bemused, shell-shocked, but otherwise, yes." He looked at her. "It's a long time since I killed anyone, Jess."

"I know."

"You're not condemning me?"

"How can I? It must have been intolerable for you when you saw what was going on. I might have done the same in your position."

"Not you, you'd have reasoned it through."

A flicker of a sad smile crossed Jessica's face. "Perhaps you're right. How did you know where they'd be, incidentally?"

"I didn't. It was coincidence."

"You don't usually ride on a Sunday afternoon."

"I felt in need of the exercise."

If Jessica suspected there was more to Harry's explanation than met the eye, she was wise enough to keep her own counsel.

"I'll have to go with her, of course, with Jenny. For a week or two. Perhaps longer."

"I understand that. Where will you go?"

"I'll need to think about it. Out of state, possibly."

"There's Richard's Hill."

"Too close." Jessica hesitated. "It might be as well if you weren't here when she woke up," she suggested gently. "She's going to feel terrible enough as it is, and she and I have some serious talking to do before I get in touch with Bill Hyde. Stay in Kuala Kelan for a couple of days. We'll be gone by then. I'll leave you a long letter."

Harry drained his glass and stood up.

"I'll pack a few things now and be ready to pull out at first light."

He tried a grin, which didn't come off. "I'd go now except I'd more than likely drive into the river."

She watched him leave the room, shoulders hunched. He'd get over it, of course, but she hadn't seen him so down since that day in France, in the emergency aid station west of St. Omer. In 1915, the third week in May, toward the close of the Second Battle of Ypres.

At first she paid no more attention to the good-looking lieutenant from the British 27th Division than she did to any of her other patients. She had enough on her hands and had hardly slept for thirty hours, during which time she had lost count of the number of her charges who had died.

She hadn't thought it possible that anything could be like this when she'd volunteered as a nurse, paying her own fare from Edinburgh to London to do so. Nursing, for middle-class girls back in Scotland, was a way of feeling useful, of contributing something to the local community, and it meant mostly looking after the young or the elderly and infirm. She had seen dead bodies, of course, had Jessica Munroe, and had even attended post mortems out of curiosity. At twenty-two she thought she'd seen it all.

Jessica's "ward" was a tent holding twenty-four junior officers who were either recovering from minor surgery or whose wounds were not serious enough for them to be sent further to the rear. It was her third day here. Her previous ward had been for other ranks, and they were crowded sixty or more to a tent, when a tent could be found. More often than not they lay in the open. She had been transferred here after four weeks with the ORs. It was meant to be a "rest." And so it would have been, comparatively, had she only had the officers to look after. But she had volunteered for double shifts, to help nurse the ORs outside. They were the ones who were dying.

The good-looking 27th Division lieutenant, according to the chart at the end of his bunk, had taken a minor whiff of gas and had shrapnel wounds in his right shoulder and both legs. Although the wounds weren't serious, they had been sufficient to incapacitate him. He was one of the lucky ones, though to hear him talk to those around him you wouldn't think it.

"The General Staff need shooting, ours and theirs, but ours especially. They're killing tens of thousands of good men by their idiocy. We should have pulled back to the Yser Canal, not try to hold a reduced salient."

The RAMC doctor, an Ulsterman named O'Brien, coughed discreetly.

"We try to keep the war out of here, Lieutenant Cameron."

"Then you're not making a very good job of it, which means you're either a fool or as blind as some of your patients."

"Perhaps." O'Brien was too tired to take offense. He'd heard it all before anyway, how doctors patched up and healed the wounded only to send them back to be killed. There was some truth in it. To Jessica he said: "Change the dressings, nurse. I'd pay particular attention to the buttock wounds, and I wouldn't be too gentle."

Jessica wasn't. Lieutenant Cameron had no right to talk to the doctor like that.

"I'm not here to mother you, Lieutenant."

"Thank God for small mercies."

"Nor is it my fault you don't believe in the war."

"You make it sound like a rumor."

Except when his injuries needed attention, they kept a civil distance from one another after that, though occasionally she would catch him looking at her, studying her. He was obsessed with the war, or rather what he believed to be the mismanagement of it. Whenever she came to check his dressings or simply take his temperature, he was always holding forth to whoever was nearest about the incompetence of the General Staff.

Within a week he was ready to be discharged.

"My platoon needs me. Some of them are only kids."

She had to smile at that. He was exactly four months older than her according to his records. And curiously, although British, his home was in Malaya. In spite of herself, she couldn't resist asking him why he was in Europe.

"I thought it was my fight too. I could have been wrong. Anyway, why are *you*?" he countered. "The last I heard they weren't conscripting nurses."

He was "walking wounded" now, on his feet, and, even though he leaned on a stick and she was quite tall herself at five feet seven, he towered above her. He was too thin by a half a stone and his dark curly hair, worn longer than regulation, could have done with a wash, but some of the other nurses considered him the most handsome occupant of Jessica's ward, one describing his features as those of a dissolute saint. This nurse thought Jessica lucky. Jessica thought otherwise. He was loud-mouthed, self-opinionated, arrogant, and the Military Cross ribbon on his tunic, designating him as an officially accredited hero, did not give him license to be boorish.

"I volunteered," she said coolly.

They were outside the hospital tent. In the distance the heavy artillery volleyed and thundered, the pyrotechnics visible for fifty miles.

"For some idiotic female reason, I expect, seeing yourself as Florence Nightingale, a ministering angel playing dolls with live human beings."

To her mortification she suddenly found herself crying; huge, silent, unstoppable tears that rolled down her cheeks.

"Oh Christ," he said helplessly, and spun on his heel, limping away on his cane.

The following day there was another officer in his cot.

He turned up again a week later, carrying a small bunch of wild flowers, and sought her out.

"Go away," she said.

"I've come to apologize."

He thrust the flowers at her. She had no option but to accept them.

"You've deserted to say you're sorry?"

"I haven't deserted. My regiment's regrouping and they've no use for me while I can't lead a bayonet charge." He still had his stick, she noticed, though he was hardly limping at all now. "I've three days' local leave and I thought I'd spend it with you."

"You're insane."

"Highly probable, but we can't discuss my mental state standing here. There's an *estaminet* in the village. We can decide how we'll spend the three days there, over a bottle of wine."

"I can't simply walk off like that."

"I know, but you finish your shift in two hours. I checked with O'Brien. He confirmed that you're due for some leave too."

"Which I'm going to spend asleep."

"We can debate it over the wine. I'll expect you at six thirty, say."

"No."

"Please."

"Why? You don't even like me."

"You're quite wrong. I not only like you, I want to marry you."

He tapped his tunic. "I have the necessary permission here, but we only have three days for the wedding and the honeymoon. We shouldn't waste any of it."

Jessica's jaw dropped. She took an involuntary step backward. "You *are* insane."

"I thought we were going to discuss that in the *estaminet*. Six thirty." He started to walk off.

"I won't be there," she called after him.

But she was. The wine was already on the table, her glass filled. She sat down primly and collected her thoughts.

"I want you to know that I'm only here because I wish to make it perfectly clear I will not be seeing you again."

"That's a terribly clumsy sentence. Are you a Protestant?"

"Presbyterian." Jessica gulped.

"That's the same thing. There's a Protestant church on the outskirts of the village. I've already had a word with the minister. He can fit us in any time. Poor old chap, he hasn't had much trade since the war started."

"Now see here," said Jessica firmly, her head spinning, "I am not going to marry you—not in a Protestant church, not here, not anywhere."

"Why not?"

"Why not? Why *not*? That's a maniacal question."

"And that's not an answer. Look, if this were peacetime and I'd met you in London or Kuala Lumpur, we could have taken it more slowly. I'd have invited you out, called on your parents, taken you for picnics and dinners, driven you into the country. After a few months we'd have announced our engagement. Six months after that we'd have got married. We've no time for such niceties. There's a war on. It may last for years. If I don't marry you now I may never see you again."

"Marry me," said Jessica flatly. "When did you decide all this? A week ago you accused me of playing games with real lives."

"The moment I saw you."

Jessica thought she'd misheard. "I beg your pardon?"

"I knew I wanted to marry you the second I set eyes on you. I didn't know how to ask you so I acted stupidly, belligerently."

"The moment you saw me," said Jessica weakly.

"You're repeating everything I say."

"That's because you're sweeping me off my feet and I don't like it." *Liar*, an inner voice said. "I'm a practical, down-to-earth Scots girl who doesn't do anything without considering the pros and cons. I know nothing about you and you know nothing about me."

"I know I want to marry you. Isn't that enough?"

"You're . . . you're a lunatic."

"We can't keep on discussing my sanity, but if I am a lunatic I'm one who saw a lovely young woman standing in a hospital tent on the fringes of the most terrible war imaginable, and decided—instantly—that she was for me."

"But you live in Malaya. God, I'm not even sure I know where Malaya is."

"You turn left at India and keep going. It's quite civilized. You'll get used to it. Listen, I asked the *patronne* to put some champagne to one side. Perhaps you think better with champagne than with red wine. We don't have much time. I promised the minister we'd be there by eight o'clock."

"Tonight!" squealed Jessica.

"Of course tonight. He's bending the rules a little because there are various formalities one should go through before a church wedding, but he assures me it's all legal. Now, what about that champagne?"

"Please," said Jessica faintly.

She was still protesting at the madness of it all half a bottle of champagne and one hour later, but she was protesting outside the *estaminet*, on the way to the church.

She couldn't possibly marry a man she didn't know. She couldn't live on a rubber plantation in Malaya. Good grief, she knew nothing about rubber or Malaya. What earthly use would she be? What if his father didn't like her? What if . . . What if . . .

Then, quite suddenly, she felt calm and secure, as if marrying Harry Cameron was the most natural thing in the world. It *would* have been been absurd had she been in Edinburgh, but she was in France, and in France all things were possible.

By fifteen minutes past eight, in the presence of half a dozen witnesses drummed up by the minister, they were married. For form's sake, although the minister spoke reasonable English, the service was conducted entirely in French, of which neither of them understood more than one word in three. They took their cues from the clergyman. Jessica's wedding-ring was Harry's signet ring; he promised to buy her something more appropriate when the war permitted.

Outside, Jessica said: "Harry."

"Yes?"

"Nothing. I'm just trying to get used to it. Apart from the service, that's the first time I've called you by name. And you haven't kissed me except to seal the knot."

He kissed her then, deeply and passionately, watched by a group of street urchins who cheered lustily and shouted something, probably obscene. Harry waved to them. Jessica clung to his arm feeling marvellously safe and content.

"There is one thing, of course," she said as they walked back to the village. The guns were still pounding in the east and it was growing dark with a possibility of rain, but nothing could spoil the day. "You've been very efficient, I grant you, in arranging the papers and the church and even—even—talking me into it. But you seem to have forgotten that we have nowhere to stay tonight."

"Wrong. The *estaminet* has a spare room above the bar. The sheets will probably be damp as they always are in France, but it's ours for three days. I arranged it with the *patronne* before you arrived earlier."

"Good God," said Jessica.

"I also arranged with her son to take a note to O'Brien if you hadn't returned to the hospital by eight o'clock. In that event, O'Brien was to assume that you were on three days' leave beginning immediately and the boy was to bring your clothes to the *estaminet*."

"*If* I hadn't returned by eight o'clock," said Jessica archly. "You weren't one hundred percent confident then?"

"Ninety-eight percent."

"If you don't finish this war as a brigadier at least, I'll start to believe there's something in this theory of yours about the General Staff."

"I'll be happy just to finish the war."

Later, in bed, when they had explored all the unknown folds and crevices of each other's bodies and made love until they were empty of desire, Jessica said, in between sipping champagne,

"You know, throughout all this you haven't once told me you love me."

"I just did."

"That was during sex. I mean otherwise—otherwise you haven't said you love me."

"You may be assured absolutely that I do."

Their three days flew past at the speed of light. Harry returned to his regiment. Neither knew when they would see each other again, if ever.

Within a month Jessica suspected she was pregnant. Doctor O'Brien confirmed it.

"We'll be sorry to lose you, but your place is at home, young lady."

Jessica went back to Scotland, to her parents, who, already primed by letter and happy to see their daughter safely home from the dangers of war-ravaged Europe, accepted her whirlwind marriage and impending motherhood with equanimity. When their granddaughter was born in the spring of 1916, they had no objection to the child being christened Jeanne Helen; Helen after Jessica's mother and Jeanne after the *patronne* of the *estaminet*. But because Scottish tongues could not manage Jeanne, she was quickly nicknamed Jen and thereafter Jenny.

Harry was not given home leave for the remainder of the Great War, though in the summer of 1917 he was sent to London with important dispatches that had to be taken by hand. He managed to let Jessica know of his plans and she travelled down by train to be with him, bringing Jenny. They spent a blissful forty-eight hours in an hotel in Russell Square, and it was there that their second child and first son was conceived.

During the next eighteen months Harry's letters arrived at irregular intervals and said little. He received promotions. In the autumn of 1917 he was a captain; in the spring of 1918 a major. She only found out about the Bar to his Military Cross from the *London Gazette*.

It was far from an easy time for Jessica, but she was no worse off than any other young wife and mother, who 'all dreaded the yellow War Office telegram that would inform them a husband or son was dead.

Jessica followed the campaigns in the newspapers. Cambrai; the breakthrough to the Marne; the Second Battle of the Marne; St. Mihiel; Amiens. She had seen at first hand what war could be like, and she knew what Harry must be going through. She prayed for him nightly, prayed for his safety, that he would not risk too much.

Then came that marvellous morning in November, the news that Ludendorff had fallen from power. Ten days later it was all over.

Harry was home for Christmas, which he spent in Scotland with her parents. In February 1919, Harry and Jessica, Jenny and Jeff, sailed for Singapore.

When Harry returned from Kuala Kelan on the Wednesday morning following Rashid's death, Jessica and Jenny had gone. Jessica's letter told him that they had left to stay with the Drummonds at Batu Ferringhi on Penang Island. Harry remembered the Drummonds, who were more friends of Jess's than they were of his. They were a childless couple in their middle thirties who had both been employed by an American bank in Kuala Kelan until one of them—the wife, he thought it was—had inherited some money, a considerable sum. They had then set about fulfilling a dream, that of building an hotel overlooking a beach and watching it prosper. The last he heard the hotel idea had turned out to be a flop, and they'd converted the few rooms already constructed into a beach house for themselves. Neither worked any longer. They had enough capital to see them through and no one to care about if they spent it all.

Jenny (Jess wrote) had seen sense after some persuading. She had made a statement to Bill Hyde to the effect that she had been attacked and raped by Rashid. Bill reckoned that would be the end of it, especially as Alan Fielding would corroborate Jenny's testimony. Bill would, however, be calling on Harry shortly, to finalize matters. He did so the following morning. Thursday.

He drove out to the bungalow alone.

"You look bloody awful," he said to Harry, accepting a beer.

"Thanks."

"My pleasure. I solved the mystery of the anonymous note, by the way."

"Who?"

"Jamie Harrison, Clive Harrison's brat."

"The little bastard. I'd like to wring his neck."

"His father's way ahead of you. He took his belt to Jamie, who was, in any case, pretty ashamed of what he'd done."

"So that's two more who know, three if we include Peggy Harrison."

"They know nothing for certain. Jamie wasn't around last Sunday. I established that."

"They can add two and two together and wonder why the official verdict is rape."

"They won't say anything. I made it clear I'd hound Jamie from now till kingdom come if even just one word appears as gossip. He won't want it spread around that he writes poison pen letters. Besides, they're thinking of sending him to school in England. You and Jess have started a trend."

"How did you find out it was Jamie?"

"From Jenny in a roundabout way. It seems he was smitten with her but she wasn't interested. So he took to spying on her. She's no fool, that daughter of yours. She suspected you just didn't happen along out of the blue. I asked her if she had any enemies, anyone who might have dropped a word in your ear. I mentioned about the letter, of course, which I've now burned. The only person she could think of was Jamie, so I tackled him. He denied it at first, but he's not much of a man. He cracked when I leaned on him. So there's an end to it. Well, almost. I need your formal statement to close the file."

"I still have to see Rashid's mother and father," said Harry.

Hyde looked at him curiously. Harry misunderstood.

"Yes, I'm not looking forward to it, but I can't duck it. It's something I have to do."

"You won't have heard, of course. I was forgetting."

"Heard what?"

"I couldn't leave them in the dark, naturally, so I sent one of my sergeants to see them on Monday, after you'd left."

"Go on."

"They took it badly, not so much Rashid's death as the disgrace. You know how proud some of these Malays are. For a son—he was their eldest, by the way—to attack and rape a European girl was, apparently, too much. They were found in the Pakelan river Monday evening. Drowned. There were heavy boulders around their necks. They'd evidently paddled down there from here and done the deed."

"Christ."

Harry remembered that Rashid was not the only child, nor the only son, for that matter. There were three others, two boys and a girl, ranging in age from six to fourteen.

"You mean the parents killed themselves, just the parents?"

"No, the whole family. Look, you don't want to hear this."

"I do, damn you!"

"Please yourself." Bill Hyde was not going to indulge Harry Cameron's sensibilities. "The children went first. They were hit over the head and then drowned. After that the mother and father." Hyde appeared uncomfortable. He was being too harsh. "I'm sorry, but you did ask. I'd forgotten you'd have no way of knowing."

"Jesus Christ," said Harry, softly.

"Jess doesn't know about any of this, incidentally," said Hyde. "Nor does Jenny, obviously. They'd gone before it happened. For my part, I'll try to keep them in ignorance."

If Harry Cameron thought his misfortunes for the year 1932 were over, he was mistaken. Jessica did not return after one week or even two, either alone or with Jenny. Nor did his wife contact him. He did not even contemplate getting in touch with Batu Ferringhi. Jess knew what she was doing. She'd be back when she was ready.

It took six weeks. When she returned, she did so without her daughter. She looked tired and pale, utterly worn out. She'd also lost weight. It was Alan Fielding's car that drove her up to the bungalow, though Fielding had gone before Harry reached the verandah.

"How's Jenny?" was his first question.

"She's fine." Jessica sighed and shrugged. "Well, no, she's not fine. She's quite the reverse. She's pregnant. Rashid's child, of course."

She watched her husband cross to the drinks table and pour her a brandy without being asked. He took nothing for himself.

"Did you hear what I said?"

"I heard. For some reason it doesn't surprise me. It's this bloody country."

"Harry!" she said sharply.

"No, you were right a couple of months ago, when you said that young girls behave properly in England. This wouldn't have happened there."

"You can't be sure of that."

"It wouldn't have happened with a Malay."

"You're stating the obvious."

"Perhaps." Harry passed Jessica her drink. "Did I ever tell you what my grandfather used to say about Malaya, why he came down here from India?"

"Many times. In any case, Richard Cameron was a bandit."

Harry wasn't listening.

"My grandfather used to say he could hear music in Malaya, the music of faraway drums. I didn't understand what he was talking about, not until I read the Edward Fitzgerald translation of Omar Khayyam. What is it? Something about 'take the cash in hand and waive the rest'? I wonder if it's worth it. Has Fielding been up to Penang?"

"Yes. I didn't want to use the Drummonds' doctor but I needed confirmation. Alan confirmed."

"And?"

"Jenny doesn't want an abortion. She's frightened. Nor would Alan perform one without a great deal of persuading, and I wouldn't trust anyone else."

"So she'll give birth to a half-caste."

"Yes."

"The Drummonds are childless."

"It's crossed my mind."

"But they wouldn't . . . ?"

"I don't think so. I'm not going to ask them. They're off to America in a week. Something to do with that money she inherited. They'll be away for a year. The house is ours for as long as we want. They don't suspect anything. They think Jenny has had a bad love affair with an older man and that you sent her away to get over it. I had to tell them something," Jessica finished lamely.

"What about the child?"

Jessica hesitated. "I hope Jenny's going to be sensible. She realizes she's made a dreadful mistake, and it's scared her. The baby will be placed in a home."

"She's agreed to that?"

"Let's say that she's accepted she can't possibly turn up back here with a Eurasian child without the scandal ruining the rest of her life."

"Don't women—girls—occasionally make decisions like that at the beginning then change their minds when the child's born?"

"They do. But if she so much as hints that Rashid's family take it in as one of their own, I'll make sure she knows it's a bad idea."

"It's no idea at all."

Harry explained what had happened to Rashid's father and mother, his brothers and sister.

"My God," said Jessica, appalled at the number of lives one girl's foolish mistake could touch.

She was silent for a long time. Finally she said that Jenny must never be told. She would blame herself. Harry agreed.

"I'll have to stay with her, you understand," said Jessica. "We'll invent some story that she's gone to England because she was missing Mike and Jeff. It's weak, but it will have to do. I'll come home whenever I can, but it won't be often."

"It'll be better if you stay away. I can fabricate something to cover a long absence, but it's going to be tricky if you keep turning up from time to time. I'll say you've *both* gone to England. A sudden decision. Apart from the Drummonds, we don't know anyone in Penang. It should work. Alan Fielding will keep his mouth shut, I suppose?"

"He promised he'd say nothing, not even to Bill Hyde." Jessica yawned. "Sorry, but I'm exhausted," she said sleepily. "I'm going to miss you."

"I'll come to you."

"Would you mind very much if you didn't? Jenny's very confused right now, especially where you're concerned. I want her to stay healthy. I don't want her worried about seeing you as she grows larger. But we can meet periodically providing it's well out of the way."

Harry grunted. "We can pretend we're having an affair."

"Sorry?"

"I said . . . "

But Jessica had fallen asleep where she sat. Harry removed the empty brandy glass from her fingers. For not the first time in his life, he was glad he'd convinced Jessica Munroe to marry him that day west of St. Omer.

3

Jenny's child, not due until January, was born prematurely during the middle of the monsoon season on west coast Malaya, in November 1932. A fine, healthy boy whose palish skin belied his miscegenate parentage, his features were nevertheless more Malay than European.

The signs that the child would be early had been present since October, but Jessica had not wanted to summon Alan Fielding unnecessarily. She was a trained nurse as well as the mother of three. She could cope unless there were complications. As it happened there were none, and it was fortunate that she, alone, acted as midwife, for it quickly became apparent that Jenny did not want to give up her son, place him in a church orphanage and never see him again.

When her daughter had regained her strength, Jessica attempted to reason with her.

"We agreed."

"We didn't agree. Even if we did, he wasn't born then."

"We agreed that you couldn't possibly take him back to the estate on your own."

"There are other alternatives."

"Rashid's parents have moved away," lied Jessica. "I explained that."

"I know. It wasn't my intention to give him to Rashid's family, anyway. What I did was stupid. I've admitted that a thousand times over, and I'm sorry that I hurt you and Daddy and caused Rashid's death. But Jean is part of me." She pronounced the name in the French manner.

"Jean?"

"That's what I'm calling him. I'm Jeanne, he's Jean. Or Johnny

56

if that becomes too cumbersome. But I'm not giving him up, no matter what you say."

"We'll talk about it," said Jessica, marvelling at how like her father Jenny was, how she had inherited so much of Harry's determination. "No one is to know that the child was premature. We have weeks to discuss it."

"There's nothing to discuss."

Days later, having tried reason, Jessica got angry.

"You're a selfish young woman. You're also far less intelligent than I gave you credit for. You admit you can't take him back as your own, but you want to hand him over to some Malay family to raise as their own. What sort of chance is that giving him? At least in a church orphanage he'll get a rudimentary education."

"And end up as a servant."

"Isn't that better than ending up as a rubber tapper? You've seen how they live, what they earn. What kind of future is that?"

"It's one where I'll be able to keep an eye on him, which I wouldn't be able to do if I never saw him again. I can see to it that he gets advantages. Oh, I know he'll never be accepted as a Cameron," Jenny went on sarcastically, "and perhaps he'll never amount to much in a European-dominated society. But I'd do what I could."

"Your father would never agree."

"I wasn't thinking we'd tell Daddy."

Jessica was shocked.

"You're out of your mind!"

"Not at all. He doesn't have to become a tapper. Even if he did, not all tappers live on the estate. Some live in the river kampongs. They're poor by European standards, I agree, but they want for nothing in the way of food. And they're healthy. We could find a family to bring him up, tell them that he's an orphan, pay them well for looking after him. I'm sure you could arrange it. Daddy need never know."

"And how do we explain the vanishing child trick?"

"We do what we agreed. We tell Daddy that he's been placed in a church home. He won't ask questions, Daddy. I know him. He'll want to forget it."

Jessica gave her daughter a long, calculated look.

"It's hard for me to believe you're only sixteen, the way you scheme."

"I'm almost seventeen."

"You're asking me to tell a lie to your father and live with it for ever."

Jenny leaned forward and took her mother's hand. Outside, the monsoon rains were lashing the beach house.

"I'm asking you for help. Take a peek next door. Whoever the father was, that's your grandchild. Are you telling me you don't want to see him again?"

"Of course not."

"Then where's your sense of adventure? You told me that you and Daddy were married within a couple of hours, and that I was conceived almost immediately. If you could do that, you can do this."

"He'd be raised a Muslim."

"The river people don't bother much with religion. Nor do I."

"He won't be called Jean. Or Johnny."

"I already have a Malay name picked out for him. Hamid."

"How on earth . . . ?"

"It's the name of a small boy I met on the shore while you were off seeing Daddy on the Peninsula. Johnny or Hamid, it doesn't matter. I'll call him Johnny Hamid."

Jessica thought it all over while Jenny fed her son. It was a crazy idea. There was no hope of it working. She would find it impossible to keep that sort of secret from Harry. Wouldn't she? No, she wouldn't. Pale-skinned Malays were nothing unusual. But . . . But . . .

"Mummy," called Jenny.

Jessica went into her daughter's bedroom. Jenny handed her mother her grandson.

"We can't do this by ourselves," said Jessica.

It was Christmas week before they sent for Alan Fielding. To begin with, he wanted nothing to do with the sub-terfuge. He had come to Penang, he said, only because Jessica's message had sounded urgent, and he had thought there might be a problem. He hadn't expected the problem to be this.

"No," he said, and kept on saying no for an hour.

"But you could do it if you wanted to, find a Malay family in a kampong close to the estate?"

"I suppose so. But I won't."

"That's a pity," said Jessica, glancing at her daughter. "We'll have to think of something else for Alain."

"Alain?"

"French for Alan. Actually, Jenny's called him Jean Alain—John Alan Hamid, in English. Jean being the masculine of her own name, Hamid the Malay name she's chosen—and Alan after you."

Fielding was bewildered. "After me?"

"You've been such a marvellous help throughout all this, Doctor Fielding," said Jenny demurely. "I thought it only right. If he were to be christened properly, I'd want you to be a godfather."

Fielding shook his head, accepting that he'd been out-maneuvered.

"I hope I never have to play cards against you, young woman. Is he ready to travel?"

"It won't take me a moment. Will the ferry be running?"

"You know how it is in a monsoon—wind and rain one moment, sunshine the next. The ferrymen know what they're doing."

Jenny left the room.

"That's a hell of a daughter you have there," said Fielding.

"Don't I know it. Do you think you'll be able to manage it?"

"Without too much trouble. I'll keep him in the hospital in Kuala Kelan until he's a bit older, though. What about Harry?"

"Did he know you were coming up here?"

"I thought I'd better tell him. He's been worried about Jen since he last saw you."

"So he'll be expecting a report?"

"I'll tell him the baby was premature—accurate—that we've done what was necessary—true enough—and that you and Jenny will be home for Christmas."

Which Jessica and Jenny were. Harry embraced his wife and daughter.

"It's over now," he said. "Let's not mention it again."

4

Events outside Malaya in the years leading up to September 1939, though heatedly debated by the Europeans in clubs and over dinner tables and stengahs, hardly seemed to touch them. Mussolini invaded Abyssinia and the Spanish Civil War started and finished. Hitler reoccupied the Rhineland and the Sudetenland, and added his native Austria to the Third Reich. Prime Minister Chamberlain waved a sheet of paper at Heston Airport and promised peace for the foreseeable future. King Edward VIII decided that the love of an American divorcée was more important than a throne and an Empire, and abdicated. The Japanese, potentially a far more dangerous threat in the eyes of the Malayan Europeans, became the third member of the Rome-Berlin Axis, but were being held by the Chinese Nationalist forces under Chiang Kai shek three thousand miles to the north, and indeed had suffered a major defeat at Shanghai. No one doubted that, in the event of a global war, to the Japanese Malaya was a great prize, producing, as it did, forty percent of the world's rubber and sixty percent of its tin, but to win the garland Japan would have to beat the Chinese, occupy Indo-China and Thailand, and advance down the Peninsula, laying open one of its flanks to the British Army in Burma. It was either that or a seaborne assault on the east coast. Those who remembered Gallipoli suggested that a seaborne assault was a non-starter, being the type of operation that was hardest on the attackers and easiest for the defenders. The mountainous backbone of Malaya, too, with ranges up to 7,000 feet all covered with dense jungle, would militate against an invader landing on the east coast and crossing to the west, where the roads down to Singapore, which had to be the ultimate objective, were better. Although exact numbers were a military secret, it was estimated that 80,000 troops were available for the defense of Malaya, albeit that more than fifty percent were Indians or Malays.

Until realizing it was impossible under the circumstances, Jessica tried to ban any discussion of war over meals while her sons were home for the long vacation in the summer of 1939; Jeff from university, where he would shortly be entering his final year, and Mike from school. Commercial air travel from the U.K. still took almost a week, but there had been flights to Singapore since 1934.

She was in two minds whether or not to allow Mike to return to England. If war came, it would not be like the last time, fought largely on foreign soil. The United Kingdom would be in the front line. But *if* war came, Mike argued with all the insouciance of a fifteen-year-old, he was as safe there as he would be here. Great Britain had the Royal Air Force, the Royal Navy, and the Channel. Hitler couldn't beat all three. Jessica wasn't so sure, but Harry sided with Mike.

"We can't interfere with his schooling because of an event that may never take place."

As far as Jeff was concerned, there was no question that he would go back.

"If I don't get my degree, it will all have been for nothing."

They were only home for a month, until the second week in August. Jeff had an invitation to visit France, stay in a château with a real French nobleman, and he didn't want to miss out; Mike was going to Ross and Cromarty in the Scottish Highlands to fish for salmon.

Jessica accepted that she was losing them to adulthood, and was wise enough not to show her disappointment that they wouldn't stay until the last moment. At their age—and she felt sure there was a girl involved as far as Jeff was concerned—they had immediate appetites that needed satisfying.

Nor, if she were honest with herself, would she have had it any other way. She was proud of both her sons, but Mike especially. Although six years younger than Jeff, he was almost as tall and broad, and both stood way above her. She could see something of the Munroes in each, but basically they were Camerons: dark hair that became unruly if not tended regularly, grayish-blue eyes with something of the devil in them, faces that were a mixture of athlete and aesthete.

After the first four days of his vacation Jeff had had enough of the estate. One day part of it would be his, and a damned good living it would provide. But there was little to do except talk rubber with his father's friends or have dinner with planters or tin miners or civil servants from other parts of the state, either at the bungalow or as a guest at other's homes. Even Kuala Kelan palled, with endless stengahs at the Planters' Club or watching cricket on the *padang*, a smaller replica of the one in Kuala Lumpur. After university, it was all too parochial for words. None of the young women he was introduced to impressed him in the least; the younger ones were either plain or giggly or so self-evidently virginal that pursuit would be a waste of energy, and he hadn't time to cultivate the occasional married one who looked as if she might be fun. He had friends in Singapore and KL; he also had money in his pocket. He hadn't been to bed with a woman since Easter. He thought that should be remedied.

Jenny drove him to the main line station in Kuala Kelan. From there he was going to KL and, afterward, Singapore. He would be back in ten days, more than enough time to spend at home before he and Mike had to take the flight to England.

"You're selfish, Jeff, you know that," said Jenny, cooling herself with a hand-held fan. The Kuala Kelan station, completed in 1919, was a Moorish colonial structure which, to a stranger, resembled a temple. Usually it was airy, but today the overhead fans in the waiting-room were out of action. "It wouldn't have hurt you to stay at home a little longer."

"I'm afraid that's not for me."

"I recognize that, which is why I'm calling you selfish."

"And you're not, of course."

"I didn't say that, but I'm always here. You're only here twice a year."

"For now. That'll change once I've graduated."

"So you say."

"Do you think Dad will allow it otherwise? I'm the elder son. He wants me here."

"You flatter yourself."

"Perhaps. How old are they now, he and Mum? Forty-seven, forty-eight?"

"Forty-seven."

"Which is not exactly getting any younger, is it? Time to hand over the reins. Not now, but soon."

"You make it sound as though you're going to inherit the entire estate."

"That wasn't my intention, but it's obvious that someone, sooner or later, has to take over, whether there's a war or not. It can't be you. You're not married, and I don't see Dad giving you much of a say in running the place until you are. Mike won't be ready for six or seven years."

A Malay railway official came into the waiting-room and announced that the train for KL would be arriving shortly. Would all those wishing to travel please make their way to the platform. The European carriages would be at the front of the train. Thank you.

"Why aren't you married, by the way?" asked Jeff. "Why isn't there even anyone on the horizon? God knows, you're attractive enough."

"What's that got to do with it?"

"Nothing, I expect. But in the few days I've been here I haven't seen anyone in whom you've shown the remotest interest, though I'll wager I could name half a dozen who have designs on you."

She had had offers, of course, though she'd be damned before she'd discuss those with Jeff. She'd also had several lovers in the past year, something that not even her mother knew about. One was a banker in Kuala Kelan, the other an Intelligence Corps major based in the Batu Mersa barracks. The banker was married and they had to meet in an apartment he rented; she wasn't sure of the major's status though he claimed to be single. She didn't care either way, and sometimes thought she had chosen lovers it was unlikely she could wed in order to avoid a commitment. If the truth were known she wasn't interested in marriage just for the sake of the institution, or possibly she hadn't yet met anyone with whom she could say with confidence she would be happy to spend the remainder of her life. Unlike many girls her age, she was wealthy in her own right, thanks to her stake in the plantation, and would one day be rather rich. If marriage happened, so be it. If it didn't, it wouldn't bother her. She was still only twenty-three. There was plenty of time.

She walked with Jeff to the train, keeping her parasol between her shoulders and the sun. Opposite the non-European carriages hordes of Malays, Indians and Chinese, most with live produce in wicker cages, fought to be the first aboard. Occasionally minor squabbles broke out, with the aggressive Chinese generally winning. Jenny couldn't be sure, but she sensed that Jeff felt superior to all this now, and partly despised the natives, seeing them as riffraff to be avoided when possible and treated as lower forms of existence when not.

"What will you do if there is a war," she asked, "and it's still on after your university deferment has expired?"

"I'll try for a comfortable job in the War House. It shouldn't be too hard with a Cambridge degree. I've no intention of seeing it close up from the sharp end, if that's what you want to know."

"Have you told Daddy this?"

Jeff laughed. "The hero? Not likely. Dad's a great believer in duty. Mike is too, I suppose, and I'm not sure about you. Romantics all. But there's no percentage in getting one's head blown off in the dubious name of patriotism. That's for fools, Dad's two MCs notwithstanding. Wars come and go, and no one remembers the dead except the widows. If Dad hadn't the estate, his medals wouldn't have bought him so much as a meal in 1919."

While Jeff was away, Jenny rode every morning with Mike early, before the sun was too blisteringly hot and the humidity index rose in concert. She still had Spartan although he was getting on in years now.

Out of devilment, only realizing later what a risk she had taken, one day she steered Mike in the direction of the river kampong where Johnny Hamid lived with his adopted parents. Alan Fielding had chosen them wisely, and he had grown up to be a fine, sturdy boy, going on now for seven years of age. She tried to see him several times a week. Since the early years, in order to allay suspicion, she had brought small gifts for every child in the kampong. Though shy, he had come to look forward to her visits. She sometimes called him Johnny but more usually Hamid, and he addressed her as Miss Jenny, as she had encouraged all the children to do. The headman of this village considered his charges fortunate since they had their own primary school and a teacher who came three times a week, all courtesy of Miss Jenny. She did not keep her apparent altruism a secret; that could have been dangerous. Europeans who knew of her interest in the village school put it down to something she would grow out of when she had a family of her own.

The boy's light-colored skin had stayed with him, and to anyone with half an eye one of his parents must have been European. There was nothing unusual in that, though the customary state of affairs was for the father to be European and the mother Malay. To anyone with a *quarter* of an eye, Jenny frequently thought, he looked uncannily like her. Mike didn't see it, though, to be fair, for the moment her son was playing with his friends in the sungei and only waved to her from a distance.

They dismounted and watered the horses. Jenny asked Mike what his plans were when he left school. He pulled a face.

"I thought I could at least rely upon you not to grill me. I've had that from Mum and Dad ever since I arrived."

"And what have you been telling them?"

"That I don't know. It's three years before I have to think about university, and if there's a war . . . "

"Please, Mike, not today."

"Okay, sorry. Anyway, I'm not sure I'll bother going up. I like England, I like it a lot. I've spent more time there than I have here over the last seven years. But I'm not the same animal as Jeff."

"Same animal," muttered Jenny. "Is that how they teach you to speak?"

Mike grinned. "Same sort of person. Jeff's happy at Cambridge. It suits him. Parties, dinners, punting on the Cam. Picnics. I'm not sure it would suit me."

"How so? It sounds idyllic."

"You haven't suffered an English winter."

"I was over in October two years ago with Mum. I grant you it was cold."

"Cold in October!" scoffed Mike. "You should try it in January. Even the sparrows get bronchitis."

Jenny chuckled. "So it's just the winters you object to. That's a funny reason for not wanting to take a degree."

"No, there's more to it than that. Take a look around you."

Jenny did so. She saw the sungei, the Malay children splashing and shouting to one another, flowers of every hue and texture. She heard monkeys and gibbons. She felt the sun's climbing heat. To her it was home and perhaps overfamiliar. But she loved it and understood that Mike did too.

"So you're getting homesick."

"Odd, isn't it? You'd think I'd be more at home over there."

"Maybe not so odd. I was born in England. Well, Scotland, rather. So was Jeff. You were born here. It's probably something in the blood."

"And it's probably malaria," said Mike, swatting his arm. "We've got company, by the way."

Jenny turned. Hamid, his sarong dripping wet, was standing a few yards away, uncertain whether or not to approach. Jenny beckoned.

"Come here," she said in Malay. "He won't bite."

Hamid said something very fast. Mike caught only the word *Tuan*.

"I *have* been away too long," he said. "I hardly understood any of that."

"He asked if the *Tuan* would mind if he rode his horse."

"Not a bit of it." Mike scrambled to his feet. "Do you know him?"

"Yes."

"What's his name?"

"Try it yourself."

"*Siapa nama anda?*"

"Hamid."

"Well then, Hamid," said Mike, walking the boy across to the horses, "let's see what you're made of."

Mike swung the giggling boy into the saddle and told him to hang on. Then, holding the reins, Mike trotted the horse fifty yards in one direction, fifty yards in the other.

My God, thought Jenny, watching them together. Surely Mike would see some vague family resemblance. To her mind Hamid could have been a younger, darker version of Mike. But that was probably just the way a mother saw things, she told herself, for Mike said nothing.

Soon the other children arrived and everyone wanted a turn. Hamid marshalled them into a queue with not a little bullying. Mike did his best until he was exhausted, and somehow Hamid managed to have three rides to everyone else's one.

"That's it," said Mike finally, panting heavily, his face glistening with sweat. "Home now."

The children ran off, Hamid last of all. He gave a final wave before diving into the sungei. Jenny would have liked to hug her son but knew better. Instead she hugged Mike.

"Hey, take it easy. What's that in aid of?"

"Nothing. You're my favorite brother, that's all."

Mike looked over to where the children were swimming, most of them now minus their sarongs.

"He's a pleasant little chap, isn't he?"

"Hamid?" said Jenny casually.

"Yes, Hamid. Only half the size of some of them, but did you see how he organized them? Does he work on the estate?"

"His parents do and a couple of their older children, as casuals. Hamid's generally around to help out."

"You should have a word with Dad about him. He'd go far, given half the chance."

The night before Mike and Jeff travelled down to Singapore for the flight home, the Camerons held a private party, just family. Harry insisted on opening some champagne he said he'd been saving for a special occasion. Jessica wasn't keen on the idea at first—it seemed too much of a final goodbye instead of au revoir—but she became as merry as everyone else before the evening was over, and at one point was discovered in the kitchen trying to explain to the Chinese cook how to make Scottish potato cakes.

Nursing massive hangovers, everyone went to see Mike and Jeff off the following morning on the early train. As was the family custom, no one went with them to Singapore. Goodbyes were painful enough without prolonging the agony.

Two weeks after they arrived in England, Hitler marched into Poland and World War II had begun.

If residents of the United Kingdom and France considered the next few months as the "phoney" war, in Malaya for civilians nothing much happened at all apart from rubber production being stepped up as far as the various estates could manage. Some able-bodied men were called up or volunteered. Some set sail for, or flew to, England, where the real fighting would be taking place, if it took place at all. One school of thought considered there would be none. Germany and Russia would carve up Poland between them, and peace talks be held before Christmas.

As for Japan, the Rising Sun Empire, finding the Chinese a more troublesome foe than had been anticipated, and being forced to fight a guerrilla-style war that was not to its liking, sought a solution to its problems by driving south along the Chinese coastal regions in an attempt to cut off its huge enemy from maritime supplies. The threat to Malaya became more real, whatever happened in Europe. The next strategic objective had to be Hongkong. If that fell, and once France had been conquered in June 1940, French Indo-China lay wide open. Abutting French Indo-China was Thailand. South of Thailand lay Malaya.

In the summer of 1941 Harry discussed the impending crisis with Jessica and Jenny. The state rubber planters had held a meeting in Kuala Kelan, the consensus being that they could do nothing but soldier on. Informal gatherings of planters representing the entire country had also taken place in Kuala Lumpur, in the Selangor Club, colloquially known as the Spotted Dog. Those, too, had delivered the same verdict. Whether independent owners or managers for international organizations, Malaya was their home, rubber their trade. Until the Japs arrived, it was business as usual. *If* the Japs came, a majority voted to stay and fight, support the military or form guerrilla bands. Should the soldiers be beaten, so what? No one knew the country the way the planters and tin miners did. They could create some havoc. In any event, they couldn't simply turn it all over to the Japs without a scrap.

But that decision applied only to the men—planters, miners, policemen, members of the armed forces who were not put in the bag. For them it might even be necessary to form temporary alliances with the Communists, Mao Tse-tung's vanguard, who were fleeing south ahead of the Japanese. As for the women and children, they would have to leave where troopships were available, go to the U.K. via Australia. But go, anyway.

Jessica disagreed. Jenny sided with her mother. It was as much their country as the men's. The discussion became quite heated.

Harry had to spell it out. If it came to guerrilla warfare, it would mean that the Allies were losing or had lost, the Japanese winning. A guerrilla campaign in the jungles and mountains of Malaya was no place for a woman. He would brook no argument.

"All right, if we've got to go, I want you to come with us," said Jessica finally, accepting that Harry would not change his mind. "The plantation's not worth risking your life for. You're almost fifty, for the love of God."

"Churchill's almost seventy," retorted Harry. "Besides, I'm fitter than most of these soldiers half my age. And acclimatized. In any case, there won't be room on the ships for any of us, the men, if it comes down to it. So it's either fight or be put in a POW camp. I don't relish that. The Japs won't torch the estate. They'll run it themselves because they need the rubber. I want to be around when it's all over to pick up the pieces."

"You talk as though we've already been invaded. We're not even at war with Japan yet."

Jenny feared for Hamid. In a private conversation with her mother, she confessed her anxiety. Jessica didn't think the Japanese would hurt non-combatant Malays. "Their propaganda is talking about an Asian Co-Prosperity Sphere. They want the Malays, among others, to be anti-European, not anti-Japanese."

But Jenny still worried.

With only a few hiccups, mail from England had hardly been interrupted since the outbreak of war and continued to arrive during the latter months of 1941, occasionally, it would seem, via eccentric routes as Sweden and Australia. Though the letters were heavily censored, Jessica managed to learn that Jeff had been commissioned a second lieutenant and was doing war work in London, and that Mike had made the First XV.

English newspapers, too, were rarely in short supply, and on days when they didn't arrive there was always the reliable *Straits Times*, plus the Armed Forces' bulletins and the wireless. Thus Europeans in Malaya got to hear that the short-lived German-Soviet Pact had ended with a dramatic bang when the Wehrmacht invaded Russia. "When thieves fall out," one or two graybeards nodded sagely. But too soon.

The next series of events in the Far East and the Pacific happened with such astonishing rapidity that no one could keep up with the dominoes tumbling; disaster followed disaster without respite.

Unoccupied France finally wilted under Japanese pressure and French Indo-China fell, albeit that Tokyo termed the occupation as "protective." Shortly afterward, in the space of three days between December 7 and December 10, 1941, in a series of brilliantly coordinated attacks, the Japanese hit Pearl Harbor, the Philippines, Hongkong—and Malaya, the Japanese 25th Army under Yamashita landing and establishing beachheads at Kota Bharu, capital of Kelantan state, on the northeast coast, while simultaneously assaulting and capturing the seaports of Singora and Patani in Thailand, violating that country's neutrality.

The Kota Bharu offensive and the feint down the east coast was soon diagnosed for what it was, but by that time a Japanese division had already swung across the Kra Isthmus to the west coast and penetrated the northern Malay state of Kedah. As if that wasn't enough, the battleship *Prince of Wales* and the battle cruiser *Repulse*, designated to strike at the Japanese convoys supplying the Kota Bharu beachhead, were sunk by bombers and torpedo bombers on December 12.

By December 16 Yamashita's forces had swept south a hundred miles and occupied Penang. The Allied armies under the overall command of General Percival were falling back everywhere in disarray. They had little or no air support, and the Japanese air force controlled the skies.

Kuala Kelan was two hundred and twenty miles south of Penang. Naturally the Japanese would sooner or later outrun their supply lines and there was little chance that they could cover the second hundred miles as rapidly as they had the first, but nothing, now, could stop them occupying the whole of the Peninsula, though there were some optimists who considered that

Singapore, with its 15-inch-gun shore batteries, would not fall.
Harry Cameron was not among them. Neither were his friends.
Before it was too late, it was time to send wives and daughters,
mothers, aunts, nieces and children, to Singapore for evacuation,
and for the men to head for the jungle-covered mountains. In
cooperation with the army, transport would be laid on for the
women and their charges, and collecting points had long ago
been arranged. The army had requisitioned most private cars,
but for outlying families such as the Camerons one vehicle had
been left for each, in order that they could drive to Kuala Kelan
to be picked up by trucks. Thereafter the Camerons' last car would
be handed over to the MPs, either to be used in some capacity
or destroyed. Trains were still running, and roads, though in
many places crowded with non-European refugees—who were
not inclined to stay put, no matter what the army said—were still
passable. Both trucks and trains, however, were under the constant
threat of being strafed by Japanese fighters freelancing for targets.
It was almost as dangerous to make for Singapore as it was to stay
behind. Harry warned his wife and daughter to be careful.

"I can't tell you how, just use your heads. Don't forget you're in
the hands of the army, and much good they've been up to now."

Harry and his group were leaving forty-eight hours before
Jessica was to drive Jenny into Kuala Kelan. Bill Hyde was
collecting Harry, bringing with him Alan Fielding. At the age
of sixty-four Fielding was feeling his years and was also not in
the best of health. But he was not going to be taken prisoner and
he was, as he pointed out, a qualified doctor, albeit retired. They
would head north for Kota Napek, collecting others on the way.
Afterward they would retreat to the hills. Contingency plans
had been laid for just this emergency and over the past three
months caches of tinned food, medical supplies, ammunition, and
weapons that could not be carried had been buried or otherwise
hidden. There were dumps all over the state, and others in other
states. How long they would last, and whether or not they would
rot before being used, no one knew.

Harry's friends were not expected to do much, not a handful
here, a handful there; nor had they been advised to by the
Intelligence colonel who had briefed them, in total secrecy, a
week earlier. Their aim for the moment was not to get caught.
As civilians bearing arms, they would be executed on the spot.

"This show's over. I'm not betraying military secrets in telling
you that. The Japs are pouring in, and all we're doing is holding

them at the rivers until they outflank us. They have tanks, we have none. Nor do we have a single long-range bomber to take the battle to them.

"I can't tell you when the next show will begin. It could take years. But with the United States now in the war, the Japs won't be here for ever. On the other hand, I expect that this theatre of operations will take a back seat compared to Europe. We're a long way from London and it's natural enough that the War Cabinet will want to deal with the most immediate threat first. The thinking seems to be that it's Hitler and Mussolini before Tojo. You're on your own for the foreseeable future. One day, however, we and the Americans and the Aussies will be doing something about putting special forces into this theatre. Experts in demolition, sabotage, and the like. It'll be your job to keep them alive and point them at targets. I doubt if more than one in a thousand will be familiar with Malaya."

When the time came for Harry to leave, he said goodbye to Jenny first. His daughter tried hard not to, but couldn't avoid crying. Harry held on to her, feeling thoroughly helpless.

"It'll be all right, you'll see."

"Please take care of yourself."

"I will. I know this country like the back of my hand. They won't get me, or any of us."

Jessica had promised herself she wouldn't cry and didn't, even though this was the second occasion in her life she had been forced to abandon her husband to a war. There had been artillery bursts in the distance then too.

"I thought of setting fire to it, you know," said Harry, his arm around his wife's waist, looking back at the bungalow.

"Don't you dare."

"The Japs'll commandeer it, use it as an HQ for a senior officer."

"Let them. We'll fumigate it when we return."

They strolled hand in hand around the garden Jessica had planted. Down on the sungei that led to the Pakelan river they could see rafts top-heavy with all the worldly possessions of the Malay and Chinese families paddling them. God only knew where they thought they were going. There was no escape. Harry guessed they'd return when it was all over.

Christ, it was such a waste! Three generations, four counting Jenny and the boys, spent planting and hacking a living out of the jungle. And now the bastard Japs would reap the benefits. Damn them, and damn the quality of leadership in the British Army.

Some planters had given instructions to their workers to slash the rubber trees, render them useless. Harry hadn't. You couldn't slash millions of trees. Besides, that would have been like setting the bungalow alight.

Bill Hyde drove up in his Chevrolet, horn blaring. Alan Fielding was in the passenger seat. There was another European policeman in the back.

"Time to go, Harry."

Hyde, Fielding and the third man stayed in the car. Goodbyes between husbands and wives were private affairs.

Harry's equipment was already stacked on the verandah; a rucksack, water-canteen, two rifles, two bandoliers of ammunition, a parang. He already had his pistols strapped on. That was as much as he could carry. It was pointless taking more, for they would be abandoning Hyde's Chevy before nightfall.

"Take a look around before you leave," he said to Jessica. "If you see anything that might be useful to the Japs that I've forgotten, destroy it. Put salt in any of the spirits you can't take."

He kissed Jessica on the lips. She clung to him longer than he wanted her to. Finally he had to ease her gently away.

"Jess."

"I know. I know." She brushed non-existent lint from his shirt. "Good luck, darling."

Bill and Alan Fielding waved as Bill slipped the car into gear and roared off. Harry didn't. Only when they were out of sight did Jessica permit herself the luxury of a damned good cry.

Two afternoons later, she and Jenny had visited Hamid in the morning and had returned pale-faced and tight-lipped. Jessica did not inquire what had transpired.

The road down to Kuala Kelan was swarming with vehicles of every description, military as well as civilian. Much of the military traffic was heading north, toward KL, which was certain to be a major Japanese objective. Mercifully, the enemy air force was now here in evidence.

At the mustering-point outside the state secretariat pandemonium raged. Jenny offered to drive the car to the MPs' compound while Jessica checked their names off with the officer in charge. It took several hours before her turn came, and afterward there was still no sign of Jenny.

The open-topped lorries were to travel in convoys as soon as darkness fell; there were a hundred or more of them, all packed to bursting with women and children. Many of the grown-ups were openly weeping; many of the children thought they were on a great adventure, but even they became fractious after a while. It was no picnic, alternatively being baked by the afternoon sun and then soaked to the skin by the monsoon rains which swept inland from the coast, and army nurses were on hand to offer advice and medication as required.

Jessica was aboard a 3-tonner in the middle of the column, balancing an infant, whose mother was preoccupied with two more under five years old, on one knee. Close to departure time, when whistles were suddenly blown and engines revved to let latecomers know that zero-hour was approaching, there was still no sign of Jenny. All the trucks were numbered and everyone had been allocated a berth. No one was supposed to move once seated, but some women had changed berths to be near friends in other vehicles; others, caught exercising their legs when the whistles sounded, climbed on to the nearest truck. Jenny could be anywhere, but Jessica wanted to be absolutely certain she had joined the convoy. Something could have gone wrong at the vehicle pound; there might be a queue or other difficulties.

Jessica handed the infant back to its mother and scrambled over the tailboard. An MP tried to bar her way.

"You've no time to go wandering about, ma'am."

"I am *not* wandering about," snapped Jessica crustily. "My daughter's missing and I'm concerned." She immediately regretted her tone of voice. With any luck, she would be aboard a troopship sailing for Australia within a week or so; this young lad was staying put, to be killed or captured. "I must find my daughter. Please," she insisted.

The MP took pity on her.

"Okay, but don't be long. We're pulling out in a couple of minutes. I wouldn't worry about her if I were you," he added kindly. "It's more than my stripes are worth to leave anyone behind. She'll be around somewhere, but look if you must."

Jessica hurried first of all toward the head of the column, then toward the rear. Then she realized it was hopeless. Her 3-tonner was about number fifty of a hundred. Jenny could be in any of the other ninety-nine, and the convoy stretched for half a mile in either direction.

She heard someone call her name. Molly Hyde, Bill Hyde's

wife, waved down at her from the cab of a 3-tonner. Trust Molly to grab a comfortable seat, thought Jessica with uncharacteristic pettiness.

"Have you seen Jenny?"

"Yes. I saw her about half an hour ago in that Humber of yours. At least, I think it was your Humber. Sorry, but it's been a very confusing day. Did Bill pick Harry up?"

But Jessica wasn't listening.

More whistles blew. Impatient male voices yelled through loud-hailers for everyone in the Singapore convoy to embus. Jessica ran back to her allotted vehicle, hoping that Jenny was already there. She wasn't.

"Find her?" asked the MP, whose unhappy task it was, among others, to prevent Chinese and Malay families utilizing space reserved for Europeans.

"No."

"Never mind, she'll turn up."

He helped her over the tailboard. The convoy pulled out.

From Kuala Kelan to Singapore was 160 miles. Because of darkness restricting speed, false alarm air-raid warnings, other traffic on the road, and the need to stop periodically in order that the women and children could attend to personal hygiene, the first vehicles did not cross the 1,100-yards causeway connecting Johore Bahru to Singapore Island until daybreak. At each stop Jessica went from vehicle to vehicle, calling her daughter's name and asking people she knew whether they had seen Jenny. No one had.

The evacuees were kept well away from Singapore City, which was reputed to be a madhouse. Temporarily they were billeted in the Tengah Airfield barracks three miles northwest. In due course they would be leaving on the same ships that were bringing in reinforcements, men of the Indian Infantry Brigade, the 18th British Division, and two thousand Australians. Some evacuees suspected that they were being isolated from the docks until the troops had disembarked and were convoyed north. It would do the soldiers' morale no good at all to see the women and children leaving.

Rumors abounded. There had just been an air-raid or there was about to be an air-raid. Japanese submarines were submerged in deep water outside the mouth of the Strait of Johore. Japanese commandos were already ashore. Fifth-columns were abroad in Singapore City, where there was rioting as the inhabitants attempted to flee. British firing squads were executing looters whatever their race. Troops were deserting.

Jessica was waiting for each new convoy as it arrived, but now they were coming from other states and she hardly recognized anyone. Jenny was in none of the vehicles.

In desperation Jessica sought out the senior officer in charge of embarkation. She got no further than a staff sergeant, and was told to leave her name and join a queue. She was not alone in having a relative missing. The Tengah Airfield barracks were full. Newcomers were being directed to Bukit Timah and the Naval Base. The best the staff sergeant could suggest was to write a note and pin it to the massive bulletin board under the initial of her surname, telling her daughter where she was. She should also check the board each morning and afternoon, in case her daughter had adopted the same strategy.

Jessica scribbled a short letter without having much faith in the outcome. There were hundreds of similar letters thumb-tacked to the board, many overlapping the neighbors; many under the wrong initial. In a rage she tore some of these off and hurled them to the floor. Then, ashamed, she pinned them back. She felt in her bones that Jenny had missed the convoy. Why, she didn't know.

She was tempted to return to Kuala Kelan, but there was no transport other than that carrying soldiers, and they wouldn't take her. She was advised, anyway, that Kuala Kelan was now directly in the path of the Japanese advance. Kuala Lumpur had already been occupied. The British were pulling back, hoping to bottleneck the Japs in Johore.

Shortly, any question of returning for Jenny became academic. One morning her name and number were called, and she was shepherded out to a waiting 3-tonner. Her ship was the *Duchess of Bedford*.

Before she left she paid one more visit to the bulletin board. Her letter was where she had left it, but she found one from Jenny, tucked underneath several others. How long it had been there she had no idea, but she suspected the worst before opening it.

Darling Mummy: I can't leave without Hamid and I realize I can't take him with us. I'm sorry. Please forgive me. It was all done pretty much on the spur of the moment. I was waiting to put the car into the pound when it came to me. Hamid is my son, after all. I saw Molly Hyde and thought of telling her, but then I decided otherwise. I knew you wouldn't go if I wasn't. I'll give this letter to an officer to hand to you later or turn over to the senior embarkation officer. I hope you receive it safely.

We'll be all right, Hamid and I. I'll pick him up and head for Richard's Hill. I'll probably take some of the other kampong children also. The Japanese won't hurt a woman with children. I love you very much. I could not have wished for a better mother.

The *Duchess of Bedford* sailed with the tide, with Jessica aboard. It was the last ship out of Singapore. On February 15, 1942, the city was surrounded. Allied losses were 9,000 killed and wounded, and 130,000 captured. The Japanese campaign had lasted 73 days.

5

Jenny had been next in line outside the vehicle compound before she finally made up her mind she would not be accompanying her mother to Singapore. She apologized to the MP with the clipboard.

"Sorry, there's something I forgot to do."

"You don't have long, Miss."

She eased out of the traffic and turned around. Once away from the compound, she pulled over to the side of the road, found a pencil and a sheet of paper in the glove compartment, and composed a note to her mother. She saw Molly Hyde and thought of giving it to her, but Molly would read it and then the balloon would go up. Instead, she found a second lieutenant travelling with the convoy and entrusted it to him. She made it clear that he was not to attempt to locate her mother until the trucks reached Singapore.

"You're not going with us?"

"Not for now."

"There won't be many more convoys out of here."

"Don't worry, I'll be all right."

She would be, too, she reassured herself. In any case, she couldn't leave Hamid behind. He'd seemed bewildered when she saw him that morning, as had the other children. Some families were fleeing on rafts, some were staying. They didn't understand what was going on, and their parents were not much the wiser.

She ran into a heavy rainstorm driving back to the bungalow, and her windscreen wipers gave up the ghost. She had to pull over until the storm passed.

They had set the horses loose, she and her mother, to forage for themselves, but Spartan, also confused at this unaccustomed freedom, hadn't wandered far. He came to her whistle. She saddled him and set off for Hamid's kampong.

77

He was delighted to see her, as were his friends, but she had to do some hard talking to the parents who had stayed behind before any of them would agree to let their children go with her. She told downright lies to persuade them. The Japanese would use the children as slave labor. Either that, or for bayonet practice. You couldn't believe Japanese promises. They had to be barbarians, or why else would they be invading Malaya? The parents could trust the children with her. She would take them to Bukit Sedikit, Richard's Hill.

In the end, not everyone saw it her way, and she was left with a tiny band of ten children ranging from five to thirteen. Hamid was among them. She would bring them all back when the Japanese had passed through and the danger was over. It was most unlikely that the invaders had sufficient manpower to garrison every kampong.

Using Spartan as a pack animal, the children taking it in turns to ride, they backtracked to the bungalow. By now it was dark and they stayed there overnight. For the children this was a great treat. Not one of them had been inside a European house before.

They were up at first light. After breakfast, somehow Jenny squeezed them all into the Humber.

To get to Richard's Hill it was necessary to join the main highway between Kota Napek and Kuala Kelan, and travel south a few miles before turning left. A couple of miles further on the road ran out. Spartan had been left behind, and it would then be necessary to climb the last two thousand feet to the hill station. This was a six-room wood-and-stone structure started by Jenny's great-grandfather and added to by her grandfather and father. It had a diesel-driven generator for electricity, running water piped in and purified from the sungei, and reasonably modern plumbing. But more important it had huge stocks of tinned food—or so Jenny thought. It wasn't until she got there that she discovered her father had cleaned out every last can. However, fresh fruit was available simply by stepping outside, and fish could be trapped or speared in the sungei. The children were used to such a diet and she could survive on it for now.

For several days Jenny pondered her next move while the fighting got closer from the north. She had half-expected to find Richard's Hill occupied by British soldiers using the high ground as an observation post. But none ever came anywhere near her. The artillery barrages did, however. So did the Japanese air force. Each morning and afternoon planes made low, terrifyingly noisy, swoops overhead, but they did not attack. Nevertheless, she accepted she could not remain where she was for ever. She might not always be so lucky with the aircraft, not if a pilot spotted any sign of life, and the Japanese were bound to overrun the hill sooner or later. She didn't choose to dwell on what would happen to her then.

Her only option was to make for the interior and hope, perhaps, to meet up with her father or another group of planters. That would mean quite a trek and she was not sure the smaller children were up to it. Or whether she was, for that matter. She had no compass, no weapons, no medical supplies, and she would have to keep away from the roads, using only jungle trails. For the first time she saw her gesture in going back for Hamid as meaningless, and this led to inertia. She'd been foolhardy. Out of maternal selfishness she had endangered him and the others by taking them away from their kampong. The Japanese would probably have left them alone; they might not do so if they were caught in the company of a European woman.

Christmas 1941 came and went without her noticing it. So did the New Year. Some of her flock, the very tiny ones, were becoming distressed, pining for their families. She promised she would take them back soon, not knowing how she could do it.

The decision to move on was made for her during the opening days of 1942, when Hamid came rushing in one daybreak to wake her with the news that there were scores ("Many, many!") of Japanese soldiers moving up the trail from the road.

Jenny dashed outside. She could see nothing or hear nothing, but that was neither here nor there. Away from the clearing in which the house stood, the jungle began in earnest.

"How far off?"

Thanks to the elementary schooling Jenny had arranged for the kampong children, Hamid understood the concept of distance.

"About halfway between here and the road."

"Did they see you?"

"No."

"Find all the others, please. Round them up and bring them to the front of the house."

Hamid ran off.

Jenny thought quickly. Halfway between the house and the road, if the soldiers hadn't seen Hamid and were in no hurry, gave her about thirty minutes. Several of the jungle trails behind the house led north. Or rather, started off by heading north. And north of the hill station was Kota Napek, where she remembered her father saying they would be dumping Bill Hyde's Chevrolet. That was the direction they would take and hope for good fortune, for once in the jungle the massive trees blotted out all sunlight and she wouldn't know which way she was going until she came across another clearing. The Japanese would see that the house had been recently occupied, but that couldn't be helped. They might follow one of the northern trails, they might not.

Hamid came to tell her that everyone was present. She counted heads to be sure. She started to explain what they were about to do, trying and not wholly succeeding to keep the fear from her voice, when there was a mighty roar of engines. In her anxiety to leave she had forgotten all about the aircraft sorties, though in this instance they were several hours ahead of their normal schedule. Not knowing anything about military tactics, she was unaware that at least one plane would sweep the terrain in front of the ground troops, especially since reconnaissance had already established the presence of a house on Richard's Hill—a house that the Japanese could use for their own purposes if captured intact but which might, for now, be occupied by British soldiers.

She had her charges outside ready to file off when two fighters came out of the morning sun in line astern and scarcely above tree-top height. Although she had no means of knowing it, they were Mitsubishi Zeros, Japan's front-line fighter, each armed with two 20mm cannon and two 7.7mm machine guns.

The pilot of the leading plane must have been half asleep or startled to see a handful of figures where on previous sorties there had been no sign of life, for he overshot them and was putting his airplane into a sixty-degree banking turn before thumbing his gun-button. The second flier had more time to react and let loose with a long burst from virtually point-blank range. Whether he knew his target was no more hostile than a woman and a group of young children was impossible to say. In any case, the cannon shells and machine gun bullets were ripping and tearing their way through flesh fractions of a second before he threw the Zero into a climbing turn and came in behind his flight commander for another pass.

Jenny knew she was screaming but couldn't hear the sound of her own voice. By some miracle she hadn't been hit, but she was nevertheless covered in blood. To her horror she saw that one little girl had been cut in two, the upper half of the tiny body lying twenty feet from the legs. Another child had been decapitated. Three others were sprawled in a single, bloody heap. A teenage boy was sitting up on the ground, his legs splayed out in front of him, apparently examining the entrails cascading from his stomach. He folded over even as she watched. Out of the ten children, six were already dead or dying, and two more were so badly mangled that it could only be a matter of minutes before they, too, died. Hamid had escaped unscathed, as had another boy the same age.

Jenny's hysterical screams went on and on. She wanted to run, race for the house or the jungle, but found that her legs refused to obey her mind. She felt Hamid tugging at her skirt, heard him shouting at her, but couldn't understand a word he was saying.

What she could hear, and understand, was the frightening roar of the planes coming back, and, with some sixth sense taking over, she grabbed each of the survivors by the hand and sprinted for the safety of the jungle. Halfway there the second boy panicked, slipped free, and galloped in the other direction, down the trail. She yelled after him. He ignored her. A moment later there came a fusillade of rifle fire and a shriek of agony. Then the planes were upon her and Hamid—but not before they reached the jungle, where she dived for the earth, pulling Hamid with her, burying him beneath her in the automatic gesture of a mother protecting her young. Machine gun bullets and cannon shells hammered into the trees above their heads. Then the planes were gone again.

She lay where she was, covering Hamid, for ten, fifteen minutes, unable to stop shaking. Finally she sat up, allowing Hamid up also. He was unhurt but terrified.

She had the presence of mind to put a finger to her lips. The rifle fire they had heard must mean that the Japanese soldiers were closer than Hamid had calculated. Or some of them were. As if to confirm that she heard several of them calling to one another. Impossible to tell how far away. The jungle muffled voices and a distance of a few yards meant invisibility. But the aircraft pilots had doubtless reported that they had seen someone run into the jungle.

The soldiers got closer. From the noise they were making there had to be twenty or more of them in line abreast. With mounting terror she realized they were stabbing at the undergrowth with their bayonets, trying to flush out their quarry. That wouldn't take long.

Suddenly she was quite calm. She knew precisely what she had to do and didn't bother thinking any deeper once the decision had been taken. If they found Hamid with her they would kill him, for he was a witness that they had killed children. They would kill her anyway. After they'd raped her.

"Listen," she said to Hamid, putting her mouth close to his ear and whispering. "In a few moments I'm going to talk to the Japanese. The second—the absolute second—you hear me do so, you must creep away."

"But . . . "

"Listen! They'll kill you if they find you. You don't want that, do you? Of course you don't. Do you know which direction north is?" Hamid nodded. "Good, then head north. Try to find Tuan Cameron. Ask any Europeans you meet for his whereabouts. Tell him what happened. Have you got that?"

"Yes, but . . . "

"No, no buts, please, Hamid. Please!"

The Japanese soldiers were very close now, twenty or thirty yards at a guess, still probing with their bayonets.

Jenny hugged her son, held him for longer than she should have. Then just as abruptly she pushed him away and stood up, stepping out on the trail. She made plenty of noise, though that wasn't necessary. There were three Japanese soldiers not twenty feet away. They jabbered excitedly on seeing her, and soon they were joined by many others. All had their bayonets pointed at her, as if suspecting a trick.

She stood perfectly still until one of the soldiers, the leader judging by the star on his collar, said something to his companions. They all laughed. It was a hideous sound, the more so to a European because they were all so ugly.

The leader grounded his rifle, took off his belt and webbing, and started toward her, fiddling with his flies. She had no doubt that he would be the first and then the others would take it in turns.

As seductively as she could she smiled at the leader and sauntered to meet him, exaggerating her hip movements. When she was within a few feet she broke into a run, dashed past him, and threw herself on to the blade of the nearest bayonet. So quickly was she moving that the bayonet went straight through her, piercing her heart and lungs. She was dead before the petrified soldier who was her unwilling executioner could drop his rifle.

Hamid had disobeyed Jenny's instructions and witnessed it all. Only when he was convinced she was dead did he creep silently away, biting back his tears.

6

The United States had been in the war for six months. Dan Holden wasn't in it at all, and he resented the fact. He didn't consider himself to be more than averagely patriotic, but the fact remained that his country was now a co-belligerent with Great Britain and the Empire, and the Soviet Union. He should be doing more than sitting on his backside.

Without telling Barbara, he'd had a few quiet words with some influential friends at the country club directly after Pearl Harbor; men who would soon be sitting on draft boards or who had connections in Washington. They couldn't believe he was serious.

"For Christ's sake, Dan, you're coming up to thirty-six. You've got a wife, two children under ten, and a thriving business. Let the professionals fight the war, and the youngsters. That's who wars are for. You can be Caspar Milquetoast for the duration without anyone pointing the finger at you. Besides, what would Barbara do if you arrived home one evening wearing a uniform?"

Barbara would doubtless hit the ceiling of their hideously expensive house, that's what Barbara would do.

Still, he hadn't been put off. He'd obtained a few Washington names and a few Pentagon names, and fired off a dozen letters, giving his qualifications. He had a pilot's license (though he realized he was too old for combat flying); he'd skippered boats (the largest being a six-berth cruiser); he'd spent several years in India and the Far East.

That had been in December 1941. Now it was June 1942 and, of those who had taken the trouble to reply, they had all said the same thing: Thanks very much but no thanks. You're doing a great job where you are. The country needs industrialists. Stick with it.

Industrialist my ass. He was doing okay, that much was true. Many of his contemporaries envied him. But AT & T, General

Motors, or US Steel he was not. Being the chief executive of Holden Office Supplies Inc. wasn't going to win the war. Not unless it was being fought with typewriters and quarto.

From his office on the tenth floor of the Brycom Building—the only office, as befitted the chief executive, that had two outside windows—he could look down on Jefferson Avenue on one side and Liberty Street on the other. The juxtaposition of the thoroughfares often amused him, since Thomas Jefferson had drawn up the Declaration of Independence and he, Dan Holden, was neither independent nor at liberty according to his definitions. Fifty miles southwest of the Brycom Building was Fort Worth, where he had a paper plant; fifty miles southeast was Dallas, where he had a factory producing typewriters and other business machines, and a regional sales office. He was at the apex, geographically speaking, of this Texas triangle. It felt the reverse, that he was in the crapper. If the Pentagon wasn't careful he'd volunteer for the other side.

When Dan Holden finally arrived home from Singapore in 1932, his father had been dead for three weeks and his mother was on the way to the nursing home that would claim her for the rest of her life. The family company was doing well but not, in Dan's opinion, well enough. If he had to stay with it for the remainder of his days to pass on to his own children, he was going to try and make it rival IBM. He didn't succeed because his heart was on a ship somewhere but, by the time he took up where he'd left off with Barbara Ravenhill, he was making ten times as much money as most young men his age.

He had known Barbara since high school, since her family moved to Texas from the West Coast. They had dated at sixteen and seventeen, and many were the frantic, passionate sessions they'd had in the back of his father's car or her father's, mostly culminating in a hasty orgasm, hand induced, into a handkerchief. There were no fourth bases with Barbara; there weren't too many first bases. She was lovely and lissom and he adored her, but she seemed to be saving herself for the wedding-ring and the honeymoon.

At college, the same college, they went their separate ways, and once they were out of college he definitely went his own way by several thousands miles. Which was the last he saw of her until he got home from Singapore.

She called, once she learned he was back, to offer commiserations at his father's death. She also expressed the hope that they could get together when the pressure of business permitted. He was surprised to learn that she wasn't married or had even been engaged. She was only a year younger than he.

She laughed and said, no, she hadn't got engaged; she was waiting for him to ask her. It didn't sound like a joke.

She was lovelier than he remembered when they met up for their first date, a word they both loathed and soon dropped. She had lost none of her blonde, cheer-leader good looks, and she was also as sexy as hell. When her mouth said "how are you?" her eyes said "will someone for Chrissake please lay me?" They were too old, they considered, for drive-ins, and too young for the country club. They settled for dinner, during which she listened with genuine fascination to the account of his years overseas. He was much more of a man than her lawyer-accountant-broker acquaintances, and she told him so. It was hard to resist such flattery.

They had reached the coffee stage before he recalled that this was no gold-digger, no pretty face on the make. If her parents' style of living was anything to go by—and like himself she was an only child—she was considerably better off than he.

They got along, enjoyed each other's company to the exclusion of everyone else. The adolescent, back-seat fumblings of yester-year were soon forgotten. Within weeks they were booking into out-of-town motels under assumed names as man and wife, and he was not surprised that her performance in bed lived up to the packaging. Texas morality could be a curse, but none of the moteliers queried their status. They were, after all, no chickens.

Which was something Barbara brought up in the summer of 1933.

"Don't you think we should legalize this relationship or whatever?"

He couldn't see any reason not to. If he had to get married—and a man in his position was viewed with a certain suspicion if he didn't have a wife—he could do a hell of a sight worse than Barbara Ravenhill.

They made it the autumn of that year, a minor society wedding. He brought his mother out of the nursing home for the occasion, but it had to be reckoned doubtful whether the old lady understood what was taking place. The honeymoon was in Hawaii, and Barbara was pregnant before they returned.

David Holden was born in 1934, Laura Holden in 1935. A third child, another girl, was born in 1938 but died in infancy. Dan got over the bereavement fairly quickly; Barbara didn't. He came home from a business trip one evening to find that she'd moved her things into a spare bedroom. She was sleeping badly, she offered by way of an explanation. It would just be for a couple of weeks.

It became a couple of months, then six. Then permanently. Only occasionally did they get it together, and afterward she went back to her own room.

Their doctor told Dan privately that it was psychosomatic depression. She had lost one child and was frightened of lovemaking for fear of conceiving and possibly losing another. Analysis might help, but the best remedy was time.

They talked about their problems openly and still professed to love each other. And they both adored their children. Barbara would not accept the depression theory and scorned analysis; it was just a phase they were going through in her view. All married couples hit choppy water every so often once the first flames of passion had dwindled.

Dan threw himself into his work. He had little alternative. The company was growing and demanding much more of him. He began staying at the office later and found reasons to remain overnight in Dallas or Fort Worth. Sometimes he headed a sales team into the barren hinterland of the Mid-West states. Any excuse to get away.

He had affairs, though nothing very serious. He wasn't going to get involved to the extent that divorce became an option. He was pretty sure she hadn't found anyone else, but suspected she had regular afternoon sessions with the martini pitcher. He couldn't really blame her, for he wasn't being much help. The older he grew, the more frustrated he became. He hadn't been born to live the life of an ass-on-the-seat company executive. The clever thing to do would be to sell up and get out. All of them—he, Barbara and the kids. Head for the mountains or get a boat and mooch around the Pacific. But he knew he was crying for the moon.

Even so, he suggested it. She turned him down.

"Look, darling, I know you miss it all and there are days when I can be a pain. But that sort of life's not for me. There's nothing to prevent you getting a boat, however, taking a long vacation."

"With the children?"

"They're a bit young, don't you think, for globe-trotting?"

He tried it alone, but it didn't work. He didn't want to set off for four weeks or six. He wanted to change his whole life, *their* whole life. He craved excitement.

Then came Pearl Harbor, the perfect opportunity. And nobody wanted him.

Paradoxically, the war did wonders for Barbara. She joined every voluntary organization that would have her. She was still a lovely woman and could perform minor miracles selling War Bonds and boosting morale at recruiting stations.

Dan prayed for a miracle of his own. It arrived in the form of a letter from Washington in August 1942, and was signed by a two-star general by the name of Mason. It requested his presence at the Pentagon three days hence at 0900 sharp.

Mason turned out to be a dapper little man in his fifties wearing World War One combat ribbons. After the formalities, he got straight down to business. Only he and Dan were in the general's office.

"It says here you've spent some time in India and Malaya." He waved a letter Dan recognized as one of his own. "When was that?"

"Late Twenties and early Thirties, general."

Mason seemed disappointed. "Ten years ago. As long as that."

"Yes, sir."

"Tell me about it."

Dan did so. When he had finished, Mason said: "You're married with two children according to this. You also have your own business. What does your wife think about you wanting to get into uniform?"

"We've hardly discussed it. I fired off that letter and a dozen like it without telling her. There didn't seem any point until I had something to tell."

Mason managed a flicker of a smile. "Everyone else turning you down, huh?"

"That's about the size of it. Incidentally, I don't remember writing to you."

"You didn't, but these things have a way of being passed around until they land on the desk of someone who might be interested."

"Interested in what?"

"We'll come to that. And when we do, by the way—and whether or not you decide to come aboard—you're to forget everything we've discussed. Got that?"

Dan said he'd got it.

"Good. You're thirty-five it says here."

"Thirty-six now."

"Fit?"

"Not as much as I could be, but I keep in shape. And I'll do just about anything to get into this war."

"Will you now? We're not looking for heroes, you know."

"And I'm not looking to be one."

"Hmmm." Mason put a match to a cigar. He did not offer Dan one. "Have you heard of General Joe Stillwell?"

Dan had. Vinegar Joe as the newspapers termed him.

"Yes, sir."

"Fine. I'm not betraying any state secrets when I tell you that General Stillwell is now in command of the China-Burma-India Theatre of Operations, and that he's not having things all his own way. The Japanese might have lost four aircraft carriers at Midway in June, but that doesn't mean they're beaten, not by a long shot. If anything, because their navy has received a bloody nose, they're fighting with greater determination on land. And they're used to the climate and the terrain.

"General Stillwell has asked the Pentagon to put together small groups of special forces—and I mean handfuls—to be parachuted behind the lines or put ashore by submarines in Burma and Malaya. The task of these special forces will be to link up with British and British Empire units already active and cause as much damage as they can, compel Tojo to deploy more divisions than he'd like to away from the front. Naturally the army first of all explored the possibility of using regular soldiers and officers, but we don't seem to have too many who know that part of the world, and local knowledge will be essential if the units are to survive and be effective. These aren't suicide missions. There's a lot more I can't tell you and there'll be a rigorous training program to weed out all those who might become liabilities. But, as of now, how does it sound?"

It was manna from heaven, but Dan resisted the impulse to leap up and hug General Mason.

"It sounds fine. When do I start?"

Mason grunted. "Well, you're enthusiastic, I'll say that for you, but we're a long way from the off yet. You'll need to undergo a routine medical, for openers. I can arrange that for you here, before you leave. But I also want you to think it over. It's going to be a long war. The newspapers are talking about it not ending until 1950. I don't know about that, but I do know there are a thousand islands between Java and Tokyo, and the Japs are going to make us fight for every one. What about your business?"

"It can get along without me. Even if it couldn't, can't you draft me?"

"Not for this unit. Strictly volunteers only. Then there's your wife."

Dan thought about Barbara. Before Christmas he'd have laid odds she'd have hit the roof. Maybe now she wouldn't, not now she was so involved with her war work. In any case, he was volunteering, and that was that.

"There'll be no trouble there," he said.

"You won't be able to discuss your eventual theater of operations with her, of course," cautioned General Mason. "Or with anyone else. Not that you or I know it ourselves for the moment. And it's always on the cards that you won't make the cut. Training will take place either in Louisiana or Florida, maybe both, and many of the others will be much younger than you. You'll need to be dedicated to keep up."

"I'll keep up," promised Dan.

"Yes, I reckon you might. Your wife will have to know where you're training, of course, and with what object. We're working on a cover story for that because some of the others are in the same boat as you—civilian volunteers with families. Your papers will probably say something to the effect that you're undertaking a special instructor's course for men with your sort of experience. You can give the impression that all you'll be doing at the end of it will be teaching others how to survive in swamp and jungle."

General Mason lifted the telephone.

"Now let's see about that medical. We'll talk further once I'm sure you're not going to drop dead on us."

"How did it go?" asked Barbara when he returned home. Dan put a clamp on his enthusiasm.

"Not bad, I suppose. They're looking for instructors."

"Instructing what?"

"Survival techniques. I saw a two-star general. He seems to think that the time I spent in India and Malaya might be useful. It'll mean a few months in Louisiana or Florida. After that, who knows? I may not make the grade."

"They've accepted you, then?"

"Looks like it."

"And you're going?"

"Yes."

"When?"

"General Mason thought my papers should be here before the end of the month. Soon after that, I guess. The beginning of September."

"And the company, Holden Office Supplies Incorporated?"

"Well, there'll be a lot of loose ends to tidy up, but the company can run itself, you know that. Frank Bailey and Eddie Moxx have been with it since my father's days. They know as much about the business as I do, more in some areas."

He waited for the storm. It didn't come. Instead she nodded quietly and left the room.

Later that evening she came to his bedroom as he was undressing for his shower. She had a large gin and tonic in one hand but she wasn't drunk. Nor was the mixture for her. She handed him the glass.

"Sit down," she said, patting the bed.

He sat beside her.

"This is important to you, isn't it, getting into uniform?"

"Very. It's not going to be easy, leaving you and the children, but there are millions like us."

"I know." She looked at him steadily, her blue eyes troubled. "Did you expect me to make a scene?"

"Well . . ."

"I would have done a few months ago. I would have demanded to know how you could be so inconsiderate as to leave me and the children, let alone the company. I would have called you selfish and immature, a little boy wanting to play soldiers."

"But . . . ?"

"But—I'm seeing things differently now. Two days a week I'm at the recruiting booth, passing out coffee and doughnuts to young men I could just about be a mother to. I smile at them and share their jokes, and even fend off one or two clumsy passes. Some of them aren't going to come back. I know that for a fact. Ruth Stone—you won't be acquainted with the family but Ruth's one of my helpers—lost a son on the *Yorktown* at Midway, and God knows how many others I've seen pass through the recruiting station are now dead. I'm not sure what you'll be doing in Louisiana, but if it can help save just a couple of lives, it's worth it. You'd tell me if it was more than instructing, wouldn't you? If it was combat."

"If it comes to that, you'll be the first to know." Dan hesitated. "And thanks."

"For being reasonable? I've given you a hard time since the baby died. I didn't mean to. It just happened."

"As you said, all married couples hit choppy water."

When Dan got out of the shower Barbara was in his bed. She didn't leave it that night or any other night until he went away.

Half the time Dan didn't know whether he was in the Louisiana bayous or the Florida Everglades. Most of the time he didn't know whether he was coming or going.

To begin with there were sixty or so recruits in CWG (1)—Clandestine Warfare Group Number One. After a week there were between fifty and sixty; after three weeks there were under fifty. Each Friday evening a notice was posted on the bulletin board giving the names of those who were to report to the company offices for travel warrants. These names hadn't made the weekly cut and there was no appeal.

One or two of the recruits were older than Dan though not by very much. The majority were a lot younger, men who'd worked for U.S. tin mining interests in Malaya, or for rubber interests, or for timber and tobacco consortia in Burma. Some were ex-merchant marine who knew the coastlines; some were born wanderers, misfits. Very few were less than as hard as nails, if not always physically then mentally. Surprisingly there were few fights among such a disparate mob, mostly because fighting meant instant ejection from the outfit.

There were no ranks above private among the newcomers; nor were there likely to be. When the time came, they'd be led by professional officers and non-coms. If anything happened to the officers and the NCOs once they were on a war footing, the natural leaders among the men would take over. That was partly what the course was for, to see who stood out, and for all of them to get to know and trust, or otherwise, each other.

Dan lost ten pounds in the first week. Another four during the second week. Then his weight stabilized and he even put some on. He'd never felt so fit, or so tired. He'd also never been happier.

As a Texan he had grown up with guns, sporting rifles and the like. He considered himself to be something of a shot. But he had never aimed at anything more vicious than game, or fired a military carbine or submachine gun. Grenades were a mystery, as were bazookas. He had to try much harder than the rest, which was what kept him, in his view, from seeing his name on the bulletin board.

Every six weeks a new batch of recruits arrived—CWG (2), CWG (3), and so on. It wasn't until the survivors of CWG (1) saw the flabby bellies and pale complexions of each new intake that they realized just how far they had come in such a short time.

Prior to enlistment, only a handful had had any form of military training. They thus had to learn a whole set of new rules for survival, rules that would have put them beyond the pale in civilian life. To be called mean, deceitful, vicious, sly and a back-stabber in CWG (1) was the highest accolade.

Apart from physical and weapons training, they were taught how to build bridges and then how to blow them up. Those with aptitude were instructed in the use of wireless, how to strip them and how to put them together again. In twos and threes and occasionally alone, they were dumped in the middle of the Everglades without food or water and told to find their way out. Not everyone did, and those who did not found themselves dismissed or, if eligible, transferred to another branch of the services.

Parachute training sorted many of them out. It was still in the balance whether they would be sent in by air or put ashore from a submarine. Much would depend upon the circumstances in their theatre of operations when they joined the war. So they had to know how to jump, by day and night. They were not going to be regular members of the airborne infantry so the course was compressed to ground training, one balloon jump, and three static-line jumps, two by day and one by night. Some couldn't get out of the DC3 with the best will in the world; one or two couldn't even leave the balloon. These were rejected. Being a pilot of small aircraft Dan had no fear of heights, but he prayed that his entry into the war would not be by air at night. It took a superhuman effort to step into the darkness from the Dakota, and this was over a drop-zone where there were no obstacles and no jungle. And no Japanese.

They practiced live-firing assaults by day and live-fire assaults by night. When they weren't doing anything physical they had their heads stuck into maps, memorizing features and terrain. The maps were of northern Malaya. There seemed little doubt that that was where they were going.

October became November, November December. There were less than forty of them now, though some who hadn't made it were out because of injury or illness.

Although the course had been hammered out on paper in Washington months earlier, because CWG (1) were guinea pigs the Army had not been sure just how long it would take to bring a group of civilians assigned to special duties to fighting fitness. Take it too easy and the training would be meaningless; push them too hard and too few to make a viable unit might make the grade. The optimum now seemed to be three months, and by the middle of December 1942 CWG (1) was deemed to be ready for combat.

There had been no furloughs during their training, not even for the married men. That, too, was part of the course. There would be no "weekends off" in Malaya until the Japanese were beaten, and any man who showed too much distress at being separated from his wife and family would have been unsuitable. But now they could be given ten days' leave. Major-General Mason flew down from Washington to tell them as much. They would be released on December 17. They would report back on December 26. They should consider themselves lucky, getting Christmas at home; tens of thousands of American boys were nowhere near so fortunate. They should also take it easy and not eat too much or drink too much. Any man who reported back overweight or otherwise unfit would be back-squadded to CWG (3) and made to do the course all over again. And they should say nothing to anyone about the maps they had been studying, or their probable destination. To do so could jeopardize their lives. They were going overseas, that was all.

Barbara took the news in her stride. She had, she said, half been expecting it from the tone of Dan's letters, and she knew better than to ask questions.

Dan was again amazed at how different, how understanding, his wife had become. He hoped she would not revert to her earlier self while he was away. He didn't doubt that he would survive the war; nor did Barbara. And, once they had established their mutual optimism, they did not discuss his impending departure until it was time to go.

She drove him to the railroad station the morning after Christmas, leaving David and Laura with a neighbor. The platform was crowded with men and women in service dress, but Dan was in civilian clothes. Unit identification flashes—crossed daggers—had been designed for the Clandestine Warfare Group, but, as there were so few of them, General Mason had directed that unit members should travel out of uniform to avoid the attention of the curious.

Barbara left the platform before the train pulled out since she and Dan both disliked drawn-out goodbyes. She said she loved her husband. Dan told her that he loved her, and meant it wholeheartedly. Sex notwithstanding—and whether or not it was his months of abstinence, the sex during his furlough had been magnificent, aggressive as well as tender—she was once again the woman he had married.

That evening—and to everyone's astonishment not one man out of the thirty-six had gone AWOL—CWG (1) flew to the West Coast and thereafter to Wheeler Field, just north of Pearl Harbor, on the Hawaiian island of Oahu. By the second week of January 1943, they were in Sydney, Australia, where they were incarcerated in barracks and not allowed to sample the undoubted charms of the Australian female population, much to the chagrin of everyone who had visited the country before and remembered the generosity of the Aussie women only too well.

In Sydney they kicked their heels for ten days while senior officers digested intelligence data, considered rendezvous map references and diversionary tactics, and figured out whether it was advisable to fly them up to Malaya and parachute them in, or whether a submarine was a better option. To everyone's relief the submarine got the vote, though once they were aboard with all their equipment and no room to swing a cat, they wondered if parachuting might not have been preferable.

Because the Japanese controlled much of the territory north of Darwin, surface travel was only possible by night, and then only with great caution. For the rest of the time they were submerged, mobile or stationary according to where they were and what the latest intelligence on Japanese dispositions was.

From northern Australia they sailed west a thousand miles through the Timor Sea before running the gauntlet through the Lombok Strait between the islands of Bali and Lombok. Then west again, with the Dutch East Indies to the south and Borneo to the north, and out into the South China Sea.

It was the middle of February before they were told that they were heading north thirty miles off the east coast of Malaya, and that they would be put ashore that night under cover of darkness somewhere between Kampong Marang and Kuala Trengganu, coastal towns in the state of Trengganu. They would be met by members of a British group already in situ. That much had been arranged weeks before. It was unlikely that the landing of such of a small force would be detected, but radio silence would be observed. They would be taking only small arms, submachine guns, wirelesses and rifles. Everything else would be provided by the British Force 136 or other outfits, who had been at this game of outwitting the Japs since the fall of Singapore and who received regular supply drops from the north. They would sink their inflatables on beaching. At H-Hour, 0100 hours, there would be a diversionary raid by carrier-borne aircraft further down the coast. That was it. Good luck and Godspeed.

The submarine surfaced at 0050 hours. CWG (1) together with their officers and NCOs came up on deck. There was a half-moon. The coast of Malaya was a thousand yards away. Ten miles downcoast anti-aircraft batteries told them that the diversionary raid had begun. Dan would have preferred to do without it. What was the point in waking up sleepy Japs?

But it all went off without a hitch. The inflatables were slipped overboard and held in position while the men of CWG (1) climbed down scramble netting. A masked torch morsed Charlie William George from the shore.

The first person to meet CWG (1) was Bill Hyde. He was accompanied by a young Malay boy whom he addressed as Hamid. In the small hours they met up with the leader of the group nicknamed Cameron's Cossacks. Dan recognized him almost instantly as the man he had encountered aboard an Australian freighter eleven years earlier.

7

When Hamid crept away after Jenny's death, his first thoughts were to return to his own kampong, to the security of the man and woman he knew as his parents. Then he realized that between him and them were hordes of Japanese soldiers, who were killing, as he had just witnessed, anyone who was not Japanese. He must do as Miss Jenny had said, find Tuan Cameron, tell him what had happened.

It took him three months, using jungle trails, and where he could, rivers and streams, paddling down the deepest astride fallen tree trunks or abandoned rafts, always with one wary eye open for crocodiles. For the first month he was totally alone, a terrifying experience for a boy not ten years old who had never been without company in his life. He slept fitfully, usually only after he was completely exhausted, for before then there were too many frightening natural enemies, tigers and leopards, huge pythons and spitting cobras for peaceful somnolence. Sometimes he slept in the lower forks of trees, sometimes on makeshift charpoys, but never for more than a few minutes at a time. A moving shadow could mean sudden death. Weariness was a constant companion, as was loneliness, for he avoided strange kampongs after, on approaching one, he saw two Japanese soldiers drag a sobbing Malay girl into a hut. It seemed to him that he was likely to find Japanese wherever he went, that the invading army would have left behind handfuls of soldiers in every kampong they overran.

He survived on raw fish and fruit, and, once, gorged himself into a stupor on a feast of cooked rice from an iron pot in a kampong that, for a reason he never established, was deserted when he found it.

He kept on heading north, as Miss Jenny had instructed, up into the mountains. He saw Japanese patrols on many occasions, but those that spotted him ignored him, and after a while, in any case, he had acquired enough cunning to avoid them altogether.

At the end of the first month he came upon four Europeans in a clearing, three in tattered British army uniform and one civilian. All were armed. He approached them shyly and asked if they knew the whereabouts of Tuan Cameron. Only the civilian had heard of the tuan, but did not know where he was. However, the four were also heading north and he stayed with them for a week, helping them to catch fish in the mountain sungeis and advising them on what fruit to eat and what to leave alone. The men had the means of making fire and he was able to enjoy hot food. One of the soldiers gave him a knife in a leather sheath, which he strapped to his waist using plaited vines as a belt. With the knife he fashioned a fishing spear out of bamboo.

One evening this same soldier, who had always seemed friendlier than the others, lured Hamid away from the camp and tried to assault him sexually. He would have succeeded had Hamid not sunk his sharp teeth into the man's arm, biting until he reached the bone. The soldier screamed in agony and released him, whereupon Hamid ran off as fast as his legs would carry him, determined to be more careful in future. Some of the Europeans were obviously as brutal as the Japanese.

Toward the end of the second month he was beginning to despair. Many evenings, especially if he had covered a long distance that day and was tired, he sat down and wept, hating himself for crying but unable to stop the tears. Until he went with Miss Jenny and the children, he had never been further than a couple of miles from his own kampong. He'd had no idea that Malaya was so huge, though the village teacher had tried to instill rudimentary geography into all the pupils. But seeing his country drawn in chalk on a blackboard, with Thailand to the north and Burma to the west of Thailand, had not prepared him for the reality.

At the beginning of March 1942—though Hamid had no idea of the date—he awoke from an uneasy sleep one morning to hear voices close by. European voices conversing in English. From their discussion he gathered that they were tin miners from near Sungei Siput in the state of Perak, though at present—as near as they could judge—they were in the state of Kelantan.

Remembering his experience with the soldier, Hamid remained concealed for some time. Then he realized he would never find Tuan Cameron unless he asked.

They were startled when he suddenly put in an appearance at the sungei's edge, where several of them were washing. He had been just a few yards from them and they had neither seen nor heard him. Half a dozen rifles forced a round into half a dozen breeches before they discerned that the newcomer was just a child.

There were ten of them, all bearded, all heavily armed. One of them was crouched over a wireless from which no sound came. Their spokesman asked him who he was, where he had come from. What he wanted. He told them.

They knew Tuan Cameron, the spokesman said, and approximately where he was. It was their intention to join him. But— what did Hamid want with the tuan? It was not until later that Hamid understood their mistrust, that he learned that the Japanese were offering rewards to any Malay who would direct them to Europeans.

Hamid explained haltingly what had happened to the other children and Miss Jenny, and what, before she was killed, Miss Jenny had asked him to do. They listened in silence until he was through, then questioned him at length until they were sure he was telling the truth. They didn't seem to find it credible that someone his size could have travelled over one hundred miles alone. But finally they were satisfied. And one of them said to his companions: "Christ, I knew young Jenny Cameron. Harry's going to lose his mind when he hears about this."

They agreed that Hamid could come with them. Harry Cameron's last location, before the wireless batteries had given up the ghost, was rumored to be near the Gua Musang limestone caves, fifty miles due east of Sungei Siput or about twenty-five miles from where they now stood. The miners' leader reckoned it would take them about a week. In actuality, travelling only a few hours a day out of the worst of the heat, from sun-up to mid-morning, and taking evasive action when Hamid, in the role of scout, warned them of approaching Japanese patrols, it took them four. And in the end it was one of Harry's men, a Chinese lookout, who spotted them, not the other way around. For that matter, the other way around would have been impossible, for the camp was a mile and a half from the Gua Musang caves, in the deepest jungle and invisible from ground and air because of the protective canopy of trees. The Japanese would need a lot of luck to find it, and the system of sentries was such that, even given luck, the camp's occupants would have vanished into the jungle an hour or more before any Jap patrol got close.

Whatever the miners had been expecting to see, it wasn't the sight that greeted their eyes. Because there were only ten of them and they had been living rough, they assumed that Cameron's group was also small, probably underfed, and doubtless skulking in the jungle. Which was as far from reality as it was possible to get.

The camp was in a natural clearing which had been widened and lengthened until it measured approximately one hundred yards by eighty. Thirty yards from the perimeter a jungle trail led to a fast-flowing sungei which would provide fish and fresh water. At the head of the trail stood an armed guard, in case the Japanese had boats, though the sungei didn't seem broad enough to be navigable. A score or more bashas, each capable of holding half a dozen men, had been constructed out of atap and bamboo. They were far from makeshift. In front of the bashas was a square measuring seventy feet by seventy and in which, when the miners arrived, thirty or so Chinese were being instructed by a European in the use of firearms, the demonstration weapon being a short-muzzle Lee-Enfield. Another, smaller, group of Chinese were huddled over a radio, trying to fathom its mysteries. Yet a third group were practicing throwing grenades—hopefully unfused. Several fires were burning. Above each, slung from a tripod, was a kawah, a cooking pot from which the most delicious smells emanated. Next to each fire was a pail of water. In an emergency the fires could be doused within seconds. Including the Chinese, the miners counted upward of eighty men, and there were probably more taking into consideration unseen sentries. Some sported beards, but this appeared to be out of choice; the majority of the Europeans and all the Chinese were clean-shaven. A few men wore army uniforms. One or two were evidently Australians judging by their headgear. There was an air of efficiency and calm about the whole encampment, astonishing when it was remembered that they were in the middle of Japanese-occupied Malaya.

Harry Cameron emerged from one of the bashas. The miners' leader, Craig Bellamy, an Englishman who had been working for an American concern before the invasion, recognized him immediately, as did several other miners. Flanking Harry were two other figures familiar to anyone who had spent time in Kuala Kelan before the war: Alan Fielding and Bill Hyde. Apart from the fact that all three men had lost some weight, they seemed in perfect physical condition.

Harry shook hands with Bellamy and nodded to the others.

"Glad to see you. We need someone who knows something about demolition, but we thought you'd been captured when you went off the air."

"Bloody batteries," grunted Bellamy. "And, things being what they are, we couldn't hop into Ipoh to get some more." He indicated the camp. "This is incredible. How the hell did you manage it?"

"With a lot of help from our Chinese friends over there."

"Who are they?"

"Well, they are, or they will be when we've trained them, part of the MPAJA—the Malayan Peoples' Anti-Japanese Army. There are several hundred groups like this one, maybe more. Precise figures are hard to come by, as you'll appreciate, but Colonel Chapman and Chin Peng reckon they'll be able to field five thousand or so before the next monsoons."

"Colonel Chapman? Chin Peng?"

"Colonel Spencer Chapman. He's one of those who stayed behind and evaded the net when the Japs invaded, and he's head of something we call Force 136. We don't see much of him but we keep in touch via radio if he's within range and by courier otherwise. The Japs think they've got this country cracked. They haven't, not by a long chalk. Chin Peng's the driving force behind the MPAJA, alongside Shorty Kuk, Lau Yew and Hor Lung. We don't see much of them, either. They're disciples of Mao Tse-tung, naturally, but very useful for all that. In fact, indispensable. Without the Chinese there wouldn't be much resistance in this theatre, if you can call it a theatre."

"Communists? For Christ's sake let's not train them too well."

"We don't have many options. The Chinese hate the Japanese, and anyone who hates the Japanese will do for me for now."

"Have you seen any action?"

"Not yet. The Japs aren't going to go away in a hurry, if we can eject them at all. There'll be plenty of time for action once the Chinese know one end of a rifle from the other. But they're fast learners and as brave as lions. Unlike the Malays, I regret to say, who've more or less chucked their hand in. But the Chinese aren't going to forget who did the fighting when peace comes."

"What about supplies?"

"We've got our own for the moment, here and elsewhere. They won't last for ever, of course, and this climate's hell on small-arms' maintenance and ammunition dumps, but Colonel Chapman's got his end of things organized. He doesn't give much away in case one or more of us is captured and interrogated by the Kempetai, but I've reason to believe that he's in touch with the fighting in Burma and India. When they've fought the Japs to a standstill up there, we'll receive our supply drops. In the meantime, we carry on as best we can and avoid trouble until we're ready.

"Now, we'll get you and your team fed and watered and then I'll require a complete report on where you've been and what you've seen, chapter and verse."

"That won't be much. We've seen patrols of about platoon strength, which could mean there's a battalion in the area. On the other hand, we've also come across kampongs where there were just half a dozen Japs in residence. It would seem to me," said Bellamy, "that they won't have more than a few hundred men deployed outside the main towns. What would be the point? The army in Malaya surrendered, the war here is over. They'd need a hundred thousand men just to comb a few square miles of jungle. They must know they haven't put all the Europeans in the bag, but, the way I see it, they won't bother us until we bother them. And bothering them will mean ambushing convoys on the main roads or sabotaging the railways."

"That seems logical," agreed Harry. "It's the way we're thinking, too. Still, this is closer to your neck of the woods than mine, and any information you can give me may save all our lives."

"Yes, you're a long way from home, aren't you? I was a bit surprised to learn you were this far north."

"There are reasons. The first is that you set up camp where you can. The second is that we might become more useful the closer we are to the Thai border. What I'm telling you is only an unconfirmed rumor, but the story is that the Japs are about to move thousands of British and Australian troops out of Changi Gaol in Singapore and other camps, and send them up north to work on a railway link between Bangkok and Moulmein in southern Burma, where, as you know, there isn't a railway at present. Anything we can do to prevent that must obviously be a help to our side. Apart from that, we may be able to liberate a few souls. Japan didn't sign the Geneva Convention insofar as it applies to prisoners-of-war, and something else we've learned is that the Japs are adopting a particularly harsh attitude toward their captives. Their military code equates surrender with dishonor, and forbids it. They cannot understand, apparently, why the rest of the belligerents don't forbid it also. Some of my Australians here, and all of the Chinese, think we should be hitting back."

Craig Bellamy had forgotten about Hamid. Now the Eurasian boy pushed himself forward and planted himself in front of Harry.

"Oh, Jesus," muttered Bellamy. The other miners, knowing what was coming, shuffled their feet uncomfortably and averted their eyes. "Look, this lad's got something to tell you and it's not pleasant."

Harry recognized Hamid as one of his daughter's lame ducks, though he was somewhat taken aback to see the boy so far from the estate and his own kampong. So the damned Japs had torched the bungalow, had they? Or aircraft had bombed the hell out of the plantation.

"Tell away."

Bellamy hesitated. "Maybe in private—you, me and the lad."

"Okay," agreed Harry, puzzled. "Bill," he said to Hyde, "you and Alan see to it that these men get fed and sort them out some accommodation."

"What's going on?" Bill Hyde asked generally of the remaining miners, as Harry, Bellamy and Hamid disappeared into Harry's basha.

"It's Jenny," answered one of them reluctantly. "According to the kid, she was killed by the Japs, bayoneted. He's a bit vague on time, but I'd say it was around the beginning of the year."

"My God," said Hyde.

"He's made a mistake," said Alan Fielding, who had also recognized Hamid. "Jenny and her mother were joining the convoy for Singapore just after we left. The Japs were miles away." Fielding had an horrific thought. Was it possible that Jenny had persuaded Jessica to take Hamid with them down to Singapore, and that, en route, something appalling had occurred? "Did he say where this reputedly happened?"

"Bukit Sedikit. That's Harry's hill station, isn't it? It was something of a massacre, by all accounts. A couple of planes shooting up the place ahead of the Jap infantry. Jenny wasn't the only one who died. A lot of children did also."

Dear Christ, thought Fielding, knowing instinctively what had taken place. In the final analysis Jenny had been unable to leave her son behind to the tender mercies of the Japs. She'd either persuaded her mother to go on ahead, pretending she would follow, or had abandoned Jessica somewhere on the road and returned for Hamid. To make it look good, she'd taken other kampong children with her, hoping to hide out on Richard's Hill until the danger was past. It had to be that. And Harry would still not know, couldn't know, must never know, that the child who had brought him the news of Jenny's death was his own grandson. He had enough on his plate, fighting a war, did Harry Cameron. To allow him to know that Hamid was his grandson was equally to inform him that he, Harry, had killed Hamid's father.

Fielding glanced across at Bill Hyde. He could expect no help there. Hyde knew of the original "rape" and the subsequent cover-up; he did not know about Hamid.

"There's food in the cook-pots," said Hyde to the miners. "Help yourselves. We'll sort out somewhere for you to sleep later. Have you got anything in your bag of tricks?" he asked Fielding.

"Morphine tablets. They're at a premium, though. God only knows when we may need them for an emergency."

"You don't think *this* is an emergency?"

"I'll allow Harry to be the judge. It's a terrible thing, I know, but we'll face worse."

"*We'll* face worse?"

"All right, Harry will."

"I don't think so. Harry's no way of knowing whether Jess made it out of Singapore. I don't know if Molly did. But we didn't have children. If Harry's lost Jess, at least Jess had almost fifty years of her life, and a damned good life at that. Molly too. I can't imagine anything worse than knowing your daughter's been killed and not being able to do a thing about it."

"Harry will do something about it. This unit hasn't been on the active list since the capitulation. I have a feeling all that's going to change."

Fielding's sentiments were more prophetic than he realized. They stood, he and Bill Hyde, a respectful distance from Harry's basha until Bellamy and Hamid emerged after fifteen minutes. The miner was ashen, the boy trembling, clearly shaken. Bellamy shook his head grimly before leading Hamid over to where the miners were eating. For compassion's sake. Hyde and Fielding gave it another couple of minutes before joining Harry, who was sitting on his charpoy, his head in his hands. When he became aware of the others' presence, he looked up. His eyes were moist. He wiped them as best he could with the crown of his wide-brimmed terai.

"You heard?" His voice was steady but it was apparent he was only keeping it under control by a supreme effort of will.

"They told us outside," said Fielding awkwardly.

"Do you believe it?"

"We got it second-hand. You spoke to the boy."

"He convinced me even though he was a bit hazy on detail. He's a spunky little bastard, too, trekking a hundred-odd miles because that's what Jenny told him to do. Christ," he said softly, "what could she have been thinking of? What the hell could she have been thinking of?"

"We'll never know," said Hyde. "Look, I know it's no help, but we're all old friends here and Alan and I partly understand what you're going through. If there's anything we can do . . . She was a fine girl, a lovely girl . . . " He tailed off, turning his palms upward and shrugging his shoulders. There were no words that could possibly ease the pain.

"You could use some sleep," suggested Fielding. "A few hours, maybe. I've got some stuff that will work the oracle."

"No, thanks. I don't need a sedative if that's what you're offering." His tone was unnaturally normal, as if he were refusing one drink for the road—*No, thanks, old chap, three's my limit*. He drifted for a few seconds, his demeanor almost catatonic. Fielding suspected he was keeping a tight rein on hysteria and wished to God he would let himself go, get it out of his system. That was always the best way, a good weep, a good scream. Knowing Harry, however, that was the last thing that would happen. "I've got some thinking to do. Alone. I'd appreciate it if you'd see I'm not disturbed outside of an emergency."

There was a fine dividing line between carrying out a private vendetta that might bring down the wrath of the Japanese army upon their heads before they were ready and without the returns being worth it in terms of matériel and personnel destroyed, and revenge that would satisfy a bloodlust without attracting too much attention. Harry trod the line with considerable virtuosity and consummate patience.

Beginning that same evening he sent out two-man patrols, all Chinese, to scout the area around the encampment for a mile in every direction. They were to report the number and disposition of Japanese troops in neighboring kampongs. They were to do nothing else. They should also let him know if they saw any Negritos or Sakai, Malayan aboriginals. It was hardly likely that these people, notoriously shy, would reveal the presence of strangers to the Japanese, but forewarned was forearmed.

By now everyone knew about Jenny's death. They also knew, because Fielding had told them, not to mention it unless Harry did first. Which Harry never did.

The leader of the Chinese, Lee Swee Peng, a slight individual in his middle twenties who spoke immaculate English learned at Singapore's Victoria School, was delighted at this early prospect of action. To him, as to his men, it didn't matter one iota whether they were destroying Japanese rail or road convoys or executing Japanese soldiers one by one. He had left behind a family in China; they were all wiped out when the Japanese invaded. He respected Harry because Harry could teach him things he could not learn elsewhere, and he was aware that the Japanese had proved, and were continuing to prove, formidable jungle fighters. But he was conversant with Mao Tse-tung's classic guerrilla warfare doctrine of falling back before superior strength. When the enemy advances, retreat. Pick him off piecemeal.

At the end of a week Harry had a dozen potential targets, all within a day's march. Craig Bellamy's assessment of Japanese forces turned out to be accurate. There could be no more than a scattered battalion in the vicinity of the Gua Musang caves. Which was logical when he thought about it. The Japanese would be garrisoning the larger cities and seaports, protecting the few major roads and railway lines in Malaya, guarding their logistics. There was no point in deploying a couple of divisions in the mountains, divisions that were needed in Burma. What possible damage could a tiny force of irregulars inflict? Well, the bastards would find out.

Harry led the first sortie, as he was to lead many others, accompanied by Lee Swee Peng and a dozen of his Chinese. The Australians, remnants of the 8th Division with not an officer among them, were peeved at being left behind. Harry promised them they would get their share.

Harry's party was away all night. When they returned at first light they were carrying, Hyde and Fielding spotted on being awoken by an excited chattering, a couple of sacks. Lee Swee Peng did the honors, emptying the sacks on to the ground in the square in front of the bashas. Out tumbled four Jap heads. One of Peng's Chinese who had not been on the raid gave a delighted whoop and kicked the nearest head. Until Harry put a stop to it, at Fielding's request, the Chinese played a scratch game of soccer with that head and the others. Then the heads were jammed on bamboo spikes at the perimeter of the camp. Within no time at all the ants left only skulls.

The second sortie ended up the same way, but this time with only a single head. The third sortie produced two. One of the Aussies was the first to understand what Harry was doing. "They'll think it's a bunch of Abos gone berserk," he said with admiration.

Then Harry laid off for a week, sending out only scouting patrols. Wisely, as it transpired. The kampongs that had been attacked had been reinforced. Occasionally aircraft were heard overhead. Once in a while Peng's Chinese reported that reprisals were being taken against the kampongs where Japanese deaths had occurred. Harry wasn't unhappy.

"The more the Japs punish the Malays, the more the Malays will become their enemy. Anyway, we're all in this war."

By the middle of the year Craig Bellamy was calling Harry, in no manner critically, a Cossack. Harry liked it, and thereafter his group was known as Cameron's Cossacks. Wingate had his Chindits up north, and Merrill his Marauders. Why shouldn't Cameron have his Cossacks?

Bill Hyde and Alan Fielding were worried about their old friend. They discussed it at length from time to time.

"He's crazy, you know that?" offered Hyde one quiet afternoon. "Jenny's death has sent him around the bend."

"I doubt that," countered Fielding. "Not unless you're calling everyone involved in this war crazy, wherein I might agree with you. I heard one of the Australians talking the other day. Actually he was writing a spoof letter, one he knows he can never send. It read, and I quote: 'Dear Mum, You ought to see it out here. The blood and guts, men going crazy, the swearing and the butchery. Then there's the war, of course.' No, I don't think Harry's out of his mind. They'll pin more medals on him at the end of this."

"If he lives until the end."

"He'll live, all right."

As the only medico Fielding had his own problems unconnected with what went on after Harry left the encampment. As far as it went, food was adequate, more than capable of sustaining life. But there was the occasional case of dysentery which nothing in his "bag of tricks" could cure, and which meant, more often than not, the sufferer dying. Cholera had not, mercifully, reared its ugly head, but malaria had, since many mosquito nets had rotted long ago. As had much else, including footwear. There was no way of escaping the dampness, and few ways of drying anything once it was wet. Then there was the awful, all-pervading greenness, which affected men's minds more than their bodies, and about which he could do nothing. Soon, too, he would be unable to do anything about their physical ailments either, for his stocks of medicines and salves grew smaller by the month.

Lee Swee Peng solved that. With Harry's permission he disappeared for a week, along with three henchmen. When he returned he came with a complete set of medical supplies, obviously from his Communist friends elsewhere though he would not confirm that. As had become a working rule between the Chinese and the Europeans, no one asked too many questions unless the answers were essential.

After a few months Fielding noticed that Hamid was beginning to accompany Harry everywhere, not only around the encampment but on sorties also. He tackled Harry on the subject.

"He's very useful," explained Harry, as if talking to a simpleton. "He can go places the rest of us cannot. He's the perfect chameleon, worth as much as six of Peng's men, and that's saying something."

"He's not yet ten, for God's sake," retorted Fielding.

"How do you know that?" asked Harry curiously. "He could be anything between eight and twelve."

"Well, he looks between nine and ten," said Fielding lamely, and left it at that.

In truth he was tired. The war in Malaya was less than a year old and he was feeling his age. His sixty-fifth birthday had come and gone. His function was nothing more than that of camp doctor—as Bill Hyde seemed to have become camp quartermaster—but he wasn't sure how much more he could take of living like an aboriginal. Oh, for a porch to rock on, a huge Tiger beer and a gigantic White Horse to top it off.

Not that a shortage of liquor was a problem. The Chinese had managed to brew a variation of *samsu*. But it was rationed by Harry for the sake of discipline, and it left the drinker with a fearful headache.

One remarkable feature of Harry's campaign of terror was that not once since it began had a shot been fired by his men, nor had any of them been captured or killed. Although they carried rifles, shotguns, handguns and submachine guns on every sortie, the firearms were not for use except in an emergency, unless they were cornered. Which they never were. Their main weapons were parangs, machetes and other assorted blades. Plus stealth, local knowledge, and the night hours.

The Japanese skulls continued to mount until Japanese soldiers in the area implemented the same tactics, with Malay villagers and Sakai as the victims. For every Imperial soldier killed and decapitated, half a dozen Malay—men, women and children— were beheaded, their heads displayed outside the kampong where the executions had taken place. Crude notices in poor English tacked to the stakes on which the heads were mounted left Harry in no doubt that the Japanese knew that their own casualties were the result of European and Chinese guerrilla activity. They had also evidently reasoned that, with such a small force in the mountains, they stood no chance of rooting out the guerrillas. They had therefore upped the stakes, believing that the Malays, much though they hated their conquerors, would sooner or later betray the whereabouts of the guerrillas rather than see their families killed.

Harry was inclined to agree with the thinking behind the strategy, and he had little option but to stop his raids before matters got as far as betrayal. It was either that or move away from the area. He was not ready to do that, though he accepted they could not remain where they were for the rest of the war.

In September, after a month of inactivity, Lee Swee Pen began complaining. Cameron's Cossacks were not only doing nothing about military convoys, road and rail, conveying matériel and manpower up north; they were not, now, even killing Japanese individually. Surely they should be doing something?

Harry took the point but disagreed with the concept, arguing that attacks on distant convoys were tantamount to suicide. They were fifty miles from Ipoh, fifty miles from the major road and rail arteries that ran all the way from Singapore to the Thai border. It would take a massive operation, with weeks of planning, to get them there and get them back. Besides, he had it on good authority that there were other guerrilla units attacking the convoys. That was the luck of the draw. Those groups had either been formed in, or found a base near, major towns.

This wasn't good enough for Lee Swee Peng. If they couldn't kill Japanese in the Gua Musang district because it was getting too dangerous, and they couldn't raid convoys because the convoys were too far away, what was the point of their existence?

Be patient, counselled Harry, who alone knew from Colonel Chapman that his small, mostly non-military force would one day over the next few months be augmented by American commandos. When, though, Colonel Chapman had been unable to say. Harry concluded that he must have a personal word with the leader of Force 136. The present state of affairs could not be allowed to continue for much longer without morale being affected adversely. Already the camp was dividing into factions, the Europeans siding with Harry, the Chinese, for whom the end and the means were identical, supporting Peng, who wanted action. It would not take much, in Harry's opinion, for Peng to opt to go it alone.

In November Colonel Chapman sent a courier for Harry. After some private soul-searching, Harry took Lee Swee Peng with him. They were away several weeks. When they returned the Chinese was much happier. Small units of American Clandestine Warfare personnel were even now under training in the United States. The first CWG was expected to arrive early in 1943, possibly being parachuted in but, more likely, landing from a submarine somewhere on the northeast coast. More details would be available nearer the date. If they came by sea, Colonel Chapman wished them to join forces with Cameron's Cossacks. The northeast coast was close on a hundred miles from Gua Musang, a hundred miles of rugged mountains, jungle and enemy troops. Since it was manifestly absurd for Harry's unit to trek a hundred miles one way to link up with the Americans, and then retrace its steps a hundred miles in the other direction, the present camp would have to be abandoned sooner or later. The enlarged unit's new area of operations would probably be in northeast Kelantan or Trengganu to begin with. Therefore—and this was what had pleased Lee Swee Peng—the wraps were off as far as creating mayhem in their present location was concerned. They should do as much damage as they could before, inevitably, the camp was discovered either by stepped-up Jap activity or informers, or both.

Harry was no less happy than Peng that, once again, the business of killing Japanese could continue. The nightly sorties resumed. Then the inevitable happened. One morning in the middle of December a patrol comprising four Chinese, two Australians and two of Bellamy's miners did not return. Their target had been a kampong two miles away, and during the hours of darkness shots had been heard, heavy machine-gun fire as well as small arms. This didn't necessarily mean anything. Shots were often heard by day and night, whether there was a patrol out or not; nervous Japs shooting at shadows.

Harry gave the patrol a further twenty-four hours before sending out a reconnaissance party, two of Peng's men. They reported back that all eight Cossacks were dead. They had been found lashed to trees near their target. Their eyes had been put out and it seemed that the Japs had used them for bayonet practice. It was impossible to say if any of them had been taken alive. Harry doubted it. If one or more of them had, they would surely have talked under torture, given away the camp's location. Yet the camp had not been raided. They must have all been killed outright or so badly wounded as to be useless for interrogation purposes. Putting out their eyes and bayoneting them was meant as a warning—to the guerrillas who, the Japs could be sure, would learn about it, as well as the Malays.

The two scouts also had other information. There appeared to be many more Japanese in the vicinity than a week earlier, two or three times the number. Was it possible, wondered Harry, that the Japanese could at last spare the manpower to do something about his guerrillas?

He did not have to wait long for his answer. Japanese air activity increased threefold during the third week in December, the aircraft, invisible above the trees, dropping HE at random. None of the bombs came anywhere near the camp so it was obvious the enemy was still guessing, but it could only be a matter of time before a pilot or a Japanese foot patrol got lucky. The moment had come to pull out, start making for the northeast coast. Since one hundred men on the march might attract unwelcome attention, they would leave in groups of ten at half-daily intervals, heading for a rendezvous in the hills outside Kuala Berang south of the River Trengganu.

Alan Fielding wasn't sure he was up to such a journey. The Chinese solved that, over Fielding's protests, by rigging up a litter for him to use when his aging limbs became tired. They could not afford to lose their only doctor.

Harry was saddened by his first casualties and enraged that their corpses had been mutilated. He was also reluctant to leave without having one more crack at the Japs.

He discussed ways and means with Hyde, Bellamy, Lee Swee Peng and some of the senior Chinese. All-out assaults against kampongs where the Japanese were present in some strength were rejected. So too were piecemeal attacks against smaller Japanese units. Craig Bellamy came up with the answer. Since the Japs were looking for the camp and Harry was going to abandon it anyway, why not let the Japs find it? Booby-trap the bashas with grenades and trip-wires and whatever else was available and could be spared, then get the hell out of it. The rear party, the last group of ten to leave, could make a fire before they went, to attract the Japs" attention.

It wasn't perfect but it was better than nothing. Lee Swee Peng suggested an alternative plan, that of using Hamid to direct the Japanese to the camp, ostensibly for a reward. Harry turned him down. It was too dangerous for the boy.

Bill Hyde, as quartermaster, had been hoarding half a dozen two-gallon jerrycans of petrol from a pre-war cache in case he could ever find a use for them. Now he could, because they were far too heavy to manhandle a hundred miles.

On December 24 Hyde removed the screw-caps of five cans and placed them in five bashas, a petrol-soaked rag depending from each. Harry, Bellamy, Lee Swee Peng and the others who were left primed all the' grenades they could spare and wedged them behind each jerrycan, with trip-wires made of vine attached to the safety pins at ankle height. The bashas had been built so near to one another for reasons of space that it would only need a single grenade to detonate and ignite the petrol for the whole camp to blow up in flames. Any Jap close by would receive a nasty flashburn if nothing more serious.

The sixth jerrycan was poured over damp-wood kindling already soaked with gun oil, and lit. A column of black smoke shot upward, through the trees.

"They'll see that in Kuala Lumpur," said Bellamy.

Harry and Hamid were the last to leave, Hamid, as was now customary, reluctant to move without Tuan Cameron unless the tuan had some special task for him. The time was a little before seven A.M., and they travelled as fast as was humanly possible under the conditions until eleven A.M., anxious to put as much mileage as they could between themselves and the camp. They heard aircraft overhead, at tree-top height by the sound of the engines, but no bombs were dropped. A little later it started to rain in earnest, and the aircraft, presumably because of poor visibility, went away. Harry estimated they were between four and six miles from the camp before he called a halt until evening, when it would be cooler.

It was two o'clock in the afternoon when they heard the explosion behind them, in the west. Although impossible to tell from where they were whether it was caused by a bomb or whether their trap had been successfully sprung, Harry was inclined to be optimistic.

"Merry Christmas," he said to no one in particular.

* * *

Six weeks after the Americans of CWG (1) landed and were led by Bill Hyde and Hamid to Harry's base in the hills above Kuala Berang, Harry received an urgent message via Chinese courier to rendezvous with Major Peter Benson, one of Colonel Chapman's adjutants, six miles away at Kampong Serit, which was known to be secure.

Since arriving the Americans had done little more than get acclimatized. The heat and humidity of the Louisiana bayous and the Florida Everglades had not prepared them for Malaya's climate. Even the civilian volunteers, Dan Holden among them, who knew the country from previous experience had forgotten just how debilitating the weather could be. On top of everything, CWG (1) had spent several weeks kicking its heels in Australia and several more aboard a cramped submarine. In short the Americans were not, to begin with, very fit. After six weeks they were, and their commanding officer, Captain Rufus Huxley, a crewcut career paratrooper in his thirties, was anxious to earn his per diem. Huxley was all hustle, bustle and let's-get-the-bastards. It took some time for Harry to convince him that this was a slow war and that targets of opportunity east of the central mountain range were scarce compared to those in the west. Supply drops from the north were becoming more regular, yes, and they were not short of weapons, ammunition, explosives and medical supplies. What they were short of was personnel. The loss of a few dozen men in the North African Theatre was nothing; they could be replaced. The loss of a few dozen men here in an attack that was incorrectly mounted or coordinated could be catastrophic. It was the same lesson Harry tried to drum into Lee Swee Peng— patience.

Huxley was inclined to argue the point and even debate who was in command of the enlarged outfit until Alan Fielding took the American to one side and explained that Harry was not, as Huxley had been overheard to comment, "a typical colonial Brit, hopeless without his servants and his cricket pitches"; that Harry had, in fact, lost his only daughter to a Japanese bayonet. And furthermore, in a memorable phrase, that Harry had been here since the week after Genesis while Huxley was fresh off the boat.

To his credit, Huxley was suitably chastened. He agreed that, while he must keep overall command of CWG (1), he wouldn't make waves if Harry seemed to take more time than Huxley thought strictly necessary in getting CWG (1) into the war.

Dan Holden only vaguely remembered Jenny Cameron, but the little he did recall was of a pretty, vivacious young lady. If what had happened to Jenny had happened instead to his own Laura, he thought he would have gone out of his mind. He wasn't sure Harry hadn't. There was an odd, maniacal glitter in his eyes whenever he talked about past operations against the Japs.

Harry accepted Dan's commiserations with a brief nod. "You were wise not to accept that job I offered you," he said, forgetting the circumstances under which Dan had continued aboard the SS *Southern Pride* to Singapore.

As instructed, Harry went alone with the returning Chinese courier to meet Major Benson, who looked ill, Harry thought; more ill, anyway, since the last time he had seen the British major with Colonel Chapman. Then again, only the recently arrived Americans appeared anywhere near healthy, and even they were beginning to show signs of jungle pallor, the result of living almost permanently away from the light of the sun. That plus a shortage of essential vitamins, in spite of the supply drops and the sterling efforts of Alan Fielding and others like him, would probably see them all in their graves before the Japanese could.

Benson's first question was about the Americans. How were they settling in?

"They're champing at the bit. Their CO's a real fire-eater. He can't wait to see some action."

"I'll try not to hog it all for myself," said Benson with heavy irony.

He had a large-scale map of northeast Malaya spread out in front of him. A red asterisk had been marked on it near Kota Bharu, where the Japanese invasion had started. A red asterisk was the symbol for a POW camp. It hadn't been on the map last time.

"Another camp?"

Benson folded the map. "Not really your concern," he said pleasantly, "but yes, another camp. The Japanese have kept the rubber estates in that area producing, using mostly Malay, Indian and Chinese labor until recently. Now they've established a European camp, two hundred and fifty to three hundred POWs from Changi." Benson mopped his brow wearily. "I doubt if conditions are as appalling as they are for the men building the rail link through the Kwai valley between Bangkok and Moulmein, but our intelligence tells us they're bad enough. The prisoners are underfed and overworked; sick men have their rations reduced because, according to Japanese logic, sick men can't work and therefore don't need as much food; officers and other ranks labor alongside one another because the Japanese don't recognize that part of the Geneva Convention. They have few medical supplies. Disease is rife, the biggest killer being dysentery. The Japs don't care. The guards, many of them Korean, are brutal. A single infraction of the rules is good enough to cost you your life. So what? If two hundred die, there are hundreds more in Changi. The wretched Japanese don't appear to follow any code of ethics whatsoever, not one that's acceptable to a western mind, anyway. For example, they starve the prisoners and beat them, but they actually pay them a wage, about two pounds a month for officers, half that for other ranks. It's money without any real backing, of course, though I understand it can be used to purchase extra food from the locals. God knows what they think they're going to do with it."

"Does anyone ever escape?"

"Very occasionally. Colonel Chapman has one or two under his wing that he protects like a mother hen. There'll come a day of reckoning, war crimes tribunals, when all this is over. Colonel Chapman wants witnesses who can testify. It has to be considered doubtful if anyone who spends the war in a POW camp will live to tell the tale."

Benson acknowledged the hovering presence of a Chinese and spoke to him rapidly in Cantonese. The man inclined his head and went away.

"You know," said Benson, "I used to wonder, as a boy, how such structures as the Great Pyramids at Giza could be built. I don't wonder any longer. With an endless supply of slave labor, anything can be achieved. But you don't want to sit here listening to me wax philosophical, and I have another visitor just arrived. The reason I asked you to meet me is because we're worried about the supply drops. The supply aircraft from India and northern Burma barely make it here and back. In fact, many don't make it back. But not all the containers that are parachuted in are seeing the light of day. Of course, some fall into impenetrable jungle and are lost, but that's only half the story. One out of three that should be turning up are not. We believe that the missing thirty percent are being hidden, buried or otherwise, by the MPAJA for some sort of post-war revolution. The Chinese—which is largely what the MPAJA is—are Communists to a man, as you know. If, with their help, we beat the Japanese, they are not going to want to see the state of affairs that existed in pre-war Malaya return, with British and American commercial interests taking up where they left off. This country will doubtless be independent of the Crown one day. Whitehall would rather like it not to be under Communist influence. So too, I'm sure, would people like you, rubber planters and tin miners. And I'm fairly certain that the majority of non-Chinese Malayans are as far removed from Communism as it's possible to be, though here we have another problem. The MPAJA's leaders are already subtly propagandizing that it is they who are doing most of the guerrilla fighting with only a little help from the Europeans. Malays have also seen that the European is not invincible, that he was defeated in just a few short weeks by the Japs. In effect the Communists are saying that it wasn't too bad in Malaya while the Europeans, however paternally, could protect it and employ its citizens. But, as it is self-evident now that the Europeans cannot protect them, wouldn't they like a slice of the country for themselves—under the Red Banner, of course?

"If there is to be a post-war revolution, it is obviously important, for us, to prevent the Chinese immediately laying their hands on vast caches of arms and ammunition, never mind that losing a third of our drops is impeding our efforts here. I'm not asking you to do anything specific, just keep your eyes open and make Lee Swee Peng aware, if the occasion arises, that you know what he's up to. We need the Chinese right now, need them badly. But we don't want to store up trouble for ourselves in the future."

Benson stood up and extended his hand. Harry shook it.

"You can tell Captain Huxley I guarantee he'll be seeing some action before long."

Major Benson was as good as his word. Throughout the remainder of 1943 and much of 1944, Harry's Cossacks and CWG (1) were ordered to step up their activity, mining a river crossing here, a road there; ambushing convoys on the east coast road, harassing the enemy at every opportunity. The pattern never varied: hit and run, do the job then slink back into the jungle where the Japanese could not spare sufficient manpower to root them out. Move on when an area became too hot. Huxley could no longer protest that his men were under-used. Nor could Dan Holden complain that his life lacked excitement. In fact, he once confessed to Harry that he'd had enough excitement to last him a decade.

Harry saw the funny side of it. "So you won't be staying on after the war?"

"I didn't say that. As I've mentioned before, I love this country. Is that job still open?"

"I don't know yet if I'll have a job myself, or an estate. The Japs will doubtless have looked after it if they've got any sense, but Christ knows what sort of condition they'll leave it in. I haven't been earning since 1941, don't forget. If we win, as seems possible, I'll be going on my bended knees to financiers."

"There'll be war reparations, surely?"

"And how are the Japs going to pay, and when? If they lose, that presumably means we've bombed their economy to smithereens."

"I have money," said Dan, "quite a lot of it, actually."

"You mean buy in?" Harry didn't take him seriously. "And what would your wife and children think of that?"

"I haven't a clue."

Other American CWGs were in the theatre now, as were additional British and Australian clandestine units, albeit only in handfuls. But Harry thought that had to be a good sign, if they could be spared from the fighting elsewhere.

Except for word of mouth from newcomers, war news from the outside world was in short supply since wireless batteries had to be conserved for communications between guerrilla units, and copies of the Japanese English language newspaper, the *Mala Sinpo*, published in Kuala Lumpur and smuggled at great risk by sympathetic Malays out to the mountains, were always months out of date. But Harry and his friends learned of Italy's surrender and of D-Day; that the Allies had liberated Paris and were sweeping up through the Low Countries toward Germany; of Hitler's last major throw of the dice in the Ardennes, the Battle of the Bulge; of the Russians attacking from the east. And they all asked themselves the same question: would the Japs continue to fight on once their co-belligerent was defeated, as Germany must be defeated some time in the spring of 1945. They all came up with the same answer. Japan would. Its troops were on the defensive in Burma but—irony of ironies—below Burma lay Malaya. At a pinch, the Japs could retreat all the way down to Singapore, as the British had in 1941. The guerrillas didn't care to dwell on what would happen to them then. Overnight the size of their enemy would increase from a few thousand to hundreds of thousands.

They were taking casualties now, the guerrillas, more in the spring of 1945 than ever before since the high command in Burma and India wanted to prevent precisely what the guerrillas feared would happen, the Japanese retreating down the Peninsula. They hadn't started pulling back yet, but the high command didn't want them to, not along unmined roads and railways. Guerrilla activity was thus stepped up, more risks taken.

In northeast Malaya, at Kampong Buloh, three-quarters of the newly arrived CWG (6) along with a dozen Australians walked into a trap while preparing to ambush a convoy carrying rubber from the estates surrounding Kota Bharu. The majority were wiped out. The survivors were executed, some by firing squad, some by the sword.

In April Bill Hyde, with an escort of Lee Swee Peng's Chinese, was making his way along a jungle trail from Kuala Berang to Kampong Serit, to report in person on supplies to Major Benson, when his group came face to face with a Japanese patrol which should not have been anywhere near the area. In the brisk firefight that followed, three of Peng's Chinese were killed and Hyde became separated from the other three. He hit the dirt and stayed there for two whole days and nights, being assailed relentlessly by mosquitoes, not daring to move and hardly daring to breathe. Once a poisonous viper slithered over his exposed neck. Ten or twenty times the Japanese patrol came within a few feet, firing at random into clumps of jungle, probing with their bayonets. Finally they went away—or at least stopped making a noise. Nevertheless, Hyde gave it another whole day. He knew the Japanese, understood their methods. They invariably left one or two men behind, waiting for the guerrilla they were sure must be somewhere around to be lulled into a sense of false security and reveal himself.

It was a wise move on Hyde's part. Toward nightfall on the third day, he heard two, perhaps three, Japanese chattering to one another, the rear party. Then they left.

As it turned out he would not have met Major Benson. In what for many of the Cossacks and many of the original CWG (1) was one of the saddest incidents of the war, Peter Benson died in late April—not through enemy action or any definable disease but because of overwork and stress. The man had simply been broken by his responsibilities. He was a few months short of his thirtieth birthday.

The news that the war in Europe was over and Hitler dead was greeted with only two cheers by the men in Malaya. Hopefully it meant that troops could be spared for their theatre to polish off Japan, but Europe was many thousands of miles away and it would all take time.

In July Harry contracted malaria. He couldn't believe it at first, assuming that the rise in temperature accompanied by shivering was no more than a chill before accepting the inevitable. "Christ, I've lived here all my life without so much as a head cold."

Alan Fielding, who had seen it all before, confirmed Harry's self-diagnosis. "The race is not always to the swift nor the battle to the strong."

For ten days it was touch and go whether Harry would even survive. They covered him as best they could with spare clothing and forced quinine, the one drug that was in every supply container, down his throat. They made fires when it was safe to do so and fed him hot fish soups, which mostly his body promptly rejected.

He lapsed into delirium, his words largely incomprehensible. But those who tended him heard him talk of Jess and Mike and Jeff—and Jenny, Jenny more than any of the others and always with great pain in his voice, pain that could not be attributed to his illness. Fielding understood, not for the first time, what a terrible strain Harry had been under for the past three and a half years.

Hamid looked after him more than anyone else, cooling his brow with cold water from the sungei, sleeping at his feet like a faithful labrador; awaking Fielding when the fever became too much and Harry, only semi-conscious, tried to shuck off his excess clothing.

On the eleventh day the fever broke and he slept peacefully. On the twelfth day he sat up and complained that he was hungry.

"You're a tough bastard," said Fielding with grudging admiration. "Men of your age don't often survive malaria."

"Men of my age my foot," retorted Harry. "You're the tough one in this outfit."

"Maybe," said Fielding. "But I made a pact with myself when I heard about D-Day. Two pacts, actually. One, that I wasn't going to die of old age or anything else until I'd had another drink in the Spotted Dog. Two, that I'd live long enough to stay good and drunk for a week when the Jap brass are hanged."

During the last week in July and the first week in August something extraordinary happened: supply drops came in like peacetime mail and there were many more aircraft overhead, Allied aircraft unharassed by Japanese fighters. The guerrillas returned their radios. On August 6 they heard that something called an atomic bomb had been dropped on a Japanese seaport no one had ever heard of, Hiroshima. Three days later another flattened Nagasaki. There were reports of thousands of Japanese dead. The guerrillas were jubilant. Serve the bastards right.

On August 10 they learned that Japan had announced its willingness to surrender unconditionally, and on August 15 Emperor Hirohito broadcast the decision to the Japanese nation. The guerrillas were warned by radio still to be careful, to stay in hiding for the time being; that a decision taken in Tokyo might be disregarded by Japanese forces elsewhere. It was all over but some Japanese troops might elect to fight to the death.

Many guerrillas decided to ignore the "safety first" caveat and formed up in larger parties, heading for the POW camps they knew about, there to free the prisoners and do something about their captors. All Lee Swee Peng's men disappeared overnight; so did half of CWG (1) and a number of Australians who had fought with Cameron's Cossacks. Realizing he was still too weak to be much help, Harry opted to stay where he was. Bill Hyde and Alan Fielding stayed with him, as did Hamid.

On the morning of September 2, the day the surrender was to be formally signed aboard the battleship *Missouri*, Harry left the camp and wandered down to the sungei. As usual, Hamid went to accompany him. Fielding told the boy, kindly, to leave Harry by himself.

Harry cut himself a stick with his parang and tossed it into the sungei, watching it flow downstream, the way he would soon be heading, back to his estate. He was fifty-three years of age. Except for rare moments of self-indulgence he had not allowed himself to think about Jess, Jeff and Mike since the Japanese invasion. But if they had survived the war they would be, respectively, fifty-three, twenty-seven and twenty-one. If they had survived.

8

Jessica had reached England in mid-1942 and found a tiny flat in London in order to be near her boys. Throughout the Blitz and the remainder of the war she worked as a voluntary nurse.

Jeff had survived. As he had vowed to his sister many years earlier, waiting for the train in Kuala Kelan, he used his degree to find a comfortable job behind a desk in the War Office. His chest was empty of medal ribbons, but in 1945 he held the rank of captain.

Mike forewent university although, with very little string-pulling, he could have got himself deferred for the duration. Or used Jeff's influence to obtain a posting well away from the fighting. Instead, in mid-1942 when he was eighteen, and much against his mother's wishes, he volunteered without waiting to be called up. After basic training he found himself in North Africa just in time to take part in the second battle of El Alamein. Later he was with his infantry battalion when it was a minor cog in the invasion of Sicily, where he won the Military Medal and was promoted to corporal. His CO wanted to put him forward for a commission. He turned the colonel down, though he couldn't give a good reason other than he preferred to stay with people he knew and trusted, and who trusted him.

His whole brigade was withdrawn from the Italian campaign to prepare for D-Day, where it landed on Gold Beach as part of the 50th Infantry Division. In the Normandy hedgerows he won a Bar to his Military Medal and received another offer of a commission. He again said no.

When the end in Europe came he was a staff sergeant and in the city of Magdeburg. Two months later he was with the British occupation forces in Berlin.

He was rotated to London and demobilized in 1946. A "grateful" government decided that he would have to wait his turn in the queue to pay his own passage back to Malaya. He opted for the latter. Jess had already gone, as had Jeff. Letters from his mother never caught up with him, and it was not until he arrived home that he learned Jenny had been killed by the Japanese.

Part Two

May 1947–June 1948

9

David Holden advanced on his sister brandishing the tree rat. Shrieking, Laura raced for the sungei and dived in. She came up spluttering. David swung the rat by its tail and threw it in after her, missing by ten yards. "It's dead, stupid."

Laura tried to brazen it out, although she was shaking.

"I knew that all along. I knew you wouldn't pick up a live rat."

"Oh no, you didn't . . . "

In the house, in the master bedroom, Barbara Holden overheard the commotion but ignored it. She could see her children from the window and knew they were in no danger. Besides, there was a Malay servant close by.

Naked and sipping a long gin and tonic, Barbara examined herself in the full-length mirror, standing, after a moment, and putting herself in profile to obtain a better view. She patted her stomach. She'd kept her figure even after two children. No, three children, she reminded herself. She wasn't in bad condition at all for a woman who, in another year, would be staring forty in the face. Jesus, forty. Over halfway toward the casket. Still, in this climate many women of forty looked ten years older, American women as well as the Brits, and, as yet, she didn't. Though she wondered if she would wind up like them, like the other expatriate American wives. She could sure drink along with the best of them, but she'd been able to do that back in Texas. What she hadn't done up to now was screw around the way some of them did. That was probably the next stage. Booze and fucking; the American way, Mr. Truman.

Dan came in, also naked but in his case from the shower. He was towelling his hair dry.

"Waal, now," drawled Barbara, accentuating the Texas twang, "maybe this is my day to go to the paddock."

"Huh?" Dan peered at her from under the towel.

"You're hung like a horse. Let's see if you can fuck like one."

"For Chrissake . . . "

"What's the matter, my dirty mouth? You don't like my language, huh? What's wrong with the word 'horse'?"

Dan picked up her glass, sniffed at it then tasted the contents.

"That's as near as dammit straight gin. What are you chasing, a new record? You're hostessing a party in less than three hours. You'll be flat on your back before then."

"If I were flat on my back more often, or other interesting variations on the same theme, maybe I wouldn't tipple so much gin. So how's about a little screw, hey? A nice little screw to take away some of the tension. Then I'll switch to vodka and orange. Screwdrivers, dummy. Come on, a little bit of service for the memsahib."

She reached for his penis, stroking it between thumb and forefinger. He was aroused immediately, stiffening under her touch. She gave a tiny smile of triumph. What the hell, he thought, she was still a beautiful woman.

"Jesus," she breathed, drawing him into her without any foreplay, "that thing could stop traffic."

She climaxed quickly, as she always did recently, not bothering to try for a second orgasm, not even caring, it seemed. Waiting, rather; waiting for him to finish like a downtown whore with one eye on the clock and the next customer.

Finally he rolled away from her, empty but unsatisfied, feeling slightly disgusted. He wasn't sure she didn't feel the same way. What had just passed between them wasn't love-making. It would have been in keeping to leave twenty dollars on the mantelpiece. Except a double sawbuck was about nineteen dollars overpayment and, in any case, she'd probably pocket it.

She leaned across him for a tissue. "Not exactly an Oscar-winning performance, but you might get a nomination for best support."

She left the bed and went over to the dressing-table, where her drink was.

"Take it easy," he said.

"Why? Frightened I might make a fool of myself in front of your precious Camerons and their friends?"

"Not really." He fought to keep the irritation from his voice. She would see it as a challenge and become combative. Unless he trod carefully, this was likely to be one of those evenings, and he could do without that in front of spectators. Up to now they'd managed to keep their arguments private. "But this is your house and it's your first party."

"*My* house? *My* first party? It's your house, dear man, and it's the cook's and the servants' party. All I have to do is be decorative—and not fall off the verandah." She pronounced "verandah" with an outrageous English accent.

"If you didn't want a party you only had to say."

"And spoil it for you? I wouldn't dreeeeeam of it, my deah. I wouldn't dreeeeeam of being a killjoy and spoiling your entrance into Anglo-Malayan society."

"Hardly society. A few of our friends, that's all."

"A few of *your* friends."

"No, *our* friends."

"Bull!"

The house, the old McFee bungalow which Dan had extended and added another storey to, had been completed just a fortnight earlier, the first week in May. It was large by most Malayan standards, bigger even than the Cameron place six hundred yards away and hidden from it by the jungle. A new road connected the two houses, snaking its way through the trees, following the old trail that Richard Cameron had once used when visiting Michael McFee.

Apart from the kitchen and usual offices on the ground floor, it had a spacious entrance hall, a large dining-room and five reception rooms, two of which opened out on to the verandah. Beyond the cloakroom was the gun-room. On the upper floor were five bedrooms and two bathrooms, while at the rear of the building, abutting the servants' quarters, was a shack housing a modern generator, one capable of producing sufficient power to light every room and the spotlights outside, run the electrical gadgets in the kitchen and elsewhere, and drive the water purification unit. A smaller auxiliary generator stood next to its big brother. In front, three acres of jungle leading down to the sungei had been cleared and laid to lawn.

The entire conversion and clearance had taken almost exactly four months from the day Dan gave the go-ahead. Earlier, Harry Cameron had estimated it would take nearer six and probably eight, and so it would had Dan not waved fistfuls of American dollars. While trying to find a name for the house he had been going over the contractors' accounts, wincing at the amount of money he had spent and muttering, "Mahal, mahal"—the Malay word for expensive. It seemed natural to call it Mahal Rumah—expensive house.

Dan thought he understood his wife's reservations about the house-warming—or house-cooling as it should be in Malaya. She was a naturalized Texan a little out of her depth among the colonial British. Although, as far as he knew, she had received nothing but kindness, she was, perhaps, somewhat scared of making a gaff. In Texas she had been a biggish fish, a rich biggish fish. Here she was just another Yank.

"They won't eat you, you know."

"Who?"

"Your guests. There's no reason to be frightened of them."

"Who's frightened of them?" She studied her empty glass. "It's not that at all. It's just that sometimes I ask myself what the hell I'm doing here. I mean, there I was in Texas with two small children growing up to be good Americans when home comes my husband from the war. After a couple of months' bliss he begins to fret, signs I recognize only too well from when he *went* to war. A few months later he announces that he wants us all to live in Malaya, let someone else take care of the business. Plow a few hundred thousand dollars into Cameron Rubber. Rubber! Hah! You may have become Anglified but in Texas a rubber is still something that prevents life."

"We discussed it a hundred times," said Dan wearily. "We agreed to give it three years. You can't judge anything in a few months. If it didn't work out by the fall of 1949, we'd go home."

Though maybe she was right, thought Dan. Maybe he'd been foolish or selfish, or both. What was it they said? You could take the girl—however rich—out of the small town; you couldn't take the small town out of the girl.

When he arrived home in time for Christmas the year the war ended, for a while everything was fine. The kids quickly got used to this stranger who announced he was their father, and Barbara was overjoyed to see him. She was loving and tender and their sex life could not be faulted. If she'd had affairs during the war, and she'd have been almost unique if she hadn't, she'd evidently been discreet for he heard not a whisper of gossip.

As he predicted, Frank Bailey and Eddie Moxx had run the Holden Office Supplies Inc. with commendable efficiency and had even, using the power of attorney Dan had vested in them, expanded and diversified. Give or take a dollar or two, he was worth, cash money, in the region of two million bucks. Adding Barbara's wealth to his own, the Holden clan could have gone to a bank with confidence and asked for a three-million dollar overdraft.

He had told Harry Cameron the morning in the jungle that he'd had enough excitement to last him a decade. He'd meant it too. But waking up each day fearing that, before evening, he would be facing the business end of a Jap bayonet was one thing; realizing that the rest of his life would involve nothing more exhilarating than selling office equipment was another.

Without saying anything to Barbara, by April 1946 he was writing to Harry. How was he? How were Alan Fielding and Bill Hyde, and the other former Cossacks? How was Hamid? And—how was Harry faring financially? Was there any room for investment capital provided by someone who wanted to be more than a sleeping partner, who wanted to learn the rubber business?

Harry replied by return. Alan Fielding was thriving. He was still awaiting the Tojo trial and verdict, and the execution. Bill Hyde was back in his former job. Hamid had been sent to school but hadn't liked it, had found it difficult to settle down to classroom routine. He was now working as a tapper on the estate. Jess was giving him lessons in her spare time, and his. There was certainly room for venture capital, especially from someone who didn't want interest but was willing to work his passage and share in the profits of the estate. Was there any chance that Dan could visit Malaya, when perhaps some sort of deal could be thrashed out to everyone's mutual satisfaction?

Telling Barbara no more than that he needed to go to Malaya to discuss some business with former wartime colleagues, Dan flew to Singapore and took the train to Kuala Kelan, where Harry met him. He recognized Jess even though fourteen years had passed since their meeting aboard the *Southern Pride*. He liked the grown-up Mike. He wasn't so sure about Jeff. After an evening of reminiscing and too much whisky, the following morning Harry and Dan got down to brass tacks.

In return for three hundred thousand dollars Dan could have a forty percent share of Cameron Rubber. There were two provisos. If Dan's wife and children could not take to the way of life after, say, three years and wanted to return to the

United States, the three hundred thousand would be treated as an interest-free loan not repayable for ten years. Alternatively, if Dan wanted to retain his shares and receive dividends without taking an active part any longer, he could not sell his stock to anyone other than the Camerons. Not to Dunlop or Goodyear, for example.

Dan agreed. Then came the hard bit.

Barbara put up every objection she could think of. She didn't want her children brought up on the other side of the world. She didn't want to live in Malaya, a country about which she knew little except that it was hot and humid. He'd hardly been home from the war five minutes, for God's sake. Why did he want to go globe-trotting again? Wasn't he happy with her, with his children? She was happy with him; they all were.

Dan countered all her arguments with a single one of his own. The long summer vacation from school was only two months off. Why didn't they spend it in Malaya, to see how she and the children liked it? If they didn't, that would be the end of it. Even if they did, they need only give it three years. At the end of that time they could call it quits.

They flew out in July. The children fell in love with the magic of the country immediately. Dan made sure that Barbara was entertained by other American families whose business in tin, rubber and banking kept them in Malaya, who could reassure her on such matters as schooling. The Camerons were charming to her, partly because they genuinely liked her and partly because it wasn't every day three hundred thousand interest-free dollars fell out of the trees. Dan showed her where they would live, his plans for the old McFee place. It would be one of the finest residences in this part of the state. He and Harry drove her and the children up country, pointed out the areas where they had fought the war against the Japanese. By the end of the holiday she had agreed to give it a try.

It took the remainder of 1946 for Dan to tie up his business affairs and raise the three hundred thousand in cash without getting too deeply in hock to the banks or selling too much stock to Bailey and Moxx, who were only too anxious to buy into a thriving concern. They were vice-presidents, naturally, but Dan and Barbara, between them, held most of the equity. To keep the two men sweet, however, Dan increased their salaries by fifty percent. They would run the company in his absence. Dan and Barbara still owned it.

They arrived in Malaya on New Year's Day 1947 and moved into the house on Richard's Hill while Mahal Rumah was being built. The children went to day school in Kuala Kelan, an estate employee driving them there each morning and picking them up each afternoon. Dan threw himself into learning about the rubber business while simultaneously overseeing the conversion of McFee's bungalow. Periodically Barbara threw herself into a gin bottle. She wasn't constantly drunk or even regularly. Days would pass when she didn't touch a drop. Had it been otherwise, Dan would have made her seek medical help. On the days she did drink, however, the evening would invariably end up in an argument.

In view of the way she'd started this particular day, the house-warming went better than Dan had any right to expect. Whether she'd thought it all over and concluded that falling down drunk in front of the Brits wasn't a good idea, he didn't know. But she didn't refill her gin glass and by the time the first guests arrived, driving first of all to the Cameron house and then along the jungle road to Mahal Rumah, she was sober. And staying sober, drinking only lemonade. Dan shook his head in amazement. For not the first time in his life he considered his wife an enigma. Maybe she was right in saying they should spend more time in bed.

It was a perfect afternoon with a slight breeze blunting the worst of the heat. There were between sixty and seventy guests—miners, planters, state officials, bankers, policemen. In the shade, a six-piece police band, slightly out of tune, played popular songs. The ladies had donned their finery, floral prints, batik, silks. Most wore floppy hats and carried parasols which they opened when leaving the verandah to stroll around the lawn or down to the sungei. The men were in shirt-sleeves. Malay servants wearing white tunics and songkoks, a round velvet hat, flitted from group to group bearing silver trays of canapés, white wine and champagne. The heavy scents of frangipani blossoms, bougainvillaea and wild hibiscus filled the air.

Barbara looked sensational, everyone agreed, wearing an eau-de-nil dress that was shorter than the current fashion but which showed off her long legs to perfection. Everyone also loved the house, and told her so. She was the centre of the whole tableau—to her mind something she'd seen in magazines about Edwardian England—and she adored it.

Harry was talking to Bill Hyde, Mike and Jeff about the recent trial and execution of Colonel Tanaguchi, former commandant of the POW camp at Kota Bharu.

"He had it a bit too easy if you want my view," said Hyde. "A quick drop through a trapdoor and it's all over. The punishment just doesn't fit the crime. You can't beat, starve and murder hundreds of blokes for close on four years and get away with it as easily as that."

Though Harry agreed in principle—over 12,000 men had died on the Kwai valley project alone—Hyde was more vehement on the subject of Japanese war criminals than most, and frequently fired off letters to the War Crimes Court at Victoria Memorial Hall in Singapore. He had good reason to be bitter, for just before the fall of Singapore the governor had urged the police to remain at their posts until the flag was hauled down. With defeat inevitable, many felt that that was an idiotic exhortation, that they could serve Malaya and the Crown better by getting out while there was still time, either taking to the mountains as Hyde had already done or leaving on a troopship if they could obtain a passage. Those who obeyed the governor ended up in Changi or another camp and could not forgive those who left, even though many of the men who did not join a guerrilla unit were parachuted back as part of Force 136. Including Hyde, seventeen officers had opted not to go meekly into the bag, policemen from all over Malaya. They were, even now, accused of "running away."

Hyde had had a terrible time of it to begin with, for which he blamed the entire Japanese nation. Other officers would pointedly leave a room he entered; men junior in rank would be openly insubordinate. He once thought of quitting the police force. Things improved after Harry wrote an open letter to the *Straits Times*, cataloguing Hyde's exploits in the guerrilla war, for Harry's reputation in Malaya since the existence of Cameron's Cossacks became public knowledge was unparalleled. However, there were still some officers, mainly from other states, who would not talk to Hyde even if he telephoned them on police business. They especially resented Hyde being a member of the official Malayan delegation at the Victory Parade in London the previous year, a mission led by the Chinese Chin Peng, Lau Yew and Lee Swee Peng.

"Bill's trying to figure out a method of hanging each Japanese colonel fifty times," smiled Harry.

"Damned right," grunted Hyde.

On other parts of the lawn, while the women discussed fashions and the latest films—Fredric March in *The Best Years of Our Lives* and Olivia de Havilland in *To Each His Own* were playing to packed houses in Kuala Kelan, while outlying estates could have the films brought to them by an organization called Caravan Films Ltd.— the men talked politics.

The British Cabinet was planning to incorporate the Federated and Unfederated states, together with the Settlements of Penang and Malacca, into a Malayan Union with a central government and a governor, and sovereign power transferred from the sultans to the British Crown. Neither the sultans nor the Europeans were very happy about the proposal, preferring a loose federation to a single unified state. The Communists didn't want either. The MPAJA had been disbanded after the war, but no one thought for a moment that that was the last Malaya had heard from Chin Peng, Lau Yew, Shorty Kuk and Lee Swee Peng. Recent strikes, totally legal, were evidently well organized and few of the Europeans had any doubts that the Chinese were behind them, the object being to acquire positions of power before any question of independence arose. Independence would have to come sooner or later was the consensus, but it was unlikely to be for ten years or so. In that time there were fortunes to be made.

In a cool corner of the verandah Jessica was talking to Molly Hyde and an upstate planter's wife, Pauline Oates. Or, rather, she was listening. Molly and Pauline were doing most of the talking.

"If you ask me, that dress is far too short and the woman herself too racy for her own good. Look at her, she's got every man eating out of her hand."

"I'm sorry?" said Jess.

"Barbara Holden, my dear. Our very own Lana Turner."

"Veronica Lake, more like," said Pauline Oates.

"A little too long in the tooth, don't you think, for Veronica Lake?"

"Carole Lombard, then."

"Jean Harlow."

They played the film-star game while Jess allowed her thoughts to wander although nodding instinctively once in a while, as if Molly's gossip were Holy Writ. Jenny would have just passed her thirty-first birthday had she lived, would probably be married now and raising a family. She thought of her dead daughter almost every day, as she surmised Harry did. But they didn't talk about her often; it was still too painful and, for Harry, too bewildering. He'd asked her time after time how she'd allowed Jenny to give her the slip and not join the convoy for Singapore. Jessica couldn't answer that, not the "how." She knew the "why," of course, but there was no way she could tell Harry that Jenny had gone back for her son.

She scanned the lawn for her husband and eventually found him talking to Jeff and Mike and Bill Hyde. Politics or war criminals, she thought. Her husband's hair was graying at the temples now, though he had regained most of the weight he had lost fighting the Japanese and, from a distance, could almost be taken for the older brother of his two sons, not their father.

She wondered how long it would be before Mike and Jeff got married and presented her with grandchildren. Years, as far as Jeff was concerned, if she were any judge. He was absurdly handsome—tall, dark-haired and slim—more like a younger version of his father than Mike. But, physical characteristics aside, there the resemblance ended. There was something faintly weak about Jeff. There was nothing wrong in not wanting to settle down, in wanting to play the field. But Jeff was too much of a lady's man, never happier than when he was charming them at a bridge party or a dinner party or after two sets of tennis. He was a metropolitan creature, more content in the big cities than on the estate. If there was business to be done in Singapore, Kuala Kelan or KL, you could bet your boots Jeff would volunteer for the assignment. He'd had a whale of a time in London during the war judging by the number of letters that regularly arrived from England addressed in a female hand, and not always the same hand, and he'd tried to persuade Harry, on his return, that they should open a London office for him to run instead of relying upon brokers. Harry had turned him down flat, understanding what his elder son was up to and making it quite clear that, unless Jeff did his share on the estate, Mike would more than likely inherit everything when the time came. They'd had quite an argument about it, and it was partly to shake Jeff that Harry had been so keen to enlist Dan Holden and his dollars.

Nor could Harry entirely forgive Jeff for having spent the war behind a desk. They had rows about that too.

"You'd have preferred me to go off and get killed."

"I'd have preferred you to have done your bit."

"Like Mike."

"Like Mike, if you insist."

The rows never lasted long and Jess suspected that Harry wasn't too unhappy that Jeff had had an easy war. Harry knew that Jeff would probably not have lasted ten minutes anywhere near the front line, and he was not wishing his son dead.

Mike was the same height as his brother but appeared shorter because he was much broader about the shoulders, more husky in general. And the differences didn't end there. Where Jeff played an excellent game of tennis and became sullen, unless he was trying to impress a girl by his sportsmanship, when losing, Mike would fling himself around the court like a maniac, not giving a damn whether he won or lost. Mike loved the estate. When other business permitted he'd either saddle a horse or jump into a car and ride or drive around it, frequently stopping by a sungei and staring into the middle distance, absorbed by the beauty about him. Jeff looked like a poet—Byron, probably—but it was actually Mike who felt the poetry. Nor was he entirely at ease in the company of women, although he had several girlfriends he saw on a more or less regular basis. One of them, in Jessica's opinion, would make an ideal wife in a few years. Diana Ashford, slightly younger than Mike at twenty-one, was a delightful strawberry blonde, impishly coquettish, and obviously madly in love with Mike. Where he was sometimes shy, she was vivacious. Together with her daughter, Melanie Ashford, Diana's mother, had also been aboard the *Duchess of Bedford* when it sailed from Singapore in 1942 with the last refugees. Frank Ashford, Diana's father, had spent the war in Changi and barely survived. He now managed an estate for an American consortium near Batu Mersa.

"Rita Hayworth," Jess heard Molly say.

"How about Ginger Rogers?" Pauline Oates riposted.

"Donald Duck," said Jess.

"Excuse me?"

"Are you two still at it?" queried Jess. "You've been through half of Hollywood."

"At *it?* At what?"

"Pulling our hostess apart."

"We're not pulling her apart at all," protested Molly. "But it's coming to something, I have to admit, when American matrons can *buy* their way into Malaya."

"So by implication you're criticizing Harry."

"I didn't mean that," blustered Molly.

Jessica stood up.

"Molly," she said with feigned dignity, "I've known you for years and I can, I'm sure, count you among my closest friends." Molly nodded, eager to please. "And it's because I count you thus that I can tell you that you probably have the most vituperative tongue I've ever come across."

Twirling her parasol, Jess left the verandah and descended to the lawn.

"Well!" said Molly.

"What's vituperative?" asked Pauline.

The six-piece band had now, somehow, managed to start playing in tune and impromptu dancing had begun on the lawn, none of it very successful until the ladies slipped off their shoes. Jessica marched up to Harry. "Your name was on my card earlier, I believe," she said, smiling.

"Oh, come on, Jess," pleaded Harry. "You know I'm not much good at this. We were about to disappear indoors for a stengah or two before the mosquitoes come out."

"That," said Jessica firmly, "you most certainly won't do. At your own parties you can behave how you like. Here you're a guest."

"The whisky was for my malaria," said Harry, clutching at straws.

"You've had one *minor* recurrence of malaria since I came home and, however you're feeling, whisky is not the answer."

"If whisky's not the answer it's a bloody silly question," said Harry. But he raised his shoulders in mock surrender and allowed Jess to lead him away.

"I don't know about you two," said Bill Hyde to Mike and Jeff, "but I feel malaria coming on also."

"When did you catch malaria?" asked Jeff.

"About three minutes ago. Anyway, I'm getting the hell out of here before Molly gets the same idea as your mother."

With that, Hyde disappeared indoors.

Mike studied his glass of champagne.

"I like this stuff, got a taste for it in France where you could get around eight bottles of it for about one pound sterling, but maybe whisky's not such a bad idea."

"We had a rougher war in London," said Jeff jokingly. "We could hardly get any of the better vintages after Dunkirk. In any case, I think you're too late. If I'm not mistaken, the delicious Miss Ashford is making a beeline in our direction and I'll wager a fiver she's not looking for me. What's going on between the pair of you, by the way, or is that a leading question?"

"Nothing's going on. Well, not very much."

"That's the very devil of a waste, if I can believe you."

"You can. Even if you can't, isn't there something in the officer code that forbids such talk?"

"I'll never know. I wasn't that sort of officer."

Diana appeared, breathless from running across the lawn. Jeff's description was absolutely right, thought Mike. She looked delicious with her hair hanging loose beneath her wide-brimmed hat and her peaches-and-cream complexion slightly flushed. Her bright-blue eyes were full of mischief and she was so tiny in stature he could have picked her up with one hand. He'd known her for two months, had seen her a dozen times during that period. They hadn't made love yet because, she'd confessed, she hadn't made love to anyone ever and was a little scared of going the whole route. They'd done everything but, however, and it couldn't be long before she got over her fears. He hoped not, anyway.

"Mummy said," said Diana, joshing Mike, "that you can either dance with me or dance with her, but you have to dance with one of us."

"If he won't," said Jeff, not meaning it for a second because obvious virgins were not his line of country and, in any case, his eyes were already on bigger game, "I will."

"Mummy also says," said Diana, straight-faced, "that I mustn't dance with older men. Well, not that much older."

"Ouch," groaned Jeff. "Off you pop, youngsters. I'll go and see where I parked my wheelchair."

Diana led Mike by the hand over to where the band was playing.

"You can grip me tighter than that," she said. "I won't break."

Jeff made his way over to where Barbara was holding court. He'd flirted with her more than mildly on previous occasions and had not been rebuffed. Once he'd visited her at Richard's Hill while her children were in school and her husband in KL. With servants hovering in the background nothing had happened between them, but he'd read the signs and knew it could if he played his cards correctly. He judged her to be the sort of woman who enjoyed risks, who would be disappointed by the conventional and thrilled by the daring.

She saw him approach and handed her lemonade to the nearest bystander. She kicked off her sandals.

"I think I have a partner," she said.

"Why isn't your husband doing this?" Jeff asked, dancing her in the direction of the frangipani shrubs where they could be seen but not overheard.

"Oh, he's got two left feet. Besides, he's talking war or business with someone. He generally is."

There was something in her manner that told Jeff she'd had sex with her husband before the party started and that, her libido aroused, she was in the mood for more. It excited him and he wondered if he could get away with it. It was almost dusk and the floodlights were on, but there were dozens of dark corners away from the lawn.

"That must get pretty dull for you."

"It does."

"For me too."

"How so? I mean, I don't understand."

"Well, the war's been over for near enough two years and business is, generally speaking, pretty boring. If you have enough money, have some fun. That's my motto."

She looked up at him. His eyelashes really belonged on a girl but, she could feel through his shirt, he had muscles in all the right places. Yet there was a certain softness about him. He didn't have the steeliness of her husband, or of Harry Cameron, say. She quite liked the contrast. Men's men could be a royal pain in the ass.

"You're right, of course," she said. "Except, what do you do for fun in this hell-hole? I've had more kicks watching planks warp."

"I thought you were having fun right now."

"Right now I am. But otherwise?"

"There's Singapore. There's KL. There's Kuala Kelan."

"Kuala Kelan's too near."

"Too near for what?"

"For whatever it is you have in mind."

"You might be shocked by what I have in mind."

"I'd only be shocked and maybe disappointed if what I think you have in mind isn't there. If it's no more than an auto trip up country."

"It's a long way from that."

"Good."

They were dancing very close and by now he had a total erection, which Barbara certainly knew about. He put some space between their hips. If she reacted with embarrassment he would mumble some sort of apology and make himself scarce. If she didn't, he'd know he was on to a good thing.

She pulled him back toward her, pressing up against him.

"My, my," she murmured throatily, "is this how you are with all the girls?"

"No, not all. Anyway, you must know how I feel about you. You're a bit different from most of them around here."

"In what way?" Barbara was enjoying her sexual power over Jeff and was far from being unaffected herself. The thought of screwing this handsome young man within shouting distance of her husband and guests made her heart beat faster. But, Christ, there were sixty or seventy people within twenty or thirty yards. There was no one in the vicinity of the frangipani, however, and just beyond the shrubs the jungle began.

"You're more beautiful, for a start."

"I'm also married, for a start. I'm no danger to your bachelorhood."

At the mention of her marriage, Jeff thought he'd fouled up. He could not have been more wrong.

"No, don't move away," she said. The feel of an erection not Dan's was electrifying. She'd not had a man other than her husband since the war and even that minor fling, with a naval commander home on leave, had been more out of loneliness than desire.

"I'm afraid I'm going to have to. If you'll excuse the expression, I'm beginning to ache."

"You're not the only one."

She threw a quick glance about her. Against the floodlights most of her guests were merely silhouettes and no one was paying her and Jeff the slightest attention. Those who weren't dancing were talking. Dan, she observed, recognizing her husband's figure even from a distance, was by the verandah, deep in conversation with a group of men.

"Come with me."

She took his hand and led him behind the frangipani. A dozen steps later they were beyond the jungle fringes. Over her shoulder she could still hear the party but could see none of the guests, and only a trickle of light permeated the trees.

"This is crazy," Jeff said.

"I feel like being crazy."

She wrapped her arms around his neck and kissed him deeply. He responded, almost beside himself with lust. He tried to ease her gently down, on to the permanently damp jungle floor. She resisted, realizing that she would stain her dress in a manner she'd never be able to explain away.

"No, like this," she murmured.

Her heels were against a fallen tree trunk. She stood on it, her hips now on the same level as his. Feverishly he unbuttoned his trousers. She took his engorged penis in both hands, feeling the glans' wetness. It wasn't as large as Dan's but it felt beautiful. Exquisite.

"You'll have me coming," he moaned.

"For God's sake not yet."

She hiked up her dress around her waist. She was barelegged because of the heat. He fumbled with her briefs, not removing them but pushing them to one side, fingering her moistness. She raised herself on tiptoe and guided him inside her with one hand, allowing only the tip to penetrate at first, teasing herself. He shook his head angrily and pushed hard with his entire length.

She exhaled a gasp of delight and raised one leg, placing it around his waist, balancing it on his hip. They rocked there for a second and then he could wait no longer. He began thrusting in earnest, slapping against her, holding her buttocks, digging into them fiercely with his fingers. She matched his urgency with frantic pelvic movements of her own, groaning softly.

"I won't be able to last," he panted.

"Nor me, nor me. Just let it go, let it go."

He ejaculated almost instantly, his semen discharging deep inside her. And she was coming too, there was no way she could stop herself. Shuddering with ecstasy, it was the most marvellous orgasm she could ever remember. She knew she was whinnying with pleasure but she had no control over her vocal chords; she could not have remained silent even if she'd tried. He buckled at the knees and had to hang on to her to stop himself collapsing.

When it was over they leaned against each other like drunks until their breathing returned to normal. Finally he withdrew from her and took out his handkerchief, cleaning himself as best he could before handing it to her. She kept it.

She smoothed down her dress and kissed him again, on the lips, on this occasion without passion.

"That was very, very good," she murmured.

"For me too," he said, meaning it. "That was also one hell of a way to end a party. We'll be doing it again, I hope."

"And again and again if you don't mind the risks."

"To the devil with the risks. I'm not giving you up in a hurry, not after a performance like that."

She left the undergrowth ahead of him. He gave her a couple of minutes then rejoined the party. If anyone saw him emerging from behind the frangipani they'd assume he had been relieving himself. Which in some respects was the absolute truth.

When he saw her again she was talking to his mother and father, and laughing with them. No one, it seemed, had missed either of them.

The party began to break up shortly afterward, many of the guests having a long way to travel. The Camerons were among the last to leave. The Ashfords, who were staying overnight with Harry and Jess, left with them.

Jeff shook hands formally with Dan and pecked Barbara on the cheek.

"Marvellous party," he said.

Alone with Dan Barbara poured herself a long gin and tonic. Under the floodlights the servants were still cleaning up the lawn. David and Laura were upstairs preparing for bed.

"Jeff was right," said Dan, sipping a whisky. "That was a marvellous party and you were great."

Barbara smiled and said nothing. She felt wonderfully wicked and, surprisingly, by no means guilty. If she used her head and played it cool, Malaya might not be such a bad place after all.

From the edge of the road that linked the Camerons' house with Mahal Rumah, Hamid watched the Malay servants tidy the lawn. Deep within him was an emotion he could not put a name to but which was a combination of envy and anger. It was wrong that the Europeans had everything and the Malays, whose country it was, had nothing. It was wrong that Tuan Cameron, at whose side he had stood for four years, hardly ever spoke to him these days except to give orders. Lee Swee Peng had warned him that would happen, that he would become a second-class citizen once the Japanese were beaten. Memsahib Cameron treated him like an idiot child. What was the point of learning to read and write? Where would that ever get him? Frankly, Hamid had preferred the war.

10

In November 1947 a meeting between a score of leading Communists took place deep in the jungle near the village of Lembingan on the Selangor-Paselabilan border. The Malayan Communist Party had been recognized as a legitimate political organization after the war, but none of its senior members expected that state of affairs to continue after the first few months of 1948, not with what they had in mind. There would be other gatherings like this, and gatherings with other leaders in other states, before they could go into action. But action there would be, direct action. Labor disruption in key industries had proved less than successful. The majority of the country's 5 million-plus inhabitants were simply not interested in revolution. They would have to be taught where their future lay.

The undisputed high priest of the group was Chin Peng, the Secretary-General of the Party in Malaya, a quietly-spoken innocuous-looking young man of twenty-six who walked with a limp and who spoke several languages fluently, including English. A dedicated Communist since his teens, ironically the policy of terror that he was shortly to put into practice had been learned with the British of Force 136 and refined against the Japanese. He was a tireless individual. Today he was in Lembingan. Tomorrow he would be elsewhere preaching the gospel of insurrection to his deputies, who in turn would be expected to disseminate the message, by violence if need be.

His senior deputies, who would accompany him everywhere until the time came to take over their own killer squads, were Lau Yew, Hor Lung and Shorty Kuk, all former associates of Force 136. Today's meeting was, in the main, to brief the two men who would run the terrorist campaign in Paselabilan, Lee Swee Peng and a Malay Communist, Abdullah bin Halim. The

Malays were outnumbered in the Party in a ratio of 95:5, but, in Chin Peng's view, were essential to ultimate victory. Malays might not listen to a Chinese regardless of how much pressure was put on them; they might listen to another Malay. Abdullah bin Halim was two years older than Chin Peng and had been born with a slight squint, about which he was self-conscious. He also had a reputation for ruthlessness. Many of the men wore khaki uniforms and soft caps with a red star in the centre. It was hoped that, in time, everyone would be issued with a uniform.

The clearing where the meeting was taking place would one day soon be Lee Swee Peng's permanent base in the state, and already there were signs that he had learned a great deal from his days with Force 136 and Cameron's Cossacks. Although the camp began two hundred yards from the road that connected Batu Mersa with Lembingan and was invisible, because of the jungle and lallang, elephant grass, from ground and air, sentries were posted. Each sentry held a cord which was attached to, at the edge of the camp, a row of tin cans. One tug on the cord and the warning was given. All personnel could be evacuated in minutes via an escape path that led deeper into the jungle. In the centre of the clearing stood a pole from which hung the Red Flag. Sleeping accommodation under construction was far removed from the bashas used during the war against the Japanese; they were far sturdier with mosquito screens covering each aperture. The largest of the huts would be a lecture room, for Peng realized that indoctrination was a major part of the battle, one that would make his cadre superior to the British running dogs. His "soldiers" could never be allowed to forget what they were fighting for, and he didn't just mean a country. It was an ideal, and it was part of his task to urge that ideal constantly upon them. Those who were not impressed by rhetoric would have to be persuaded by other means. In the words of an ancient Chinese warrior, Sun-Zu: Kill one; frighten a thousand. Separate quarters were being built for female guerrillas, though promiscuity would be frowned upon as counter-revolutionary.

Lee Swee Peng's camp was only one of dozens scattered throughout Malaya, many of them old Force 136 bases. Some would hold several hundred, some only scores; a few just a handful of the elite killer squads. The men would be paid thirty Malay dollars a month, roughly the equivalent of four English pounds. The money was to be raised by blackmail and terror.

There was no shortage of weapons. Even if the omnipresent humidity had rendered useless many of the rifles, grenades and submachine guns parachuted down to Force 136 during the war, and hidden by the Chinese, when the MPAJA was disbanded in 1945 and each member given a £45 bounty, most soldiers had accepted the money gratefully, handed over to the British what the British *thought* were the only weapons they had, and disappeared with captured Japanese rifles and automatic weapons.

Logistical support would be vital once the terror started in earnest, and to back up the fighting troops there were Communists in all walks of life—waiters, cinema attendants, house servants, club servants, rubber tappers, tin miners. Chin Peng had designated these men and women, and sometimes children, as the Min Yuen, the Masses' Movement. They would never hold a gun or throw a grenade into a crowded restaurant; their function was to keep the fighters supplied with intelligence and, to a lesser extent, food. Every community of any size, from kampongs upward, had its "Chinatown"; potentially Chin Peng had a Min Yuen two million strong. In the big cities Chinese prostitutes, whose clients were mainly European or wealthy Malays, would be encouraged to report whether a particular customer paid her regular visits. If so, that customer might, one day, not live to return to the brothel.

Chin Peng had also decided that calling his guerrilla force the MPABA—the Malayan Peoples' Anti-British Army, just a change of one letter from the MPAJA—was inadequate and possibly counter-productive. As the British intention was a slow and democratic route to independence for Malaya, it was pointless having "anti-British" in the designation. The British were leaving anyway, sooner or later. He therefore rechristened his organization the MRLA—the Malayan Races' Liberation Army, for the proletariat had to be made to see that being ruled by Malay princes and plutocrats was as injurious to their future as being ruled by the British.

The Secretary-General envisaged the campaign in three phases. In Phase One his guerrillas would attack isolated rubber estates and tin mines, police stations and government offices in small towns and villages. In theory this should compel the British and their Malayan lackeys to evacuate the countryside and retreat to the safety of the larger towns and cities. It would also disrupt the economy to the point of ruination. Phase Two would begin by expanding his army with recruits from the Min Yuen and training them in the now deserted rural areas, where food, because of the rice paddies, would no longer be even a marginal problem. In Phase Three the enlarged army would take the fight to the British in the cities, a full-scale war backed if necessary by China. He had no doubt victory could be achieved. He had private knowledge that identical actions were being contemplated against the French colonial power in Indo-China, and in Korea. If the present strength of his army, under five thousand, seemed pitifully small, he remembered, and often lectured upon, three things. The first was that the British were exhausted physically and financially from the recent war, had no troops in numbers in Malaya, and would have to bring in, if they chose to fight, men whose knowledge of jungle warfare was nil. The second were the words of Mao Tse-tung: "The longest march begins with but a single step." And the third was the example of his hated enemy, the British Empire. For several hundred years the tiny island nation had ruled half the world. Size was nothing, determination everything.

As mid-afternoon approached and the rains came, Chin Peng, Lee Swee Peng and Abdullah bin Halim took shelter in one of the half-completed huts. The remaining Chinese shared another hut. A stranger stumbling upon the scene would have noticed something odd. The clearing was now deserted except for three Malays, all men of mature age. All three were tied to separate trees and all three appeared terrified.

Sometimes individually and sometimes together, Lee Swee Peng and Abdullah explained to the Secretary-General the progress they had made since their last meeting.

"Some Malay villages are proving difficult," said Abdullah, almost apologetically, speaking in English, "although I have to confess we have covered only a handful up to now. The three men out there are typical. They are the headmen of neighboring kampongs and they are not concerned with revolution. They just wish to be left alone. Comrade Peng will support me in this."

"Will you, Comrade?" asked Chin Peng.

"Up to a point. I have accompanied Comrade Abdullah on several occasions. It is my opinion that harsher methods are needed than the ones he has adopted up to now."

"I agree," said Abdullah anxiously. "However, you made it clear when we last met that the time was not yet ripe for open violence, in case we alert the British before we are ready."

"I did not say *precisely* that the time was not yet ripe for open violence. I think I said the time was not here for *general* violence, violence on a large scale. There's a difference."

"I apologize," said Abdullah, contrite. "I misunderstood."

"It's of no importance," said Chin Peng pleasantly, "and it's good that you understand your error and confess it. You did right to bring the three intransigents with you. You can, perhaps, set them an example after I've gone. However, those three and some others like them apart, would you say you were making progress?"

"Yes, Comrade," answered Lee Swee Peng. "Generally, yes, we are making progress. Specifically, perhaps more so."

Peng explained that, quite by accident in a kampong visited by Abdullah and himself, he had become reacquainted with a Malay youth he had known during the war.

"His name is Hamid and he is employed as a tapper on the Cameron estate."

"Yes, I know of this Cameron," nodded Chin Peng.

"I've spoken to him and he is disillusioned. He scarcely left Cameron's side in the war and I think he expected something more from his life when the war ended. Cameron did indeed send him to school, but Hamid found it difficult to learn, pick up where he left off when the Japanese invaded. Cameron's wife now teaches him. In my opinion he is highly intelligent."

"And how can he be of service to our cause?"

"The Cameron estate will be one of my prime targets when the revolution starts. I may find a way to use him then. In any case, I will feed his disillusion at every opportunity, explain that he is still being used and that he can never hope to achieve anything while the Europeans rule."

"Do you agree, Comrade Abdullah?" asked Chin Peng.

"I do, Comrade. As the youth is a Malay, I would have done more myself were it not that he trusts Comrade Peng since they fought the Japanese together."

"Excellent," said Chin Peng. "You will keep me informed, of course."

They discussed logistics and potential targets for another hour and then Chin Peng left, together with Lau Yew, Shorty Kuk, Hor Lung and the majority of the other Chinese. They had another meeting in Pahang the following day and many miles to cover before then. Apart from Lee Swee Peng and Abdullah, only the invisible sentries and the two men's personal bodyguards remained in the camp.

"I think you should do it," said Lee Swee Peng. "It will be more appropriate, Malay to Malay."

Abdullah squinted at the Chinese. "All of them?"

"What would be the point in all of them? Remember Sun-Zu—kill one, terrify a thousand. In this instance, perhaps two."

"Which two?"

Peng sighed inwardly and hoped it would not always be like this.

"You choose, Comrade. They're your people. It's a matter of complete indifference to me."

Peng accompanied Abdullah to where the three headmen were bound to the trees. The Malays' eyes widened with terror when Abdullah produced his parang and ran a thumb along the cutting edge.

"You have been in error," he said to the first man, his voice even.

"You were offered a revolution but preferred slavery. For that you have to die."

With a sudden movement he severed the man's head from his shoulders. Blood spurted, some of it landing on Abdullah. Peng took a step backward in order to avoid his own clothes being stained. The two surviving Malays let out wails of anguish and began begging for their lives, protesting that it was all a mistake, that they hated the British and would conform.

"Too late," said Abdullah.

With the second man he removed both arms above the elbow with two swift slashes. He gave him half a minute to experience the pain before beheading him also.

The third man had urinated down his legs and evacuated his bowels. His howls of fear sent birds screeching from the trees in alarm. Abdullah raised his parang for a third time—and cut the man's bonds.

"Go," he said. "Go and tell everyone you meet what happens to those who side with the running dogs."

Abdullah and Peng turned their backs. After a moment, the survivor staggered away in his own filth.

"Excellent, Comrade," said Peng.

11

Over Easter 1948 Dan had to fly to the States to sort out some minor problems concerning Holden Office Supplies that could not be resolved by letter or telephone. He would be away about a week. The children had arranged to spend the holidays cruising on a schoolfriend's father's yacht berthed at Kota Jaya, and had already left. Thus Barbara would be by herself. Dan asked her if she would like to fly with him, for a break.

"No," she said. "It's too far for just a week. You go, darling, I'll be fine here."

If Dan was surprised, he was also delighted. His wife was settling down after all. She'd hardly uttered a word of complaint about "this bloody country" for almost a year.

The day after Dan left Barbara travelled by train down to Singapore, where she had taken a three-year lease on a two-bedroom apartment using her own money. Only she and Jeff knew of its existence and they used it whenever they could both find an excuse for being away. Hotels were too dangerous. Jeff being a Cameron, there was always the danger they would bump into someone he knew, or who knew them both. For the same reason they hardly ever left the apartment, and never together, once installed. Not that either of them wanted to. Their relationship was almost exclusively physical.

Dan being called back to Texas could not have worked out better for Barbara. Her affair with Jeff was almost a year old, but recently she'd sensed a certain coolness in him.

The trouble was, they didn't see each other often enough. From the crazy beginning, they'd only managed to be alone once or twice a month. That wasn't enough for her. It surely couldn't be enough for someone with Jeff's appetite. He was bound to have other girls in between, albeit that they'd agreed early on that inquisitions on that subject were taboo.

When they were together the sex was marvellous, although that was probably all there was to their relationship, sex. Nothing anyway, that would cause more than a few ephemeral tears when it was all over. She hoped. She was a little in love with him while accepting that he was in no manner in love with her. Never mind what he said on occasions. He was, if the truth were known, something of a selfish bastard. Somehow it didn't seem to matter. She needed him for now. Afterward, who could possibly tell?

He was an hour late arriving. She was beginning to think he'd missed the train in Kuala Kelan when she heard his key in the door. "Christ, what a journey," he said wearily, depositing his suitcase on a chair.

"And hello to you too."

Jeff grinned. "Sorry."

He kissed her. She'd had his whisky and water already poured in anticipation, but the ice had melted long ago. She fixed him another.

"Thanks," he said, slumping into an armchair.

She curled up on the floor at his feet, resting her arms on his knees and her chin on her arms. "Was the train delayed?"

"No, not the train. That was right on schedule give or take a minute or two. But I got caught up in some sort of political demonstration. It was getting quite nasty and the police had their batons out. So I paid off the taxi and walked, taking the long way around. That bloody suitcase weighs a ton. I've got arms like King Kong."

"There was something happening in Kuala Kelan just before I left. The police were out in force there too."

"Yes, I saw the remains of that. I heard somebody say that one of the demonstrators had been killed."

"It's getting worse, isn't it?"

Jeff nodded. The political situation had deteriorated since the Federation of Malaya was officially created on February 1, with state sovereignty remaining with the sultans instead of transferring to the British Crown. The Malayan Communist Party seemed to see this as some sort of threat to their ambitions, and it had been widely reported that its leaders had attended the Russian-sponsored conference of Asian Communists in Calcutta, also in February. God knows what they had discussed during the closed-door sessions. *That* had not been reported. But a one-eyed man could see that the British were being given the runaround in Palestine and India while in China Mao Tse-tung had all but defeated the Nationalist forces under Chiang Kai-shek. Malaya must appear ripe to be plucked.

"It's certainly not getting any better. Beginning to regret Dan investing in Cameron Rubber?"

"You know better than that. Have you decided how long you can stay?"

"Tonight and possibly tomorrow night. No longer. My mother gave me a very peculiar look when I told her I had business in Singapore. You didn't tell her you were coming down here, did you?"

"No. I just said I was going away for a few days."

"Still, she knows Dan's in the States and the children are on that yacht. She's no idiot, my mother. She'll go over it in her mind and try to remember how often we've been away from the estate simultaneously."

"What would you do if she challenged you?"

"Deny it, of course."

"Of course." Barbara levered herself up. "Well, if it's only tonight and tomorrow night . . ."

"I could use a shower. I smell like a yak."

"Elegantly put. I'll join you." She held out her hand. "Come on, let's commit a little adultery."

They made love in the shower and then sat around in their robes in front of the open window, relishing the breeze blowing off the Strait. Barbara made them a light snack around nine, which they polished off with a bottle of champagne. By eleven they were in bed and making love again. Afterward they both dozed.

Around midnight there was a thunderous crash outside. It could have been a car backfiring, it could have been a gunshot. Jeff sat up with a start.

"What the hell was that?"

"Probably another commandment breaking," said Barbara sleepily.

In the middle of April Jess began worrying about Harry. For a man of fifty-six who had fought in two wars he appeared outwardly to be in remarkably good health and he had no financial worries; business was booming. But she had recently woken up beside him in the small hours to find him covered in sweat and muttering in his sleep. At first she feared a recurrence of his malaria, but that proved not to be the case. He'd only had the one bout since the war ended. Nor was he aware that he had been talking in his sleep, or concerned about it. "Everyone does that from time to time."

She wanted him to see a doctor. He refused. There was nothing wrong with him. He was as fit as a fiddle. But once or twice a week she'd be awakened by his murmurings and touch his forehead to find it soaking. The only words she could make out were "bastard Japs."

She spoke to Alan Fielding, without telling Harry. Fielding was pushing seventy and of course no longer practiced medicine. But he thought he had the answer for her. Or at least a sort of answer.

"In the first place you have to remember that Jenny was killed by the Japanese." Jessica's face clouded over. Fielding apologized. "I'm sorry to remind you of that but you are asking for a diagnosis. I know from what you've told me on other occasions that you and Harry rarely talk about Jenny. What is repressed when he's awake, therefore, surfaces when he's asleep. Secondly, and more important in my view, Harry spent four years under the most enormous pressure. We all did, of course, but it was Harry's outfit and he kept us together. I'm not going to give you chapter and verse about what we did in the jungle because it's ugly and you wouldn't want to hear it. But it was a rough war, Jess, very rough. We had to be brutal to survive and some of us didn't.

"I've had dreams like Harry's myself. That is, I've woken up in a cold sweat convinced that I'm back up country and that there's a Jap patrol just a few feet away. Some others who were with us have told me they've dreamt the same. I guess a doctor never actually retires. My dreams—or nightmares I suppose we should be calling them—happened directly after the war. It's just taken Harry's subconscious a little longer than mine to click into gear. But they'll go away in time, the dreams. Mine did. They may not go away for ever, but it'll become easier."

"I hope you're right," said Jess. "It's unforgivable, I know, but in England we were so wrapped up with our European war that I don't think we ever appreciated what you all went through."

"Yes," agreed Fielding, "anyone who fought in this theatre, military or civilian, can claim to belong to a forgotten army."

Also in April the Ashfords, Diana included, flew to Australia, where they had friends, for two weeks' leave. Mike was surprised that Diana chose to accompany her parents; it seemed an oddly immature act for a twenty-two-year-old girl, especially as they had been seeing more and more of each other to the exclusion of anyone else, and Diana had, the previous October during a shared holiday in Penang, overcome fears about her virginity and surrendered it willingly and enthusiastically. It would have been more logical, in Mike's opinion, for Diana to remain behind. Unless she was getting fed up with him.

For the first few days Mike hardly missed her; he had too much on his plate. His father was in Kuala Lumpur on business and Dan's problems in the States had proved more troublesome than was first thought. He cabled it would take a further week to sort them out. Jeff, back from whatever had taken him to Singapore, was around, but he had his own work to do. The estate employed several European and Indian clerks and a dozen Krani, Tamil overseers, but Harry Cameron had a rule that at least one member of the family, or Dan when available, had to do the rounds each day.

Mike was awake before sun-up every morning and off on his horse or in the estate Jeep. The Chinese, Malay and Tamil tappers, male and female, were all trained on the estate and in theory knew their jobs. But too deep a cut could destroy a rubber tree.

Long before noon the trees ceased to yield latex and work stopped. Each tapper's crop, collected in large buckets, was then carefully weighed and carried to temporary storage tanks prior to removal to the estate factory, where it was poured into troughs and mixed with chemicals. Lengths of tin were then placed in slots in the trough, and twenty-four hours later strips of rubber could be lifted out for drying and compressing into bales. A clerk paid each tapper's wages, on average two or three Malay dollars a day or one pound sterling every three days, but Mike liked to make unscheduled visits to the estate office to ensure that the tappers were only receiving what they'd weighed-in for. He had no reason to doubt the honesty of his clerks, but as everyone was paid in cash there could always be a first time for larceny.

It was after lunch toward the end of the first week Diana was away that he started to feel her absence. Batu Mersa, where her father ran a plantation, was a considerable distance from the Cameron estate, but it was on the main highway linking Singapore to KL and most afternoons or evenings they managed to meet halfway. On days they didn't meet they would either telephone each other or talk over the radio net.

Jessica observed that he was pining.

"You'd better snap her up before someone else does," she remarked.

"Huh?"

"Don't be obtuse, Mike. Diana."

"If you mean what I think you mean, I've no intention of getting married for a few years yet."

"That's up to you, of course, but don't blame me if, when you decide to ask her, she's found someone else."

"I won't," said Mike grumpily. He collected a cold beer and went out on to the verandah, where he sat with his feet up on the balustrade. Behind him, Jess smiled to herself. Clever girl, young Diana, going off to Australia like that.

Each afternoon when he had finished work and every day when he was not on supervisory or other duties, Mike saddled a horse and went for long rides. Sometimes he took his 12-bore or a hunting rifle, but his heart wasn't in killing game that was not for the pot.

He wondered if his mother was right, that Diana might find someone else if he didn't propose. Diana had never even hinted at getting married, never complained that she was unhappy as they were. Anyway, why the hell should he propose just for the sake of it? He was too young to get married. Jeff was still playing the field and Jeff was six years older. Let his mother tackle Jeff if she was so anxious for grandchildren.

The second week of Diana's absence dragged its heels. Mike went through it like a zombie. Each day seemed to have about sixty hours, and each night was twice as long.

Most evenings he drove into Kuala Kelan and met up with some friends at the club for a few beers and a little hell-raising. He could remember a time when he'd enjoyed getting legless and roaring around the back streets in his car, racing a couple of other guys equally drunk. Or dropping in on one of the more salubrious brothels in Chinatown for either the whole works or a relief massage. He didn't enjoy it any longer. He was becoming a dull old stick, blast it. He blamed Diana, stupid little girl. What a juvenile thing to do, go on holiday with your parents.

The day she was due back he made himself scarce. He'd show her.

He made his usual evening trip into Kuala Kelan and had a quiet dinner at the club, a good bottle of wine and several glasses of cognac. He drove back at a leisurely speed and arrived home around eleven thirty. Only his mother was still awake.

"Hi," he said casually. "Everyone else in bed?"

"It would seem so."

"Any calls?"

"A few."

Mike waited. "And?"

"And nothing. One was for me and the others were for your father. Why, were you expecting someone to telephone?"

"Well, I thought. . . . No, I guess not."

Jessica removed her spectacles and polished them with the hem of her skirt. "Do you mind if I offer you some advice?"

"Fire away."

"You call her. And for God's sake stop looking at me like that. You know perfectly well what I'm talking about. Call her now."

"It's almost midnight."

"And don't you think she's sitting up there in Batu Mersa waiting for the phone to ring? Do it, for heaven's sake."

"Well, I suppose it would be polite, just making sure they all got back safely."

"Mike," said Jess severely, "there are times when I could throttle you. I never thought that you, of all people, could be so humorless and insensitive. Jeff, yes. Although I love him dearly Jeff has the sensitivity of a flat rock. Diana's missed you as much as you've missed her. Now call her before I forget how old you are and take a rattan switch to you."

He was on the phone for twenty minutes. When he returned he was beaming.

"Look," he said, "I know I'm supposed to be on early duty tomorrow but I thought I'd drive up to Batu Mersa tonight. Diana says it's okay with her parents. I can be there in two hours."

"Don't you worry about early duty. Jeff can cover for you. You'll need this." Jessica indicated the overnight bag at her feet. "I've packed a change of clothing and underwear, your shaving tackle and a toothbrush."

"How on earth could you possibly have known I'd be driving up tonight?" asked Mike, amazed. "I didn't know myself until five minutes ago."

"Intuition."

Mike kissed his mother on the cheek.

"You're a wise old owl," he said fondly.

"Less of the old, if you don't mind. Drive carefully and give Diana my love."

Within forty-eight hours Mike and Diana had announced their engagement, the wedding to take place in August.

Late in May Laura Holden celebrated her thirteenth birthday with a party on the lawn of Mahal Rumah. Since she now considered she was, in her own words, "on the threshold of womanhood," she insisted that it shouldn't merely be a children's party but that grown-ups, particularly the Camerons, should be invited also, if only for an hour. She begged her mother to arrange it. Barbara readily agreed, seeing it as an opportunity to spend some time with Jeff, albeit that they would be in public.

Diana was staying with the Camerons for the weekend, and Mike asked Barbara if he could bring his fiancée. Barbara told him of course without checking with her daughter.

Another unexpected guest was the twenty-five-year-old niece of a friend Jessica had known in London during the war. Anne-Marie Tate, golden-haired, with a ready smile and an easy manner, was a newly qualified doctor on her way to New Zealand for two years. Since she wanted to see as much of the world as possible on what might be her only overseas assignment, and as one of her stopovers was Singapore, Jessica's friend had written to ask if Anne-Marie could possibly spend a few days with the Camerons if she made her own way up to Paselabilan. Naturally Jess had replied she could and, equally naturally, Anne-Marie went to Laura's party.

Laura was the first to show her displeasure.

Dan had hired a firm of contractors to erect a marquee wherein the children could shelter and have tea if it rained, and also a bus to collect and then return Laura's guests, to save their respective parents the trouble. There were a dozen girls of Laura's age present, but no boys. Laura didn't want any and wild horses would not have persuaded David to stay anywhere near the house on such an occasion. There was dancing, the girls taking each other as partners, to an electric record-player, a relatively new mass market invention Dan had discovered in the States and brought back as a birthday present for Laura. The girls drank fresh lemonade and bottled soft drinks, while the adults settled for wine.

Laura was fine and happily dancing with Mike until Diana and Anne-Marie turned up in a separate car. The two women had been applying finishing touches to their make-up and getting along famously together when it was time to leave. They sent Jessica, Mike and Jeff on ahead. Harry was having nothing to do with the party, not under any circumstances.

"I didn't invite *her*," pouted Laura on seeing Diana drive up.

"Well, no," agreed Mike puzzled by the teenager's fierce expression. "But I asked your mother and she said it would be all right."

"Well, it isn't and she shouldn't have done," snapped Laura, almost in tears. "She's spoiled everything! Wait till I find her."

She broke away in the middle of the dance and ran off toward the house, looking for Barbara. Mike was bewildered. Diana caught the tail-end of the conversation. She smiled sympathetically.

"I think you have a problem and I have a rival."

"Laura? She's only thirteen years of age."

"You'd be surprised how deeply thirteen-year-old girls can feel. Believe me, darling, she's jealous."

She wasn't the only one. By the time Barbara appeared Jeff was dancing with Anne-Marie, not closely but close enough. Barbara recalled only too well her first dance with Jeff a year ago. To make matters worse, Anne-Marie was the same physical type as Barbara but with fifteen years on her side.

Damn him, she thought. He didn't have to flaunt his interest in the young British doctor in front of her, the bastard.

Being new to Malaya, Anne-Marie was visibly melting in the afternoon heat but still an attractive challenge to Jeff. Although Barbara couldn't know it, the feeling wasn't mutual. Anne-Marie saw him for what he was, a hunter looking for scalps. She was determined to keep her own hair, and made her intentions clear by holding him at arm's length. Jeff accepted the rejection with good grace, but Barbara was unaware of that also.

It was forty minutes before she could get him to one side. She had a glass of wine in her hand, her fourth of the afternoon. She wasn't drunk, but she wasn't entirely sober.

"I suppose she's next on your list. Where do you plan to have her, in your bed or hers?"

"Don't be ridiculous," said Jeff, irritated. He wasn't in the mood for a public squabble that would be hard to explain away.

"Ridiculous am I? I've seen that look in your eye before."

"For God's sake keep your voice down." Jeff gripped her forearm and dug his fingers into her flesh. She bit her lip but wouldn't give him the satisfaction of wincing. "You know we agreed to live our own lives. If I've got to look over my shoulder to see your reaction every time I talk to an attractive girl, there's no future in our relationship."

"There isn't anyway. All I am is a convenient lay when you're not getting enough elsewhere."

Jeff glared at her, tried to shock her out of making a scene.

"You're a very stupid woman and not a very pretty one when you snarl," he said cruelly. "If you want to know why I'm dancing with Anne-Marie and not you, take a look in a mirror when you're in this mood."

"You bastard!" she hissed. She would have thrown the contents of her glass in his face, but he kept hold of her arm until she calmed down. Then she tried a different tack. "I've hardly seen you since Singapore," she said, trying to please him by keeping her voice low. "What about this afternoon, just for an hour? I could meet you at Richard's Hill. The party will be over by four, I could be there by five."

"I won't be able to get away."

"You could try."

"It's not possible. We have house guests in case you've forgotten."

"Just for an hour. Please." She was begging and hating herself for it. "Please."

"It can't be done."

"I'll be there anyway. Please try."

"Watch it, here's Dan."

The Camerons and their guests left soon afterward. Mike made a special point of saying goodbye to Laura, who was still sulking.

Toward four o'clock Barbara told Dan she had to get away from the house for a while—a dozen teenage girls laughing and squealing were driving her mad—and would he mind seeing them all safely on the bus to take them home? Dan didn't mind in the least. He was accustomed to the minor eccentricities his wife had developed during the past twelve months, one of them being the need to take off for long drives every now and then.

Barbara drove to Richard's Hill, parking where the road ran out. Jeff's car wasn't there, which meant neither was Jeff. There was nowhere else to park.

It began to rain with a vengeance, huge drops that drummed maniacally on the roof of her Ford. The rain could have delayed him, she attempted to reassure herself. But after an hour she knew it hadn't, that he wasn't coming at all.

She drove back savagely, gunning the accelerator where the main road was free of other traffic. Passing the Camerons', she leaned heavily on the klaxon. At least that would tell him that *she'd* been up to Richard's Hill.

It had stopped raining now but she was travelling far too fast along the road that linked the Camerons' to Mahal Rumah. She didn't see the bicycle until it was almost too late, and she only managed to avoid what would have been a fatal collision by wrenching the wheel over and skidding to a halt. Even so, the rider tumbled off his bicycle, and fell. He was unhurt and the bicycle undamaged, but he was shaken.

Barbara leaned out of the window.

"Watch where you're going, you clumsy little bastard!" she yelled before slipping into gear and driving off.

Hamid, on his way to receive his afternoon lesson from Jessica, later than usual because of the party, picked himself up and dusted himself down. He'd recognized the car and the driver, and knew that it was the memsahib's fault, not his, that he had come close to being killed. And if he'd died Tuan Holden's wife would have been acquitted in a court of law. What did the death of one Malay matter? It didn't; Lee Swee Peng and Abdullah bin Halim had taught him that much.

There was a small summerhouse surrounded by frangipani a hundred yards from the bungalow. This was where Jessica tutored Hamid. She was waiting for him when he arrived, a jug of iced lemonade and two glasses on the table.

Today's lesson was reading, and the book they were studying was *Treasure Island*—a boy's adventure story that transcended, in Jessica's opinion, all race and religion. They sat alongside one another, Hamid following the words with a finger and pronouncing them aloud. Jess only helped out when Hamid was totally stuck, which wasn't often these days.

Jeff called to his mother from the verandah. She didn't hear him; nor could she see him when he waved, for the frangipani acted as a screen.

It was Anne-Marie's last evening; tomorrow she would take the train to Singapore and then fly to New Zealand. She and Jeff, Mike and Diana, had decided to make an evening of it in Kuala Kelan. Jeff had already informed the cook that there would be four less for dinner, but he wanted to tell his mother their plans.

He strolled toward the summerhouse. When he was within a few yards he came to an abrupt halt, his face white. "Jenny," he

whispered, knowing that, in the dusk, his eyes must be playing
tricks.

Through a gap in the frangipani and silhouetted against the
kerosene lamp, Hamid was in profile. His hair was quite long
and curly, and he was the image of Jenny when she was sixteen—
which was how, in his mind's eye, Jeff always remembered his
sister, from the day he and Mike flew to England to school
from Karachi. Although he saw her several times subsequently in
England and Malaya, the mental picture he always carried was of a
sixteen-year-old girl waving goodbye from the Karachi airstrip.

"We're going out," he said to Jessica, explaining where while
continuing to study Hamid. He could see now that his mother's
companion was the young Malay she tutored, but the resemblance
between the boy and his dead sister was uncanny. They could
have been mother and son. He couldn't understand why he'd never noticed it before. Same eyes, same nose, same mouth. He'd
be about sixteen, too, and he was obviously Eurasian, not pure-
blooded Malay.

"Are you sure you're okay to drive?" asked Jessica lightly.
"You look as if you've seen a ghost."

"I thought I had," said Jeff. "For a moment there, I really
thought I had."

Instinctively Jessica understood. Oh my God, she thought.

Jeff was dull company that evening, paying hardly any attention to the conversation of his brother and the two girls. *Mother
and son*. He could scarcely credit it but, unless he was losing
his sanity or had witnessed a million to one chance, Hamid was
Jenny's child.

He went over what he knew. One of the boy's parents had to
be European; nothing else would account for that skin coloring
or those features. Jessica paid Hamid a great deal of attention;
exclusively, for none of the other estate children received private
tuition. Okay, perhaps that could be explained because Hamid had
fought alongside Harry Cameron in the war, and Harry might feel
obliged to do something about giving the boy an education. But
Jenny did not join the convoy heading for Singapore when the
Japanese invaded. Instead, she'd eventually ended up on Richard's
Hill with a group of Malay children. That had never been explained
satisfactorily, why she had elected, in effect, to sign her own death
warrant. Unless Jenny had found herself unable to leave without
her son, and had gone back to be with him.

If he was right, who was the father and where was he now? And who else knew that Jenny had given birth to an illegitimate child by a Malay? Not Mike, he'd stake his life on that. And not their father, because he and Mike had often heard him asking Jessica the same question: why had Jenny missed the convoy? That left only his mother.

But no, it couldn't be. How could it be? It was a secret almost impossible to keep. Yet the evidence, as he interpreted it, seemed conclusive.

The following morning Mike took Anne-Marie to the station before driving Diana home to Batu Mersa, where he was to spend the night. While Harry was making his rounds of the estate, Jeff tackled his mother, coming straight to the point. At first she told him he was out of his mind.

"That's an evil thing to say about your sister. Good God, what sort of girl do you think she was? And, if it's so obvious, why hasn't anyone else spotted the likeness?"

"I don't know," admitted Jeff. "Probably because they're not looking. I only saw it myself due to a trick of the light. If I'm wrong and you convince me I'm wrong, that's an end to it. But, if I'm right, the boy's half Cameron. He's my nephew and your grandson. And if I saw the resemblance it's possible Dad or Mike will one of these days. You should be prepared."

Jessica accepted that it was impossible to keep the truth from him any longer without constantly lying.

"Oh Jeff," she said in a tone that left him in no doubt he'd hit the nail on the head.

He put his arms around his mother's shoulders.

"Jenny's gone, God rest her soul. There can be no scandal attached to her now."

"But it's not just Jenny, don't you see? You don't understand a fraction of it."

"I'd like to try. Who else knows?"

"Just Alan Fielding."

Jeff nodded. A doctor. That made sense.

"Don't you want to tell me about it?"

"I don't want to, but I suppose I must. I'll call Alan. I think he should be here too."

Fielding drove out at four o'clock. He, Jessica, Jeff and Harry had drinks on the verandah before Harry excused himself on the grounds that he had some paperwork to do.

"But you'll stay for dinner?"

"I'm afraid I can't," said Fielding. "Some other time."

To keep out of Harry's earshot, Fielding, Jessica and Jeff, taking their drinks, went down to the summerhouse.

"Well," said Fielding, "where to begin? At the beginning, I suppose."

He started with the day Harry caught Jenny and Rashid, Hamid's father, making love.

"God alone knows why she did it, and with a Malay. She could never explain it herself. All we could come up with was that she was lonely now that you and Mike were in England. Anyway, Harry thought she was being raped, of course—at least to begin with—and went berserk. So berserk that he killed Rashid, throwing him sixty feet off an escarpment and breaking his neck. Then the trouble really started because Jenny, who'd obviously witnessed Rashid's death, confessed that she'd been a willing party to everything that happened. By this time Bill Hyde and myself were on the scene."

"Christ," said Jeff.

"Between us we got Jenny to change her statement. She didn't want to until we pointed out the alternative, that she would be the chief prosecution witness at her father's trial and that she wouldn't come out of it smelling of roses, either. So she agreed, and that, we thought, was the end of that. Harry had caught a Malay raping his daughter and killed him in a frenzy. Bill Hyde saw to it that there was no indictment. You won't remember how it was in 1932, but that sort of thing could be done."

"You told me only you and Alan knew about Jenny's child," Jeff said to his mother. "What about Bill Hyde?"

"Bill knew about the 'rape' but not the pregnancy," said Jessica.

"Harry knew, of course," added Fielding.

Jeff's head was spinning.

"Dad *knew*? About the pregnancy? I don't understand."

"Bear with us," said Fielding. "When Jenny told your mother she was pregnant, your mother contacted me. I confirmed it. I suppose we all considered an abortion, but Jenny didn't want one. There was no way of keeping Jenny's condition from Harry so Jess told him. And persuaded him that the child would be fostered out as soon as it was born, which it was in November 1932, on Penang. Then Jenny complicated matters by refusing to give up Hamid to a church orphanage. If she did that, she would never see him again, she argued. She wanted me to place him with a Malay family in a kampong on the estate. Against my better judgement I went along with her wishes."

"So Rashid's parents brought him up as their own?"

"No." Fielding shook his head sadly. "Rashid's parents believed the story of the rape and couldn't stand the shame. They drowned themselves and their other children in the Pakelan river. Hamid was brought up by total strangers as one of their own. They were well paid for their services during their lifetime, but they never knew the truth about Hamid's parentage."

"During their lifetime?" queried Jeff.

"They were killed in the war," said Jessica. "When I got back from England and heard from your father that a boy called Hamid had brought him the news of Jenny's death, I knew it had to be Jenny's Hamid. I went looking for him. I found him but not his parents. He lives with another family now."

"And as far as your father's concerned," said Fielding, "Jenny's child was handed over to a church orphanage just before Christmas 1932. He doesn't know—nor must he ever know—that the boy who was with him throughout the war is his own grandson."

"Why not?" asked Jeff. "I can understand no one wanting to tell him while Jenny was alive because he would have been furious, mostly with Jenny, at being deceived. But now?"

"There are several reasons," said Fielding after Jessica indicated she was happy for him to continue as spokesman. "Number one, you're doubtless right about your father's fury, which, now, would be directed against Jess and me. We're the ones who've lied to him for sixteen years. Two, what's the object? He would never acknowledge a Eurasian grandchild because that would besmirch Jenny's memory. Don't forget he as much as any of us went to great lengths to cover up the pregnancy. Three, Jenny missed the convoy because she went back for Hamid. That was why she died. How would your father view a grandchild who'd brought about, however inadvertently, his only daughter's death? Harry's very fond of Hamid, which is why he sent him to school. Which is equally why he encouraged Jess to tutor him privately when the lad found he couldn't settle down in school. But he's fond of him only as some Malay kid he spent the war with, not as Hamid his grandson. Four, even if by some miracle he accepted Hamid as his own flesh and blood, which would probably mean Hamid himself finding out about it some day, how does he explain to the boy that he, Harry, killed the boy's father? How would Hamid take it? It's no use saying he'd never find out. Once you open Pandora's box you can't choose what you'd like to reveal and what you'd prefer remained locked away. No, let sleeping dogs lie."

"You're right, of course," said Jeff. Hell, he thought, he'd be laughed out of every club between KL and Singapore if it came out. It was all right to sire a Eurasian bastard; it wasn't all right for your sister to be the dam. "My only worry is that, one day, Dad'll see the likeness."

"That's a risk we have to take," said Fielding. "I don't think there's much danger of Harry being as observant as you. He saw Hamid grow up, don't forget, from a boy to a teenager over three and a half years. You detected a likeness because you hardly know Hamid, and when you saw him yesterday you automatically connected his looks with the image you have of your sister when she was the same age. Harry's perception is clouded by familiarity. It's like a school friend you haven't seen for twenty years. You remember him as he was, without the wrinkles or the paunch. Anyway, for the reasons I've given we have no option. It's our secret, just the three of us."

But Alan Fielding was wrong. Four now shared the secret. The fourth was Hamid. The day's events had caused Jessica to forget that this afternoon was one of the afternoons her protégé had a lesson.

When Hamid approached the summerhouse for his reading lesson he observed, as he got closer, that the memsahid was in conversation with Tuan Fielding and Tuan Jeff. Their heads were together and they did not see him. He'd intended to make his presence known and wait until the mem was ready for him until he heard his own name mentioned. Intrigued, he crouched behind the cover of the frangipani and listened. Thirty minutes later he crept away, back to where he had left his bicycle, fighting tears of rage, his mind reeling at what he had learned.

He was Miss Jenny's son. He could hardly believe it but he had heard it with his own ears. He'd been forced to watch his own mother, whom he'd thought of only as a kindly European, bayoneted to death. Tuan Cameron had murdered his natural father and had escaped the penalty of the law because he was European. Memsahib Cameron had known the truth since the day of his birth and had kept it from him. He was part Cameron but would never be recognized as such. The Camerons were rich, as rich as sultans and princes, and they had stolen his birthright. Not the wealth, that was unimportant, but his name, his real name. They had told him lies to protect themselves and, as a result, his father's parents, his Malay grandparents, had killed themselves rather than face the shame that had not existed. He was almost sixteen years old and he hadn't even known that.

The man and woman he'd thought were his parents, whose deaths at the hands of the Japanese he'd mourned when he learned of them after the war, had been paid by the Camerons to bring him up as their own. It was money again, European money and European power. It corrupted, as Lee Swee Peng had taught him. If he could have laid his hands on a rifle he would have killed the Camerons, all of them.

But perhaps he could obtain a weapon. Lee Swee Peng would know where.

It was a week, the longest week in Hamid's life, before the Chinese visited Hamid's kampong again. During that week he attended his work as a tapper as usual but declined to take lessons. When the men sought him out to ask about his absence, he merely smiled and said he needed a rest from books. She accepted his explanation, and he was proud of his ability to lie convincingly. Not only Europeans could do *that*.

Lee Swee Peng noticed the change in him immediately, but it took an afternoon for the whole story to be told. And told again, for the Chinese could not believe his good luck. As a propaganda weapon the information was next to useless. Scurrilous pamphlets could be circulated by the Party accusing Harry Cameron of getting away, literally, with murder, but the contents would be denied and there was no way of proving them. However, Hamid's hatred for the Camerons was genuine and could certainly be channelled in the right direction. Give him a gun and he would do the job today— and probably be caught tomorrow. In the terror to come, Hamid was going to be very valuable. Once he'd killed, there would be no turning back.

He dismissed the boy's request for a rifle.

"No, there's a better way of doing it than that."

12

During the first two weeks of June, attacks against rubber estate workers throughout Malaya became more commonplace. The usual targets were of the "soft" variety, Tamil overseers and tappers of all races who, their working day over, returned to their kampongs and villages which were not, for the moment, protected. Many of the attacks proved fatal; even those that did not ended up with the victims being mutilated, usually by having hands or whole limbs chopped off with parangs. The attackers were almost exclusively Chinese, who appeared from the jungle, selected and dealt with their prey, then disappeared as silently as they had come. Invariably they left behind handwritten caveats. The most common wording was: "Death to the running dogs and their lackeys. Malaya must be free." Police interviewed surviving victims and dead victims' families without much success. They were too scared to give descriptions.

No Europeans had been attacked to date and there were some planters who thought they never would be, that the Communists—the assailants' collective identity was no secret—wouldn't dare and hadn't the means; that they would only try to intimidate the workforce, which in itself should be enough since without labor the rubber industry would grind to a halt.

Harry Cameron wasn't one of those who subscribed to the theory of European inviolability. These were just the opening shots in the battle. Sooner or later the terrorists—or bandits as they were known until it was realized that the word tended to glamorize men who were essentially murderers—would become more daring although, so far, no one connected with Cameron Rubber had received so much as a warning. For that matter, Paselabilan was the only rubber-producing state that was attack-free.

Harry had no means of knowing that Lee Swee Peng was biding his time in the state, wanting to begin the insurrection with a spectacular coup, which he would not be able to promote if the Europeans took fright and posted armed sentries around their houses.

From June 1 to June 10 Harry and his sons worked hard to drum up support for a general meeting in KL for the 14th, where, hopefully, the planters could agree upon a common policy and present a united front to the High Commissioner, currently Sir Edward Gent, who did not appear to be taking the crisis seriously. Harry also made it an estate rule that all Europeans be armed, even the clerks in the estate office. Jessica objected to bearing arms herself, although she could handle a rifle and pistol competently. "They will not attack Europeans," she insisted.

Harry let her have her way for the present. Mike and Jeff were more than capable of looking after themselves and their mother.

On the afternoon of the 14th Dan drove his wife and children to the Camerons' before setting off, with Harry, for Kuala Lumpur. They were staying in the federal capital overnight, and it might have been asking for trouble to leave Barbara, David and Laura alone in Mahal Rumah.

Jeff had seen Barbara only twice, both times in the company of other people, since the afternoon of Laura's birthday party, and on both occasions she had treated him coolly, making obvious her annoyance that he had not met her at Richard's Hill. Today he went out of his way to be charming to her. In the first place he didn't want to make an enemy of her, whereupon she might do something stupid like confessing to Dan that they'd been having a torrid affair. In the second place, he had far from written her off as a lover. Although familiarity had dulled the edge of excitement, he still remembered how it used to be, and how it could still be when their needs coincided.

After several drinks she responded to his overtures by making one or two risqué comments. At the head of the dinner table Jessica exuded general disapproval. Was it possible, she wondered, that something was going on there that she knew nothing about? Perhaps. Jeff was a lady's man and no mistake and, for her age, Barbara Holden was an extremely good-looking woman in that peculiarly brittle way some Americans had.

When dinner was over and David and Laura packed off to bed, Mike responded to his mother's cue by pushing back his chair and getting to his feet.

"Time for evening rounds," he announced.

"Do you need any help?" asked Jeff.

"No, I can handle it."

"Bloody country," said Barbara to no one in particular.

Mike rolled his eyes at his mother. He selected a rifle from the gun-rack and checked the magazine before stepping outside.

Jeff excused himself from the table by saying he had some wireless calls to make, the most important being to the estate office, where a European duty clerk would be expecting him to check in. This was another of Harry's recent rules, having at least one clerk sleep in the estate office.

When Jeff returned, Barbara was nowhere to be seen. Jessica was in the drawing-room, where Jeff joined her.

"Barbara gone to bed?" he asked casually.

"She went outside for a breath of fresh air. Which she could certainly use, in my opinion."

"She's harmless, just a little the worse for wear."

"A too frequent occurrence from what I've seen."

"Would you like me to make sure she's all right?"

"I'd like you to stay precisely where you are. As soon as the servants have cleared up and retired to their quarters, I suggest we all go to bed."

"You may have to think about the servants soon," said Jeff seriously. "The Chinese anyway."

"I'm not going to lose a perfectly good cook because he's Chinese. He's as loyal to your father and me as anyone."

Outside Mike glanced up as a cloud passed over the three-quarter moon. Somewhere in the distance a leopard snarled.

He held his rifle by the stock. Funny, he thought, I never thought I'd be using one of these again in anger after the war. But it was coming, all right, trouble, if he were any judge. The strikes and agitprop in the cities and the intimidation of plantation workers were just the beginning. God help them all if the Communists were really serious and started a guerrilla campaign. Using the jungle, where it was possible to pass within a few yards of someone or some animal without seeing him or it, and hit-and-run tactics, they'd be almost impossible to defeat.

Evening rounds, too, would have to become a damned sight more comprehensive than a casual stroll around the bungalow and lawn. The U.K. would doubtless send more soldiers if the whole damned country fell apart, but a fat lot of good they'd be, straight off the boat. In any case, the British were not jungle fighters. With a handful of honorable exceptions, his father among them, the Japs had proved that.

He heard a slight noise behind him and turned on his heel, bringing the rifle to his hip and releasing the safety.

"Who's that?" he called in Malay, repeating the question in English. "*Berhenti!* Halt!"

"Hold it, hold it," he heard Barbara Holden say. A moment later she appeared out of the shadows.

"You'll get yourself killed, sneaking up on people."

"Not me, not with a rifle. I was born to be hanged."

She weaved up to him unsteadily, almost stumbling. He stretched out a hand to help her. Inadvertently, he touched one of her breasts. She covered his hand with one of her own, pressing his fingers into her flesh. In spite of himself, he felt a stirring in his groin.

"Mmm," she murmured dreamily, protesting mildly when Mike whipped his hand away as though her body were red hot. She was, she conceded, more than a little drunk.

"What are you doing out here?" Mike asked her.

"Fresh air. Your mother all but suggested I could use some."

"She told you to come out here alone knowing I was walking around with a loaded rifle?"

"Maybe not exactly. Jeff went off to the wireless room and your mother disappeared into the kitchen. So I decided to take a look at the moon."

She had been hoping that Jeff, after making his calls, might take the hint and follow her outside, but it didn't look as if he was going to, the bastard. Well, she'd show him.

She swayed against Mike. To him the smell of her hair, newly washed, was overpoweringly aphrodisiac. She flapped the collar of her dress, cooling herself. A whiff of some expensive perfume reached his nostrils.

"Christ, this heat," she complained. "I'll never get used to it."

"We'd better get back," he said uneasily.

"You'll have to lend me your arm."

He slung his rifle over one shoulder. After a couple of paces she shuffled to a halt.

"Wait a minute, let me get these damned shoes off. Keep hold of me or I'll wind up on my ass."

She stooped to unfasten the straps. While both of his hands were occupied steadying her, and with her shoes, finally, in one hand, she reached for his groin with the other, feeling his semi-erection. He pushed her away, embarrassed.

"For Christ's sake, Barbara . . . "

"For Christ's sake Barbara nothing. Your head might be telling you one thing but down in the fun factory you're thinking different. 'Could I get away with it? What would she be like? It's an offer so take it.'"

"Let's go," said Mike. "You don't need my help."

"You're not going to take advantage of my generosity? Come on, it doesn't have to be more than a quicky. It's a warm night, there are plenty of dark corners . . . "

"You're drunk."

"And you're presumably getting all you can handle up at Batu Mersa, huh? Or not interested in getting laid by a woman of forty, is that it? If it is, you're not the man your brother is."

"What does that mean?"

"Think about it."

She seemed suddenly to realize that she had said too much. At least she made an effort to sober up and walk a few steps in a straight line.

"Forget it," she said. "Just forget everything I said. You're right, I'm drunk. Let's leave it at that."

She went inside, said her goodnights and, after looking in on her children, stumbled into her bedroom. She peeled off her clothes and lay on top of the sheets. Automatically she dropped the mosquito net. Within seconds she was asleep.

By the time Mike reached the drawing-room, Jessica too was preparing for bed.

Outside the bungalow, from the shadows, Hamid had witnessed everything that had occurred between Barbara and Mike. It would have been better had Lee Swee Peng ordered him to kill Tuan Holden's men, the woman who had knocked him off his bicycle. But that wasn't to be. It was Memsahib Cameron who had to die.

Lee Swee Peng had spread his poison well, using his considerable oratorical skill to inflame Hamid, convince him that, above all, it was Jessica Cameron who had kept him from knowing his true parentage. Via the grapevine the Chinese had learned that Harry and Dan Holden were to be in KL overnight, and had concluded that this was the moment to raise the Red Banner in Paselabilan. The death of the Cameron woman would be an auspicious beginning to the revolution.

Hamid had not needed much persuading. The European woman could have done more for him, much more. What she had presented as kindness he now understood to be self-interest. He was an inferior. He could not be accepted because his skin was the wrong color. Of all of them, she was the most guilty.

He knew her bedroom. He had taken pains to establish its exact location. When the house was asleep he would do what he had to, and let them know why. Then he would disappear with Lee Swee Peng and Abdullah bin Halim and take the fight to other parts of the state. One day all Europeans would be driven out and the country would belong to Malayans. Then and only then would there be justice for all regardless of race and creed. Never again would a white man be able to murder a Malay and escape punishment. His only regret was that he could not kill Tuan Cameron as well, but Lee Swee Peng had promised him that day would come.

"You won't believe this," said Jessica returning to the drawing-room a few minutes after she had retired. "Barbara's gone to sleep in my bed."

" 'Said the mother bear,' " said Mike.

"I mean to say," grumbled Jessica, "wouldn't you think she'd know the geography of the bungalow by now? I suppose that puts me in her room."

"Let's hope Dad doesn't come home unexpectedly," said Jeff.

They were all in bed and the house in darkness by midnight, but Hamid gave it another hour to be sure. When he was satisfied he padded noiselessly across the lawn, his parang gleaming in the moonlight. Outside the bungalow he counted the windows until he found the one he wanted. Seconds later he'd pulled back the mosquito net and was standing over the motionless form of Barbara Holden.

For a moment he panicked. Had he got the wrong room? No, impossible. They must have changed rooms for some reason and he had no means of knowing which one Memsahib Cameron was in. He couldn't try them all for fear of waking somebody up, and he had seen outside that Tuan Mike carried a rifle.

But Memsahib Holden, who had hit him with her car and sworn at him, was just as good a victim, wasn't she? Almost better in some respects because, with her, he would do more than kill her. Lee Swee Peng would understand. Another day would come for Memsahib Cameron, as it would for her husband.

Still clutching the parang, he stripped off his clothes and fondled his erection.

She stirred when he parted her legs, opened her eyes and tried to scream. He knocked her unconscious with the flat of his blade before entering her with the savagery of one who knows his actions will never be brought to account.

He cried out loud when he reached orgasm and had to bite deep into her shoulder to stifle his groans. It was the most magnificent feeling he had ever experienced. When his breathing returned to normal he almost regretted having to kill her. But he did, drawing the cutting edge of his parang across her jugular with such force that he almost separated her head from her shoulders.

He used her clothes to wipe the blood from his blade and from his body, a gesture of contempt. Then he dressed.

His final act was to take from his pocket the handwritten note he had composed earlier in the day. He had thought carefully about the wording, sought Lee Swee Peng's advice. It had to be short and simple, and at the same time dramatic. It didn't matter that it was tantamount to a confession. He never expected to be caught

The note read: "You betrayed Hamid, the son of your daughter. This is his revenge. Death to all running dogs."

The wording wasn't accurate now, of course, because his victim was not the one originally intended. But it would have to do.

He propped the note against Barbara Holden's still bleeding corpse and left the way he had come in. By dawn he was many miles away.

13

With a grief-stricken David and Laura beside him, Dan flew to America with Barbara's body as soon as the coroner gave permission for the corpse to leave the country. He wasn't sure he was coming back to Malaya. He was certain his children weren't. If he returned, they would remain with their maternal grandparents.

Jessica, who had discovered Barbara's body and Hamid's note, was still in a state of shock three days after the killing. Although she could scarcely credit it, she now accepted that she had been Hamid's target. The blood-soaked single sheet of paper left her in no doubt about that. Nor could the identity of the killer be disputed; Jessica had more reason than anyone to recognize Hamid's handwriting.

Because of his mother's health it was left to Jeff, himself numbed by Barbara's murder, to explain to his father, Dan and Mike the circumstances of Hamid's upbringing and how Jessica had conspired with Jenny and Alan Fielding to keep it all a secret. He could not, however, account for how Hamid had learned of his true parentage. Nor to begin with was it clear whether Hamid's action was one of personal vengeance or whether it was political, though the reference to "running dogs" seemed to indicate that Hamid had joined the terrorists.

For Harry, pieces of a hitherto unsolved jigsaw fell into place. It was now obvious why Jenny had not embussed with the convoy for Singapore after the Japanese invasion; it was equally apparent why Jess had taken such an interest in the boy. No, not just "the boy," he had to keep reminding himself. Jenny's son, his own grandson. His own flesh and blood was a murderer. Considering how Rashid had met his end, there was a bitter irony about it all.

It wasn't hard for Harry, as it was for Jess, to understand how a youth still several months short of his sixteenth birthday could kill in cold blood and rape his victim. Hamid had spent close on four years in the jungle war against the Japanese and had witnessed atrocities few other youngsters had. He had been brought up on death and reprisals.

The Camerons had little chance to dwell upon the tragedy, however, for within twenty-four hours of Barbara Holden's death the terrorists began attacking other Europeans, exclusively those in outlying districts. Whether Barbara's murder was the trigger for general insurrection no one ever found out, but on the morning of June 16, on a rubber estate a few miles east of Sungei Siput in the state of Perak, terrorists executed an estate manager named Walker, shooting him through the head and heart. Half an hour later, a dozen miles away, a manager called Allison and his young European assistant were bound to chairs and shot. In both instances cash in safes was left untouched and Malayan workers told: "Our war is not with you unless you make it so. We're only out to kill the running dogs."

That Europeans were the sole targets was proved to be untrue the same afternoon. In the state of Johore a group of Chinese emerged from the jungle wielding parangs and brandishing automatic weapons, mainly Sten guns. All wore green combat uniforms and caps with red stars in the center. They approached a tappers' compound and asked for the headman. When he, also Chinese, appeared, they demanded money. The headman complained that he had no means of raising money, that they were all poor. The terrorists' leader listened in silence. Then he summoned the remaining tappers and their families. While they watched, the terrorist chopped off both the tapper's arms above the elbow. "Let that be a lesson to you. When we next ask for money, however little, provide it."

Strictly speaking money was not the purpose of the mutilation; thousands of Malay dollars had been left untouched in earlier executions. Discipline was the object. Obey, or else.

Before the day was out a State of Emergency had been declared, and before the week was over Malaya had become a country at war, one where no European walked about unarmed. Driveway approaches to estate houses were blocked with barbed-wire barricades and the walls of the houses themselves reinforced with sandbags. Trees that might obscure a field of fire were removed. Europeans tried not to motor except in groups and never drove after dark. On the rubber estates the tappers were watched over by armed guards during working hours then, those that lived on the estates, locked up in compounds for their own safety at night. There wasn't sufficient manpower to safeguard those who lived in their own kampongs; they had to take care of themselves, protected wherever possible by Malay policemen carrying Stens. Domestic servants, Malay and Chinese, were questioned closely regarding their political allegiances, and only those who passed the test were permitted to retain their jobs. But they too were confined to their quarters at dusk.

The Communists made no secret of their intentions or their identities. Their leaders even signed revolutionary documents and were, in any case, known to the police. Chin Peng, Lau Yew, Shorty Kuk, Liew Kon Kim, Ah Hoi, Goh Peng Tun, Lee Swee Peng, Abdullah bin Halim. And Hamid, occasionally known as Johnny Hamid.

There were few troops in Malaya, few British troops. Those that were there were mainly Gurkhas. The Devonshires and Seaforth Highlanders were in Singapore, the King's Own Yorkshire Light Infantry on Penang. They were soon to be redeployed.

The Malayan Police Force, to whose aid the soldiers were to come, was unprepared for battle on anything like a large scale. It was still split from top to bottom, with men like Bill Hyde— and others who sympathized with them—at constant odds with the European officers who had spent World War II in Changi or other POW camps. The majority of the rank-and-file were Malay and they were affected by the dissension. Morale was low, disenchantment high. Police guards were, before long, posted around rubber estates and tin mines, but only after the planters and miners made the strongest possible representation to the High Commissioner's office. In spite of the evidence, Sir Edward Gent was still disinclined to believe that the terrorists were anything more than a ragbag collection of freebooters who would soon be brought to heel.

Outside the Camerons' bungalow, which, with the sandbagging, resembled a wartime air-raid shelter within a week of Barbara Holden's murder, the floodlights were switched on each evening. To date the terrorists had not threatened any of Harry's workers or attacked his home, as they had attacked other planters' homes. But that day would surely come and he wanted to be ready for it. To that end he instituted certain security measures. Extra weapons and ammunition were not hard to obtain through the proper channels, and senior Malay estate workers, those whose loyalty was indisputable, were trained in the use of firearms and acted as a sort of

home guard. No one left the bungalow after dark unaccompanied
and no one left it at all unless it was essential. Storm shutters
on windows and doors were locked at dusk regardless of how
unpleasant that made the atmosphere inside. Even before dusk
no one walked into a lighted room without first checking that
the windows were covered. Harry bought three fierce German
shepherd attack dogs which were, to begin with, let loose in the
grounds at night to roam at will. But they couldn't tell friend
from foe and were impossible to control. After they savaged a
Special Constable, he had to shoot them. All planters in a given
area checked in with their nearest police station at two-hourly
intervals throughout the night. Since the telephone lines were
frequently sabotaged, communication with the police and with
other planters was largely by wireless. Which was no way to run
a romance, as Diana Ashford and Mike soon found out.

Due to the Emergency they couldn't meet as often as they had
in the past because police escorts could not be spared except for
essential journeys and it wasn't always possible to round up
enough civilian vehicles to form an armed convoy all heading in
the same direction and wanting to return at the same time. While
single-vehicle travel was undertaken by everyone on occasion,
usually without incident, it was still a risky business since a
solitary car or truck, no matter how expertly armor-plated by
the owner, was an obvious candidate for an ambush. What was
more, the workload of the average planter had doubled since the
Emergency. Where before he could do his morning rounds as and
when it suited him, now he had to stand guard over his tappers in
case they were intimidated or the rubber trees slashed. If a planter
couldn't make a living there was no point in staying in Malaya.
Some didn't the moment the first shots were fired, but they were
in a minority.

For Diana and Mike it became a question of getting married at
once or putting off the wedding until things looked as if they might
return to normal. The original plan had been for them to move into
his parents' bungalow directly after the August wedding while a
house was built for them on the estate. Now Diana didn't feel
inclined to leave home. Her father had never entirely recovered
from his experiences in Changi, and she pulled her weight on
the plantation whenever he was laid low. She could handle a rifle
and handgun as well as any man, and it didn't seem fair to her to
abandon her mother and father in the present circumstances. Mike
obviously couldn't leave the Cameron estate, which was part his

and where he earned his living. Nor was it possible to construct a house with everything else that was happening. After much soul-searching they decided to call off the wedding until 1949.

It was going to be hard for them, they accepted, because they were very much in love, but the Emergency was hard on every-body. To Mike's surprise Diana quoted his own father as an exam-ple.

"He fought in the First World War in those dreadful trenches, then for three and a half years against the Japanese. Now he has to start all over again against the Communists. It seems that his generation has always been in one war or another."

Mike spent every hour they were apart worried sick about Diana's safety. The Batu Mersa plantation her father managed was more isolated than most. But there was nothing he could do to change her mind. Nor did he want to. She had her responsibilities as he had his. They would meet whenever they could and pine for each other when they couldn't.

Although three months were to pass before Whitehall appointed another High Commissioner, at the end of June Sir Edward Gent was recalled to London to be told that his services were no longer required. Two weeks after that, a month almost to the day since his wife was killed, Dan Holden arrived back in Malaya. Without his children. He told Harry that he'd thought it all over and that no bloody terrorists were going to drive him out. Besides, he had a score to settle. He'd been following events in Malaya closely from the United States and it seemed to him that any troops the British Government sent were likely to be unaccustomed to the jungle and going to need all the help they could get. Even if they didn't, one way or another he was going to see to it that Hamid paid the penalty for Barbara's murder.

Part Three

July 1948–May 1957

14

Luke Ross arrived by train in Kuala Kelan and checked into the Regency Hotel four days after the security forces achieved their first major success of the war when, on July 16, a squad of detectives under the command of a Police Superintendent named Stafford killed Lau Yew, a former member of Force 136 and Chin Peng's leading military adviser. Acting on information received, Stafford led his squad into the jungle near the town of Kajang, ten miles south of Kuala Lumpur. What he had hoped would be a surprise attack was foiled when a Chinese woman outside the hut where Lau Yew and others were reputedly holed up saw him and gave the alarm. Three men dashed out, shooting as they came. Stafford's men replied in kind and all three terrorists were killed in the opening exchange of shots, one of them being Lau Yew. Stafford arrested five Chinese women and successfully fought off a counter-attack launched by terrorists who had been in the jungle when the shooting began. In the crossfire the five Chinese women were killed. Later the detectives collected maps, rifles and several thousand rounds of ammunition before torching the main hut and the auxiliary accommodation.

Luke had been drinking with other journalists in a Kuala Lumpur hotel which was the unofficial base for the press corps in the federal capital when news of the victory percolated through, and, while the remainder hared across to police headquarters for a thorough briefing, she got on the telephone and rang the deputy press liaison officer, asking to be allowed to photograph the corpses and the area where the killings had taken place. For a sizable fee if the pictures were exclusive. Sensing a useful piece of propaganda as well as an increased bank balance, the press officer agreed and said he would have a car in front of the hotel in thirty minutes. When Luke Ross turned out to be a woman, he changed his mind. Suddenly the

Kajang area was out of bounds to journalists. "I thought, when you rang, you were Ross's secretary," said the press officer.

Luke fumed and cursed, doubted his parentage, accused him of press censorship and threatened to take her complaint all the way up to Government House. She got nowhere, and it wasn't the first time. To make matters worse, one of her colleagues—an agency employee and a man, naturally—returned that evening with a perfect portfolio of photographs, having not only taken them in situ but having used police facilities to develop the negatives. They were already on the wire to the world's newspapers.

Luke wasn't the only overseas woman journalist in KL, but she was the only freelance who dealt in hard news. The other women were reporting on "fashions during the Terror" and "how the average planter's wife copes with household management in the Emergency." Which was what her male colleagues considered she should be doing. Hard news was a man's world; war reporting was especially a man's world. It was no place for a twenty-six-year-old girl even if she could drink with the best of them, play a mean hand of five-card stud, and even if she was an eye-catcher. Her page was the woman's page—or, it was often suggested, in one of their beds if she had nothing better to occupy her time. Her answer to this was that she never slept with anyone whose IQ was less than his age.

She got her own back the following day. At eleven A.M., a battery of cameras slung around her neck, she raced into the bar and announced that Superintendent Stafford had cornered Chin Peng himself near the Batu Caves. She was literally knocked over in the rush for the door, pushed to one side with such force that she stumbled and fell. When she protested, the average response was, "Tough."

She had a quiet beer and thought about what she'd done, concluding after a while that she'd overplayed her hand. Chin Peng, as far as she knew, was nowhere near the Batu Caves, and Superintendent Stafford was unlikely to view her rumor with equanimity. Not for nothing was he known to the Chinese as Tin Sau-pah, The Iron Broom. This was an Emergency, after all, and for all she knew she'd broken some recently passed law. The best that could happen was that her colleagues would, in future, refuse to cooperate with her; the worst that Superintendent Stafford would declare her irresponsible, persona non grata, and frog-march her in the direction of the nearest flight back to Australia. She decided to pack her things and entrain for a different state. The Emergency wasn't exclusively taking place in Selangor.

Thirty minutes later she was in a taxi heading for Kuala Lumpur station. She covered her face on passing police headquarters, where, outside, a group of her colleagues seemed in mutinous mood.

The first train out was an armored express non-stop to Kuala Kelan. She took it. Apart from two young army officers taking more than a passing interest in her—which she quickly put a stop to—the journey was uneventful. Which in some respects disappointed her. The terrorists had already begun blowing up lengths of track attempting to derail trains; she could have taken some great pictures.

Lucasta Ross had been in Malaya under a week. Before then, she had last seen the country in 1940, aboard the freighter skippered by her father, the *Southern Pride*, a voyage she had regularly undertaken with the old man after her mother's death when school and, later, university permitted. Peter Ross, to her great sadness, was killed in 1941, and the *Southern Pride* sunk, by Japanese dive-bombers in the Timor Sea. Luke cried her heart out when she received the official telegram, and left university without graduating. Instead she joined a Melbourne newspaper, starting first by running copy and fixing coffee and sandwiches for the largely drunken reporters whose bylines made the front pages. With one of these men, Doug Hurst, she had her first serious affair. He was thirty years her senior and had a wife and children. He was also so frequently inebriated that he was incapable of making love or writing his piece, which she did for him. She used to ask him why he drank so much, even for an Aussie.

"Because I'm fifty and you're not. Because I've got three chapters of a novel in my desk that I've been writing for a quarter of a century. Because my eldest son is older than you are. Because there are younger men than me making the headlines because they're in combat, and because there are others, equally young, taking the pictures and writing the copy. Because the whole world's a spittoon. I sit here and shape the combat reporter's words and try to keep the subs from fucking up too much. I sit here—and I'll die here—living vicariously. Christ, how'd you think I feel when I see my name attached to something you've written? You've got talent, make no mistake. But—but, if you plan to make a career in this racket, get your press card, grab a camera, and make sure you write your own captions. And for Chrissake don't tell anyone your name's Lucasta."

Doug Hurst died of alcohol before the war was over, but Luke didn't forget his advice. She obtained her press card, learned how to use a camera and became proficient, and could type her own captions and accompanying stories before she was twenty-three. She also found out that working as staff for a large newspaper meant being given "women's" assignments. She was denied hard news material because of her sex. When she resigned, she sent the proprietor a tampon in a hot-dog bun. The note attached read: "What a prick!"

She would have starved were it not for the money her father had left her. No one would hire her, publish her pictures or her copy. You didn't offend press barons and get away with it, not in Australia and probably not anywhere.

She saw herself as Dorothy Parker but knew that she looked more like a dark-haired Katharine Hepburn. In fact, her looks were half the reason no one took her seriously. If she dressed dowdy they saw through her; if she dressed fashionably they got scared or wanted to screw her before looking at her work, sometimes instead of looking at her work. She accepted she was attractive to men; for that matter she wouldn't have had it any other way. But at five feet nine, and particularly when she was wearing high-heels, she was taller than half of them. She was certainly twice as bright as most of them but unable to hide her brightness, shelter behind fluttering femininity. If a man couldn't see further than her spread legs and tits, that was his hard luck. It was also hers, because men controlled the jobs.

She took a time-elapsed photograph of herself one day and tried to analyze the results. She saw a woman with excellent bone structure and sensual eyes, about as many teeth as Katie Hepburn—which meant enough to get worried when the winner of the Melbourne Cup got anywhere near the paddock—and close-to-black hair. She recognized she was a threat to most wives and possibly too aggressive to attract more than the most confident man. Wearing eye-glasses she didn't need didn't help either; she then resembled Mata Hari with myopia. She was, in short, an unemployable mess looking for a place to have an accident.

She found the accident in the shape of an Australian of Irish descent by the name of Sean O'Hare, a riproaring fighting man who fought her as much as anybody. So, naturally, in 1946 she married him.

The marriage would have frightened a battalion of commandos. He got drunk, she got drunk; he threw things, she threw things. He was a lousy shot, she had the eye of an eagle.

Sean also worked in the newspaper business but was a man who wanted to change the world to his own vision of it. Especially by penning plays. Unfortunately he had no talent. He could write up a storm when describing a traffic accident, a motor race, or corruption in high places. He wrote dialogue the way Donald Duck talked. Neither could he understand why, when she occasionally got a byline with pictures, she didn't announce herself as Luke O'Hare. She told him why not.

"Nobody's called Luke O'Hare. Christ, say it fast by way of introduction and it sounds like a character actor in a John Ford Western pointing out dead Indians. 'Well, looky here.' No one would take me seriously."

"No one does anyway. I thought that's what you were complaining about."

He looked like a young Clark Gable and drank like a young Scott Fitzgerald, and she didn't want to end up like Zelda. It couldn't last, and didn't. In bed they were marvellous together. She frequently passed out during orgasm. Out of bed they were the Hatfields and the McCoys, the Yankees versus the Confederates. Soon they separated and she filed for a divorce. Before the papers could be served, Sean got in touch with her.

"I forgot to tell you," he said. "We were never really married. I've got a wife in Adelaide. What I mean is, you don't need a divorce."

"You bastard. What if I'd got pregnant?"

"Not much chance of that, was there? There wouldn't be room for the four of us."

"Four of us?"

"You, me, a child and your career."

She hit him with a jug. When he recovered, they made love for the last time. Afterward she fell asleep. When she woke up, Sean had gone and so had most of the money from her purse. She didn't chase him. That wasn't her style. But she did spend a fair sum having the marriage annulled, and she never saw him again.

He'd been right in one respect, though. She was ambitious and a child would have got in the way.

With her money dwindling at an alarming rate and the prospect of regular freelance work as distant as ever, she took a long hard look at her career. Or non-career, as it seemed to be. In order to succeed she had to provide a service no one else was giving. She listed the possibilities and only one stood out: war correspondent. There were virtually no women in that field, none who took their own photographs and wrote their own copy, anyway. There was only one snag: there were no wars to report apart from the one in China between the Nationalists and the Communists, and the Chinese were letting hardly anyone in. So she did the next best thing. She obtained a visa from the U.S. Military Government in Tokyo and took a plane for Japan.

Practically everyone in the world had seen pictures of the devastation caused by the atomic bombs and the horrifying wounds and burns of the survivors. Still, she found a new angle. Instead of staying in hotels with the rest of the press corps, using American military facilities for transport and writing her copy from the luxury of a bar stool, she found a Japanese family who had lived on the outskirts of Hiroshima and who spoke rudimentary English. Although none of them had been affected by blast or radiation, at least not in a manner that would be revealed for a generation, they had lost their home and everything they possessed and now occupied a tin hut in a coastal shanty town thirty miles from the explosion's epicentre. She stayed with them for six months, going native. She shared their accommodation and food. She helped them build a fishing boat. When they didn't eat, neither did she. Her only luxuries were pen and pad, her cameras and rolls of film. She took pictures from morning to dusk and contrasted them with the way the American occupying forces lived, cleverly juxtaposing photographs of overweight generals and starving children. She had a stroke of luck, when the family's youngest child died of malnutrition toward the end of her stay, but she cried genuine tears at the funeral.

Her entire portfolio was syndicated under the heading of: The Way We Live Now. It created a sensation and her name was made. Independent agencies fell over themselves wanting to market her talent, and she chose one run by a husband and wife. They weren't the biggest or necessarily the best, but they were hungry and—a bonus—the man was only interested in her work.

Nevertheless, Japan was a one-off exercise, and what she needed was a good war. The Malayan Declaration of Emergency came at precisely, for her, the right moment. She made a few enquiries and discovered that there were Australian families in the mining and rubber industries, and that there was a possibility, if the situation deteriorated, that a squadron of RAAF Lincolns would be deployed and even Australian troops. Thus she had her home market covered, though she had no intention of making her series exclusively Australian in content. She'd simply follow her nose and see what turned up.

And so far that was precisely nothing, she reflected as she unpacked her things in the Regency Hotel. Kuala Lumpur had not been exactly a dead duck, but, whatever the condition of the carcass, there were too many other scavengers around picking at it. Maybe Kuala Kelan would prove more fruitful.

The Regency Hotel wasn't the best in the state capital, but she had her own bathroom and telephone. After showering and changing into a cream cotton shirt and dark-blue culottes, she flicked through the telephone book and ascertained that Reuters had an office on Victoria Street. She decided to give them a call and pick the bureau chief's brains. After several attempts she got through to him. He introduced himself as Jerry Appleby and agreed to meet her in the bar of the Regency at 7 P.M. for a drink.

He turned out to be another Australian, although his accent had not been evident over the phone. He was middle-aged with thinning white hair and twinkling blue eyes. He'd heard of Luke and knew her Japanese work, and asked how he could help. She was mildly surprised at his friendliness.

"Aren't you supposed to tell me to take a walk? What would Baron von Reuter say?"

"Not much unless you know a good medium. Anyway, it's not like that in Kuala Kelan. In KL or Singapore you'd get short shrift, but not here. It says Reuters in the phone book, but there's only me, two reporters and a secretary. Anyway, I won't tell if you don't, so fire away. What do you want to know?"

"Just about everything," confessed Luke. "I'm brand-new to the territory, don't forget. I read up all I could before I flew over, but, apart from seeing a lot of soldiers and police on the streets, and armed guards on the trains, it doesn't look as if the country's under siege. I'm beginning to wonder if I'm wasting my time."

"You're not." Appleby sipped his beer. "Malaya's an iceberg, if that's not an incongruous metaphor. What's happening in the main towns and cities, the tip, is nothing to what's happening out on the rubber plantations, sub-surface, shall we say. In Kuala Kelan we've had the odd grenade thrown and bomb detonated, and anyone connected with the security forces sleeps with a pistol under his pillow. But that's all. They're here, of course, the terrorists and their support organization, the Min Yuen, but they're not making too much of a nuisance of themselves because the odds against getting away are against them. The police and the army have powers of stop-and-search, and to be caught with a grenade or a gun or ammunition means the rope. However, providing you don't do anything stupid like wandering around Chinatown by yourself late at night, it's like being at home.

"But it's out on a rubber estate you want to be to see things at close quarters. Or, if you can wangle it, with a police or an army patrol, although that's almost impossible. So is travel outside all major towns. That's either restricted or suicidal. If you want to get from A to B along a lonely road—and just about every road in Malaya is lonely—it's wiser to travel in convoy or find your own armed escort. You can't just hire a car, even if there was one to be hired, and take off. For us in the bureau it's not so bad. We wait until the news breaks and then go where we're directed. If nothing happens for a month, the salary checks still get paid. I can't imagine that being much use to you."

"Right," agreed Luke. "I pay my own checks. No work, no eat. Besides, I need specifics, not the stuff I can read on the front page any morning." She had a thought. "Is there a planters' organization in Kuala Kelan?"

"There is. There's also a planters' club, very English and old school tie even though many of the members aren't English. It's a possibility for you, I suppose."

"Do you know any of the planters personally?"

"Well, yes," admitted Appleby. "As a matter of fact, the wife of a planter in this state was the first casualty of the Emergency, an American woman named Barbara Holden. She had her throat cut by one of the estate tappers, only a kid, actually."

"Did they catch him?"

"No, his picture's still on a wanted poster. You can pick up a selection of those at police headquarters."

"I already did in Kuala Lumpur. Holden, Holden," murmured Luke, trying to recall the articles she'd read before she left Australia. "Didn't she have a husband and two or three children who all went back to the States directly after the killing?"

"Yes. But he returned, the husband. There was a column on him in the *Straits Times*. He's now part of something called Ferret Force when he can be spared from the estate. Ferret Force isn't exactly a secret, but the police and the army don't go around bragging about it, either. They're a group of civilians, mostly European but with a sprinkling of Malays and non-Communist Chinese, who once belonged to Force 136, a wartime organization who fought the Japanese and who are now helping the troops and the police because they know more about the jungle and the calibre of the terrorists than just about anyone. They're not exactly youngsters, most of them."

"He sounds an interesting man, this Holden."

"Dan Holden. He is, but he won't talk to you."

"Why not?"

"Partly because his wife's death's too recent and partly because whatever he's doing with Ferret Force is hush-hush."

"He'll talk to me," said Luke confidently. "You say he has a plantation in Paselabilan?"

"He's in partnership with a man called Cameron, another wartime guerrilla and something of a legend in these parts. Their place is midway between here and Kota Napek, west of the main highway. But I don't think you understand the difficulties. You can probably reach him on the telephone if he's around and the line's not down, but then there's the problem of getting to the estate even if he'll see you. The main highway's easy enough. There are always military convoys motoring up and down it. But the estate's way off the road. You'll have to wait until someone's heading in that direction unless you can beg, borrow or steal a car and don't mind sticking your neck out. If he doesn't want to see you—and he won't—you'll be marooned out there."

"Well, that's my job," smiled Luke. "How dangerous is it— I mean, *really* how dangerous—to drive around the countryside alone?"

"Very. Don't get me wrong, it's done all the time, mostly without incident. But it's done by men, rarely women alone, who know the risks and are prepared to take them. People have to travel, trucks deliver produce, buses take children to school. We'll never know, but the terrorists seem to be attacking mainly police vehicles and troop convoys. God knows how many others they let through unmolested waiting for bigger game. Let me put it this way. The country's at war. Actually, the word 'war' is never used because the London insurance companies, upon whom just about everyone here relies for protection, don't cover loss of property in a war but do cover it against riot and civil commotion risks. Still, it's a war. And, as in any war, you pay your penny and take your chances. Ninety-nine times out of a hundred you'll get away with it. I wouldn't drive myself unless I had to, although I own a gun. But I'm no expert. It's a senior policeman you should be talking to. You should introduce yourself at police HQ anyway. They like to know who's in town from the press."

"Anyone in particular?"

"My regular contact is Chief Inspector Hyde. In fact, it's not a bad idea that you meet Hyde. He knows Dan Holden and Harry Cameron intimately. He would have retired this year or next, I think, but because of the Emergency they want anyone with any kind of experience to stay on. I'll give him a call in a moment and see if he's still there. If he is, I'll walk you over and do the honors."

"I'd appreciate that."

Luke signalled a uniformed Malay waiter for refills. "Unless you'd prefer something stronger," she said to Appleby.

"No, beer's fine. Is there anything else I can do to help?" he asked once the fresh drinks were served.

"I'd appreciate looking through your morgue for whatever you have on Dan Holden and Harry Cameron."

"That can be arranged. You'll find more on Cameron than you will on Holden. Cameron's family has been here since before the turn of the century. We've got a pretty good morgue, actually. As good as anything the *Straits Times* has, anyway, and in some respects superior. I wasn't here before the war, but the bureau chief then, even before the Japanese landed, saw the writing on the wall and transported all his files down to Singapore for shipment to Australia. I came back with them in '46."

"A wise move. We'd be lost without our records."

"Wise for the records, yes. Wise for the bureau chief, no. He was from the old school of journalism, battered hat and sixty cigarettes a day from what I was told. He stuck around until the last minute and didn't get out. He died in the street fighting here."

"That's rough."

"It is. You wouldn't catch me being that valiant." Appleby got to his feet. "Look, I'll give police HQ a ring from the lobby. If Hyde's there, we'll go across and see him. It's not far. After that, as you're a stranger in town I'll buy you some dinner."

"Well," said Luke doubtfully.

Appleby chuckled, understanding.

"I was also thinking of inviting my wife."

"Then I'd be delighted to accept."

Appleby was away ten minutes.

"Hyde was there, but he's going to be busy for the remainder of the evening. He'll see you at two o'clock tomorrow afternoon. I arranged for my wife to meet us here in half an hour. Do you like fresh seafood?"

"Are you kidding?"

"Then I've got just the place. You know, there's only one sure way the terrorists can win this fight. They should forget about attacking rubber estates and tin mines, and ambush the trucks that bring the day's catch up from Kota Jaya. A week without seafood and the Europeans would settle for a draw."

Luke was in the Reuters office in Victoria Street shortly after eight A.M. the following morning. Appleby's secretary, Ellen Mount, a widow in her forties, showed her the ropes.

"The cuttings are in these binders, not just Reuters stuff but clippings from the *Straits Times* and other newspapers and magazines. Everything's in date order. There's a card index over there which lists names of individuals and organizations and is cross-referenced with the appropriate binder. It's not as up to date as I'd like it to be, but it's close. There's not much before 1920, which was when we set up a bureau here. There's nothing at all for the war years, of course.

"Most of the material concerns people in this state. We haven't room for much else. Jerry said you were interested in Harry Cameron."

"And Dan Holden, yes."

"I doubt we'll have much on Dan Holden that doesn't concern the last few weeks. But the Camerons have been here as long as rubber. Anyway, I'll leave you to it. Call me if you need any help."

Luke began with the most recent entries and worked backward, starting with Dan Holden. She wasn't looking for anything specific, just general background material, something to tell her about the man she wanted to interview.

Ellen Mount was right. There was virtually nothing on him that didn't concern his wife's murder, and on that there was a great deal. There was no clipping covering his return to Malaya from the United States; presumably that was one Ellen still had to index. The first cutting concerned his original arrival in the country to buy into Cameron Rubber. There were several grainy photographs of him—a good, strong face, she thought idly—and of his wife and children. And that was all, apart from brief details of his wartime involvement with Cameron's Cossacks.

Also, as Ellen Mount had predicted, there were dozens of entries under Cameron. It took her a while to sort out which Cameron she was interested in and which were other Cameron families.

As with Dan Holden, she began with the most recent cuttings and worked her way backward. By the time she reached the early 1930s she was getting bored and almost missed a clipping and photograph about the Camerons and their three children taking a ship to Karachi where the two sons would be put on a plane for England. But there it was in black and white.

WELL-KNOWN LOCAL PLANTER OPTS FOR ENGLISH SCHOOLING

Harry Cameron and his wife, Jessica, pictured here with their children, Jenny, Jeff and Mike, en route to Penang where they will board the Australian freighter Southern Pride *for Karachi. When asked why he considered English schooling . . .*

But Luke was already open-mouthed with astonishment. There simply couldn't be two Australian freighters called *Southern Pride*. She knew enough about maritime law to be sure of that. Therefore this *Southern Pride* had to be her dead father's vessel, now at the bottom of the Timor Sea.

She checked the year of the clipping. 1932. That made her ten years old. And the chances were that she would have been aboard when the Camerons were. If that was so, it was the most unbelievable stroke of good fortune.

She racked her brains and tried to remember. Her father had often carried fare-paying passengers; she'd met dozens of them over the years but their faces were just a blur. Nothing about the name Cameron rang any bells. After all, it was sixteen years ago, but the name Jessica seemed familiar. It wasn't quite as unusual as Lucasta—God damn her mother—but it was rare enough. Somewhere along the line she seemed to recall an "Aunt" Jessica, a woman who'd befriended her. But the grainy photograph offered no clues. However, it had to be her father's ship. Furthermore, while she didn't remember Jessica Cameron, the odds were Jessica Cameron would remember her. It would be a unique occasion in the Cameron family annals, sending their two boys to an English school for the first time. Their mother, at least, would probably recall every detail of the voyages to and from Karachi. Anyway, it was all the introduction Luke needed.

At a few minutes before two o'clock she thanked Ellen Mount for her help and poked her head inside Jerry Appleby's office to express the same sentiment. He wasn't there. It didn't matter. She would almost certainly be bumping into him again.

Ellen gave her directions for police headquarters, and she left the bureau. The afternoon heat hit her in the face like a slamming door, and she was perspiring freely before she'd covered a hundred yards.

To get to the central police station she had to cross the edge of Chinatown with its bewildering array of shops and food stalls, vendors selling fruit, vegetables, meats and fish standing cheek by jowl with merchants displaying exquisite jewelry and gold ornaments, Indian silks, Persian rugs and lengths of multi-colored hand-dyed batik. Snake charmers competed with fortune tellers for attention; bare-headed Chinese vied with Malays wearing sarongs and songkoks for the shoppers' coin. If there was a war on, these people seemed unconcerned.

She liked Bill Hyde on sight and spent an hour in his company while he briefed her on current terrorist activity in the state, telling her as much as he felt able but parrying any questions that came too near operational security. She learned that the leader of the terrorists in Paselabilan was a Chinese named Lee Swee Peng, who had a bounty of 40,000 Malay dollars on his head; that his deputy was a Malay, Abdullah bin Halim, valued at 30,000 dollars, and that their gang reputedly included Hamid, the murderer of Barbara Holden, whose skull, to anyone who brought it in, would also earn 30,000 dollars.

It was no secret how the police obtained information on the chief terrorists. Lee Swee Peng appended his signature to the notices tacked to rubber trees after an atrocity. As in any war, it was no use gaining a victory if the men behind it went unacknowledged. This was part of the terrorists' doctrine. But knowing who they were was not the same as capturing them and executing them. Hyde was fairly sure that Lee Swee Peng paid occasional visits to Kuala Kelan and smaller towns, losing himself among the crowds and then bragging about his daring later. Luke could see Hyde's point. Lee Swee Peng could have been selling rugs in Chinatown for all she knew. 40,000 dollars—she made that about £5,000— was a small fortune, but not much use to the informer if his name became known. He would then surely be killed. The police had it all to do.

Hyde didn't seem to think it odd in the least that a twenty-six-year-old woman was doing a job usually done by men, but he gave her a qualified negative when she asked if she could be part of the next police or army sweep. She queried the qualification.

"Well, search-and-destroy missions are definitely out as far as journalists are concerned. You'd get in the way and we couldn't be held responsible for your safety. However, if I was to hear of something that was over or virtually over and you were on hand, I don't see any reason why you couldn't go along."

Toward the end of the hour she asked him how well he knew Dan Holden and Harry Cameron.

"Very well. Any particular reason for asking?"

She chose her words carefully, not wanting to be told that Dan Holden wouldn't grant her an interview. If she could use her tenuous link with the Camerons to get *them* to see her, she must surely run into Holden before long. She wanted to spend some time on a rubber estate, in any case.

"I have a feeling I met Mr. and Mrs. Cameron and their children many years ago on a ship my father skippered. If I'm right, I'd like to renew an old acquaintanceship."

"What's stopping you? Why don't you call them? They don't see many people on the estate since the Emergency. They're always glad of company."

"I intend to call them. Are the phones working?"

"Last I heard they were. The terrorists don't cut the lines that often. They've realized that all outlying plantations and mines have wireless and, up to now, they haven't found any way to jam the frequencies."

"Then it's just a matter of getting to the estate, if they'll see me and put me up for a while."

Hyde grunted. "That sounds as if you're looking for a ride."

"That sounds about right."

"Shouldn't be a problem. There are police and army patrols on the main highways every day, and the police, at least, try to visit every plantation once every four or five days, just to check. Police of some rank, I mean. Also, each estate has a squad of Malay Special Constables permanently bivouacked close to each estate bungalow. They're rotated once a week, sometimes more often if the bungalow's come under fire, which fortunately Harry Cameron's hasn't up to now. I'll look at the roster when I have a moment and see when the Cameron squad is due for relief. You could travel with them. You're at the Regency, aren't you? I'll get in touch."

Luke's conversations with Jerry Appleby hadn't prepared her for this amount of cooperation, and her expression must have revealed as much. Bill Hyde read her mind.

"Surprised at how helpful the police can be, Miss Ross? I wouldn't be. This time yesterday I would have given you the usual police handout and showed you the door. But yesterday afternoon we had a new directive from the High Commissioner's office, even though we're temporarily without a High Commissioner. I'm no authority in these matters, but reading between the lines I'd say our new instructions come all the way from Downing Street in London. Apparently some members of the international press have been complaining that they're not being allowed to do their jobs, that the security forces are being too restrictive; that the news when they're allowed to have it is days old. London evidently agrees, believes we should be publicizing our successes with more vigor. Anyway, as of today we have new instructions. We give as much help to the press as we can without risking lives. Your material will still be subject to censorship, of course, if it's to be published in this country, but I don't expect that will apply to you. You can tell Jerry Appleby if you like, though the new rules will be common knowledge by this evening."

"I think I'll let him find out for himself," said Luke, smiling.

"I thought you might. A word of caution, however. We're not fools or backwoodsmen here in Paselabilan. Or in Malaya, for that matter. When Jerry Appleby told me who wanted to see me, I took the trouble of checking your credentials. By which I mean your series on the Japanese family you lived with. As you can imagine, anything concerning the Japanese is read with interest in Malaya. I understood the point you were trying to make—indeed made—but some of us aren't too fond of the Japanese, any Japanese. What I'm trying to say is, if you play by the rules, you'll get all the cooperation we can safely give. But this is not a so-called popular war of liberation no matter what Chin Peng's propaganda says. If there's even a hint about the 'poor' Communists, I'll personally escort you to the airport and make sure you're never allowed back into Malaya."

"You don't have to worry about that, Chief Inspector," said Luke, choosing to ignore the tacit threat to press freedom because she had no alternative. "That series about the Japanese family was a one-off. The ship I mentioned earlier that the Camerons were on, the one my father skippered: that's now at the bottom of the Timor Sea, thanks to the Japanese, and so is my father."

"I'm sorry," said Hyde. "That's something I didn't know. Now I suggest you return to your hotel and give Harry Cameron a call. I'll be in touch."

Luke spoke to a houseboy and, immediately afterward, to Jessica Cameron at a few minutes before four o'clock the same afternoon. Jessica remembered her almost immediately, thanks to Luke's unusual given name and her insistence on being called Luke. Jessica also said that she and her husband would be delighted to see Luke on the estate whenever Luke could make it. Putting her up was no problem; they had plenty of room. It would be a great pleasure to have a house guest.

Luke had showered and changed her clothes, and was having a light dinner in the Regency when, shortly before ten P.M., two Malay policemen burst into the dining-room, carrying rifles. Directly behind them came Bill Hyde. He crossed swiftly to the table where she was eating alone.

"You're luckier than you know, if luck you can call it. We're on our way to the Camerons' now. They came under attack fifteen minutes ago."

Luke knocked over her wineglass in her anxiety to get to the door.

"Let me get a camera," she called.

"You've got a minute," said Hyde. "*Gopoh, gopoh!*"

15

"You must remember her," said Jessica, a few moments after she put down the telephone on Luke. "A lovely little dark-haired child, full of mischief. Hated being called Lucasta. We read that series she did about the Japanese family outside Hiroshima. I didn't make any connection with the names at the time, of course."

"Christ, Jess, that's sixteen years ago. I can hardly remember what happened last week apart from Billy Hemmings being killed down at Ulu Pangam. Anyway, why are you telling me all this?"

"Because she's coming to stay with us for a few days, perhaps longer. She's going to take some photographs and write about how the planters live with the Emergency."

"Can she shoot?"

"Harry, dear," said Jess gently, "that wasn't the first thing I asked her."

Jessica had found Harry sitting on the verandah with his feet on the balustrade, looking out across the lawn. On his lap was a U.S. Army-issue Colt .45 automatic, with a spare clip for the weapon in the top pocket of his bush jacket. By his side lay a Lee-Enfield .303 rifle and a Sten gun. In a basket on his other side sat three hand grenades, with 7-second fuses, like oversized hen's eggs. Jess didn't scoff at such precautions. Although it was almost unheard of for the terrorists to attack an estate house in broad daylight, it wasn't unique. She herself never went anywhere without a .38 Webley in a canvas holster strapped to her hip. The days for being squeamish about guns had passed. If she were only supervising the collecting of flowers from the garden, or collecting them herself, she took the basket containing the grenades. She knew how to remove the pin and throw one with a reasonable chance of destroying what she aimed at. Elsewhere in the bungalow, apart from Harry's collection of hunting rifles and shotguns, there were two Brens and enough ammunition to ward off anything but the most determined siege until help arrived. The bungalow was the last line of defense, if any attacker got beyond the Malay Special Constables in their sandbagged bunkers. Each constable had a hand-held gong which he sounded once every half hour after dark, the signal that all was well. If anyone missed his cue, a full-scale alert was implemented.

"Which reminds me," said Jess, "Luke must have met Dan also. That was the voyage we first met him, wasn't it?"

Harry didn't hear her above the sudden roar of aero engines. As she spoke, a flight of RAF Spitfires, Merlins snarling, swept overhead only feet above the trees, beating the way for two lumbering Dakotas, though it was known that the terrorists didn't have anti-aircraft guns. Still, the Dakotas, used for dropping leaflets and, occasionally, as "voice" aircraft, with an officer on a loud-hailer calling on the terrorists to surrender, were slow and, at the altitude they flew, vulnerable to machine gun fire from the ground. Harry was far from sure how much good the leaflets did. They advised, so far without much success, terrorists "without blood on their hands" to give themselves up. It was also ironic, Harry often thought, to see so many aircraft carrying RAF roundels. There had hardly been any in Malayan air space until near the end of the war against the Japanese.

"I was saying," said Jessica, removing her hands from her ears, "that Luke must have met Dan also. It was coming back from Karachi that we first met him, if you remember."

"If you say so." Harry got to his feet. "I'm going to lower the flag."

"A little early, isn't it?"

"I don't want to get into the habit of lowering it at the same time every day. Any habits I pick up, the terrorists might pick up also."

The raising and lowering of the Union Jack, hung from a thirty-foot pole in the middle of the lawn, was a recent innovation. Before the Emergency Harry hadn't felt it necessary to trumpet his loyalties. Now he did, more as a gesture of defiance than anything else. The flag was hoisted as soon after first light as was practicable and lowered any time before dusk. An identical ceremony was enacted on every estate where the owner or manager owed his allegiance to the Crown, and some American managers of plantations and mines did the same with Old Glory. No one thought it absurd.

Unless Harry was absent or incapacitated, only he reefed in the Union Jack. Jessica accepted this display of eccentric bravado on the part of her husband without demur. Other wartime guerrillas, when available, scouted with Ferret Force, but Harry had realized from the unit's inauguration that he was far too old to spend what could be weeks living rough in the jungle. He could play his part in protecting his own property and family, but that was as far as it went. Apart from anything else, if he had a recurrence of his malaria while on patrol, he would become a liability.

Jessica's heart had gone out to her husband when she observed him defer to advancing age. It hurt more, she could see, that Dan Holden was a fully-fledged member of Ferret Force, though as yet there had been little for Dan to do. He and others like him in Paselabilan were waiting for the arrival in the state of the 1st Battalion the Royal West Bedfordshire Regiment, fresh out from the U.K. and now undergoing acclimatization and rudimentary jungle training in Johore.

The police had their own trackers, Dyaks from the Iban tribe in Borneo, who were reputedly brilliant. They were strange little men with long hair dangling down their backs. They carried blow pipes armed with poison darts, gleaming jungle knives, and were said to collect the heads of their victims. Jess wasn't sure what impression they would make on the Communists but, by God, they terrified her. Then again, this was a war of terror, fire fighting fire. Billy Hemmings had been decapitated when ambushed on his rounds, and his wife was now hospitalized suffering from a nervous breakdown. His daughter and son-in-law had vowed publicly, in the press and on the radio, that they would not be driven out of their home, but how long that attitude would last no one could possibly tell. Independence for Malaya was still many years away, but when it came, with it would come an inevitable policy of Malayanization, whereby European planters would be replaced by Malayans if they chose not to take out Malayan nationality. Many managers probably wouldn't, would go "home," back to the U.K. The independents such as Harry would have the choice of Malayan citizenship or forming a new company where key positions would be held by Malayans, to comply with the law. Harry thought he could live with that. There were always ways of circumventing the letter of the law when a lot of money was involved. As for the managers, American and Australian as well as British, Jessica occasionally wondered why they stayed on and risked their lives. Sheer bloody-mindedness, she supposed.

After completing their afternoon rounds and ensuring that estate workers in their care were safely locked up in their compounds for the night, at six o'clock Jeff and Mike drove up in their armored Ford, which was nothing more than a production line Ford reinforced externally where possible by sheets of steel plating. Over the windscreen was an ingeniously designed latticed grille, also steel, which could be opened and closed from within the vehicle at the tug of a cord. When only the pair of them were traveling, the non-driver always sat in the rear seat, a Sten by his side. The driver kept his own submachine gun next to him on the front passenger seat.

While Mike went immediately to the telephone to call Diana, Jeff poured himself a drink and sank into an armchair, making his report to his father and mother. Along with other planters, Harry had experimented with wirelesses in all estate vehicles, in order that the drivers could keep in touch with each other and base when out on rounds. The experiment had proved a flop. Without a huge aerial, which was impractical on a moving vehicle, the jungle had the effect of muffling signals more often than not.

"Some trees slashed on the north side," said Jeff wearily. "About a hundred. They won't produce again. As usual, nobody saw anything."

"Any casualties?" asked Harry.

"None reported. There were quite a few Specials around. Must have scared them off. Still, those trees were producing yesterday. We have to assume Lee Swee Peng is in the area. Time to circle the wagons, as Dan would say."

"Did you see Dan?"

"At the estate office, drumming up morale. Some of the clerks are getting nervous about sleeping there overnight. He'll be along later."

On returning from America Dan had intended remaining in Mahal Rumah until he realized he was being foolish. Two Malay constables guarded the house as a matter of course, but more couldn't be spared. If the terrorists attacked in strength, he'd be in trouble. Furthermore, splitting forces was poor strategy. The Camerons might need his assistance as much as he might need theirs. So he let his servants go, keeping them on half pay until he could take them on again, and moved into one of Harry's empty bedrooms. If the terrorists wanted to burn down Mahal Rumah, there was nothing he could do about it.

Mike came in from the telephone and poured himself a whisky.

"Is Diana all right?" asked Jessica. "Her mother and father?"

"Yes," nodded Mike. "I'd like to go up and see her at the weekend if you can do without me for forty-eight hours. I'll leave with the Malays when they change shifts and join a convoy in Kuala Kelan."

"That shouldn't be a problem," said Harry. "God knows, we've got to try and live some kind of normal lives until we can get the upper hand."

Dan arrived at six forty-five and dinner was at seven fifteen in order that the table could be cleared and the servants escorted to their own quarters before it got too late.

Harry was right, thought Jess while coffee was being served, in saying that they should all try to live some kind of normal life. Although the Emergency was only a few weeks old, the strain was already beginning to show on her sons' faces. On Dan too, who had lost a lot of weight and who seemed constantly on edge. She understood why; the whole family did. Dan wanted to be out there hunting the terrorists, hunting Hamid in particular. For him, the arrival of the Royal West Beds could not come too soon.

They never discussed Hamid by name any more, and Jessica, at least, tried hard not to think about him. He was Jenny's flesh and blood but he was also a killer; he had to be caught. She sometimes found herself wishing that he would be shot dead in the jungle or, a treachery she never revealed to a soul, that he had escaped to Thailand and was taking no further part in the terror. What she would do if he were captured and brought to trial she didn't dare think.

At eight o'clock the searchlights were switched on. Dan and Jeff escorted the servants to their quarters and checked that the generator house was secure. Then Dan, Jeff and Mike drove as far as the barbed-wire barricade at the entrance to the drive and confirmed that the sentries were awake and alert. From eight fifteen onward, when they returned to the bungalow, all doors and windows would be locked and bolted, all shutters closed.

Lights-out was generally any time between ten P.M. and midnight, depending upon how tired everyone was. They had considered someone remaining awake all night and rejected it at the start of the Emergency. The Malay policemen were there for that purpose, and a rubber plantation could not be run efficiently if the owners were exhausted.

Between last rounds and whenever they went to bed, they usually sat in the sitting-room and talked. Whisky was drunk sparingly.

It wouldn't do to be intoxicated if there was an attack. Whenever anyone moved out of one room into another, even if it was only to the cloakroom or the lavatory, his weapon went with him. The men took it in turns to ensure that the Bren guns—one behind sandbags, in the window of the upper storey observatory, and one in the room immediately to the right of the front door—were well oiled and functional, that the magazines were full. From time to time the wireless would burst into life with a nearby neighbor establishing that all was well, or the police station doing the same thing. There were few phone calls at night. Mike was the only one who made them or received them regularly, in order to have some private conversation with his fiancée. She generally called at nine thirty on the dot. Punctuality meant more than politeness these days; it could be the difference between life or death.

By twenty minutes to ten the telephone hadn't rung, and Mike was getting edgy.

"Take it easy," grinned Jeff. "She's probably in the bath."

Mike didn't want to panic but resolved to give Diana two more minutes only. But before thirty seconds were up he heard a voice coming over the wireless transceiver, which was switched to loud-speaker when no one was actually on watch. Even though the set was twenty yards from where he was sitting, and behind a half-closed door, he recognized the voice as Diana's.

He leaped to his feet and ran to the radio room. His parents, brother and Dan were instantly alert. This was out of the ordinary, and anything out of the ordinary had to be viewed with alarm.

They couldn't hear what was being said until Mike closed with: "I'll get back to you."

"What is it?" asked Harry.

"Diana's been trying to get through on the phone for the last quarter of an hour. Her line's not cut. She tried another number. It must be ours."

A well-rehearsed plan went immediately into action. On her way to the radio room, where she would operate the set if necessary, Jess threw a master switch which instantly extinguished all internal lights save two on dim bulbs, one in the hall and one above the wireless. Flashlights were always kept in the same place, next to the gun rack. Dan grabbed the nearest and ran upstairs, to the Bren in the observatory. Harry took up position behind the second Bren. Mike and Jeff, both with Sten guns, went to adjacent rooms at the rear of the house.

There was no point yet in radioing the police station at Ruang, which was in direct contact with Kuala Kelan headquarters. The Communists had given up sabotaging telephone lines unless they had cause to suspect an estate's wireless was out of action. The line could be down for reasons unconnected with terrorist activity.

But it wasn't. Cautiously Dan opened one section of the huge observatory window and pulled back the shutters. As he did so, he caught sight of a flash of gunfire coming from behind the summerhouse, which since the Emergency had been sandbagged to chest level and turned into a fortified bunker, and which was always occupied by two Malay policemen. A fraction of a second after seeing the muzzle flash, he heard the throaty rattle of a machine gun.

The searchlights made the lawn as bright as day. Dan had to shield his eyes and peer beyond the pools of light. The terrorists, at least those within his field of vision and numbering, at a rough guess, six or eight, were attacking from the jungle fringe, their immediate target being the policemen in the summerhouse, who were giving as good as they got. The terrorists all seemed to have automatic weapons, some heavy, probably Bren guns. He debated holding his own fire until he could see what he was aiming at. Then he thought, the hell with it. The police would be expecting support and might get scared if it wasn't forthcoming.

Dan pulled back the cocking-piece and let fly. Each 28-round magazine held tracer in a ratio of one in five. His first burst arced over the summerhouse and was way off target. He adjusted his sights and fired again. Pretty red lights like a fairy bridge hosed into the fringes of the jungle. A second later his own position came under attack and glass in the picture window to his right shattered.

Downstairs in the radio room, her heart thumping wildly, at the first sound of gunfire Jessica called up the police station at Ruang and told them what was happening. With an effort she managed to keep her voice calm. "I'm logging this call at 9:46," she concluded.

"We'll have someone with you as soon as we can," said the policeman at the other end, equally calm, and sounding for all the world as though he'd been contacted about faulty plumbing.

Jessica's function from now on was to stay with the radio. Absentmindedly she wondered if she should call Diana Ashford and let her know that the bungalow was under attack. She smiled when she realized how idiotic that notion was. The air-waves were open. Half of Paselabilan would know precisely what was going on by now and would keep the frequency clear unless they, too, were besieged.

Harry heard Dan open fire above his head and a moment later the sound of shattering glass. He had his own window and shutters open, but he couldn't see anything to shoot at; the terrorists, those who had revealed themselves up to now, had the summerhouse between him and them. He had to get outside, on to the verandah, which itself had sandbags running its length to the height of the balustrade.

Keeping low, he picked up the Bren and bipod with one hand and an ammunition box containing six full magazines with the other. In all, the weight he was carrying amounted to some forty pounds. It felt like forty ounces. The adrenaline was flowing.

He unbolted the main door and wrenched it open. Behind him he thought he heard Jessica calling something, but he wasn't sure.

Still at the crouch, he ran along the verandah, to his right, until he could see beyond the summerhouse. Then he folded the bipod and placed the Bren on top of the balustrade. Terrorist fire was still hosing over his head, in Dan's direction. And those bloody windows were going to need the attention of an expert glazier. He wondered if his insurance policy covered replacements. He also wondered if the six to eight terrorists out front were the total complement. He rather doubted it.

At the back of the house Mike and Jeff could hear the commotion behind them. So far, however, no terrorist fire was being aimed at them. Nor, as far as they could judge, were the guards at the barbed-wire barricade under attack. Mike hoped to God the Malays at the end of the drive and those outside Mahal Rumah knew their job and would not be enticed out of position, even if they didn't fire a shot or have one fired at them all night.

"It's all out front," he called to Jeff.

"I think you're right."

"Can you hang on here? I'll see if I can give Dad a hand. Give me a yell if you come under fire."

"You'll be the first to know."

Mike ran toward the front of the house. At least one terrorist heavy machine gun was strafing the ground floor now. Glass shattered and a fusillade stitched its way across the upper shelf of a bookcase as he made his way toward his father's post. En route, he looked in on the radio room. He could barely see his mother in the dim light, but she gave him a wave to let him know she was fine, and sitting over the wireless, waiting. Not for the first time in his life he recognized her as being a marvellous woman, not just his mother.

Mike was momentarily alarmed to see the front door ajar and no sign of his father until he realized that Harry Cameron was not the sort of man to cower behind sandbags and wait for targets of opportunity. He ran on to the verandah in the same second as one of the searchlights received a direct hit and went out, and the bungalow came under attack from the other side of the lawn, five or six guns by the sound of it. The terrorists had split their forces, six or eight on one side, five or six on the other. Mike sincerely hoped that that was all. The summerhouse was already in the crossfire and they could well do without another dozen Chinese attacking Jeff's position.

"How's your mother?" shouted Harry, as Mike took cover at the other end of the verandah from his father.

Mike elected to hold his fire for now. A Sten was very useful for house clearing and in a confined space, but its range was limited and the nearest patch of jungle a hundred yards from his side of the verandah. The Brens were the weapons to sort out the attackers for the moment. He wondered, in passing, if Dan, overhead, had seen the new threat and would move to another part of the observatory. He needn't have bothered. Even as the thought occurred, he heard Dan's Bren open up on the left-hand group.

"She's fine," called Mike. "She's doing her Marconi act. Are you okay?"

"Never felt better in years." Harry punctuated his enthusiasm with a short burst into the jungle. "These buggers don't know what they're doing. I've half a mind to douse the lights and get among them."

"Don't even think about it," said Mike. "If this attack follows the pattern we've heard about on other estates, they'll pack it in before long. They'll know the police are on the way."

"Not necessarily," Harry reminded him. "They cut the phone wires. That means they think the radio is out of action."

"So they made a mistake. Thank God they're capable of one."

"I'll second that, but you're missing the point. They won't be expecting the cavalry. They could stick around until the police are halfway up the drive. That's what I meant about getting among them. The more they keep shooting, the more chance there is of one of us getting hurt."

In the radio room, a policeman from Ruang came through and

asked Jessica what she estimated the size of the attacking force to be. Jess said she'd find out and made her way toward the front door. On her hands and knees she relayed the policeman's question.

"Ten to fifteen," said Harry just as a machine gun tattooed a dozen neat holes in the woodwork above Jess's head. Without a word she shook the splinters from her hair and returned to the wireless, where she passed on the information.

After thirty minutes the terrorists' fire had diminished to a trickle. They were still there but they were conserving their ammunition. So far they'd hit nothing apart from glass, woodwork and a few books, and they couldn't cross the lawn and launch a full-scale assault because of the searchlights, only two of which had they succeeded in putting out of action. Nevertheless, thought Mike, his father was right. The police from Ruang wouldn't be on the estate for another half hour, and they'd only be a small force as Ruang was a sub-station. The main force from Kuala Kelan could be a further thirty minutes even assuming everything was running like clockwork. There was a chance of somebody getting hurt.

He had an idea that might swing the battle in the defenders' favor. If they extinguished all the searchlights—suddenly and completely—and then raised their voices in feigned panic to give the terrorists the impression that the generator and auxiliary generator had failed, there was a possibility that they would come out of their funk-holes and approach the bungalow under cover of darkness. Give it a couple of minutes, say, then snap on the lights again. With luck they might catch some of the bastards in the open.

He crawled across to his father and explained what he had in mind.

"Might work," said Harry. "How was it you never accepted that commission?"

"Dad," said Mike patiently, "can we talk about that some other time? I think we should still leave Jeff as backstop, just for safety's sake, but bring Dan down with us. If it works and they get close, he won't be able to bring his Bren to bear from the observatory. Mum can do the lights. Okay?"

"You're the boss. You tell them. I'll stay here."

Mike was away five minutes. When he got back Dan was with him and Jessica within earshot, standing over the switch that controlled the searchlights, waiting for the signal. Dan and his Bren took up a position at the other end of the verandah from Harry.

"Now," said Mike.

The entire lawn area was immediately plunged into darkness. On cue, Harry, Dan and Mike started calling to one another. As acting performances, Mike was to think later, none of them would have got anywhere near the nominations, let alone the Oscar-winner's rostrum. But most of their Chinese adversaries would certainly speak English. Jess added her own twopennyworth by letting loose an ear-piercing scream that was unscripted and didn't do much for anyone's nerves.

"For Christ's sake, what's happened to the lights?"

"I can't see a damned thing!"

"They must have hit the generator."

"Do something, for the love of God!"

It seemed to be working because, after a brief fusillade when the lights went out, all shooting from the jungle ceased. The defenders peered into the darkness, but it was impossible to see anything. To keep up the illusion of panic, they fired a few rounds themselves, deliberately aiming high.

Mike couldn't see his wristwatch and counted up to two hundred slowly. They were the longest three minutes he'd spent since Normandy. If the Chinese were coming, they'd be in the middle of the lawn by now. In any case, he couldn't afford to wait any longer.

"Any time you're ready, Mum."

Jessica hit the switch. The searchlights came on as a battery to reveal, to those in the bungalow, a truly gratifying sight. On Harry's side, six armed Chinese were thirty yards to the right of the summerhouse and sixty yards from the bungalow, caught well and truly, he thought with grim satisfaction, with their trousers down. They froze when the searchlights came on. Harry was also temporarily blinded and he blinked a couple of times before squeezing the trigger of his Bren. At that range he couldn't miss. He saw the bullets thump home. Two of the attackers were tossed backward as though jolted by a sudden surge of electric current of huge voltage. They both twitched on hitting the ground but after that didn't move. A third man was wounded in the thigh. He fell but had the wit or desperation to begin crawling for the nearest patch of jungle. Then the Malay policemen in the summerhouse figured out what was happening and swung their own weapons on the three survivors, who themselves were heading at top speed for the trees. These three were lucky. At least they didn't appear to get hit. But they abandoned the man with the thigh wound, who was finished off by one of the Malays as he crawled like a shore-bound amphibian for the security of the shadows.

The attackers approaching the bungalow from the other side of the verandah were closer than sixty yards but at a more acute angle than their comrades. There were four of them. Three were emphatically Chinese, but the fourth, equally obviously, was a Malay. Mike couldn't be sure because it all happened so fast, but he'd have staked a lot of money that the Malay was Hamid.

He and Dan opened fire in unison. Characteristically, the Sten jammed after a couple of rounds. Rather than try and clear the stoppage, Mike threw it down and unholstered his revolver.

Dan raked the quartet with his Bren, but his aim was off. He hit only one of the Chinese, who fell with a loud scream. The other three reacted very fast. Instead of retreating the way they had come, they ran at an angle toward the bungalow, trying to put it between them and the Bren gun before Dan could get in a second burst. One of the Chinese was slightly behind his two companions. He had his arm raised. Mike knew the gesture only too well.

"Grenade!" he yelled, and ducked down behind the balustrade and the sandbags, with Dan only a fraction of a second behind him. The grenade was thrown but exploded harmlessly on the far side of the barricade.

Dan too had recognized one of the attackers as non-Chinese. After the grenade detonated, cursing, he heaved the Bren on to the sandbags and started to climb the balustrade, anxious to give chase. Mike grabbed him and pulled him back. Just in time. The quartet in the open was not the full terrorist force. They had left two men at least in the jungle as cover and, now that the surviving trio were out of the line of fire, these two opened up on the verandah with unnerving accuracy, hacking out chunks of wood and masonry above Dan's head. Had he been straddling the balustrade, he would have been shot.

"That was Hamid, fuck it!" he swore.

"I know, I know. But he's long gone now."

"They must have crossed in front of Jeff. Why the hell didn't he shoot?"

Although it took twenty minutes for them to realize it, that was the end of the battle. The Chinese had cut their losses and fled. Half a dozen Specials from the sub-station at Ruang were the first to arrive, and they were joined forty minutes later by Bill Hyde with three times that number. Before then, however, the defenders could not afford to relax, or reconnoiter to see if anyone they'd hit was still alive.

Leaving Dan and his father at either end of the verandah with their Brens, Mike went to check on his mother and Jeff. Jessica was fine if slightly shaken and pale. Jeff was another matter. Mike found him crouched beneath the window, his back to the wall. His Sten was beside him. It had not been fired.

"You okay?" asked Mike.

"They ran across in front of me," whispered Jeff, his voice scarcely recognizable, "but I couldn't shoot. I don't know what the hell happened, but I just couldn't pull the trigger. All I could think was, if I shoot at them, they'll shoot at me."

Mike averted his eyes. He'd seen extreme fear before and it was never a pleasant sight. It was even worse to witness it in one's own brother. He sometimes forgot that Jeff had spent the war behind a desk in London, out of choice. It wasn't his fault he was scared. Some people were, some weren't, and most, like himself, were frightened but overcame their fear. A cowardly streak could no more be changed than red hair and freckles.

"You won't say anything, will you?" pleaded Jeff. "Not to Dan or Mum, but especially not to Dad."

"The Sten jammed," said Mike. "It often happens. So did mine. We're going to have to see about getting a few more Brens or the Patchett I've been reading about."

By four A.M. Bill Hyde had scouted the area, posted perimeter guards and was reasonably satisfied that the surviving terrorists were now many miles away. He and his men would check the jungle fringes at first light just in case any wounded had been left behind, but he rather doubted, judging from Harry's report, that they would find anything. Luke had been introduced, or rather reacquainted with, the Camerons and Dan, and Hyde had given his permission for the house lights to be switched on.

Of the four men who had been shot, all were dead. Hyde ordered his constables to drag them to one side of the bungalow for identification. He had to speak rather sharply to Luke when the Australian journalist kept getting in the way to take her photographs. None of the dead was a pretty sight, but their mangled corpses didn't seem to affect Luke in the least. Hyde surmised that she saw them the way a painter saw nudes, as arrangements of texture and light. Still, he admired the no-nonsense manner in which she went about her work. Her only comment was that flash photography invariably lacked depth of field.

Two of the men Hyde recognized from his wanted posters, two he did not. None of the four was a kingpin, Lee Swee Peng or

Abdullah bin Halim, but a body-count of four was an excellent night's work whichever way one looked at it. It would do wonders for morale, and not only among the planters.

"You're in for a reward," he said to Harry. "They're not top-liners, but even the dregs come in at five thousand dollars a crack."

They were in the sitting-room or, rather, scattered around it and the adjacent library: Hyde, Harry, Dan, Mike, Jeff, Jessica, a couple of Hyde's European officers. Luke was talking to anyone who would talk to her, anxious to get full details of the battle while it was fresh in everyone's mind. There was a whiff of slightly hysterical excitement in the atmosphere, similar, Jessica thought, to that she'd experienced in London after the Luftwaffe bombed; idiotic jokes made people laugh more than usual. They had fought the good fight and won. Even Jeff was back to normal, though he glanced away when he caught Mike's eye.

Jessica had roused the servants and got the kitchen organized. The servants didn't object in the least. As loyalists they would have been murdered had the fight ended differently.

Huge plates of sandwiches and pots of coffee appeared at regular intervals. Harry made sure that the policemen outside, particularly those who had defended the summerhouse, were not overlooked. There was whisky and brandy for those who wanted them; most did.

"Plus fifty dollars for each automatic weapon and a dollar per bullet," went on Hyde. "We haven't counted those yet, but you're twenty thousand minimum up on the night. Say three thousand pounds in all. Not bad. You could make a living out of this."

"Can they come back tomorrow?" asked Mike, which everyone thought uproariously funny.

Mike had just left the wireless room after talking to Diana. Hyde's men had hogged the air-waves for an hour after they arrived, giving details of the fight to headquarters. Listening in, Diana had known long before Mike called that there had been no European casualties, but it was a relief to hear his voice. She told him she loved him, unconcerned that her admission was being overheard by several hundred pairs of ears. Mike reciprocated, equally unworried. He said he would see her at the weekend.

"One of the kills was down to the Malays in the summerhouse," said Harry. "Is there anything in the rules that says they can't share five thousand dollars?"

"There is," said Hyde, "but we'll work something out."

Hyde was interested in the apparent sighting of a Malay terror-ist; they were few and far between. Could it have been Abdullah bin Halim? It could not, Dan and Mike agreed, both being familiar with Abdullah's wanted portrait. This terrorist was much younger. If it wasn't Hamid, it was someone very like him.

"And the bastard got away," said Dan angrily. "Mind you, if Mike hadn't dragged me back, I'd probably now be another statistic."

Luke's journalistic antennae twitched.

"What's so special about Hamid?" she asked innocently.

"Nothing," said Dan.

Luke left it. She'd fallen on her feet by actually meeting Dan Holden, and there would be other times to broach the subject.

A little later she collared Harry. Although like any good journalist she knew the answers to some of the questions she was about to pose, it was Rule One that you appeared ignorant and got the subject to talk about himself. Harry was slightly drunk, part whisky, part tiredness.

"Let's see if I've got this straight," said Luke. "I'm new here so excuse me if I seem to be ignorant. The Malays and the non-Communist Chinese are going to take over this country sooner or later anyway. That's been decided or will shortly be decided in London. Only the timing has to be worked out. If the Communists win, they'll take over. Whatever happens, one day the Europeans will not wield the power they do now."

"They don't wield that much anyhow," said Harry. "There are sultans, princes. A British High Commissioner, when we get another one, admittedly, and British advisers in each state . . . "

"That's not what I mean," interrupted Luke. "I mean the way of life. Any dark-skinned country, once it gets independence, is not going to take kindly to its citizens functioning as no more than lackeys to a white community."

"Right," agreed Harry.

"Then I don't see the point," said Luke. "What can it possibly matter to you, or any other European stroke white man, who wins? You're in the front line. I can see that for myself." She gestured around her at the bullet holes, the broken glass. "But your days are numbered. Why bother?"

"Because we're not about to be beaten," said Harry. "It may sound paternal, but what would happen to the non-Communist Malayans—not Malays, understand—if the Communists win? It's a bit more complicated than that, but that's broadly it."

"Still sounds like capitalism to me," said Luke provocatively.

Harry roared with laughter.

"So it is, so it is. What's wrong with capitalism? There are Malay capitalists and Chinese capitalists, some of them doing a hell of a sight better than I am. Anyway, what's the alternative? As long as we're here, the terrorists are going to try and kill us. We might as well try and kill them first."

"You could leave, sell up. I'm not expert, but from what I've read there are people, wealthy Chinese mostly, who are willing to buy rubber estates. Why take chances?"

"What country were you born in?" asked Harry shrewdly.

"Australia."

"Your father?"

"Australia also."

"Your grandfather?"

"England."

"And what nationality do you think of yourself as being?"

"Australian."

"Exactly," said Harry. "Except you're not. Your Aborigines are Australian. You're English twice removed."

"Clever," said L/uke.

"Not intended as such. Just practical. We live here," said Harry. "I was born here. So was my younger son. I'm not going to be chased out. Whatever happens after independence, the Camerons aren't leaving. You can bet your boots on that. There'll be change, certainly, but we'll adapt to it."

"On the record?" queried Luke.

"On the record," nodded Harry.

Luke made a note on a her pad before switching tack.

"They were talking about Hamid across the room earlier," she said casually, "but I didn't quite hear it all. Mr. Holden seemed particularly upset. Can you give me the details?"

Forty minutes later, as dawn was breaking, Luke had most of the story. What she didn't have was Hamid being Harry's grandson. Excusing herself, she sought out Jessica.

"In all the excitement I haven't really had a chance to thank you in person for agreeing to put me up."

"Don't mention it. We're delighted to have you. I'm just glad you didn't arrive yesterday."

"I'm not," said Luke with feeling. "However, that's part of the problem. Chief Inspector Hyde informs me the roads aren't safe to travel alone, but he dragged me out of my hotel so fast last night that I only had time to snatch a camera. All of my things are still in Kuala Kelan. I can't bother the chief inspector again, but your husband said something about Mr. Holden occasionally running the gauntlet into Kuala Kelan."

"Hardly running the gauntlet." Jessica frowned. "I'm not sure I should be telling a journalist this, but Dan is part of Ferret Force. He's in Kuala Kelan periodically talking to the advance party of the Bedfordshires. The rest of the battalion is due here in three weeks or so. Dan will then join it, at least for a time. He'll be travelling into Kuala Kelan on Friday, when the Specials change over, and probably come back the following day. You could possibly go with him if you can do without your things for the time being. You can ask him, anyway."

"I will."

She did. In fact she spent forty-eight hours asking him because, at first, he wasn't keen on the added responsibility of a woman passenger. But in the end he relented, partly because he recognized, as she did, that there was some sort of chemistry between them. For his part he considered ninety percent of the formula to be loneliness. For her, he was an attractive man made more attractive by his recent bereavement. She was also a woman with a normal sexual appetite and it had been too long since her last affair. Jessica saw what was going on almost at once and passed it on as tea-time gossip to her husband.

Thus none of the Camerons was entirely surprised when Dan and Luke—"the Testament Twins," as Jeff quickly dubbed them—did not return to the estate immediately from the capital. Nor were they more than mildly shocked when, the day after they got back, Luke made her apologies and announced that she was moving her belongings over to Mahal Rumah, which Dan was reopening. She still wanted to report on the activities of the estate, if that was all right with the Camerons. It was. Their only concern was the security problem. Dan solved that by teaching two of his male servants how to shoot and allowing them to live in.

"A damned good thing," declared Harry. "That's just the sort of young woman he needs to help him forget about Barbara."

"It wouldn't have happened before the war," said Jessica primly, but mostly for the sake of form. She liked Luke, she liked Dan. And Luke was much more spunky than Barbara had ever been.

"It won't be for long anyway," said Mike.

Nor was it. The Royal West Beds arrived four weeks after the attack on the bungalow. Dan joined them in Kuala Kelan. Luke went with him; there were other parts of Malaya to see and report on. Mahal Rumah closed its shutters.

16

Regularly from September onward, frequently with precious little rest between sorties, Dan accompanied patrols of the Royal West Bedfordshires in their area of operations, northeast Paselabilan in the region of the Gulangor Pass, a natural divide through which a road had been constructed prior to World War Two. Flanking the pass were two major mountains, Gunong Kesenangan and Gunong Sa-tuju, roughly translatable as Mount Peace and Mount Harmony. One was 2,800 feet in height, the other 3,200. Primary jungle covered much of each, and that was bad enough. But secondary jungle, virgin jungle that had been cleared and allowed to grow again, covered huge tracts of the lower slopes, and that was much worse. There were few trails. Those that existed had to be treated with caution for fear of booby-traps. Where there was no obvious path, a track had to be hacked out with parangs and machetes. When that was the case, covering a thousand yards a day was considered good going. It was suspected that the terrorists had a major base somewhere in the area, but no one had been able to find it. Small wonder, Dan often thought. In this sort of terrain it was better to be the pursued than the pursuer. He remembered only too clearly how he and Harry, Bill Hyde and the other members of Cameron's Cossacks had evaded the Japanese for three years, and the Japanese had understood the jungle. Most of the newly arrived soldiers did not.

Many were National Servicemen, what he knew as draftees, youngsters conscripted for a two-year period and largely shoved into infantry regiments whether they liked it or not. Few were older than eighteen or nineteen, and the junior officers, some of them also draftees and upon whom so much depended, were the same age. All were green. Four weeks in the jungle warfare school at Kota Tinggi in Johore couldn't turn them into seasoned fighters.

During the day they suffered almost constantly from what they quickly came to call "jungle blues," a peculiar state of melancholy brought about by living in a perpetual twilight, and at night the cacophony of jungle noises scared them half to death and largely kept them from enjoying the deep sleep they needed in order to be efficient. Add to those factors the need to operate in silence, permanently wet feet, jungle sores, mosquitoes, leeches, the decaying smell of rotting vegetation, the shivers from the regular evening downpour and the threat of snakes, and Dan wondered how these people could hope to defeat the likes of Lee Swee Peng. Or how to help them. About all he could do was tell them to watch him and the Dyak trackers, and the Malay Special Constables who sometimes came with a patrol, and do as they did; teach them the rudiments of survival, and hope for the best.

Behind his back, using the few words of Malay they had picked up in Johore that had nothing to do with ordering beer or enquiring how much a whore charged, the troops called him *Berdarah Penganiaya*, which was as close as they could get to "bloody slave-driver."

He did drive them too. Officially he and several others like him from Ferret Force were with the regiment as advisers, which meant, in practical terms, that he went wherever the commanding officer wanted him to go, or elsewhere if he thought the CO was making a mistake and could convince him as much. Some of the senior officers and NCOs had served during the war in Burma and India, and it was with these men, paradoxically enough, that he had the least trouble. They were only too aware how lethal the jungle could be for the uninitiated and attended his lectures at the regiment's permanent base in the Batu Mersa barracks with enthusiasm. The junior officers, the platoon commanders, were also keen to learn anything that might help save their lives and those of their men. But there were a handful of middle-ranking field officers who looked upon him as an uncouth know-all, and an American uncouth know-all at that. Somehow one or two of them had learned that his wife had been murdered by terrorists and that he was in this for personal vengeance, which went against the Code. Nor did they approve of his appearance. He invariably didn't bother to shave unless his beard became an irritation, and the weapons he sported made him look like a brigand. They avoided him in the mess when the regiment was in barracks and steered clear of him in the tented encampments the regiment sometimes occupied when on local field-and-firing exercises. Being ostracized didn't bother him; he knew that few armies were fond of irregulars, who some-how managed to break rules that, if broken, would mean a court martial for anyone else. In any case, not many of them would sur-vive their first encounter with the enemy if that was their attitude.

Two, a major and a captain, the company commander and his 2 i/c, did not.

On Operation Hector in October, an incursive drive centered on the Gulangor Pass where the regiment was supported by a battalion of Gurkhas and one of Guards, the leading company's vehicles came under fire from ambush before the debussing point was reached. The terrorists had set their ambush cleverly, but predictably, on a bend in the road. They raked the vanguard vehicles with machine-gun fire but failed to hit the drivers. Thus the vehicles could have continued, which was what Dan had told them to do if caught on a bend. Instead—on the company com-mander's orders—they stopped and the men piled out, heading for the supposed safety of the jungle on the opposite side of the road to the terrorists and impaling themselves on sharpened bamboo spikes smeared with human excrement placed in the undergrowth. The major and his second-in-command were among those to die, but they took three soldiers with them and a fourth and fifth were badly wounded. What was more, because the leading vehicles stopped they blocked the road. The follow-up companies were forced to halt also, the rearguard half a mile from the vanguard. By the time the troops got their bearings, the terrorists had gone. These were the regiment's first casualties, and it shook them.

There were other things the troops had to learn. Dan had warned them until he was purple in the face not to step off jungle trails even if they were faced with a pool of water a foot deep. Their damned feet were wet anyway, weren't they? What the hell did it matter if they got wet further? But still the soldiers found it hard to break the habit of a lifetime, that of automatically avoiding puddles or pools. And the terrorists, knowing the idiosyncrasies of the British as well as those areas of jungle trail where water naturally gathered after a downpour, booby-trapped either side of various pools with land-mines. When a man stepped sideways, he was on his way to his Creator, usually in fragments. Men lost life and limb because they wouldn't listen or couldn't learn the lessons. Dan had no doubts that the British Army, given time, was as good as any army on the planet and better than most. But the terrorists were not about to give it time and the jungle was unforgiving of the incautious.

Other booby-traps were not so easy to read without the eye of a hawk and the acumen of a Comanche warrior. A favorite terrorist stratagem was to fill a sack with fifty pounds of earth in which were embedded iron spikes. The sack was tied to a long rope of vines and suspended, hidden by the foliage, from a tree. The other end of the rope was attached to a trip-wire, which, when sprung by the leading man of a patrol, caused the sack to swing into the remainder. Fifty pounds of earth were enough to take a man's head clean off his shoulders, and it was a cheap method of terror.

The regiment had some success late in November when, acting on information received, two companies raided a terrorist encampment near the Lamir Caves on Bukit Lamir, killing two and capturing one and uncovering a cache of ammunition and tinned food. But in the attack—two hundred men against three—the regiment lost a subaltern and a corporal. The men still hadn't learned that this wasn't a street fight in England or maneuvers on Salisbury Plain, that the enemy was ruthless and playing for high stakes. For many of the troops, half the time their minds were on getting the patrol over and done with and returning to Batu Mersa, to beers in the Naafi, the latest film and the latest screen goddesses.

But the Lamir Caves encounter *was* a success, and elsewhere other regiments were having their own, thanks partly to the new High Commissioner—Sir Henry Gurney, who had arrived in October—insisting that everyone in Malaya carry an identity card; insisting also on powers to deport any undesirable who was not a Malayan citizen and implementing Regulation 17D, whereby inhabitants of whole villages could be placed in detention if the High Commissioner's office was satisfied they had abetted or were in any way connected with the terrorists.

Ferret Force was gradually wound down as the army gained expertise, although volunteers, while no longer under contract, were welcome to stay on or return on a casual basis from time to time, as and when needed.

Two weeks before Christmas 1948 Dan found himself in Kuala Kelan on his way back from Johore, where he had spent ten days lecturing to jungle warfare instructors. He'd been dropped in the capital by an armored patrol of the Seaforths, which was going no further. Now he needed a lift home.

Dan called in at police headquarters to see if Bill Hyde had anything going down to the estate. Hyde's deputy told him that the chief inspector was out.

"He's having lunch with a friend of yours, actually, Mr. Holden. Luke Ross."

Dan fingered his beard. He had a three-day growth. He also smelled a goat, and everything in his bag smelled like a herd of them.

"Do you know where they are?"

"They're at the Regency." Hyde's deputy didn't have to check his pad. "Miss Ross is staying there."

He hadn't seen Luke since August; he hadn't even known if she was still in Malaya. She'd promised to keep in touch but there was no way, she'd said, that she could guarantee her movements. At least not for now.

"I've got to go where the job takes me. When I've got enough material I'll go back to Australia for a while. The people who market my stuff are excellent, but the bastards who run the newspaper industry have different ideas from me about what makes a series. I have to raise my voice at them every so often. But I'll be back. As they say in Hollywood, this war will run and run."

There were many, many more uniforms on the streets than the last time he was in Kuala Kelan, Dan reflected as he made his way to the hotel. Taking advantage of the new regulations, patrols were stopping Chinese and Malay civilians at random and demanding identity cards. Military Police were also present in greater numbers than he remembered, but for different reasons. They guarded the red light districts of Chinatown, which was out of bounds to soldiers of every rank. A man with his trousers down was a perfect target for an assassin, and Chin Peng was known to use whores as informants.

Dan made directly for the dining-room, which was half-empty. The maître d'hotel came toward him, more, Dan suspected, to forbid such a scruffy individual access than to offer him a menu. Dan studied him coldly without breaking step. The man dropped his eyes and backed off.

Hyde and Luke had reached the coffee stage of their lunch. They were sitting at a table away from the window. In fact, everyone was sitting at a table away from the window. Although it was covered with wire mesh as a precaution against a grenade attack, they hadn't invented the mesh that would stop machine gun bullets.

"I'll take mine black, no sugar," he said, sitting down.

Luke stared at him. "For Christ's sake, Holden, you look like you died a week ago."

Hyde had to leave after fifteen minutes. Dan promised to call in on him later and bring him up to date on events in the northeast.

Luke signalled for another round of drinks after the policeman had gone, a brandy for her, a whisky and beer chaser for Dan.

"On my room number," she said to the waiter when the drinks arrived.

"They'll have to be," said Dan. "I've got about ten dollars and change in my pockets."

"Think nothing of it. It's tax deductible. Now, where the hell have you been? I mean it, you look terrible."

"You first. Mine's run of the mill stuff."

"Okay. Since I last saw you I've been back to Australia twice, mostly to punch a few jaws. I flew into Singapore two days ago and hitched a ride with some British soldiers up here. Christ, are they horny. I got propositioned every five miles, sometimes by youngsters who didn't look as if they were shaving yet. Did you see my stuff about the raid on the Camerons?"

"No, I haven't had a good look at a newspaper or magazine for weeks."

"Pity. You figured very prominently. Anyway, what with that and some material I collected while in Johore, I became the flavor of the month. At the last count I'd been syndicated to sixty different outlets throughout the world. The checks are rolling in like merry hell. And they want more, which is why I came back. 'Five thousand words plus pix by our glamour girl with the troops.'"

Luke rolled her eyes in mock dismay, but Dan could tell she was delighted by her success.

"No, that's not altogether true, why I came back. I did so partly to earn my bread and butter and partly to see if you'd managed to avoid the bullet with your name on it. I called Jessica yesterday. She said she didn't know where you were. They've been having some fun down there, by the way. Jess said the bungalow came under attack three times in October, all unsuccessful though no more kills for our side. Since then, nothing. Bill Hyde, so he just told me, considered the Camerons a front line target and gave them another dozen Specials. They've also got half a company of soldiers on the estate—not just for their protection, of course, but as a base to strike against Lee Swee Peng.

"Hyde reckons Peng has changed his tactics. They tried to scare off the planters and it didn't work. Sure they killed a few and a few more tappers, but rubber's still being produced and no one's run for cover." Luke shook her head. "As another colonial I'm not that fond of colonials who are so obviously British, but you've got to admit that when they get stuck in nothing's going to move them.

"Now there are more soldiers in Malaya, it will probably never work, jitter tactics on the planters. Peng'll keep on hitting the estates and the tin mines, of course, but it's getting more dangerous without producing the desired result. He's better off ambushing army convoys and attacking isolated police stations. Hyde reckons he can't win now, not in this state, but the thing is neither can the British, not for years. It's a stand-off for the moment. Peng's also troubled by deserters. Those leaflets that the Dakotas drop and Harry Cameron's always scorning are having some effect. Terrorists without a capital crime against their names are starting to surrender. Not many, but enough to worry Lee Swee Peng. There are rumors that he's begun executing his own men, waverers. There are other rumors that Gurney is about to start clearing the squatters away from the jungle fringes, move them to what he calls New Villages. Heard anything about that?"

Dan had. There were half a million squatters, mainly Chinese, who had lived at the jungle's edge since before the Japanese invasion, occupying land to which they had no title, living in bashas or kongsis, communal huts which could house several families, and eating what they could fish out of the sungeis or pick from the trees. They were a natural target for the terrorists, being made to give food or information concerning troop movements, occasionally money. Anyone who didn't comply was murdered or mutilated. Gurney's plan was to shift them all, lock, stock and barrel, to proper villages, real housing, with armed guards to protect them. They would still be able to fish or collect fruit, but they would no longer be a source of information to Lee Swee Peng, or other leaders in other states. At a stroke, the terrorists would lose a valuable source of supply.

"I've heard something about it," said Dan cautiously.

"Jessica's invited me for Christmas," said Luke, changing tack with bewildering speed. "If I'm here. There's no reason why I shouldn't be, but I'm not sure I'll go."

"Why not?"

"Where will you be? What about those children of yours?"

"I'll be with them, in the States."

"Why can't I come? I could do some business in the States."

"In Texas?"

"Okay, I can't do any business in the States. Where's Texas, anyway? But I could come. You could pass me off to your kids as their new governess."

"My kids, as you call them, are not that much younger than you."

Luke spluttered over her brandy goblet.

"Jesus, Holden, are we going to start all that again? If you think it's too soon after your wife died to introduce another woman into your life, I'll accept that. But forget the age bullshit. You're forty-two, I'm twenty-six. So what? My first lover was a man older than you are now when I was younger than I am now. Is that English?"

"It's never going to win a Pulitzer. Is this a spur of the moment decision?"

"Yes."

"Well, you're honest."

Luke recoiled in mock horror. "Never say that to a journalist. It offends them. It's like telling a nun she has impure thoughts. Well?"

"What about your piece entitled: 'Christmas With Terrorism— A Review of the First Months'?"

"Don't be cynical, it doesn't become you. Are you checked in here, by the way?"

"No."

"Good. I've got a big double room—I like to spread myself around—and you need a bath and a shave."

Dan shook his head. "This is Malaya, not New York. If you don't want to find yourself the object of gossip from one end of the state to the other, I'd better take my own room."

Luke was surprised to see he was serious. "I didn't know you were that conservative."

Dan grinned. "I'm not. I just told you I've only got a few dollars on me. You'll be paying for my room as well as your own, and once I've ruffled the sheets I don't expect to be seeing mine again."

"In that case get yourself a cheap single. I suppose I'll be paying for your laundry as well?"

"Somebody had better. If these clothes aren't cleaned soon they're going to march away."

"You've lost weight," Luke was saying half an hour later as Dan emerged from the bathroom, a towel wrapped around his middle, newly shaved and bathed and drying his hair. Half the dust and dirt of Johore had vanished down the waste pipe.

Luke had considered joining him in the bath before realizing that he probably needed a little privacy in order to clean up. But she had taken advantage of his absence to undress. Now she was lying naked under a single sheet.

"I mean it. You've got positively skinny."

"It's the jungle diet. Is there anything to drink around here?"

Luke sat up, allowing the sheet to fall from her breasts. She tossed her head impatiently.

"Christ," she said petulantly, only half of it feigned. "Here I am lying waiting for you and all you can think of is booze."

Dan turned to face her. Now that he was shaved she could see that there were huge dark rings under his eyes. He looked exhausted.

"To tell you the truth," he said, "I need the drink. This may sound crazy considering the time we spent together a few months ago, but you're making me nervous. I guess that doesn't sound very masculine."

Luke could have bitten her aggressive tongue off. Here was a man almost straight out of the jungle after witnessing Christ knows what horrors, and she was behaving like a nymphomaniac. And not a very intelligent nymphomaniac at that. If a man had spoken to her, treated her like a chattel, the way she'd just spoken to Dan, she'd have shown him the door in double-quick time.

"On the contrary," she said softly. "It makes you about five times as masculine as any other man I've ever known. In the matter of a drink, I'll join you. It's in the bathroom and I'll do the honors. Whisky okay?"

"Whisky's fine."

When she returned she was carrying two glasses and a bottle of Black and White. She had wrapped a spare towel around her, knotting it across her breasts.

"There's bound to be an answer to this," said Dan, who had drawn up a chair and was sitting at a small table, "but why do you keep the whisky in the bathroom?"

Luke sat opposite him and poured the drinks.

"Force of habit, old journalist's trick. If you leave it in the open it drops an inch a day whether you've touched it or not. In some countries the staff think it's part of their perks. I stash it under my dirty linen. They'll no doubt find it, but at least they'll know I'm on to them. It may make them think twice. I'm not stingy but I don't like being taken for a ride. Cheers."

They each drank their drink in one gulp. Luke re-poured.

"Rough?" she asked after a moment. "And I'm not talking about the scotch."

"I know. Not as rough as the war, the Big War, I mean, but I was younger then. And not rough at all in some respects. I can get out. The soldiers can't. I can get the hell out of Malaya, for that matter. Christ knows, I'm rich enough. Harry and Jess can't. It's just that I started to think on the way up from Johore. What's the point? When I came back from the States after Barbara was buried, I guess I had some crazy idea that I'd find her killer, execute him, and then everything would be okay. Abracadabra. An eye for an eye. But it's not going to be that simple. I'd forgotten what the jungle was like, its density. I may never find Hamid. Maybe nobody else ever will. If they do and kill him, will that be enough?"

"You said execute," said Luke. "That's a curious expression. It implies formality. It also implies solitary formality. *You'd* execute him, not the state or the security forces."

"I'm not as exact with words as you are. It's all a lousy waste, that's what I mean. I kill him, Peng kills Harry, Mike kills Peng. Abdullah kills—well, you." Dan looked at her with mournful eyes. "Well, it's not impossible."

"No, it's not."

"Can I have some more of that?"

Dan pushed his glass forward. Luke refilled it.

"The children," said Dan, "Laura and David, asked me before I came back: 'Why are you going, Dad?' I thought I knew why, but I'm no longer sure I do. Here am I pursuing a vendetta, and there are they growing up without me. I've only spoken to them three times since August. You'd think I'd have more sense, wouldn't you? I'm not immortal. I could get killed. Oh, yeah, I think I know the ropes, but if I get careless or a terrorist gets lucky, my children are orphans. Laura, who's brighter than David, also said: 'Mom's dead. There's nothing you can do to change that.'"

"Does that mean you won't come back after Christmas?"

"No, I don't think it means that at all. You don't know this, but I pulled every string I could to get into World War Two. Barbara couldn't understand why I wanted to put my neck on the line. I said I needed the excitement. She said I was being selfish. Maybe she was right, but I'm coming back."

"I'm glad, not only for selfish reasons. I'm probably not even as bright as David, but I think there's something here you've got to do, or find out with absolute certainty that it can't be done. Never mind that you're forty-two," Luke smiled, "and according to Holden's Anatomy damn near over the hill. Unless you see it through it'll gnaw at you for ever."

"You're probably right."

"I'm glad you see it like that."

Luke stretched forward around the table, reaching for Dan's hand. Inadvertently her own touched beneath the towel. He had a huge erection.

"My, my," she said, her eyes widening with surprise and sudden lust, "what big teeth you have, Grandma. Unless I'm being too pushy or miss my guess, it's time for bed."

"Maybe not bed," said Dan roughly, his voice husky with need. "Lose the towel."

Luke whipped it away in a single movement. Dan eased the chair he was sitting on against the wall and, still sitting, untied his own towel.

"Jesus," whispered Luke, eyeing his penis.

Dan opened his arms and beckoned her urgently. Luke stood up, crossed to him and straddled him, taking his whole length inside her without preamble and locking her long legs in the rungs of the chair for support. She leaned backward while he held her hips, pressing the palms of her hands against his shoulders. Because of the way he was sitting, only she could move with any real freedom. She gave her hips full reign, pumping slowly to begin with but then faster. Dan watched her with a glazed expression, his own pleasure heightened by hers. She shook her head like a mad woman as she galloped toward orgasm. Her pupils dilated until only the whites were visible and then she'd gone somewhere, somewhere beyond her eyes. She began bucking like a horse and urging him to come, to fill her. He removed her arms from his shoulders and placed them around his neck. He dragged her mouth toward him, kissing her on the lips. She had to pull away, unable to breathe, as she climaxed with an intensity that almost made her faint with delight. A moment later he ejaculated fiercely and with a loud cry. This brought her to a second orgasm which she achieved while throwing her head back and tossing it wildly as though in pain and, before he had finished, a third. She went almost out of her mind with excitement as he came again, an orgasm he didn't know he was capable of until it happened.

Gradually their breathing returned to normal. Luke put a middle finger between their legs. She then placed the finger in Dan's mouth and kissed him through it. He was still inside her, not hard but not entirely soft either.

"I'm not sure I should be saying this, Holden," said Luke after a while, when they were lying side by side on the bed and sharing a glass of scotch, "but I think I'm half in love with you, if not more than half. Does that bother you?"

"Not at all. Tell you what, let's talk about it over Christmas, in Texas."

In February 1949, in the camp near the village of Lembingan on the state border, Hamid witnessed his first execution of guerrillas by other guerrillas.

Two of Lee Swee Peng's Chinese had been caught by perimeter guards trying to abscond. At least, that was Lee Swee Peng's interpretation of events. The men, one not much older than Hamid, protested their innocence, but they could give no convincing reason why they were leaving the camp without orders. Peng refused to accept their explanation that they were merely going hunting, but their fate was finally sealed when a British surrender leaflet was found on each of them. Peng set up a formal court martial. There could only be one verdict, and they were found guilty.

They could not be shot. Rifle bullets were scarce and, in any case, it wasn't always possible to know if the security forces were in the neighborhood, troops or police who would automatically investigate any sound of firing. Shooting was also too clean a death for traitors, as Peng raged in an hour-long harangue during which the prisoners, tied to trees as was the custom, were spat upon and generally defiled with excrement and the bloody entrails of dead animals. They would be hanged.

The sentence was carried out the morning after the verdict at first light and the whole camp summoned to witness the proceedings. The older man, though plainly frightened, went to his death with dignity, refusing even at the last to confess his errors or beg for his life. The younger man screamed and pleaded for mercy as his hands were lashed behind him and a rope placed around his neck. The logs on which they stood were then kicked away: Their bodies thrashed for several minutes afterward. They were not so much hanged as strangled. Hamid suspected that this was deliberate. There had been other defectors before the dead men, but they, succumbing to the promises of a fair hearing in the leaflets dropped by airplane, had got clean away. Lee Swee Peng was determined not to let it happen again.

Hamid never wondered whether the British promises to "those without blood on their hands" were genuine. He would not surrender as the leaflets urged. He was a murderer with a price on his head. For him there was only the jungle and the mountains until the guerrillas won the war or he was killed. He thought the second alternative more probable. It had almost happened during the first attack on the Camerons' estate, when he had barely escaped the fearful machine-gun fire coming from the verandah after the searchlights came on. It had almost happened several times during ambush. There were moments when he didn't care if it did.

In eight months his enthusiasm had waned. He still believed in the cause, that the British should be driven out of Malaya; he found it hard to live the way the Chinese did. Now that the squatters were being driven away from the jungle fringes, food—especially rice, the staple—was becoming more scarce. There were days when each guerrilla hardly had enough to eat to sustain life, especially such a demanding life. Lee Swee Peng didn't seem to think it mattered. The camp routine never varied regardless of the food stocks. There were drills in the morning, physical exercises in the afternoon. When an operation wasn't planned, there were lectures on military procedure and, most of all, Communist doctrine and the duties of a comrade. Textbooks and pamphlets printed on presses hidden deep in the jungle close to the Thai border were issued at intervals by the Central Committee, and every man in the camp had to learn their contents by heart. Those who couldn't read were taught by those who could. Every man had to subject himself to criticism and be prepared to criticize others, even his close friends.

Hamid had no friends and, cleverly, Peng had deduced that the youngest member of his guerrilla force was wavering. Not enough to surrender; Hamid could never do that. But enough to make him a liability on operations. Frequently, therefore, Hamid was left behind, to act as a sentry or help clean up the camp, for cleanliness was important.

For his part Hamid recognized that the emotion he often felt was one of loneliness. Apart from Abdullah bin Halim, he was the only Malay—or part-Malay, he occasionally had to remind himself—with Peng's guerrillas. But Abdullah, more often than not, was not true to his upbringing. When meat was available it was usually wild pig. Abdullah ate it heartily, and so did the Chinese. Hamid could not. Although he had no religious beliefs, he had been raised more a Muslim than anything else. Pork was forbidden.

There were women in the camp, exclusively Chinese women varying in age but usually in their twenties. Some took an active part in operations or acted as go-betweens, linking the guerrillas with the Min Yuen; others just laundered and cooked. Unless they were married to a male guerrilla or so involved with one, and only one, that marriage would one day be a formality, promiscuity was not encouraged and indeed punished if discovered. Women were comrades and had to be treated with respect. Sometimes, especially when a man and his woman retired to their own hut, Hamid felt a terrible need to be close to a member of the opposite sex. Not just for physical release—in part, masturbation (again discouraged but impossible to stop) provided the answer to that—but for the companionship of a female his own age. That was impossible, of course. A Chinese woman wouldn't look at him even as a permanent partner and there were no Malay girls with this guerrilla band or any other. There were no females his own age.

Hating the Camerons and wanting them dead, particularly the memsahib and the tuan, all seemed so long ago. There were times when he could barely remember why he hated them, or sustain the hate when he did. So he went from day to day, from morning to dusk, simply doing what was asked of him, and doing it mechanically. When it rained, he sheltered. When the British were near, he hid. When there were fish to be caught, he trapped them; when fruit was needed, he climbed trees. That was his whole life.

By May the house Mike was having built for himself and Diana was almost complete. It was located one hundred yards down the main drive from the bungalow and on the other side of it from Mahal Rumah. Watched over by armed guards, contractors from Kuala Kelan had begun clearing the jungle and laying the foundations in January. The finished structure would be nowhere so grand as Dan's place or as large as Mike's parents', having only four bedrooms and four reception rooms on two floors. It was designed, however, in such a manner that it could be added to when circumstances permitted or when children arrived. The armed guards had proved unnecessary; the terrorists hadn't attacked the workers or the partly completed house. Apart from the presence of soldiers and police on the estate, it wasn't hard to guess why. When it was finished, it would become a juicier target than the bungalow or Mahal Rumah because it was so obviously built for just two people, and therefore two defenders. Except the terrorists were going to be unlucky. Mike and Diana had no intention of moving into it by themselves, on a permanent basis, until it was safe to do so. They'd wanted their own place to exist instead of having to start from scratch when the Emergency was over, but for the time being they would stay, after the wedding and honeymoon, with Harry and Jessica.

The wedding date of Saturday, June 18, had been agreed before Christmas, when Diana's parents, due to her father's continuing ill-health aggravated by the Emergency, announced that Frank Ashford was retiring in June 1949 on three-quarters pension. He and Melani were going to live in Western Australia. The Batu Mersa estate would be taken over by another company manager. Thus there was no reason for Mike and Diana to delay their marriage beyond June. The ceremony would take place in the main Protestant church in Kuala Kelan because it was easier for the guests, coming from all over Malaya as well as a few from England and Australia, to get to the state capital and arrange accommodation there than it was to use the church in the smaller town of Batu Mersa. Diana would drive down the same morning from Batu Mersa with her father and an armed police and army escort. The reception was to be held on the *padang* of the Planters' Club. The honeymoon would be in Europe and Jeff Mike's best man.

Accompanied by her mother, Diana had already spent a month in London and Paris earlier in the year, choosing and being fitted for her wedding-dress and the rest of her trousseau. Knowing that Frank Ashford was not a wealthy man, Mike had offered to foot the bill for the trip. Diana's father wouldn't hear of it.

"It's a generous thought, Mike, but a gesture I can't accept. Diana's my only daughter. I've had a few thousand put away since before the war for just this occasion."

"You didn't mind me asking?"

"No, I appreciate it."

Jessica was good-humoredly concerned about a European honeymoon.

"Now remember what you're there for, if you understand me. Don't go boring the poor girl stiff by making her walk the battle-fields."

"As if I'd do such a thing."

"As if you wouldn't."

Harry overheard the conversation.

"You seem to be implying that the Cameron men aren't romantic. If I remember correctly you didn't have any complaints on that score when we got married."

"I didn't have time to complain."

Harry rolled his eyes. "There's no pleasing them, Mike. If you sweep them off their feet they're being rushed. If you plan everything down to the last detail you're temporizing."

Whenever Diana felt Batu Mersa could spare her, she travelled down by train—now generally agreed to be the safest means of getting from one major town to another—to see how the house was progressing. Like her mother, like Jessica, and like all women in Malaya during this period, she went nowhere without a pistol strapped to her hip and a rifle or shotgun close by. Mike wondered jokingly where she would keep her handgun on the day they were married.

"Under my dress, in a holster next to my thigh. Or down my stocking."

"That has to be one of the most erotic images I can think of, having your 'something blue' as a Luger next to one of the best-looking thighs in the state."

"And the 'something borrowed' can be an army-issue Sten. Luke will have a field-day with her camera."

There was a time, in January when Dan and Luke returned from the States, that Diana, who had become very friendly with the Australian woman, thought that she and Mike would be beaten to the altar. It hadn't happened. Luke confided in Diana that, while she had got along famously with Dan's children, who didn't seem to resent her interest in their father at all, neither she nor Dan felt the need to get married. They were in love with each other and, for now, that was enough. She stayed at Mahal Rumah as a matter of course whenever she was in the area, and no one any longer raised an eyebrow. But she had her career to think about.

Wedding or no wedding, the terror did not abate. Exact casualty figures were hard to come by and speculation by newspapers frowned upon by the authorities, but it was generally reckoned by those in a position to hazard educated guesses that, in the first eleven months of the Emergency, between three and four hundred civilians had been killed—native tappers as well as European planters and miners—a hundred policemen, and sixty to seventy military personnel. Officially, the terrorists were estimated to have lost, in the same period, five to six hundred killed, four hundred captured, and two hundred surrendered. Most Europeans took these latter category figures with a pinch of salt. If Chin Peng was losing men at such an alarming rate, he should hardly be able to mount a serious attack any longer. Except he could and did, regularly.

Possibly because of the presence of so many soldiers and police on the estate, the Camerons were only raided twice in the opening months of 1949. One was a daring daylight attack on the estate office in February, toward noon when the morning's work was almost over and everyone tired. As a preamble, moving swiftly but silently the terrorists rounded up six tappers virtually under the noses of some Special Constables, soaked them with petrol and set fire to them. When the Specials and half a platoon of the Royal West Beds, hearing the screams, went to investigate, the terrorists, a dozen of them, stormed the estate office, in which Jeff and his father were going over some figures. Although frightened out of his wits by the sudden ferocity of it all, Jeff grabbed the estate office Bren and, with a young European clerk, Ken Oates, carrying a Sten, in tow, left the office by the back door and took up a firing position behind some sandbags. He'd emptied one magazine without hitting anything and was on his second when the soldiers and the police, realizing that they had been duped, back-tracked and caught the terrorists with crossfire. The Chinese ran off, leaving two of their number dead. Apart from the murdered tapers, these were the only casualties of an assault that lasted less than five minutes.

When it was over and Jeff and Ken Oates returned to the estate office, they found Harry calmly reloading his Sten and three glasses of whisky on the desk. Harry took one and indicated that Jeff and Oates should take the other two. Jeff needed both hands to guide the glass to his mouth; even then, because he was trembling uncontrollably, he spilled some. He wasn't alone. Oates' teeth chattered against the rim of his own glass, revealing how scared he'd been. Only Harry seemed unaffected and, after a moment, Jeff caught his father studying him, a peculiar expression on the older man's face. It took Jeff some time to work it out.

"He thought I'd run for it," he said to Mike later. "When I went through the back door, he thought I'd skipped out on him."

"You're imagining it." Mike tried to make light of the incident, though he would not have wagered a lot of money that Jeff was wrong in his assessment. "He didn't say anything, did he?"

"He couldn't, not in front of Oates. Anyway, he didn't have to say anything. I could read what he was thinking."

"I'll have a word with him."

"And say what? It's bad enough as it is. If he thought I'd been talking to you, it would only make matters worse."

Mike felt deeply sorry for his brother. Although their father would never see it, it had taken a lot of guts for Jeff to snatch up the Bren and get out behind the sandbags.

The second attack came at night in March, but thanks to one of Bill Hyde's informers this one was expected.

Together with the company commander of the Royal West Bedfordshire detachment, Hyde set a trap for the terrorists by pretending that the troops were moving off the estate for a sortie elsewhere, suspecting that the bungalow was under observation. The troops piled into trucks and left just before last light. A mile up the highway to Kota Napek they parked their vehicles and returned to the estate on foot and noiselessly, concealing themselves in the jungle some distance from the bungalow. When the attack began, the terrorists were not only quickly outnumbered but caught in a vise, which was gradually tightened. They lost five men that night against two military casualties, neither fatal. Harry also lost a few more panels of glass. Dan Holden examined the corpses when it was all over. No Hamid. For that matter, no Lee Swee Peng or Abdullah. The king rats were letting the minions do the hard work while they did the planning. Or, more likely, there were small killer squads operating away from the main terrorist base and operating independently.

As usual after an attack was successfully repulsed, the house was thrown open and coffee, sandwiches and spirits served. Because there were so many people around, Mike didn't notice for half an hour that his brother had slipped away. He found him in his bedroom, nursing a bottle of scotch.

"You're missing the celebrations," said Mike casually.

"I doubt the celebrations are missing me." Jeff looked a wreck. His face was flushed, his speech slurred. He was also drinking the whisky straight from the bottle.

"You're imagining things."

"That's your answer to everything, isn't it? My imagination. Well, it won't wash. I didn't imagine becoming immobile the moment the first shots were fired. I froze again, Mike. I couldn't pull the blasted trigger. I knew we outnumbered them and that the army would probably polish them off before they got anywhere near the bungalow, but I froze."

"I didn't see it."

"How could you? You were out on the verandah playing commando." Jeff's tone was one of sneering, bitter reproach, but Mike chose to ignore the remark. After a moment Jeff apologized. "But that's half the trouble, nobody seeing me. If someone would spot me cowering in a corner and pin the official label of coward on me, at least it would be out in the open. Then I wouldn't have to pretend any longer."

"You're not a coward, for Christ's sake. You proved that last month outside the estate office. You've got to try and understand the difference between being scared and being a coward."

"Is there one?"

"Of course."

"Do you understand it?"

"I think so."

"And Dad?"

"Dad's a law unto himself. He's like Great-grandfather Richard Cameron in that respect."

"And I'm like Grandfather Edward, a builder of observatories."

"Don't be ridiculous. Anyway, Dad doesn't feel fear, not the way the rest of us do. Half the time, this is all an adventure to him. Oates was scared outside the estate office, wasn't he?"

"Oates is twenty years of age. He's also not a Cameron. The trouble with you is that you don't know what it's like to be frightened. Never mind Great-grandfather Richard, you're like Dad and Jenny, and Mum to a certain extent. They left one of the moving parts out of me when I was constructed."

"Balls."

Mike lost his temper—only momentarily, but he very emphatically lost it. He could take most of his brother's faults but not drunken self-pity. Besides, unless he snapped out of it, his mother or father might begin to wonder before long where their sons were. If either of them, but especially his father, caught Jeff in this mood, words could be said that were irretractable.

"The trouble with you is that you think there's only one form of cowardice, the lack of physical courage. There are more, many more. I damned near didn't get engaged to Diana because I was too slow asking. When you get right down to it, I was frightened of being rejected. What if she says no? I kept asking myself. Can I have some of that scotch or are you determined to hog it all for yourself?"

Jeff passed over the bottle. Mike took a long swig.

"What you need is a break," he said. "It was my turn to go to Singapore next week to have our regular argument with the shipping agents. Frankly I can do without it. Why don't you go in my place? It'll mean three days away from here. Book yourself into Raffles and find a friendly girl, European for preference. It'll do you the world of good. I'll square it with Dad. What with the new house, I've got enough on my plate here."

Jeff took his brother's advice, but he didn't check into Raffles when he left the train. Instead he instructed the taxi driver to take him to the apartment Barbara had leased, and which still had two years to run. Although he had been to Singapore several times since her death, the thought of visiting the apartment had never occurred to him. It was as though it had gone with her. Now he remembered otherwise. He still had his key and the lease had been paid for out of Barbara's private funds. Apart from himself and the landlord, no one knew it existed.

After he had completed his business on the second day he was there, he picked up a Canadian girl travelling alone, in Raffles. She was due to fly to Hongkong the following morning, and that suited him perfectly. Once dinner was over, he had no difficulty in persuading her to come back to "his apartment." There he made love to her until the small hours in the bed he had once shared with Barbara. It didn't trouble him, as he felt sure it would not have troubled Barbara. The girl had gone before he woke up the following morning.

Between March and the week before Mike's wedding he only managed to visit Singapore twice more. On both occasions he picked up a girl, neither time a Chinese or a Malay, and took her back to the apartment. In some way he could not define precisely, it made him feel secure that he had a bolt-hole that was totally private. It also made life on the estate more tolerable.

17

Whatever Jeff's shortcomings in other directions, he took his responsibilities as Mike's best man very seriously. Emergency or no Emergency, what the state of Paselabilan needed was a bloody good society wedding whereby everyone could forget for a while that the country was under siege. Harry and Jessica, Frank and Melanie Ashford, Mike and Diana, all agreed. It would be a marvellous boost for morale and one in the eye for the terrorists, showing them, if they needed any further showing, that life went on regardless of what they did.

With this in mind Jeff was full of advice for the guest-list long before the event. It wasn't possible to get the High Commissioner because they knew him only vaguely through meetings between the Planters' Association and his office; nor did they want to invite senior European civil servants and administrators because, to most planters, they had all been too slow in recognizing the Emergency for what it was way back the previous June. His Highness the Sultan of Paselabilan, whom Melanie Ashford had known for years because her father had taught him how to play polo, was considered then struck off. Although he had been a popular ruler before the Japanese war, and still had friends among the polo-playing fraternity, post-war investigations revealed that he had been a little too hospitable to the invaders, cooperating fully to protect his interests while his subjects suffered. He'd also been slow in releasing land he owned to rehouse the jungle squatters.

Those groupings aside, however, anyone of any importance, and quite a few who were not so important, would be invited. Ranking military personnel, and junior officers who had made themselves well-liked; senior policemen and some not so senior; middle-division civil servants, Malay and Chinese as well as European; planters; miners; bankers; personal friends of both families. In spite of the climate the occasion would be formal; morning dress for the civilians, uniform for the military and the police. As bridesmaids Diana chose the two young daughters of one of her mother's friends in Batu Mersa, Amanda and Zoe Lockyer, aged fourteen and twelve respectively. Their dresses, scaled down versions of Diana's but in pink, had also been bought during Diana's European trip, and altered to fit them. Only half seriously, Diana invited Luke to be senior bridesmaid. Horrified, Luke begged off. "Pink doesn't suit me. Besides, it's a working day for me. You wouldn't want to deny yourself the opportunity of being seen in sixty magazines and newspapers worldwide, would you?"

The first list came to four hundred and sixty guests, which turned Frank Ashford the color of clay when he calculated the cost of feeding and wining such a number. Then they took the scissors to it with a vengeance and got the final count down to two hundred and eighty.

"Better keep all the army and police personnel in," cautioned Jeff, when Ashford thought he could see a way of making it two-sixty. "We don't want to jeopardize our escorts."

It was originally suggested that Melanie Ashford stay overnight with the Camerons and travel with them to church on June 18. Melanie rejected the idea. She wanted to be with her daughter until the last moment. After all, she said, three days after the wedding she and her husband would be on their way to Australia. God knows when they would see each other again. With her own escort and the bridesmaids, therefore, she would set off from Batu Mersa half an hour ahead of Diana and her father.

Whenever Mike and Diana managed to snatch a moment alone together, they both marvelled at the number of people they knew; or in some cases did not know.

"Who's this?" asked Mike, perusing the guest-list.

"Who's who?"

"Sandra McKenzie."

"I went to school with her, in England and here. She and her parents run an hotel in the Cameron Highlands."

"Why aren't her parents on the list, then?"

"They were, in the original four-sixty. Before Daddy started counting the dollars. Besides, I don't know them that well."

"I don't know *anyone* that well," confessed Mike. "A few of the other planters and a couple of policemen. It strikes me that this wedding is more for your mother and father and mine than for us."

"Aren't they all?"

"I've no idea. This is my first."

"And last, I hope."

"You can guarantee it. I wouldn't go through all this again for a pension."

"It's that streak of romance in you that I think I love. Getting nervous?"

"No."

"Liar. But, if you're not, I am. I'm also beginning to think that we should have had a quiet civil ceremony with just friends and the families. In fact, I suggested as much to my mother last week when I was trying on my dress and finding that I seem to have put on about five pounds in all the wrong places since I last wore it. Do you know what she said?"

"Tell me."

"My dear, it's just jitters. In any case, it's too hole-in-the-corner, a civil ceremony. Everyone would assume you were pregnant."

"You're not, are you?"

"Not at the last count. Would it bother you?"

"Not really, but I'd like a couple of years to ourselves before children. It's not much of a world, anyway, to bring kids into. I was reading somewhere the other day that the Americans are now working on something called the H-bomb, which makes the A-bomb look about as lethal as a bow and arrow."

"I can't see it changing in a hurry," said Diana. "Anyway, that's probably what Og said to Mrs. Og a million years ago in their cave. 'Let's not have children yet, darling. It's not much of a world now that Glug's invented the wheel, never mind the price of dinosaur cutlets.'"

Mike wasn't keen on having a stag-night until Jess insisted.

"We've got to do this thing properly. It's not every day you get married."

"It's not *any* day *you* get married."

"I'm one of the world's natural bachelors. I'll leave it until I'm forty-five or so, and then find someone about thirty-five who won't expect me to be a paragon of virtue. Now, about dates. It would be ideal if we could make it the 17th because everyone who's coming will be around by then. But that would mean you being in a hell of a state on your wedding-day, which would also mean Diana using me as a punch-bag. So, either the 15th or the 16th. Whichever date, there won't be more than a handful of people who live locally present."

"I'd prefer it if it was only you and me, Dad and Dan."

"Don't be a spoilsport. Who do you think the wedding's for, anyway?"

They made it the 15th in order that everyone could recover in plenty of time from any hangovers they acquired and decided to stay in Kuala Kelan overnight rather than risk the roads after dark. Jeff booked a private room for dinner in the Imperial, Kuala Kelan's best hotel, and bedrooms for himself, Mike and Dan. The other guests made their own arrangements. Harry declined to attend for the sensible reason that he could hardly leave Jessica alone under the circumstances. To make doubly sure his parents were safe in the event of an attack, Jeff arranged with the company commander of the Royal West Bedfordshire detachment for him and his platoon commanders to sleep in the bungalow.

There were twenty guests at dinner, though shortly afterward Mike managed to count twice that number. Whenever his glass was empty, Jeff or whoever was nearest filled it up.

After dinner Jeff produced two Malay whores whom he'd smuggled in through a side entrance after bribing the armed policeman who guarded it with fifty dollars. Jeff had cleared the girls for security with Bill Hyde beforehand. They were both in their late teens and possessed a beauty that would soon vanish but hadn't yet, and they worked out of a Malay club in the red light district where business had been poor since the Emergency. They had a floor-show which consisted of them undressing one another to tinny gramophone music and performing various sexual acts, one of which involved covering themselves and anyone else they could persuade to join them in scented oil. Somewhere around 1 A.M. Mike remembered being manhandled toward them and being relieved of his clothes, but recalled nothing else until he woke up in bed with a raging thirst. The bedside clock said it was 2:45 A.M.

After stumbling to the bathroom and drinking copious quantities of water, he staggered back to his bed. When he climbed between the sheets he found someone lying next to him. Although the figure was fully dressed, an exploratory hand established that it was a woman.

He snapped on the bedside lights and sat up, suddenly very sober. The bastards had put one of the Malay whores in with him. Except the woman wasn't Malay. Next to him was Luke Ross, snoring her head off.

Mike left the bed as if stung, knocking his portable alarm to the floor. A split second later, the door was flung open. In the corridor stood Dan, his expression grim, brandishing a shotgun. Behind him was Jeff.

"Jesus," said Jeff, "what the hell have you done?"

Mike was naked except for his shorts. He also reeked of scented oil.

"For Christ's sake, Dan," he said, "I've no idea how Luke got in here."

"Tell that to the horse marines. You bastard," growled Dan, advancing on Mike, who backed against the wall. "You're not content with screwing those two hookers downstairs, you want icing on the cake."

"Take it easy, Dan," soothed Jeff. "He was probably too drunk. We don't know that any harm's been done."

"The hell we don't." Dan swayed unsteadily on his feet. "I'm going to blow his damned head off. Then I'm going to do the same with her."

"For God's sake, Jeff . . ." Mike looked to his brother to stop this lunatic.

Then Luke spoiled it all by sitting up, giggling helplessly. She set Dan and Jeff off, who, laughing uncontrollably, had to lean against each other and the jamb until they got their breath back. Mike glanced from one to the other, open-mouthed until he realized he was the victim of a set-up.

"You should have seen your face," spluttered Dan. "Like the end of the world was at hand."

"What in God's name did those two girls rub on you, Mike?" Luke wanted to know. "You smell like a Siamese ponce."

"Not bloody funny," muttered Mike, irritated to begin with until he, too, saw the amusing side of it and joined in the laughter, reluctantly at first. "Jesus, I thought my last hour had come. How long were you lying there next to me, anyway?" he asked Luke.

"About two minutes."

"Luke's along the corridor in Dan's room," said Jeff. "We put you in bed about half an hour ago and then just sat here watching you until you looked as if you were going to wake up. Then Luke climbed in beside you and we went out."

"You'd have all looked bloody silly if I'd thought that Luke was one of the Malay girls and tried to do what comes naturally," grumbled Mike.

"There was a moment just before you woke up," said Luke

archly, "that I thought you were going to. Just as well I had all my clothes on."

Mike grinned sheepishly. Then he remembered what Dan had said a minute earlier.

"You said something about me and those two—er—girls. Did I? I don't remember anything about it."

"And you never will." Dan winked conspiratorially. "Let's say it's our secret and one we'll keep from Diana—unless you ever step out of line."

The Friday evening before the wedding, Dan and Luke joined the Camerons for a quiet dinner. Although he was getting married at 11:30 A.M. the following morning, there were still security measures to be taken, wireless schedules kept, other calls made. Mike telephoned Diana at 10:30 and again, because she insisted, at 11 o'clock and midnight.

"What are you doing?" he asked her.

"Talking to Mummy and Daddy. I don't think I'll sleep a wink tonight."

"Leave yourself plenty of time in the morning. It's a fair drive from Batu."

"Don't fuss. I've got it all organized."

"I still think it would have been better if you'd left home from here."

"And let you see my dress before you're supposed to? Not likely. Besides, apart from the war I grew up in this house, and after Monday Mummy and Daddy won't live here any more."

Mike thought of calling her again at 1 A.M. because everyone in the bungalow was still wide awake, but decided against it. She would probably get some sleep if he left her alone.

He managed four hours but was up before the rest of the house at 5:30, long before the servants were due to be released from their quarters. He made himself a cup of coffee and, in his robe, sat on the verandah, listening to the dawn noises. Down by the summer-house he could see the Malay Specials in their bunker and, toward Mahal Rumah, hear the sound of the Royal West Beds preparing for another day. It was already becoming hot. By 11:30 it would be scorching. They were all going to suffer in their morning suits, lightweight though they were.

At 6:15 Harry joined his son on the way to unlocking the servants' compound. He had an uncorked bottle of champagne and two glasses in one hand, his Sten in the other.

"Bit early for me," grimaced Mike, as Harry poured.

"Just the one. Clear the cobwebs. The others can finish off the remainder of the bottle."

"You're right. What the hell."

Mike accepted his drink and clinked glasses with his father. "Cheers."

"Now, about the birds and the bees," said Harry.

"I bought a book. With pictures."

"Perhaps you'd lend it to me when you've finished. I'm starting to lose faith in that powdered rhino horn."

While Mike was showering, Harry, Jeff and Dan brought the cars they would be travelling in around to the front of the bungalow, two Fords and a Humber, all armor-plated. Jeff and Mike would travel in the first, Harry and Jessica in the second, Dan and Luke in the Humber. The Royal West Beds had loaned them three drivers for the day. The drivers would look after the vehicles before, during and after the ceremony and the reception. More important they would guard the weapons that the civilians were taking with them but which would not be allowed in church.

At 10 A.M. the army escort drew up in front of the bungalow, two 30-cwts, and a 15-cwt on which were mounted twin Vickers heavy machine guns. There was some light-hearted banter from the soldiers in the 30-cwts, directed at Mike, who knew most of them well. You'll be sorry. Don't do anything we wouldn't do.

Mike grinned good-naturedly as he climbed into the first Ford. Being ex-army he knew that this was what the troops would call "soft" duty, and that lots had been drawn to determine who stayed behind to guard the estate. For those who were going, it would be a pleasure, heightened by the knowledge that Mike had laid on a dozen crates of beer for them when they got back, to get out of the damned jungle for a day.

When she appeared, Luke drew admiring wolf-whistles. The troops were accustomed to seeing her in culottes or jodhpurs. Today she looked stunning in a white knee-length dress and a matching floppy hat. She acknowledged her fan club with a slight wave. As if to prove they played no favorites, the troops also whistled at Jessica, who was wearing a floral print, with blue the predominant color.

The journey to Kuala Kelan passed without incident, and the convoy arrived outside the church at a few minutes after eleven o'clock.

"Christ," muttered Mike when he saw the size of the congregation being shepherded inside by the ushers. He thanked God

Frank Ashford had scrooged the numbers down from close on five hundred. Even two hundred and sixty seemed like a multitude. "Do I have to take this damned topper with me?"

"Yes," said Jeff. "Just carry it."

Jeff then raced off to ensure the ushers were doing as he had instructed.

Melanie Ashford and the two bridesmaids were already there, standing in the porch, out of the heat. Mike went over to talk to them while Luke fluttered around with her cameras, demanding smiles and comparing notes with the photographer who was to take the pictures for the official album.

Mike shook hands with Amanda and Zoe Lockyer, who were shyly delighted to be the center of so much attention. He kissed Melanie Ashford on the cheek.

"Everything okay back at the command post?" he asked. "I was going to telephone this morning but thought better of it."

"I'm glad. Diana's taking everything in her stride, as if you wouldn't know it, but her father's been awake since five o'clock. He was fully dressed by six thirty and then he got hot and had to undress to change his shirt. But apart from that, yes, everything's fine. You look very handsome, if I may say so."

"I feel like a tailor's dummy," responded Mike, uncharacteristically churlish. "Sorry. Just nerves, I guess."

"You're not alone."

For the next twenty minutes Mike stood in the porch. He was introduced to comparative strangers whose names he immediately forgot, and had conversations with others. At 11:25 Jeff appeared.

"Time for the tumbril, old son."

He and Mike walked up the aisle to where the Reverend Arthur F. Raynor was waiting. The clergyman chatted genially to both brothers. Though responding automatically, Mike couldn't have said for a million pounds what they'd talked about.

He checked his wristwatch at 11:35 and again at 11:40.

"She's late."

"Bride's privilege," smiled Jeff.

At 11:45 he said, "I think you've been stood up." The words, meant to put Mike at his ease, didn't come out the way Jeff intended. They sounded like a death sentence.

The entire congregation, equally aware of the time, were murmuring among themselves. But they turned as one body when there was a sudden commotion just inside the porch, where the verger was standing to signal the bride's arrival to the organist. Instead of seeing the verger or the bride, they saw a dishevelled young army lieutenant accompanied by a police sergeant. For a moment the two men stood stock still, as though uncertain what to do next in front of so many people. Then the army officer, removing his cap, walked slowly forward, scanning the pews on either side, searching for someone of rank. His heels rang uncannily loud on the stone floor.

"Stay exactly where you are, Mike," snapped Jeff crisply.

"To hell with that."

"Please, Mike. Just stay where you are. I'm sure it's nothing."

Mike nodded dumbly, his heart pounding. The tension in the army officer was palpable. Something had gone terribly wrong.

Followed by several senior officers, Bill Hyde, Melanie Ashford, Harry and one or two others, Jeff walked quickly down the aisle to where the lieutenant was already in conversation with a colonel from another regiment.

"Please keep your seats, ladies and gentlemen," pleaded the rector above what was already becoming a tumult. "Remember where you are. It'll be all right, Mike, you'll see."

Mike knew it wouldn't be all right, would never be all right, when he heard Melanie Ashford's cry, "Oh my God!"—a singularly inappropriate entreaty, he was to reflect later, considering that God, on an occasion that was to take place in His house, didn't seem to care one way or another.

Jeff appeared at his side, his expression grim.

"Now please keep calm," he said softly, "but there's been an incident just north of Kota Napek. Diana's convoy was ambushed. The lieutenant hasn't any other details as yet."

"You're lying. The only way the lieutenant could have heard is by wireless, and an army operator would have said more than that."

Jeff looked at his brother steadily, his eyes full of pain.

"All right, there have been some casualties. Diana and her father have been injured but we don't know how seriously yet. I swear to you that's the truth."

"Let's get out there."

Mike tore off his tie and removed his tail-coat and waistcoat, which he flung to one side. He attempted to push past his brother. Jeff barred his way.

"You won't do any good. Leave it to the army and the police. This is their job."

"That's typical of you!" shouted Mike, regretting his words

even as they were uttered but unable, in his anxiety, to prevent them being said. "What are you worried about, that the bastard terrorists are still there? That they might take a shot at you? That's Diana out there! What do you expect me to do, wait here until they bring in her body? We've got cars and arms outside. You do what you like, I'm going."

Mike had to barge his way down the crowded aisle. By now everyone knew that an incident involving Diana and her father had taken place, and they were all leaving their pews. Mike shouldered people aside, his eyes darting right and left, hunting desperately for someone who could tell him more. He saw Bill Hyde talking to his father and Dan. Close by, Jessica was comforting Melanie Ashford.

"Diana's been killed, hasn't she?"

"We don't know that, Mike," answered Hyde coolly. "Truly we don't. She's been hurt but we don't know how badly."

"Then what are you standing here for, for Christ's sake! Like a bunch of robots. Why isn't someone doing something?"

"Reinforcements are already on their way."

"Not without me they're not."

"We'll take my Humber," said Dan. "There are arms enough in the back of that."

"Okay," said Hyde, "if that's what you want to do. I'll get some of my police and lead the way."

"I'd better stay here," said Harry, reluctantly. "Someone will have to see to the guests. Radio in when you've got hard news. I'll keep Jeff too."

"Keep him and good riddance," snarled Mike, who suddenly caught sight of Luke snapping away with her camera, instinctively if insensitively recording a unique event. He covered the ground between them in three strides and dashed the camera from her hands. "You bloody ghoul!" he yelled at her.

Shocked, Luke took a step backward.

Dan grabbed Mike by the arms.

"For Chrissake, what good is that doing? She's not your enemy."

Dan dismissed the army driver. He knew how to handle his own Humber better than anyone, though speed now, he felt sadly, was not going to be much help.

It took several minutes for Bill Hyde to round up a police vehicle. Dan tucked in behind him. The two of them were at the tail-end of a long line of vehicles, mainly military, heading north for

Kota Napek. Drivers leaning on klaxons to clear a passage added to the general air of bedlam.

Mike spent much of the journey asking questions to which he knew there were no, or too few, answers.

"Why Diana, why now, why today of all days? Is it coincidence? It can't be, but how can they have possibly known? The route, the timing?"

Dan realized that Mike wasn't thinking straight. Hardly surprising.

"You didn't exactly keep it a secret," he said. "It's been in all the newspapers, remember, state and national. Any terrorist who can read would know what was going on. That's why we arranged the army and police escort."

"But it was a heavy escort, forty or fifty blokes, armed to the teeth. They've been steering clear of those in recent months, anything big."

"You're a Cameron, Mike."

"Christ, do you think it was Lee Swee Peng? *Hamid*? That they went after her because she was marrying a Cameron?"

"I don't know."

"If she's dead, Dan . . . "

"Don't talk like that," said Dan sharply. "The wireless signal spoke of casualties, not fatalities."

"But if . . . "

Then you'll get over it, thought Dan. Sooner or later. As I did.

Diana had been dressed for an hour before her mother left with Amanda and Zoe.

"Good luck, darling," said Melanie Ashford. The next time she spoke to her daughter she would be Diana Cameron.

"See you in church," smiled Diana.

Wearing his second shirt of the morning and fingering his neck where the collar was rubbing, Diana's father was drinking a glass of beer while Diana unhurriedly made sure she had everything she should. There would be no turning back once they were on the road, in more ways than one. Not that she wanted to turn back. She loved Mike as she was sure he loved her, even though it had taken a little strategy to lasso him. God, what a performance.

Something old—well, that was a lace handkerchief her mother had carried at her own wedding and her grandmother before that. Something new was her dress, of course. Something borrowed was a thin gold chain from Amanda; and, because Zoe couldn't be left out, a silver bracelet from the youngest bridesmaid. The something blue to complete the custom was a garter around her right thigh. She intended to leave that on until Mike removed it himself this evening.

Her dress, from Paris where the fashions had appealed to her more than those in London, was traditional white ("I think I'm cheating here," she'd said to Mike, "but what the hell") and Victorian in style. It was also very heavy. In the huge armor-plated Daimler her father had borrowed from a wealthy Chinese planter, she intended riding with her veil up until they reached the church. Otherwise she'd faint in the heat.

Anything else? She asked herself, then spotted the 9mm Browning pistol on the table. She would take it because she had promised Mike she would carry a weapon and she had no intention of starting her marriage by breaking a promise. But, because it was covered with surface oil, she gingerly dropped it into a brown paper bag.

Finally her bouquet, flowers from the garden here that she would probably never see again, and made up by her mother. She had few regrets at leaving. That part of her life was over; the rest was about to begin.

"You look absolutely beautiful," said her father, who had followed her every move.

"Thank you." Diana attempted a half-curtsy, which she barely managed in the heavy dress.

She looked back only once as she entered the Daimler, the door being held open for her by a handsome second-lieutenant, who saluted her with his free hand.

"Bye, house," she said.

In front of the Daimler as it pulled out of Batu Mersa were a 15-cwt and a 30-cwt, the latter packed with troops. Behind the Daimler were a second 30-cwt and two police vehicles. The soldiers in the first 30-cwt were making faces at the Daimler over the tail-board until reprimanded by an NCO. The Daimler was being driven by a corporal, hand-picked from the motor pool because of his skill, according to her father. Next to him was a sergeant with a Bren gun across his lap. This was quite a way to go to one's wedding, thought Diana, but something she'd be able to tell her children and grandchildren in years to come.

Roadblocks, something everyone in Malaya had to suffer since the Emergency, had been warned about the convoy, and removed barricades as it approached, waving the vehicles through. Some of the troops on roadblock duty caught a glimpse of Diana's wedding-dress, and she thought she heard them cheering. She wasn't sure, though. The vehicles were travelling at speed, occasionally hitting 50 mph. They had a schedule to keep to and one thing that must not happen on this day of all days, the drivers had been warned, was for the bride to be late. Well, no more than the traditional few minutes.

They had reached the 9th-mile signpost, at a point just beyond where the road from Gulangor joined the main highway, when the leading 15-cwt hit the mine. Or perhaps there were several mines, it all happened so fast. One minute they were cruising along at a steady 35 mph, the next there was a huge explosion. The 15-cwt was flung into the air by the detonation, and turned over on its back, spilling driver and passengers in all directions. The following 30-cwt was the regulation distance behind, but the road was wet and the driver could not brake in time. The 30-cwt went into a tail-wheel skid and slammed into the remains of the smaller vehicle.

The corporal-driver of the Daimler tried to demonstrate the skill for which he'd been appointed by hurtling past the wreckage of the two vehicles in front on the inside, but there was no room. He clipped the jungle on his near-side, and his off-side wing collided with the stricken 30-cwt, sending the Daimler up a slight incline. It overturned even as the sergeant was yelling at Diana and her father to keep their heads down. Then the following 30-cwt crashed into the Daimler. Simultaneously with the four-vehicle pile-up, the terrorists opened fire with light- and heavy-machine guns from both sides of the road.

Frank Ashford had hit his head and was unconscious. Diana was dazed and bleeding and her left arm was broken. She still had her wits about her, though she realized after a moment that the Daimler was upside down and that she was lying, inside, on the roof. Her first thought was that she must cover her exposed legs; it was most unseemly to be seen like this. Her second thought was on finding the paper bag with the Browning in it.

The corporal-driver was half-in, half-out of the Daimler, dead for all she could tell. Immobile, anyway. The sergeant was alive and trying to hammer open the door, which was buckled, with the butt of the Bren. There were flames and black smoke everywhere. She didn't know if the Daimler was burning or whether it was another vehicle.

"Stay where you are, Miss, stay where you are!" bellowed the sergeant.

Diana had no intention of moving, could hardly do so without experiencing excruciating pain in her broken arm. She now had her Browning with the safety off and was concerned about her father. She slapped his face, gently at first then harder. He was breathing but didn't respond.

Bullets from the terrorists' guns hammered into the Daimler's bodywork, not so much piercing the armor-plating as finding gaps where it had been rent apart. Diana screamed in agony as a round found her shoulder and another her chest. Blood poured from the wounds, reddening her dress. Insanely she could hear a wireless breaking forth with a broken-biscuits squawk. "Hello, One-three, hello, One-three. How d'you hear me? Over."

Someone shouted "Grenades!" Another voice, almost overlapping, "Mortars!" Then the explosions followed each other so rapidly that it was impossible to distinguish one from the next. So far the action had lasted thirty seconds.

The sergeant with the Bren got out of the Daimler in time to be hurled back against the bodywork as rounds from a machine gun stitched across his chest. His blood and viscera obscured what was left of the windscreen. A moment later a slice of mortar shrapnel scythed through the car and through Frank Ashford's head, taking part of the skull with it and killing him instantly. Diana screamed before emptying the Browning's magazine into thin air, hitting nothing.

Fifty feet above the action but well hidden by the jungle, Lee Swee Peng swept his binoculars over the convoy. So far, so good. But in another minute the surviving British would be regrouping and putting his own men under fire. Surprise was everything, but he'd had his. Except for one last gesture.

He shouted orders in Cantonese. Three machine gunners with Brens concentrated on the Daimler, while two other terrorists flung grenades at the same target. The car's petrol tank caught fire and detonated. After that, Peng gave the instruction to disperse. Some of the British were already scrambling into the jungle. It was time to leave.

Before the firing stopped, three policemen and the second-lieutenant who had saluted Diana into her car sprinted for the Daimler, seeing the explosion as the tank went up. There was nothing they could do for either civilian occupant except save them both from being disfigured further by burning. The last fusillade had killed Diana Ashford, though it was hard to remember that the bloodied figure they pulled from the wreckage was the beautiful girl with the smiling eyes they had seen climb into the Daimler a short time ago. She had a Browning automatic in her right hand, and try as they might they could not prize her fingers from the butt without breaking them.

"Cover her legs, for fuck's sake," snarled the second-lieutenant. "Where the fuck do you think you are?" He bent down and picked up a blue garter, slipping it over his wrist. The policemen swore later that he was crying. "And somebody get on that bloody radio. Tell them that call-sign One-three is in trouble."

Overcome with grief, at the graveside Mike had a violent row with the officiating clergyman. Father and daughter had been buried alongside one another in the Batu Mersa Anglican churchyard, and to add gloom to an already mournful occasion torrential rain poured from the heavens as the coffins were being lowered. Aware of the suffering around him, the Reverend Mr. Barber was doing his utmost not to sound too unctuous or holy, trying to keep his voice solemn but neutral. But the words were unreal; to Mike, insulting even. "We brought nothing into this world and it is certain we can carry nothing out. The Lord gave and the Lord hath taken away. Blessed be the Name of the Lord."

All Mike could think of was the beautiful girl he should have married, and how she had looked when, against all advice at the ambush site, he lifted the waterproof cape that covered her body and saw the small hand still clutching the automatic pistol. He'd hated everyone then. He still hated everyone, especially that cruel God Barber was exalting.

"Damn your God!" he shouted, tears cascading down his cheeks. "Damn Him for the unfeeling bastard that He is. Is this how He shows His mercy, His benevolence, how He so loved the world—by allowing a young girl to be murdered?"

The cleric was taken aback by the outburst but recovered quickly. This was his church, where he was God's servant. No one could be permitted to say such things about the Almighty, no matter how they were suffering.

"I understand your sorrow, Mr. Cameron, but you have to accept that this was God's will."

For a moment the shocked onlookers thought that Mike was going to strike the clergyman. But he didn't; he vented his fury with words.

"Damn His will! Damn His will and damn you! It's all a confidence trick. Where's the sense in killing a young girl? Answer me that. Your precious God either doesn't exist or He doesn't care."

Dan and Jeff hustled Mike away from the graveside. Melanie Ashford, already on the verge of collapse, broke down completely and had to be supported by Harry and Jessica. It was the most terrible day any of them could remember.

For seventy-two hours after the funeral Mike was inconsolable, as he had been between the murders and the burial. He wouldn't accept any sedation that did not come out of a whisky bottle; nor would he eat. Taking turns, his father, Jeff and Dan sat with him, listened to his ramblings until he fell into a drunken sleep. Little work was done on the estate. Nobody cared.

On the fourth day after the funeral Mike took it into his head to bathe and shave, something he hadn't bothered with since the scene at the graveside. He also accepted some nourishment, mainly soup, which he drank with shaking hands.

Then he began behaving very strangely, apologizing, over the telephone or in person, to everyone he'd shouted at or insulted since the murders. Despite the amount of alcohol he had consumed, he appeared to have forgotten nothing.

He sought out Luke and said he was sorry for breaking her camera and calling her a ghoul. Luke was worried for him. His eyes were wild.

"No, it was my fault," she tried saying. "You were right. I should have had more sense."

Mike promised to buy her a new camera.

He apologized to Jeff for the names he had called him.

"There's nothing to apologize for."

"There is. You were only doing what you thought had to be done."

He telephoned Barber, who managed, on this occasion, to make all the right noises. "I'll remember you in my prayers, my son."

Mike thanked him.

The only person he couldn't reach was Melanie Ashford, to whom he wanted to express his regrets for his performance at the graveside. She had flown to Australia immediately after the funerals, to stay with friends. She told Jessica she would decide what to do with the house she and Frank had purchased when she felt able. But she would not be returning to Malaya.

A week after his recovery Mike disappeared late one afternoon. His father and mother, Jeff and Dan, were frantic. He hadn't taken a horse; a check of the stables revealed that. Nor had he taken an estate vehicle. But he was nowhere to be found.

Then Jeff had a brainwave. Without saying anything to anyone, he walked the hundred yards down the main drive to the house Mike had built for Diana. Although it would be dark soon, a dangerous time for anyone to be out alone, Jeff was unworried. The terrorists couldn't do any more to the Cameron family than they already had, short of killing him.

He found Mike in the sitting-room, a sledgehammer by his side. He'd demolished the fireplace and damaged some of the panelling and was in the process of making a fire in the middle of the room out of oily rags and kindling. He barely glanced up as Jeff came in.

"Don't try to stop me. This is my house and I can do what I like with it."

"I've no intention of trying to stop you."

Mike struck a match and lit the rags. They spluttered into life. Mike added kindling and some larger pieces of wood. Within a couple of minutes a good blaze was going. Within ten, at Jeff's guess, the room would be well and truly alight. The windows were open and smoke was pouring out.

Mike sat on his haunches in front of the fire, feeding it every now and then, coughing occasionally. Jeff squatted alongside him. Tentatively he placed an arm around his brother's shoulders. After a while Mike began to weep. Not tears of bewildered rage this time, but tears that came from deep down in his gut, from somewhere no one else could reach.

"That's it, old chap," said Jeff gently. "That's it. Get it all out of your system. But I don't think you should burn the house down. It was Diana's too. She wouldn't want that."

Mike nodded, and together they stamped out the fire. Then Jeff put both arms around his brother and held him until the tears were gone.

18

To the dismay of every European in Malaya, the British Labour Government of Clement Attlee recognized Mao Tse-tung's Republic of China in January 1950. In Kuala Kelan hotels and clubs, the talk was mutinous.

"It makes no bloody sense at all. Who does London think we're fighting out here?"

The decision had a profound effect on the non-Communist Chinese too. Their days were numbered if Chin Peng's guerrillas won. Where was the sense in recognizing a regime that supported the killing of your friends, which had slaughtered 860 civilians, 320 policemen, and 150 soldiers since the Emergency began?

Luke was among journalists who put that question to the new Director of Operations, Lieutenant-General Sir Harold Briggs. Sir Harold ducked the issue, claiming that he was a soldier, not a politician.

In June 1950, just back from an assignment with the 26th Gurkha Infantry Brigade in Johore, Luke heard via the bar radio in the Regency Hotel that North Korean troops had invaded South Korea. She immediately raced around to Victoria Street, where she found Appleby hunched over the teletype.

"I'm going to have to start charging you agency rates," he grunted.

"I'll buy you a drink. What's the latest?"

"President Truman has ordered all U.S. land, sea and air forces in the area to support South Korea. Does this mean you'll be leaving us?"

"Just as soon as I can get clearance. It's a new war, Jerry. This one will still be here when I get back."

"You're a bloodthirsty young woman. What will you do when they run out of wars?"

"Not possible. The disappointing thing about the future is that it's just the same as the past. There isn't any brave new world."

Luke telephoned Mahal Rumah.

"If I can get a late train to KL," she said to Dan, "I can pick up a DC3 for Singapore first thing in the morning. I might be able to arrange papers for Tokyo from there, but it might also mean going to Tokyo and rattling a few cages."

"When will you be back?"

"Next week if Truman gets antsy and drops the Bomb, but my nose tells me it's a war that will drag on. I have to go, Dan. All the agencies will have people there. I can't miss out."

"I know. Make sure you bob and weave. If they start a shooting war in earnest up there, it'll make this one look like the teddy bears' picnic."

Leaving when she did, Luke missed the first piece of hard news that year, when Lam Swee, the political commissar of the 4th Johore Regiment, surrendered to police in Pahang, claiming to be disgruntled. Because he was not a warrior and therefore "had no blood on his hands," he risked nothing by quitting. Except from Chin Peng, who put a price on his head. But the security forces' star defector was spirited away by them and kept safe until fully debriefed.

During the remainder of 1950 and much of 1951, the Cameron bungalow and Mahal Rumah came under attack a dozen times. Each assault was beaten off with little damage done, but the frequency of the attacks forced Harry and Jessica, who would both be sixty the following year, to question whether it was worthwhile staying on, much though they both loved the country and their estate. They had received substantial offers for the plantation from wealthy Chinese, non-Communists betting on a Communist defeat.

To Harry's relief, because it made the decision for him, but not entirely to his surprise, because they both had a vested interest in staying in Malaya until the last terrorist met the last bullet, Mike and Dan firmly vetoed any notion of selling out. Jeff was scarcely consulted. He was still number two son in his father's eyes but it no longer bothered him as it once had.

In October 1951 Harry lost a personal friend when the High Commissioner, Sir Henry Gurney, was ambushed and killed while driving up to Fraser's Hill in his Rolls-Royce. Two months later General Briggs was forced to retire due to ill-health, and Sir Gerald Templer replaced them both with the joint roles of High Commissioner and Director of Operations.

Templer's appointment soon paid off.

In May a leading terrorist nicknamed Manap the Jap, with 75,000 dollars on his head, was killed by a Gurkha patrol. Six weeks later Liew Kon Kim, known as The Bearded Terror because of his wispy goatee and ruthlessness, was shot dead while fleeing his hideout. The same month, July, Shorty Kuk was beheaded by two of his own men while he slept. His executioners had been unable to resist the 200,000 dollar reward, which they duly received on delivering Shorty Kuk's head in a sack, but only after Templer insisted, against the advice of his civil servants, that they be paid. If they didn't keep their promises, Templer argued, someone of the stature of Chin Peng or Lee Swee Peng would never be caught or betrayed. 200,000 dollars, £25,000, was cheap.

In August a female terrorist, Lee Meng, was put on trial for her life at Ipoh. The charge was possessing a hand grenade, and the penalty was death. Her case under the Emergency Laws was heard not in front of a jury but before a judge and two assessors. She was acquitted by the assessors, but the judge was empowered to order a retrial, and did. This time she was found guilty and sentenced to hang.

Her case attracted worldwide attention, partly because she was a woman and partly because she was a physically attractive woman. Petitions for clemency were organized around the globe, many by people who could not point with any accuracy to where Malaya was on a map, and eventually her sentence was commuted to penal servitude for life. Lee Meng was luckier than some of her less attractive female terrorists, six of whom had been hanged since the Emergency began.

Luke Ross, who was home from Korea and who had witnessed the retrial, found herself in a minority of one defending the reprieve.

"Don't get me wrong," she said one evening after dinner at the Camerons', "I'm not defending the commutation because she's a woman. But the second verdict stank. If she'd been caught in Penang or Malacca or Singapore, where they still have jury trials, the first verdict would have set her free and that would have been that. The prosecution couldn't make the hand grenade charge stick, and that should have been an end to it."

"She's a killer and a supporter of killers, for God's sake," said Dan, "and it's the court's job to make sure she doesn't kill again. There was a reward of 100,000 dollars against her name. The security forces are going to start taking the law into their own hands if there's any repetition. Terrorists won't get as far as the courtroom."

"Can I quote you?"

"Don't be ridiculous."

Dan and Luke continued the argument into their bedroom. At least, Luke thought it was an extension of the dinner debate when Dan asked her if she was returning to Korea. She'd been backward and forward on half a dozen occasions.

"I don't think so," answered Luke, "not unless something dramatic happens. I've said all I've got to say, and the major battles are being well documented by staff reporters, agencies and the newsreels. Besides, step too far off the beaten track and you could find yourself in a wooden cage eating chow mein for the rest of your days. I think I'll stay here for a while. Any objections?"

"None, except I might not be here myself."

"Come again."

"The kids. David and Laura. I had a letter a few days ago. They didn't say so in as many words, but the sentiment was there: when can we get together as a family again? David's eighteen. Laura will be eighteen in May. I speak to them pretty regularly on the phone, but I hardly ever see them. I know they worry about me, Laura especially. Since Korea took over the front pages there hasn't been a lot in the American press about Malaya, but they're aware that there's still a war on out here. I'd bring them out for a holiday, except I daren't risk anything happening to them."

"You're between a rock and a hard place, all right, but let's talk about it over Christmas, in Texas. David and Laura seem to have accepted me for now. Let's have a good drunken discussion over the turkey."

"I'll be coming back."

"I wouldn't expect any other decision."

When General Templer retired in May 1954 the Korean Armistice had been signed at Panmunjom and the word Merdeka, Malay meaning Freedom, was appearing more and more often in the newspapers. Independence was only three years away.

In his valedictory address Templer emphasized that Chin Peng's forces were still reckoned to number between 4,000 and 6,000. The rehabilitation centres at Taiping and Morib, and the female centre at Majeedi, had done and were continuing to do excellent work, making useful citizens out of former terrorists and fellow travellers. But the war was far from over yet.

For Bill Hyde, however, it was. Harry and Jessica were among the first to hear of his decision to retire when he called to see them in October 1954. He was the same age as Harry and Jess, sixty-two, and had only been kept on in the police because men of experience were desperately needed during the first years of the terror. Now, with elections to be held in July 1955 and independence to be granted at a date to be decided in 1957, throughout the police force a gradual process of Malayanization was taking place, and there was no room for old hands. That was understandable, but Harry and Jess were shocked to learn that Bill and Molly Hyde were leaving the country completely.

"We're not citizens," said Hyde.

In itself this did not mean that Hyde and his wife could not have stayed on after independence. Citizenship regardless of race had been defined as someone who'd had at least one parent born in Malaya. Thus Harry qualified as of right, and Mike and Jeff as his sons. Jess qualified because of her marriage. Dan didn't but could acquire citizenship either by registration or naturalization. He wasn't going to bother, had no intention of giving up his U.S. passport. If required, for reasons of continuing to be a forty percent stakeholder in Cameron Rubber, he would register as a resident alien. This option was open to Bill and Molly Hyde, as was naturalization.

"They wouldn't turn you down," said Harry. "Christ, they wouldn't dare. You've been here for forty years. You fought the Japs and you've been fighting the terrorists. Show me the civil servant who's told you you don't qualify, and I'll show you a man who's shortly going to be out of a job."

Hyde smiled and shook his head.

"You're not following me. I've got to retire at the end of the year, sure, but no one's kicking Molly and me out. It's just that we've decided to go. Molly has some family in England, in Devon. We're going to buy a place there or somewhere close by. I'll have my gratuity and my pension, and we've got some money saved. Quite a lot of money, as a matter of fact. Molly visited Devon during the war . . . "

"I remember," nodded Jess. "I travelled with her once during the Blitz."

" . . . and I went down to see them when I was in England for the Victory Parade in '46. Anyway, that's where she's decided she wants us to retire to, and I've agreed. We've kept renewing our British passports, thank God."

"And what the hell do you think you're going to do in Devon?" demanded Harry. He was upset at the thought of losing a very old friend, one who'd fought alongside him against the Japanese and one who, moreover, had bailed him out of trouble all those years ago when he'd come across Jenny and her Malay lover. "Grow flowers and vegetables? Where the hell is Devon, anyway? I'm as wise on that score as a Devonian must be about Paselabilan."

"It's in the southwest," said Jessica. "Dartmoor, I think. Or Exmoor."

"And bloody cold summer and winter I'll be bound," snorted Harry.

"Well, it's not Malaya," said Hyde. "I hear they think themselves lucky if the temperature reaches seventy degrees in the summer."

"And what about the winter?"

"I shudder to think."

"Shudder's right. You'll freeze to death."

They were sitting on the verandah. Harry reached for the handbell he used to summon one of the servants when he wanted a drink. Then he thought better of it and went to fetch refills himself.

"That's what I mean," said Hyde, accepting the whisky.

"I don't understand." Harry glanced at Jessica, to see if she could enlighten him. Jess shrugged.

"You wanted another whisky then," explained Hyde. "You instinctively reached for your bell. How long do you think that sort of thing can last after Merdeka?"

"People will still need jobs."

"It'll all change, Harry, you must see that. Your servants don't have a vote now. Next July they will, men and women both providing they're over twenty-one. A single vote. The same as you. The same as Jess. Of course people will still need jobs, but the government won't be keen on seeing them work as lackeys for European bosses, whether or not those bosses are citizens too. It might not happen directly after independence, it might not happen for a few years; but it *will* happen. It's only natural."

"And because of that," said Harry irritably, "you're leaving a country you've lived in for most of your life. Because things will change. I know that. I'm not a Colonel Blimp. I know there won't be exclusively European clubs and bars any longer. But I can live with it. I thought you could too. Frankly, I also thought you were made of sterner stuff."

"Harry," cautioned Jess.

"It's all right, Jess," said Hyde. "I've known Harry long enough not to take offense."

Harry tried a different tack.

"The job's not over yet," he said. "The job of fighting and beating the terrorists, I mean. Look down there." He pointed toward the summerhouse. The sandbags were still in place, as were two Malay Specials. "Templer said it himself: there are thousands of them still in the jungle and the mountains. They're not giving up, and they won't even after Merdeka. Merdeka means nothing to them. It's the country they want for Uncle Mao, never mind who's running it."

"The job's over for me," said Hyde. "Weren't you listening? They've retired me as from the end of the year. Actually they're being quite generous. I've dropped a hint in one or two senior ears that we won't be staying on, and I've more or less been told that, if I want to leave early and get settled in England before Christmas, no one will object. I'm thinking of taking them up on the offer."

Harry didn't appear to hear him.

"There's work here for you," he offered. "Security work. This estate is still a target and I'm getting a bit too old to help run the place and make sure those men I can trust with weapons know how to use them. You could organize them, form a Cameron militia. I'd pay top salary. You could live in the house Mike built. He wouldn't object. Just for a year or two, maybe. Devon won't run away."

"I don't think so, Harry. I appreciate the gesture, but I don't think so. A year or two could become three or four or even five, and I'd be pushing seventy. We've made up our minds, Molly and I. It'll be a wrench, but it's time to go."

Luke heard about Bill Hyde's decision the following day. She discussed Harry's attitude with Dan.

"He says he can tolerate change, but I don't think he's looking forward to it at all. He doesn't even want to let Bill leave. A Cameron militia, for God's sake. He's living in the past, in the days of Cameron's Cossacks. He reminds me of one of those cattle barons in a Western movie, a John Wayne character. He and his family were here first, fighting the Indians and making something out of nothing, but now there are barbed-wire fences being erected and the railroad's coming through. It's all different. He can no longer run the range like a feudal fiefdom. He's not only getting older, he's losing his power. There's a fascinating story here if I can pin it down. The next two or three years are going to be critical for men like Harry Cameron."

Bill Hyde accepted his superiors' offer to retire early in order to be in England before Christmas, and at the end of November Harry organized the biggest party Kuala Kelan had seen since pre-war days. It was held in the Planters' Club. Toasts were drunk and speeches made, and afterward everyone got down to some serious drinking. A few tears were shed, not exclusively by the ladies present. Then Bill and Molly Hyde were gone, and with them went part of the irrecoverable past.

Three months before the 1955 elections Lee Swee Peng moved his main camp for the fifth time in two years, this time settling near the Lamir Caves beneath Bukit Lamir. Gone were the heady days of the camp at Lembingan, when the guerrillas were housed in permanent huts and Lee Swee Peng commanded upward of two hundred and fifty men. Now, with deaths and desertions, and executions because of disloyalty, his force numbered less than fifty men and a few women, and they bivouacked where they could, constructing rough bashas out of atap and terrorizing nearby kampongs for food and money. The raids they mounted were concentrated on isolated police sub-stations and the occasional unescorted motorized traveller who was foolish enough to believe that the main highways were now safe. And railway trains, where sometimes rich dividends could be obtained for minimal risk.

Lee Swee Peng lived in constant fear of being betrayed by the inhabitants of the kampongs he persecuted, and slept surrounded by a bodyguard comprised of men whose loyalty was beyond question, to himself personally and to the cause in general. He had no doubts, could not afford to have any, about the eventual outcome of the struggle. There was almost no way, now, that the Central Committee could prevent Merdeka. But it wouldn't end there. In fact, after independence things might improve for the guerrillas. The British would—must—sooner or later begin to withdraw troops in large numbers. After that, it would be easier to overthrow the elected government.

In some respects he appreciated he was luckier than many of his fellow guerrilla leaders, who were now either dead or awaiting execution. Not that unfortunate, either, in having less than a quarter of his original force. With only one or two exceptions, who were carefully watched, the men presently with him were most unlikely to give themselves up or reveal his whereabouts to the authorities since they had all killed at one time or another and the security forces were no longer accepting the surrender of such individuals. One of the exceptions was Hamid.

In April 1955 he was twenty-two years of age and a strikingly handsome man, having inherited the best features of his Malay father and Jenny Cameron. He was taller than everyone in Lee Swee Peng's unit, including Abdullah bin Halim. But he wasn't trusted by the Chinese or the squint-eyed Malay. Although unable to prove it, they suspected, rightly, that on many occasions over the last few years he had examined some of the leaflets dropped by the Dakotas (for which Lee Swee Peng's penalty was death), to see if there was anything written there that would enable him to surrender without losing his life at the end of a rope. There wasn't. Although he had killed only once, it was unlikely that the American Holden would allow the authorities to forget just who had been the victim. The precedent set by the commutation of Lee Meng's sentence could, he sometimes considered, apply to him also, though he doubted it. Even if it did, on the grounds that he was very young when he committed the murder, it would certainly mean incarceration for life. On the whole, he preferred to live out the remainder of his days in the jungle.

The facial likeness, either a photograph or a drawing, that he sometimes saw on wanted posters brought in by the Min Yuen, was seven years out of date, and the description no longer fitted him. Even so, it would have been impossible for him to disappear to a different state and hope to get work. He had no papers. Nor could he hope to find a kampong where he was unknown and attempt to live there, hunting and fishing. Someone would be sure to inform on him. If the guerrillas didn't kill him, the security forces would. He occasionally found it beyond belief that Lee Swee Peng mistrusted him as he did. Where could he go? Who could he talk to?

To be accurate, the Chinese guerrilla leader did not view Hamid with suspicion every hour of every day. Were it otherwise, Hamid would not have been the unit's quartermaster. Because of his age and length of service with the guerrillas, he was no longer required to act as camp cook; but because Lee Swee Peng never accepted him as a dedicated Communist, he did not take part in operations, where his willingness to kill might be found wanting at a crucial moment.

There were days when Abdullah urged Lee Swee Peng to dispose of Hamid, remove him entirely if Peng believed him to be a threat. The Chinese always argued against such drastic action. Hamid was part Malay by birth and virtually all Malay by upbringing. Terror was not always the best weapon in bringing a kampong's inhabitants to heel, and Hamid was notoriously easygoing with the villagers. However, if that brought in fish, meat and fruit without threats, so much the better.

It was in his capacity as quartermaster that Hamid made his way to kampong Elok—literally translatable as "beautiful village"—soon after the guerrillas arrived at the Lamir Caves. He was alone, and it was his task to persuade the village headman to part with food for fifty men and women on a regular basis. Peng approved of the sympathetic approach to begin with; only if that failed were selected villagers killed or mutilated.

After making sure there were no police or soldiers in the vicinity, Hamid sought out the headman. From past experience he knew there was no point in apologizing for his demands. The villagers would have to work that much harder to feed fifty extra mouths, but the alternative was far worse.

Although Lee Swee Peng's unit was new to the area, the headman had been forced to feed other unwelcome visitors earlier in the Emergency. After weakly trying to argue that providing food for such extra numbers would place a heavy burden on his villagers, he finally agreed to do what was asked.

Hamid left. On the outskirts of the kampong he heard running footsteps behind him. Fearing that some of the younger males had disagreed with the headman's decision and were about to take the law into their own hands, he slipped into the undergrowth and unsheathed his parang. When his pursuer was level, he emerged from the jungle and seized the figure from behind, throwing "him" to the ground. A pair of huge brown frightened eyes peered up. He removed his hand from the girl's mouth and gestured her to stand. She was about eighteen, in his estimation, and the most beautiful female he had ever seen. She stood in front of him, a head smaller, scared but defiant.

"You were following me," was all he could think of saying.

"Yes." Her voice was as soft and refreshing as a cool breeze.

"Why?"

"Because we can't feed you and the others, not without it causing us a great deal of hardship."

"That can't be helped. What's it to do with you, anyway?"

"It was my father you were talking to."

"You're the headman's daughter?" She nodded. "What's your name?"

She hesitated. "Rihana."

"It has to be done, Rihana. There can be no exceptions. We need food. If it's not provided willingly, there are other ways, ways you wouldn't like."

"I know. You'll kill some of us."

"Not I, but others."

She studied him, brushing dirt absentmindedly from her sarong.

"You're not Malay."

"I'm partly Malay. My mother was European."

"And you're a terrorist."

"I suppose so. Please convince your father that he must obey. If he doesn't terrible things will happen. I'll be back tomorrow, at this time, to make sure he hasn't changed his mind. I don't want to appear in the kampong again. You bring his message. Meet me here."

There was no reason for Hamid to return within twenty-four hours. In fact, it was dangerous to do so, and not only because this young girl might alert the security forces. If he knew, Lee Swee Peng would forbid it. But Hamid wanted to see Rihana again. He particularly wanted to convince her that refusing food could be fatal. No, not could be, would definitely be.

"Why are you doing this to us?" she asked.

"I'll try to explain. Tomorrow."

She was there when he arrived, bringing her father's acceptance of the original demands. Not that Hamid had expected otherwise. She was also there the following day and the one after that, although Hamid varied the times they met, sometimes sneaking away after dark. Gradually he told her about himself, most of it. He omitted to inform her that he had killed Memsahib Holden. He judged she would find him repellent if she knew.

Within a month they were lovers. He never dared ask why she chose to let him enter her body; he was frightened in case, through curiosity, he lost her. Sometimes he wondered if she permitted him to have sex with her because it gave her power, and wielding that power she could expect him to protect her and her father and the rest of the kampong from Lee Swee Peng. Other times he knew with absolute conviction that she selected him because she felt as he did. To his most certain knowledge she never told anyone in her kampong of their intimacy. He frequently worried that it would come out anyway, that she would become pregnant. She told him to forget his fears. "There are ways." She never said she loved him. In the heat of passion she would use the words *chinta berahi*, meaning sexual desire, or *dendamkan*, meaning "long for." It was enough. Given the circumstances of their relationship, it was as much as he could expect.

If he thought his involvement with Rihana to be a closely guarded secret, he was mistaken. Almost from the first, Lee Swee Peng and some of his closest advisers knew about it. Peng opted to do nothing to interfere. Now that Hamid had his own woman, there was little likelihood he would do anything to jeopardize her safety. Nor would he contemplate surrender, even if that became feasible. Where Rihana was, there would be Hamid. It was information worth having.

The elections in July 1955 resulted in an overwhelming victory for the Triple Alliance of Malays, Malayan Chinese and Malayan Indians under the leadership of Tunku Abdul Rahman, who became Chief Minister. In September he offered an amnesty to the terrorists, the details of which were dropped from aircraft. Although it was still death to be in possession of a leaflet, Hamid obtained one and believed, for a while, even with some anxiety, that his moment to surrender had come. For the terms appeared to imply that even those guilty of murder in the past would have their crimes forgiven if they gave themselves up, together with their arms.

On the day the amnesty was made public Lee Swee Peng called his men together. There could be no surrender. Anyone who attempted to do so would be dealt with mercilessly. If a man capitulated and wasn't caught, his woman would pay the penalty; if he had no woman, his closest comrade would die. It was therefore incumbent on every man to watch his neighbor.

Hamid accepted he was lost. He remained unsure that Lee Swee Peng knew of his relationship with Rihana, but suspected the Chinese leader did know. Even if he managed to steal away— and he was as familiar with the surrounding jungle as any man in the encampment—and take Rihana with him, Lee Swee Peng would exact revenge on Rihana's father. If he managed to persuade her father to accompany them, Lee Swee Peng would destroy the remainder of the kampong and all its inhabitants. He couldn't ask Rihana or her father to leave under those circumstances. It wasn't even worthwhile mentioning the amnesty, which in any case was revoked, not to be repeated, before the end of the year.

Before that happened Chin Peng requested a meeting with the Chief Minister. This took place at the end of December at Baling, twenty miles from the Thai border, where Chin Peng made impossible conditions, demanding recognition for the Malayan Communist Party and the release of leading terrorists in detention. He was turned down, and the amnesty ended—to the relief of the security forces who, during it, had been compelled not to open fire against suspect positions unless fired on first.

Early in 1956 a final date for independence—August 31, 1957—was set. In May 1956 Alan Fielding, now a very old and feeble man, had to travel to Singapore for medical treatment. He couldn't go alone and he wasn't up to flying. Although the lease on the flat once owned by Barbara Holden had expired many years earlier, Jeff still liked to visit Singapore whenever he could, and he volunteered to accompany Fielding. Even at this late stage the roads were considered less than safe, and Jeff and Fielding chose to go by rail. A few miles south of Ulu Pangam, the train came under attack.

19

Fielding lived in a small apartment in the grounds of Sandwood Lodge, Kuala Kelan's main hospital. Although he could walk with the aid of a stick, his rate of progress was generally slow, and it was in a wheelchair that he was pushed by a pretty European nurse to the waiting ambulance. The nurse would accompany Jeff and Fielding to the train, where she would leave them. In Singapore another ambulance had been arranged to collect the former doctor.

Although it was a very hot morning, Fielding had a rug over his knees and a shawl around his shoulders. On his head he wore a battered straw hat. Jeff thought he looked a little like the Van Gogh self-portrait and tried to remember how old he was. About eighty was as close as he could get.

His mind was still razor sharp, but age had done nothing to mellow his disposition.

"I don't know why we're going to all this trouble," he grumbled on the way to the ambulance. "I know what's wrong with me. It's called old age and there's nothing they can do for that in Singapore."

"Now, now, Doctor Fielding," soothed the nurse. "You know it's for the best. They have equipment in Singapore we don't have here."

"And a fat lot of good it will do me to learn that my heart has only got two more years left pumping. Or two months. They're not keeping me there, you know. I'll stay for the tests but, if there's any suggestion they want me for more than a few days, I'm leaving and I'll make my own way home if necessary. I know how hospitals work, don't forget. They take you in for tests and the next thing you know, they're performing an exploratory operation. The step after that is the funeral."

"Don't be so morbid," the nurse reprimanded him.

That was something Jeff hadn't considered, how long he would be in Singapore. He managed to get the nurse to one side while the driver and his assistant manhandled the wheelchair into the ambulance and secured it.

"Do you think he'll be kept in long?"

"I've no means of knowing, Mr. Cameron. It is his heart, as he is only too well aware, but we'll have to wait for the results of the tests and see what is recommended."

"Attractive little thing, isn't she?" said Fielding to Jeff in the ambulance, leering at the nurse. "Nice legs."

Blushing, the nurse attempted unsuccessfully to pull her skirt lower.

They took refuge in the waiting-room with it's huge overhead fan, out of the worst of the heat, until the express pulled in. Then the nurse and one of the ambulancemen assisted Fielding to his reserved first-class seat. A porter took care of the luggage. The wheelchair was staying behind.

Jeff remained on the platform until the nurse joined him. There were fewer uniforms on the train than there had been three or four years ago, but it was still heavily guarded. Jeff recognized the regimental insignia of the Royal Australian Regiment and the Rhodesian African Rifles. Waiting to embark were men in company strength of 25 Field Regiment Royal Artillery. Judging by their high spirits they were travelling to Singapore en route to England. At either end of the train was a flat-car on which was mounted a light tank. At intervals in the coaches stood troops with light- and heavy-machine guns.

"Is there anything I should know?" Jeff asked the nurse. "I mean, is he likely to need any medication?"

"If he does he'll take it himself. In case he's unable, the pills are in his right-hand pocket. Give him one with a glass of water. In his left-hand pocket is a flask of whisky. He shouldn't really be drinking whisky, but I doubt there's anything you can do to prevent him."

The nurse proved correct in that respect. Almost before the train left the station, Fielding produced the flask. It was a handsome affair in silver and leather, capable of holding half a pint. The screw-top was the cup. In spite of his apparent frailty, Fielding managed to pour a generous measure without spilling a drop. He offered the cup to Jeff, who shook his head.

"A bit early in the morning for me. For you too, I would have thought."

"Delicately put. You've been talking to Nurse Hitler, and the answer to your unposed question is, yes, I shouldn't be drinking. On the other hand, drinking and bridge are two of the few pleasures I have left. I'm fed slops—milk puddings and the like, boiled fish—and I'm hardly allowed any salt. There's also half a case of first-rate malt hidden in various places in my flat, and I'll be damned if I'll cash in my chips before it's all drunk."

"God help the doctors in Singapore," grinned Jeff.

"Serves them right. Between them and those sawbones in Kuala Kelan, they practically bullied me into making this appointment. *And* told me I couldn't fly. We could have been there in a couple of hours by air. Which reminds me, I haven't had a proper chance to say thanks for offering to accompany me. I'd have been stuck with that damned nurse otherwise. Or someone from the same coven."

Fielding's gratitude was genuine, revealing to Jeff what he already suspected, that at least part of Fielding's irascibility was an act. Or an old man's self-indulgence.

"She's got better legs than I have."

"True, but she'd have confiscated my flask, make no mistake. They're heartless, most of them."

"I had some business to take care of in Singapore, anyway," said Jeff, not wanting Fielding to believe he was making a special trip. "It might as well be done this week as next."

"And the nightlife more than makes up for any inconvenience, right?" Fielding winked and chuckled, looking for all the world, Jeff thought, like a wicked goblin. "It's still the place to be, Singapore. Lots of beautiful girls. Makes KL look like a convent. You should be thinking of getting married, you know," he said suddenly, out of nowhere. "I was talking to your mother a week or so ago. She doesn't say it in so many words, but she'd love a grandchild. Your father too, though he's even less forthcoming. Then there's the estate to consider."

"I'll leave that department to Mike, grandchildren."

"Yes, poor Mike. I don't see as much of him as I used to, but I know he still feels deeply about Diana. How long ago was it? Six years?"

"Almost seven. Anyway," added Jeff, anxious to change the subject, "you're a fine one to talk about marriage. You never took the plunge."

"Who'd have a crusty old bastard like me?"

Fielding had a second capful of whisky and then announced that he was going to take a nap. He stirred only once, as the train came to a halt before the bridge crossing the River Selagganu, where some of the troops left their coaches and carefully checked the track for signs that anything was amiss. Nothing was, and thirty minutes later they were on their way again.

The express gathered speed. Small villages flashed past. Jeff wondered how much Merdeka would affect the inhabitants of the tinier kampongs. Not at all, if he were any judge. These people's ancestors had lived more or less like this for ten thousand years and their descendants wouldn't alter much during the next ten thousand. It wasn't as if Malaya was Europe. There would be no industrial revolution in this country.

Although the first-class coaches were air-conditioned, it was still stuffy and the motion of the train soporific, and approaching Ulu Pangam Jeff nodded off. The next thing he remembered was hearing the hideous screeching of metal on metal as the engine driver applied his emergency brakes. Then there came the sound of machine gun fire and the entire train left the tracks, bucking like a steer. Jeff was catapulted from his seat. His head crashed into a window, shattering it. Something sharp penetrated his eyes, and he screamed with pain. After that, everything went black.

Witnesses later told the investigating teams that, at first light, a gang of terrorists had removed a hundred-foot length of rail and replaced it with the same quantity of aluminum foil. From the air, therefore, on cursory examination, the track did not appear to have been tampered with. All nearby villagers had been herded back to their kampongs and kept under guard.

The few who saw the crash all told the same story. The driver had appeared to sense that something wasn't right moments before the engine hit the foil. He applied his brakes, but it was too late. The engine's momentum carried it for a dozen yards, but then it lurched sideways, tumbling down the embankment, dragging the coaches with it. In that second the terrorists opened fire. The troops aboard the train were in no position to return the fire. The action lasted under five minutes. Then the terrorists fled while the villagers did their utmost to drag battered and bleeding bodies from the wreckage or help those who, miraculously, had been thrown clear. One they pulled free was the body of a very old European whose neck had been broken. In his left hand they found a whisky flask, incredibly undamaged. Close by was a much younger man who had had recovered consciousness as they approached. His face was in a terrible condition. Slivers of glass protruded from his eyelids and the area around his eyes. He had his arms held out in front of him like a beggar. They recalled him saying, "I can't see, I can't see. Am I blind?"

"I could give you the clinical details, but they probably wouldn't mean a lot to you," Andrew McIver said to Jessica, Harry and Mike. "Briefly, the glass severed the optic nerves in both eyes. There is also some evidence that the optic lobe—that is, the dorsal lobe of the midbrain from which the optic nerves arise— was damaged. The glass and the impact of the derailment did a great deal of other harm too, but much of that is operable. I'm not sure about the eyes. I'm afraid you may have to face up to the fact that your son will never see again."

Andrew McIver was the senior consultant at Sandwood Lodge. In the ten days since the ambush he and his team had taken X-rays and performed minor surgery on Jeff before concluding that they did not have the necessary expertise to probe further in safety. What Jeff Cameron needed was a top-class ophthalmic surgeon. There was an excellent man in Kuala Lumpur, several in Singapore and several more in Tokyo. Ophthalmic surgery was not McIver's specialty, but in his view what Jeff Cameron also required was a miracle. The men McIver had in mind were first-rate, at the zenith of their profession, but they couldn't make water from wine. If such a man existed he would be found in Europe or the United States. McIver rather doubted he did exist.

"I'm very sorry."

They were in McIver's office. Total silence greeted the consultant's verdict. Harry looked from his wife to his son, and then at McIver.

"Are you saying there's nothing that can be done? Good God, that's not possible in this day and age."

"I said you *may* have to face up to the fact that your son will never see again."

"Then there's a chance?"

"I'd be misleading you if I suggested it was more than a very slim one, but surgery advances in leaps and bounds every year. There are men in England, Europe and the United States who have produced remarkable results. You must appreciate, however, that each case is different. Where sight can be restored in one instance may not apply in the next. Even the surgeons I have in mind fail more often than not. It depends on the circumstances."

"Fly the best man you can think of out here," said Harry. "Expense is no object. If you can't do it, I will. Just give me his name."

"I'm afraid it's not as easy as that." McIver shook his head. "You see, it's not just a question of performing surgery and then hoping for the best. It's not an appendectomy where the offending organ is removed. A series of operations could be involved, half a dozen of them, possibly, spread over months. Each one designed to knit together part of the broken nerves. Any one of the men I'm thinking of couldn't spare a lot of time away from his own practice. In England, Europe or the United States, they have their own facilities, their own trained staff. Sadly, we can't provide them with that here."

"Then you're saying," said Jessica, "that Jeff would have to go to them, not the other way around."

"That's correct, Mrs. Cameron." McIver hated to remove any last vestige of hope, but the rider had to be added. "However, you must understand that these surgeons are only human. They would need to see your son, examine him, take further X-rays. After all that, they may conclude that he is inoperable."

"Will you set the wheels in motion?" asked Harry. "Write letters, make telephone calls, do whatever you have to."

"I can certainly do that. It may take some time before they can even see him. But I'll get on to it directly."

"Does he know about all this?" asked Mike. "That he may be blind for the rest of his life?"

"Not in so many words because I haven't told him. However, I think he knows. Yes, I think he knows."

"When can he come home?" asked Jessica.

McIver thought about it.

"I'd liked to keep him here another week, under observation. It's not just his eyes, you understand. He was battered and bruised in that damned ambush. I suppose we have to thank God nothing was broken. He was lucky there."

"I doubt he'd agree," said Mike.

"Quite," nodded McIver.

"Go along and talk to him, Mike," said Jessica. "Your father and I need to discuss this question of European surgery with Mr. McIver. If that's all right?"

"Of course," said the consultant. "You know the way."

Jeff had a private room. He was leaning against the pillows, his eyes bandaged. There were other bandages on his hands and forearms where they had been cut, and there were sutures in his forehead and upper lip. He had the radio on, recorded dance music, but he heard the door open.

"Come in, come in, whoever you are," he said lightly. "If you've brought the violin, I'm afraid it'll be a while yet."

"Me," announced Mike, drawing up a chair to the bedside. "I forgot the fruit as well as the fiddle."

"Never mind that, what are the shift nurses like?" Jeff turned his unseeing eyes in the direction of Mike's voice.

"Not so hot. You wouldn't like the matron on this ward. She's a dragon straight out of the Brothers Grimm. As for the junior staff . . . " Mike fluttered his hands non-committally until he remembered that Jeff couldn't see him. "Nothing to write home about."

"I'll consider your verdict at a later date, when I get a glimpse of them myself."

Mike gritted his teeth. "Well, you know my judgement as far as women are concerned."

"Agreed. With the single exception of Diana, uninspiring. Trouble is, you never had my experience." Jeff hesitated. "Don't worry about it. I know the odds are against me ever seeing another pretty face."

"Don't be a bloody fool," retorted Mike gruffly. "You're not counted out yet."

"You don't think so? I'll tell you something funny about not having sight. Your hearing improves. McIver tries to keep his voice down, but I've heard a couple of whispers. If this were the races, I wouldn't risk a cent on me. Still, I suppose I'm better off than poor old Alan Fielding. I heard someone say they damned near had to use a crowbar to get that flask away from him. How are the rest of the casualties?"

The derailment had cost thirty lives, most of them civilians. A dozen others, mainly military personnel, were in as poor a state as Jeff, though none with eye damage. A further fifty had been injured in one way or another. Mike didn't bother to beat about the bush.

"Thirty fatalities at the last count, which should be the end of it. And I meant what I said a moment ago. Don't write yourself off yet. McIver's a good man, but he's not the only fish in the ocean. He's also not an eye specialist."

"Sounds like he's been having words with you."

"Well, a few."

"It doesn't bother me as much as I thought it would, you know," said Jeff after a moment, "the thought of not seeing again. Okay, okay," he added on hearing Mike grunt, and shift irritably on his chair, "the *possibility* of not seeing again. I don't suppose it's really sunk in yet. Or maybe, in spite of what I've just said, I still feel there's some hope. What are their plans for me?"

"Christ, Jeff, you can't ask me that. That's McIver's job."

"McIver isn't family, and if not you, who else? Dad would get tongue-tied—he doesn't like infirmity—and Mum wouldn't know the words, either. It might come as a bit of a shock, but I'm closer to you than to either of them."

Mike realized his brother was right. He also owed Jeff from the time directly after Diana's murder. This bloody country! Jenny, Barbara Holden, Diana—and now Jeff. Malaya seemed to have it in for the Camerons and anyone connected with them.

"They're talking about Europe or England, possibly the United States. Apparently there are specialists there, and equipment, that we don't have in Malaya. McIver's going to make some enquiries."

"Do I get a vote?"

"Of course you do, don't be idiotic."

"In case I don't, tell them to make it England." Jeff only partly managed to keep the bitterness from his voice. "As close to London as they can manage. I always wanted to go back."

At the end of the month Jeff returned to the estate, and in July flew to England, where his destination was a private clinic in Surrey for exploratory surgery. The bandages were now off his eyes and he wore, in their place, a pair of very dark sunglasses, more to hide the scars he knew must be there than for any other reason. He could still not perceive even the faintest glimmer of light.

In spite of his protests that one of McIver's staff was all that was necessary, his parents accompanied him. He did, however, make a condition, which they agreed to. As soon as he was settled in, they must fly home. He would not have them waiting around, worrying. They accepted the stipulation; they knew he was talking sense. However good the Surrey people were, it could take several months before a final verdict was delivered.

Three days after he arrived and the day after his parents left, he had a visitor. He knew it was a woman the moment she entered his room, and also one who had not visited him before. She wore an expensive perfume, which the nurses did not. Nor did she have on a uniform; his ears were attuned to the starched rustle the nurses made.

"Mr. Cameron." Her voice was vaguely familiar but he could not place where he had heard it before. "I thought it must be you when I saw your name and address on the admissions register. I can't understand how I came to miss it when Mr. McIver first contacted us."

Jeff got to his feet, feeling for his stick. He was not bed-bound. His room had its own bathroom and he was allowed to wear his ordinary clothes. Only if he wanted to go elsewhere in the clinic did he have to ring for a nurse.

"I'm afraid you have the advantage of me."

"Anne-Marie Franklyn. Well, you may remember me as Anne-Marie Tate. We met in Malaya in 1948, at your parents' house. I was on my way to New Zealand. Your mother knew my aunt during the war. I'd have been in to see you before except I only got back from a week's holiday this morning."

Jeff had an immediate mental image of a blue-eyed blonde, very lovely. She'd also kept him at arm's length, he recalled.

Jeff held out his hand. Hers was cool, the grip firm.

"Of course I remember you. What happened to New Zealand?"

"Oh, I was only going out there for two years. Actually I stayed two and a half. Since then I've had several jobs. I've been here for eighteen months."

Jeff also recalled that she was a doctor.

"Are you one of the people who'll be operating on me?"

"Good heavens, no." Her voice was bubbly, merry, full of fun. "I'm just a general practitioner. I look after various aches and pains and so on when the surgeons have done their stuff." Her tone changed. "I've read your case file and Mr. McIver's various letters. I can't tell you how sorry I am about what happened."

"Let's hope you can do something about it."

"You're in good hands. Mr. Quilter, the head of surgery here, is the best there is, a truly brilliant man."

"I met him when I arrived."

"Yes, you would have. Incidentally, I see from your case notes that you've hardly met anyone else since, that you haven't been out of your room for any length of time. I think you should make the effort. The facilities here are quite extensive—vast grounds, a common-room, a heated swimming pool, a gymnasium . . ."

"Tennis, golf, small-bore shooting, television . . ." *Damn.* Jeff swore beneath his breath. But it suddenly hit him, *really* hit him now that he had met again this woman from the past, that the mental image he had of Anne-Marie Franklyn's golden hair might be all he'd ever have. "Sorry," he apologized, "but all this is a bit new to me. I keep thinking I may have to reread the classics in Braille."

"I know, and I sympathize. And being eight thousand miles from home is a little disorientating, I accept."

"It's not that. I was here during the war, too, as well as my mother. Well, in London, which is only ten miles away. I occasionally think of London as my home."

"What a strange thing to say."

Anne-Marie made a note on her file—*Depression*? The question mark was because she was not one hundred percent sure if it was depression, or if Jeff was serious.

"Anyway, I would urge you to think earnestly about paying a visit to at least the common-room to begin with. All you have to do is ring for a nurse. And now, I'm afraid, I have other patients to see."

"But you'll be around?"

She sensed the anxiety in his voice.

"Oh yes, I'm usually somewhere to be found."

He waited until he heard her hand on the door-knob.

"What do I call you, by the way—Ann-Marie or Doctor?"

"I think we should keep it formal in public. Those are the rules."

"And Franklyn?"

"I don't understand."

"You're no longer a Tate but a Franklyn. Presumably you got married?"

"Yes."

She didn't offer any more and he didn't press her.

Also in July Laura Holden turned up in Singapore. She had attained her twenty-first birthday in May and graduated from college, majoring in English, a month later. Dan had flown to the States for her birthday and stayed on, mostly to make sure that David, who had taken his degree at Harvard Business School the previous year, was not running Holden Office Supplies into bankruptcy. Small chance of that. David had taken to commerce like a duck to water. Somewhat disappointingly in Dan's view, David appeared to want only two things from life: vaster sums of money than he already possessed and a behind-the-scenes say in Texas politics. He had no political ambitions for himself. Intelligently, Dan reluctantly granted, he had realized early on that the real power lay in pulling strings.

Luke had not been able to make Laura's birthday, being in Australia. The husband and wife team who marketed her work were considering selling out their agency to a newspaper combine, and Luke didn't want her contract with them to be part of the deal until she vetted the potential buyers.

On reaching twenty-one Laura had inherited her share of her mother's estate. Including her stock in Holden Office Supplies, she was now an extremely wealthy young woman. She was also the image of her mother except for her hair, which had become, with only a little cosmetic assistance, lightish red. A shade darker and she would have passed as the actress Arlene Dahl's younger sister, which made her staggeringly good-looking by any standards. Her problem was that she didn't know what to do with her life. A degree in English, she pointed out to her father, qualified her for very little except teaching and publishing. She'd edited her college magazine, but publishing was out. "Every deadbeat who can construct a sentence with more than the usual number of conjunctions thinks he's Hemingway. Every woman thinks she's one of the Brontës. What they can't take is that they're all a combination of Doctor Seuss and Ella Wheeler Wilcox. I couldn't handle the tears. Writing's a crying game."

As for teaching . . .

"Teaching's not what I'd consider an attractive proposition when you've got several million bucks in your portfolio. Teaching's like publishing except you're dealing with smaller egos. I don't want to wind up a drunk or a hooker with amateur status, or hang around until one of David's dreary pals decides he wants to marry me. Nor do I want to be there if I said 'yes.'"

There was a lot of him in her, Dan decided. And she was bright enough to appreciate she could make a serious mistake if she wasn't careful. While Jeff Cameron's tragedy had proved beyond question that the Emergency was far from over, Malaya wasn't as dangerous as it had been. He'd kept his daughter away from Mahal Rumah for far too long. Maybe it was time to change all that, at least in the short term.

"Why don't you take the long way around, across Europe and Asia, and come and live with Luke and me for a few months?" he suggested.

"I thought you'd never ask. Maybe I can do something to help you two make it legal. You're fifty and Luke's got to be in her mid-thirties. The hell with Europe, though. I saw the movie. I can do Europe when I'm older and grayer and wearing granny glasses. What say I take a slow boat to Japan and make my way down from there?"

Dan remembered enough about slow boats in tropical waters to worry about his daughter.

"Why not take a fast boat? Better still, a plane here and there."

"Look, Pop, I'm a big girl. It might be hard for you to accept, but I am."

Dan winced inwardly at "Pop." One time it had been Daddy, then Dad. Where on earth had Pop come from? Laura was right; he was getting old.

"I'll call you when I arrive."

Dan had a long conversation with Luke when she returned from Australia. Her agents were still undecided whether or not to sell. The trouble was, her contract with them had been written in such a manner that she was part of the agency fixtures and fittings. If they sold their company, she was in the package. It would cost her a small fortune to buy herself out, and she wasn't entirely sure she wanted to belong to the prospective owners.

"My own stupid fault," she confessed. "I didn't read the small print."

Dan got her off the subject of her own problems for a moment and told her that Laura was coming to stay. Luke couldn't have been happier.

"Though I don't know how you're going to put up with two women in the house."

"I'll get used to it. She seems to be worried about us making our relationship legal."

"Is that what we have, a relationship? And here's me thinking for the last few years that what we had was a love affair."

"Christ, you've known her too long. You're beginning to sound like each other."

"No bad thing. If she has grave doubts about writers, including me, and mistrusts publishers, she'll go a long way."

"Be serious."

"I'm being serious. Let's talk about me for a minute. I've got problems in Australia I'm not sure I can handle alone. You're a businessman. I may need your help in a sub-boardroom battle. I don't want to hand over my contract to these new idiots unless I'm sure I'm doing the right thing. Can you spare me a week or two back home? Maybe we can make the relationship legal at the same time."

Dan was astounded.

"You're kidding me."

"Not kidding in the least. God bless white weddings, but I don't see myself trotting down the aisle fluffed out like Cinderella. Why don't we fly to Australia, do some business, and then see how we feel? We can do it by special license in a couple of days."

"It's not the most romantic proposal I've ever had."

"Shut it, Holden! It's the only one you're ever going to get. I've kicked around, seen a few places. Maybe it's time. I don't want children and I don't think you want any more. So why not?"

"Harry and Jessica won't forgive us, robbing them of a formal splash."

"I'm not marrying Harry or Jessica. There's a proviso, though. Just one. I don't give up my job. If the big war blows up in Europe, I'm off."

"Who doesn't need a working wife?"

"Where will we live?"

"What's wrong with Mahal Rumah?"

"You don't want to go back to the States?"

"I don't think so, not in the foreseeable future. David's turning out to be Gulbenkian. I think we can safely leave the business in his hands."

"Then it's settled."

Dan solved Luke's agency problems within a week. Her contract with the husband and wife team only covered newspaper and magazine features, not books. Dan persuaded her to write a book about her ten years as a war correspondent, illustrated with her own photographs. With her experience and looks, it had bestseller written all over it. The agency could handle the marketing of the book worldwide, and take its percentage, providing it didn't sell out to the newspaper combine, or anyone else, for five years. At the end of five years they could do what they wished, and Luke was free to tear up her contract if she so chose.

Two days later she and Dan got married. He sent two cables announcing the nuptials, one to David, one to Harry. He had no way of knowing where Laura was. In his cable to Harry he asked if someone would be kind enough to meet Laura and look after her if she turned up before he and Luke got back. They were renting a yacht in Darwin and were off to explore New Guinea and the Spice Islands. They'd be home some time late July, early August.

When Laura telephoned from Singapore, Dan's houseboy advised her to call the Camerons. Jessica answered. After the social niceties Jess remembered to tell Laura that her father had just married Luke and was now cruising somewhere in the Spice Islands.

"Good for them," said Laura, genuinely delighted.

"You'll stay with us, of course, until they're home. That is, if you want to."

Laura thanked her and said she did. She added that she had only disembarked an hour ago and would remain overnight in Singapore. There was an early morning flight to Kuala Lumpur, which she'd reserved space on, but nothing to Kuala Kelan until later in the day. Rather than hang around KL, she thought she'd take the train. Jess told her that someone would meet her.

"How will I recognize her?" asked Mike, who volunteered for the job.

"She can't have changed that much in eight years," said Jessica.

But either she had or she'd missed the train, Mike thought the following afternoon—until this glamorous redhead walked up and planted herself in front of him. "Hi, Mike."

Mike took an involuntary pace backward.

"Good God," he stammered, immediately cursing himself for his customary gaucheness with attractive women.

"Something the matter?"

"I hardly recognized you. Was your hair always that color? You've also—er—grown," he added feebly.

"The hair's partly bottle, partly me. Mostly me. As for growing, that's what happens to people. What were you expecting, braids and braces on my teeth? I was terribly shocked to hear about Jeff, by the way. How is he?"

Laura slipped into the household routine with easy grace. Her sense of fun and her enthusiasm were infectious. She collapsed into giggles when the family occasionally used English expressions such as "I'll knock you up at six A.M." and "He's just got to keep his pecker up"—and explained that "knock up" and "pecker" meant something quite different in the States. Even though Dan was American, America was another world, familiar to Europeans in Malaya only by courtesy of the cinema. Malaya was not just a closed, semi-insular society; it was also small geographically. In area it was only slightly larger than England, and England would fit comfortably into one of the tinier states such as Arkansas. It would fit five times into Laura's home state of Texas.

She let in a breath of fresh air. Whether swimming in the sungei with Mike, watched over by armed estate guards, or going for short horseback rides, again with guards, she was fascinated by everything around her, flora and fauna. For short periods they all even managed to forget about Jeff, though Harry or Jessica made it their business to telephone the Surrey clinic every other day. So far Mr. Quilter was still studying X-rays and consulting with his colleagues.

By the time Luke and Dan returned, Laura and Mike were spending many of their waking hours together when estate business permitted, and Jess was not slow to notice that her younger son glowed whenever Laura was around. Not since Diana had she seen him look like that. Paradoxically, however, he occasionally removed his hand as if stung if Laura reached out to touch him.

Of course, Mike was eleven years older than Laura, but what did that matter? She was a sophisticated young woman who probably needed a man far senior to her in years. Jess sincerely hoped she wasn't anticipating events, and she was determined to do nothing to interfere, but she suspected that there was a real possibility of a serious romance in the offing.

Mike didn't seem quite so sure. Jess watched him carefully. That he was attracted to Laura—and what man wouldn't be— was beyond question. But there was still a reticence about him that could not be put down to shyness.

Laura also spotted it, and one afternoon down by the summer-house she resolved to do something about it. She had been in Malaya ten days. She had swum with Mike, gone riding with him; she'd had dinner alone with him in Kuala Kelan. So far he had not even kissed her except for formal pecks on the cheek.

The sandbagged bunker was still in place, but the Malaya Specials were not. During the day the bunker was unoccupied. At night, on a roster system from a pool of a dozen, pairs of the more trustworthy estate employees took up residence, both armed, all being paid danger money. It wasn't quite the militia Harry Cameron had envisaged, but it was the next best thing. Malay policemen still guarded the entrance to the main drive, and the searchlights were always switched on after dark.

The news that the former Anne-Marie Tate was one of Jeff's doctors in England was now common knowledge, and it reminded Laura of her thirteenth birthday party, which Anne-Marie had attended along with Diana.

Mike said he also remembered it.

"Your father put up a marquee on the lawn. God, was that really eight years ago?"

"It was. And I made a scene."

"I don't recall that."

"I do. Vividly. We were dancing, you and I, when Diana drove up with Anne-Marie. I got angry."

"Why?"

"Because she was your fiancée and she was taking you away from me."

Mike smiled. "At thirteen?"

"Don't patronize me. Of course at thirteen. What has age got to do with it? I'd been in love with you almost from the moment I first saw you." She paused and looked at him steadily, holding his eyes with her own. "I still am. I didn't know I would be until I saw you at the station, but I am. So there it is. Out in the open the way we Americans like it to be. Don't tell me it comes as a surprise."

It took Mike a moment or two to find his voice.

"I don't know what to say."

"There are only two things to say. The first is that you feel the same way. The second is that you don't, in which case I'll experience some embarrassment for a day or two and then pack my bags."

"It's not as easy as that."

"You're still in love with Diana, or the memory of her?"

"Yes and no."

Laura was drinking lemonade. Impatiently she flung the contents of her glass on to the lawn.

"Christ, can't you be a bit less British than that? What does yes and no mean? Either you're going to carry a torch for Diana for the rest of your life, or you're not. It's that simple. All you've got to do is say the words."

"It's more than words. Of course I love Diana's memory. I always will. She was killed on what would have been our wedding day, but I guess you're familiar with the story. I saw her body. That's something you don't forget."

"I know, I know," said Laura softly, regretting her petulance.

Mike cleared his throat nervously. "I'm not very good at this, but I could fall in love with you without any effort at all. I probably am in love with you and can't admit it. I never thought that anyone would ever replace Diana. Since her death there's been no one. If I need sex it's always available in one place or another."

He came to a full stop. Laura appeared puzzled.

"You're not telling me anything. You're probably in love with me but you can't admit it. I don't understand."

"It means I'm scared of getting involved. No, listen to me," he hurried on when Laura shook her head in despair and tried to interrupt. "We never got any absolute proof, but we suspected that Lee Swee Peng—he's the terrorist leader in these parts—set out to murder Diana because she was marrying a Cameron. I never want to put anyone in that position again. Nor do I want to be there myself."

"So you'll back off for the rest of your life?" Laura was incredulous.

Mike recalled his thoughts when sitting with Jeff in Sandwood Lodge.

"Malaya has it in for the Camerons."

"That's crazy. You're in love with me, or could be, but you won't do anything about it. That's crazier." She got to her feet. "Well, fuck you for wasting my time. I came halfway across the world to be with Rhett Butler and I wind up with Ashley Wilkes."

Luke heard the whole story from Laura the same evening.

"Give him space," she advised. "I was at that wedding. You weren't. Mike's not acting like he's out of weakness. He's a strong man but he's confused. He's also vulnerable. Mind you, tell me one worthwhile who isn't."

"The hell with his vulnerability. Either he wants me or he doesn't. If he does I'm here for the taking. If he doesn't I presume there are other men available between here and Kuala Kelan."

"With your looks? They'll be beating down the door."

"And they'll gain access."

"That would be stupid."

Laura nodded miserably. "You're right, of course. What do you think I should do?"

"Descend about ten thousand feet for a start. Get out of that rarefied atmosphere and put the brakes on your temper. Go out with other men while you're here if you want to, but, I warn you, they're a horny lot. You'll have to defend your virtue."

"That went when I was eighteen in the back of an Oldsmobile. It's a pitcher that's been taken to the well a few times since, I can tell you."

"I'm sure you could. But you're presumably *anak dara sunti*—that's Malay for virgo intacta—since you've been here?"

"I haven't had much opportunity to be otherwise."

"Keep it like that. This is a gossipy community. If you get laid in Kuala Lumpur they hear the bedsprings in Johore. It didn't bother me because I'm a thick-skinned Aussie, but when I first moved in with your father they were forecasting raining plagues of frogs."

Laura smiled. "I'm damned glad Pop married you."

"And I'm damned glad you're glad. Talk to Jessica if you get a chance. Mike's got a lot on his mind. His father's getting older and his brother may never see again. Even with Dan's investment, this is still Cameron Rubber. Mike takes things very seriously. He needs someone like you to keep him sane. All we've got to do is make *him* understand that."

Jessica had little to offer by way of advice, though she was distressed to learn of Mike's attitude. And, while she loved her younger son dearly and would have liked nothing more than to see him settle down with Laura, a phone call from England to let her know that Jeff would be undergoing surgery the following day removed everything else from her mind.

When Jeff recovered from the anesthetic Mr. Quilter had a long talk with him.

"It's neither good news nor bad, I'm afraid. There's a possibility that you'll recover partial sight. What we have to do now is see if my poor skills have helped in any manner. That will take time, a week or more before I can remove the dressings. I'd like you to remain in bed until then. It's difficult, I accept, but you must bear with me."

"What happens after a week?"

"More X-rays. Another operation, I'm sorry to say. You're in no pain, I trust?"

"It feels like a bad headache."

"That's about normal. I'll see you're prescribed some pain-killers, though I don't want to overdo them."

Quilter had a word with Anne-Marie.

"There's little hope. The X-rays didn't reveal half the problem. There's still a long way to go, of course, but I don't have to tell you that there's only so much the human body can stand. After a time I'll be doing more harm than good."

"Poor fellow. What a frightful prospect."

"Yes." Quilter had a thought. "Look, you could help, if you're willing. It's vital to keep his spirits up. You knew him in Malaya, and I saw your remarks about depression. Part of the reason for that is because he's a long way from home with none of his friends around him to take his mind off things. I know you've persuaded him to mix with the others in the common-room and take escorted walks in the grounds, but I wonder if you could do a little more. For example, if you can spare the time when he's up and about, take him for a drive. He won't be in the theater again for another two or three weeks, and I don't want him becoming despondent. Nor do I want his parents over here. They'll only remind him of home. It's unorthodox, I agree, and I certainly wouldn't suggest it under normal circumstances. But with Simon away in Ethiopia . . ."

Anne-Marie thought about her husband, now just starting a year's sabbatical with Unicef somewhere south of Addis Ababa. She hadn't wanted him to go. The holiday they had taken in the Dordogne just before Jeff Cameron arrived at the clinic had been, in part, to induce him to stay.

"I need you here."

"There are children in Ethiopia who need me too. Christ knows I'm no more than an average doctor, but I might be able to save a few lives. It's only a year."

Only a year. If they'd had children of their own he wouldn't have gone, of that she was certain. But the tests had proved they couldn't. At least she couldn't. It had been a terrible blow. He never said as much, but she felt she'd let him down.

"I don't think that's a good idea," she said to Quilter.

"Ah well, you know best."

But she changed her mind after she accidentally overheard Jeff talking to Malaya on his room telephone. He didn't hear her come in because he was in the middle of a conversation.

"No, everything's fine," he was saying. "They're doing all they can. Mr. Quilter keeps me informed and Doctor Franklyn . . ." He paused. "Yes, I told you that when we last spoke. That's what I call Anne-Marie. They like to keep it formal. Best not to get too familiar with the patients, I guess."

Anne-Marie closed the door quietly. They were not doing all they could. She wasn't, at least. It couldn't hurt to take Jeff Cameron for a short drive every now and then.

She suggested as much when Jeff was up and mobile. The dressings were off except for two small pieces of gauze taped across his eyes.

"Isn't this a little unusual? What will the other patients think?"

"The other patients won't necessarily know. If they find out, we're old friends. Don't you want to go?"

"Of course I do."

The first time they drove out to Richmond and walked along the towpath. Jeff had his cane, and his arm through one of Anne-Marie's, but his footsteps were hesitant and it took them almost an hour to cover half a mile. The second time they went to a pub for lunch, Jeff settling for sandwiches which he could guide to his mouth without help. The third occasion they went for a picnic on Epsom Downs. It was a beautiful day with just a hint of fading summer in the air. On the fourth afternoon, a fortnight after the first day at Richmond, Anne-Marie drove him into London and walked with him along Oxford Street and down Regent Street. To begin with the heavy traffic disturbed him—she could feel him tense—but slowly he got used to taxi klaxons and the rumble of London buses.

"That's got to be the best sound in the world," he said.

Later they had tea at the Ritz and, afterward, got caught in a thunderstorm and were soaked before they could make shelter.

"I'm going to have to learn to run faster if it's always going to be like this," said Jeff. "You should see the rain we have in Malaya."

Despite the fact that they could never go anywhere without linking arms, he never once tried to insinuate himself into her affections, do anything other than treat the relationship as one of doctor and patient.

Quilter delayed the second operation until the middle of September, but it proved no more successful, in the surgeon's view, than the first. He admitted to Anne-Marie that he felt it pointless to try a third.

"I'll wait until the dressings come off, of course, in case he can see even a flicker of light, but I regret I'm going to have to tell him that he'll never regain even partial sight. How do you think he'll take it? You know him better than anyone."

"A few years ago I'd have said like a child, asking, 'why me?' Now, I believe, with courage. Certainly with dignity."

"I'll call his parents before I tell him, as soon as we're sure. These sort of ill-tidings should come from me, not him. God knows, they've both suffered too."

Jessica and Harry were stunned. Before Quilter spoke to them they had felt there was some hope, albeit slim. The final verdict was hard to take.

They broke the news to Mike, who in turn drove the few hundred yards to Mahal Rumah to tell Dan, Luke and Laura. Since talking to Luke, Laura had "descended ten thousand feet" and kept off the subject of love as far as Mike was concerned, adopting instead a softly-softly approach. They had continued to ride together and swim together and even dine alone together. He'd come around to her way of thinking, lose his fears, had been her opinion. Propinquity, she considered, was the best aphrodisiac.

Now she wasn't so sure. With Jeff almost certainly blind for the rest of his life, Mike would have more responsibilities than before.

She talked it over with her father and Luke, after Mike left.

"I think it's time to move on. Not for good, you understand, but for six months or so. I'll go to Europe, as you originally suggested, Pop. Grab a gutful of culture and drive the Europeans insane with the almighty dollar. That'll give everyone a chance to adjust."

Mike was dismayed when she told him of her plans.

"Oh, hell. Look, I know I'm probably being unreasonable, but are you quite sure this is only au revoir and not goodbye?"

"It matters to you?"

"Of course it does. It might not seem like it, but I've found it very hard to keep my hands off you, these past weeks."

"Well, you don't have to bother now, do you, now that I'm leaving?"

Anne-Marie was waiting for Quilter in his office.

"How did he take it?"

"With courage, as you predicted. Hell, I thought I was used to this. I've performed surgery on children, soldiers, young women with everything to live for. I've had to tell a few of them the same thing I've just told Jeff Cameron. It doesn't get any easier."

"Did he ask to see me?"

"No, but I think he'd appreciate a visit."

He had been crying, she noticed immediately. Well, he was entitled to a moment's self-pity. She'd be howling like a banshee if Quilter had told her what he'd told Jeff.

He was sitting on the edge of the bed, facing the grounds outside he couldn't see. She sat next to him, and put a hand on his shoulder. He responded, and suddenly there was more between them than mere friendship.

She left the bed. He heard her go to the door and lock it.

"What are you doing?"

"You know very well what."

He heard her kick off her high-heels and unzip her skirt.

"No," he said. "I don't want your pity."

"It isn't pity. You know damned well it isn't pity."

"It is, even if you don't recognize it as such now."

"You don't want me?"

"Of course I do. Right now, there's nothing more I want in the whole world. But you'd hate yourself in the morning. Or the next day. You're not made for adultery, Anne-Marie. Believe me, I know." He tried to lighten the moment. "Besides, don't I remember this scene from *A Farewell To Arms?*"

She smiled to herself and then chuckled openly. Then she zipped up her skirt and put on her shoes. He held out his hands. She walked across to him and took them in her own, standing in front of him. She forced back her own tears. That wouldn't help.

"There's always America," she said, her voice full of emotion. "There are other surgeons."

"No, you said it yourself. Quilter's the best."

"What will you do?"

"Well, this afternoon, when you've finished, I'd like to go for another drive. Somewhere deep in the country."

"And after that?"

"After that I'm going home."

20

Between January and April 1957, Chin Peng left his jungle stronghold across the Thai border to visit each of his district commanders in turn. There were few left of any caliber. One of the most senior, Goh Peng Tun, had been killed in a raid on his encampment by Canberra bombers a year earlier. Of the remainder, Ah Hoi, known to the security forces as The Baby Killer because he had once, in a rage, ripped open the belly of a pregnant woman, still terrorized much of Johore, aided by the leader of the Johore Regional Committee, Hor Lung. In Negri Sembilan Teng Fook Lung commanded 3 Independent Platoon, and in Paselabilan Lee Swee Peng continued to operate from the Lamir Caves and was considered by the Central Committee to be the most successful of the surviving leaders thanks to his sensational coup in derailing the Singapore express south of Ulu Pangam. The other commanders were either emphatically second rate or immature. They needed time to develop, adjust to their responsibilities. Chin Peng was determined to buy them that time.

With Merdeka so near and more and more areas being declared, as the security forces termed it, "white," Chin Peng felt he needed a series of spectacular triumphs to show the nation that his army was not finished yet. At the very least, if total military victory was no longer feasible, Tunku Abdul Rahman must be compelled to talk to him again, perhaps recognize the Malayan Communist Party as a legitimate political organization. It was less complicated for Chin Peng to travel, with a small coterie of loyal bodyguards, to his commanders than it was for them to leave their various states and come to him. Each commander was ordered to destroy a major target before Merdeka. There was no hurry. The commander could choose his moment, but failure would not be tolerated. Maximum effort was required. The targets must be annihilated and severe casualties inflicted, whatever the cost.

Lee Swee Peng was offered options, but had no hesitation in selecting Cameron Rubber. The estate and the houses on it had been left alone long enough to have lulled the occupants into a sense of false security. It was not only a soft target, but Harry Cameron was the largest independent planter in Malaya. Furthermore, he and his family were remaining on after Merdeka. In permanent graves was Lee Swee Peng's fervent wish.

The weekend of May 18–19, four weeks off, was chosen as the date for the attack. Prior to then Lee Swee Peng's unit would stay inactive. Three days before the weekend they would leave their base in groups of six or eight, travelling an hour apart for safety's sake. Everyone was going, women as well. Fifty-six people in all, plus their weapons. The unit would not be returning to the Lamir Caves base.

Lee Swee Peng had been considering for some months whether or not to quit the Lamir Caves for good. His guerrillas had been in the same place for two years, and that, although the base had proved secure, was too long. If the destruction of the Camerons was successful, that entire corner of the state would be swarming with troops and police within hours. Attempting to get fifty-six human beings back to the Lamir Caves was unworkable. The derailment of the Singapore express had been accomplished with only a dozen men, who had easily vanished into the jungle. After the attack his guerrillas would scatter, and reform south of Ruang. From there they would make their way to the border and link up with Teng Fook Lung where Paselabilan abutted Negri Sembilan.

Hamid was appalled when he learned of the decision. He might never see Rihana again. His relationship with the Malay girl had been common knowledge among all the guerrillas for twenty months. Peng had shown no inclination to put an end to it. Where Rihana was, there would be Hamid.

Hamid went to Peng and begged to be allowed to remain behind, to leave the guerrillas, in effect, and live the rest of his life in Kampong Elok. He swore he would never do anything to endanger Peng or his men.

His request was refused. Hamid had not honestly expected the decision to be otherwise. He knew he was valuable to Peng in his role as quartermaster and, in any case, no guerrilla leader could expect to lead for long if he allowed his men to make up their own minds whether or not to continue. Nor could Hamid simply disappear, taking Rihana with him. As he had calculated two years ago, Peng would then exact revenge on Rihana's father and possibly the entire village.

Unknown to Hamid, Abdullah bin Hamid, in a private conversation with Peng, was all for killing the Eurasian and therefore removing the problem of questionable loyalty. Peng was unwilling to go that far. Hamid still had his uses. Besides, the unit had dwindled alarmingly from its original strength and did not have sufficient numbers for its commander to pass arbitrary death sentences unless the victims proved totally unmanageable.

Abdullah argued that there was nothing to prevent Hamid slipping away under the cover of darkness once the guerrillas were en route to the Cameron estate, and returning to Kampong Elok. If the unit was not coming back to the Lamir Caves, Hamid would probably be safe. There was a possibility that, on Merdeka Day or shortly afterward, Tunku Abdul Rahman would declare another general amnesty. Hamid would thus only have to remain in hiding for three months, and then give himself up.

But Lee Swee Peng had already foreseen that danger.

"One man will stay behind to guard the Malay woman and join us later at Ruang or on the border. Unless Comrade Hamid plays his full part in the attack on the Cameron estate, word will be sent back and Rihana's life will be forfeit. Comrade Hamid will be informed of this nearer the day. It would be preferable if the guard is himself a Malay. I suggest he be you, Comrade."

Abdullah's squint eyes glittered. The arrangement, though unexpected, suited him perfectly. Not only would he avoid the raid with all its inherent dangers—both during it and, more importantly, immediately afterward—he would be Rihana's jailer. On the various occasions he had visited Kampong Elok, the woman had made quite clear her contempt for him. Well, perhaps she would revise her opinion. He enjoyed the thought.

"And she is not to be harmed if Comrade Hamid does as he is instructed?"

"Not in any manner. *Any manner*," Lee Swee Peng emphasized. "Keeping her alive and unhurt is the only way we can ensure Comrade Hamid's continuing loyalty."

Abdullah nodded but said nothing. If she tried to escape, of course, it was his duty to prevent that, and he could not be held responsible for anything that happened to her.

The weeks passed too quickly for Hamid. He had not wanted to tell Rihana that the guerrillas were leaving for good, but she sensed that something was wrong and wormed it out of him. Neither of them yet knew that she was to be a hostage for Hamid's good behavior.

Whenever they found time to be alone together, they tried to resolve their future. Rihana was now twenty years of age, old for a kampong female to be unmarried. Hamid's greatest fear was that her father would compel her to marry once he had left. He would have gone through a formal ceremony with her himself except her father had refused his permission and Rihana would not marry without it. It was not unusual for kampong males and females to take lovers before marriage. It was unheard of to marry against a parent's wishes. Rihana's father accepted that Hamid was a reluctant guerrilla, but he did not want his family involved with terrorism or terrorists, men who forced his villagers to provide food for them under pain of death. Hamid could understand that.

"I'll be back."

"How? When?"

"I don't know, but I'll find a way."

The closer the day of the raid came, the more Hamid had to do. Although each guerrilla was accountable for his own personal weapons, his rifle, or submachine gun, and his parang, unit support weapons were Hamid's responsibility. Light-machine guns and 2-inch mortars had to be stripped down and checked, ammunition accounted for, and the load shared evenly between all the guerrillas since an unloaded Bren gun, for example, weighed twenty-three pounds and a 2-inch mortar the same. Many of the Brens and all of the mortars were very old, legacies of the parachute drops more than a decade earlier to Force 136. The Brens were occasionally unreliable and some of the .303 ammunition unstable. In theory each light-machine gun round was supposed to be scrutinized, but in practice there was no real method of telling whether a bullet was a dud until the gun was fired. There were a few modern Sterling submachine guns in the armory, spoils from a raid the previous year on a police outpost in Kampong Dusan, but only selected personnel had these. The other submachine guns were Stens.

Fragmentation grenade fuses had to be checked and inserted, and the firing levers tied down with thin strips of vine. Several of the 2-inch mortar bombs had been adapted to become incendiaries. Food for three days had to be collected, packed and distributed because Lee Swee Peng wanted to avoid the necessity of visiting kampongs for revictualling en route. Fifty-plus men and women on the march would attract enough unwelcome attention as it was, unless he was careful. All food would be eaten cold. No fires would be permitted.

Scouts had been dispatched to reconnoiter the trails between Bukit Lamir and the Cameron estate soon after Chin Peng and Lee Swee Peng had agreed on the target, to see what military or police units were in the area. They reported back that there was nothing to cause any great alarm. Two of the scouts had even got within a few hundred yards of the Cameron bungalow, approaching from the sungei. They confirmed that Malay policemen still guarded the main drive, but the remainder of the defenses were being taken care of by estate employees. It did not appear as if household servants were locked in their quarters at night any longer. There were no soldiers on the plantation.

Lee Swee Peng went over his battle plan with the aid of a sketch map. The attack would begin two hours before midnight on Saturday, May 18. The guerrillas would start leaving the Lamir Caves during the afternoon of May 15. They should all be in position by dawn on May 18, where they would form up at the edge of the estate and remain hidden until dark. "Here." He jabbed a finger at the map. After nightfall they would approach the bungalow from the front. The signal to begin the attack would be an HE mortar round. To make sure nothing was left behind, he and his command group would leave their present location last.

Listening without enthusiasm, Hamid was puzzled when Lee Swee Peng designated the leader of each group and the order in which they would depart without mentioning Abdullah. He did not have to wait long to find out the reason, and it was only by exercising immense willpower that he held his temper. Peng's own rages were legendary. In spite of the circumstances, it would have taken very little for the Chinese to have ordered him killed.

"There is no reason to do this, Comrade," he said through clenched teeth.

"There is every reason, *Comrade*," said Lee Swee Peng. "The woman will be quite safe providing you do as you are told."

Hamid glanced at Abdullah, who was grinning evilly, and wasn't so sure. He knew that Rihana hated Abdullah, being a Malay, more than she loathed and feared the other guerrillas.

"You will bring her to me here the morning of the day we leave," said the Chinese.

"Her father will not permit it."

"Her father will not permit it! *Her father will not permit it!*" Lee Swee Peng spat at Hamid's feet. "Her father has no option. Please make certain that he and his daughter are aware of that."

"Can her guard be someone other than Comrade Abdullah?"

"He cannot."

"I'm frightened of him," said Rihana, referring to Abdullah, when, hesitantly, Hamid explained what Lee Swee Peng had ordered.

"There's no reason to be," Hamid reassured her, with more confidence than he felt. "He won't harm you. It's more than his life's worth."

"And I have no alternative, do I?" asked Rihana sadly. "But you do. The Camerons were once your friends. They're blood relations and they're going to be murdered. You're going to help murder them."

Although he had never dared confess that he had been responsible for Barbara Holden's death, Hamid had told Rihana everything else, particularly that Jenny Cameron had been his mother. He had joined the terrorists as a youth, he'd lied, because he had believed that Malaya should be ruled by Malayans. There had been no turning back.

"Write a letter to the authorities," Rihana urged, seeing a way out for both of them. "Get it to the police at Dusan. Persuade someone in the village to deliver it. You don't have to be involved, but sign it. When they learn you've saved lives you'll receive a pardon."

Hamid considered it. If he could warn them . . . If they reacted in time . . . If Lee Swee Peng were captured or killed in the raid . . .

But there were too many ifs. The soldiers and the police were not as cunning as Lee Swee Peng, as the Chinese had proved over many years. They would arrive in battalions and Peng would realize that a trap was being set and who had sprung it. After that Rihana's life would be worth nothing. Besides, he couldn't get away unseen.

"It can't be done," he said.

On the morning of May 15 he brought Rihana to the encampment. Her father accompanied them. "I'll stay with my daughter until I know she is safe."

Lee Swee Peng dismissed him imperiously. The headman walked off, shoulders slumped. Rihana was allocated one of the empty bashas, where she would remain until Abdullah received word from a Min Yuen courier that the attack had gone according to plan. There was no need to bind her. She knew it was futile to run away. Her father would perish if she did.

The first guerrilla group moved off amid a torrential rainstorm at one o'clock; the last, including Hamid so that Lee Swee Peng could keep him under observation, at seven. Hamid was carrying a Sten and a parang as well as his share of ammunition and food, and he didn't dare look back for fear, if he saw Rihana's face, of being unable to leave.

Each group had a scout who was familiar with the trail, and the route, to begin with, took them northwest. Thereafter they would follow the River Pakelan until it ran beneath the rail bridge and the road bridge above Kota Napek. Then they would swing due south and approach the Cameron estate from the north.

For the rear echelon, camp was made after two hours and their evening meal eaten in total darkness. And almost total silence. Any conversation were held in whispers. Hamid ate alone and no one spoke to him. He wondered if he could go through with it, take part in an attack against, as Rihana called them, his blood relations. He didn't want to hurt the Camerons. All that youthful hatred and confusion was history now. They had suffered too. From newspapers smuggled in by the Min Yuen he knew that Tuan Jeff had been permanently blinded in the train derailment.

While all bar a single guard slept he racked his brains for a way out of his dilemma. He could, of course, kill Lee Swee Peng, though he himself would certainly be cut down shortly afterward. And Rihana a while after that, because the guerrillas would not allow their leader's death to go unavenged. Rihana was the key. While Abdullah held her he was helpless.

But . . . But . . .

The nearest group was one hour ahead somewhere on this trail. The leading group was six hours ahead. All he had to concern himself with were the seven men around him. One man, really, for it seemed unlikely that Lee Swee Peng would ever post more than one sentry.

Hamid examined the plan that was forming in his mind. It was imperfect, true, but it was better than nothing.

Lee Swee Peng's strategy was designed to put the whole unit in position before dawn on the 18th, a little under sixty hours off. By first light on the 17th the guerrillas would be within a day of their first objective, and it would have taken them thirty-six hours to reach it. If he could slip away then, or just before dawn, take minimum rest and travel lightly by disposing of the Sten and spare ammunition, keeping only his food and parang, he could be back, he calculated, at the Lamir Caves encampment somewhere during the small hours of the 18th. Though he might suspect, Lee Swee Peng would not know for certain where he had gone. Nor would he be able to send men after him without depleting his attacking force. He might risk one, or two, in order to inform Abdullah that he, Hamid, had defected, but they would have to use the same trail he used. And, as he would be ready for them, he considered he would have no trouble dealing with them. In all likelihood Lee Swee Peng would not waste time on what he would consider to be incidentals until the attack—ordered by the Central Committee, after all—had been carried out. And if it was to take place at all, the Chinese would have to stick to his original zero hour, or earlier, of two hours before midnight on the 18th—in case the authorities were informed.

Which Hamid intended to do. With luck he should be able to free Rihana even if it meant killing Abdullah, before acting as Rihana had suggested, writing a letter for the police at Dusan. If that letter forewarned the Camerons and saved their lives, surely the security forces would treat him leniently. Not that he intended giving himself up, but the letter would also inform the police that Kampong Elok and its inhabitants could be in danger. They would then throw a cordon around the village and keep it there if only to capture Lee Swee Peng, should he escape capture and decide to return.

Throughout the following day, with the scout always two hundred yards ahead of the main body, Lee Swee Peng cracked on the pace, once every so often glancing back at Hamid as if expecting some protest. Hamid kept his own counsel, answered if spoken to but otherwise remained silent. During the afternoon they caught up with the group ahead, which had been moving more slowly than anticipated because there were women in it. The two groups joined forces rather than waste time, and Hamid cursed his ill fortune. Now there were fifteen people he would have to be wary of when he chose to make his move.

At nightfall the two groups camped a stone's throw away from the river and almost within shouting distance of Kampong Dusan and its police station. Next day would see them beyond the railway line and the main highway.

Hamid slept easily after his evening meal. Years in the jungle had accustomed him to waking at will, and at four A.M. he stirred. Even with the usual cacophony of night sounds—birds, animals, insects—he detected the grunts and occasional pacing of the sentry. This man's watch would be the last before dawn. He'd be tired. It was time to go.

Hamid sheathed his parang. His Sten and spare ammunition were under his poncho. So was his food. He would have to leave most of that—taking only a few strips of dried and salted fish that he could conceal in his pockets—and live on what he could pluck from the trees. A man with a parang alone going to empty a full bladder was nothing unusual. But taking the submachine gun was out of the question, and the sentry might also see the bundle containing his supplies.

"*Pergi terkenching*," he said gruffly, using the vulgar Malay for pissing, and making for the river. The sentry, faultlessly hygienic as all the Chinese were, would appreciate that he was not about to urinate anywhere near the camp.

By sun-up he had covered a mile, and by noon five. Kampong Dusan was invitingly close but he dare not risk a detour. By now Lee Swee Peng would know he had gone, and might well have dispatched someone to Abdullah bin Halim. However, anyone tracking him would almost certainly have to use the same trail. He would wait and see. Better to be safe than sorry, even if it meant losing a few hours.

Mid-afternoon he rested again, only a dozen yards from the trail but invisible from it. No one was following him, he was sure of it. For food he munched some of the dried fish, chewing slowly, and a hand of bananas.

In the hours before darkness he travelled as fast as he could, occasionally breaking into a trot, something no one in Malaya ever did unless in an emergency. Twice he made a mistake with the trail, unable to judge his direction by the sun, out of sight above the thick foliage, and had to backtrack. Soon he was moving through familiar country, but he knew he would still be several miles short of his destination by sunset. It was infuriating, but his rate of progress after last light would be measurable in yards per hour rather than miles. He would exhaust himself for no reason.

He left the trail and made himself a rough cot of atap and bamboo, cutting them with his parang and lashing the pieces together with creeper. For the first time in as long as he could remember he was aware of the mosquitoes biting him, and he slept fitfully.

Fifteen minutes before dawn he was awake. He moved his bowels, ate the last of the fish, and washed his mouth and face in the nearby sungei. He was about to start the last leg of his journey when he heard a noise on the trail—*ahead* of, not behind him. He listened, and identified the sound as that of someone breathing heavily and slashing at an obstruction with a parang. It could not be troops or police. Even the best of them made a greater commotion than this individual was making, and they never patrolled singly. He would stake his life that the man, or woman, up front was alone.

He remained in hiding but in a position where he could see the trail. The sounds drew closer and then, in the half-light, he made out the unmistakable figure of Abdullah bin Halim.

For a second he froze, uncertain what to do. Abdullah here? How could that be? Hamid experienced a moment of dread. Something terrible must have happened.

However, in that he was guessing. What was certain was that Abdullah was no friend.

Hamid allowed him to pass before springing out and knocking the squint-eyed Malay to the ground with the flat of his parang. When Abdullah recovered his senses, Hamid was squatting beside him, the blade of the parang at his throat.

"Why are you here?" demanded Hamid. "Where's Rihana?"

"Permit me to sit up, Comrade."

"Answer the question. Why are you here?"

"Why are *you* here?"

Hamid pressed the parang's cutting edge into Abdullah's flesh.

"You have twenty seconds, *Comrade*, and that's all."

Beads of perspiration stood out on the Malay's forehead. He was within a hair's breadth of dying, and he knew it.

"I decided to let the girl go. Back to her father. Why should I be left out of the attack? I only agreed to guard her because Comrade Peng insisted."

"Liar."

"It's the truth, I swear."

"Then you won't object to returning with me to Elok. To verify."

"Of course not, Comrade."

Hamid rose from his haunches and retreated several feet. Abdullah had been carrying a Sterling as well as his parang. Hamid now had the submachine gun slung across his shoulders. He threw Abdullah's parang into the jungle.

"You won't be needing that. Walk ahead of me."

Hamid brought up the rear, remaining a few paces behind. The closer they got to Elok, the more nervous Abdullah became. Hamid could feel the tension. He suspected the worst, and that Abdullah would attempt to flee before the worst was discovered. He cocked the Sterling. Abdullah stiffened.

"You wouldn't shoot me in the back, Comrade?"

"Perhaps I would."

Abdullah came to a halt, and turned. They were very close to Elok now.

"It wasn't my fault, Comrade. You must understand that. You must also forgive me. That blow on the head has made me dizzy. If I may pause for a moment?"

He did not wait for permission. He sank to the ground. In an instant, before Hamid could think or object, Abdullah hurled a broken branch, which struck Hamid in the face.

But Abdullah had not learned the lessons of the past years, especially the one which taught that a man with an uncocked submachine gun in his hands will react instinctively. Hamid squeezed the trigger.

Half a magazine of ammunition hammered into Abdullah's chest, tearing chunks out of his torso and hurling him backward. He was quite dead by the time Hamid recovered his wits and bent over him. Hamid was unconcerned about the fate of Rihana's captor. He was very fearful that the man would not have made such a suicidal move without good reason.

"We tried to free her," said Rihana's father a short while later. He was the headman and could not weep, but the tears were there, hidden somewhere behind his eyes. "We suspected he would violate her if he was left alone long enough with her. So we sought to free her."

Hamid could not prevent his own tears flowing freely. He had seen Rihana's corpse, and he wept.

"We were too clumsy, or slow. The terrorist heard us. He threatened to cut her throat if we approached closer. We didn't believe him. He is a Malay, after all."

"But he killed her," said Hamid dully.

"While we watched. And then he killed some of my villagers, with the gun. I was fortunate."

"I didn't hear anything," said Hamid, knowing he was being foolish. The trees and the night sounds absorbed and drowned all noise not in the immediate area.

"Then he ran."

"I loved her," said Hamid.

"I know, I know. I know that now. I am a foolish old man."

Hamid's mind was suddenly clear. It was not enough, now, to write a letter to the police at Dusan. It would take him half a day to reach them, another half to organize troops, even if they believed his words. He was exhausted, but in sixteen hours Lee Swee Peng would be attacking the Cameron bungalow. He might make it, if he were lucky. He might yet have an opportunity to avenge Rihana's death with the death of Lee Swee Peng.

21

The attack on the bungalow began at nineteen minutes after ten o'clock when a high-explosive mortar round landed just short of the verandah and detonated with sufficient force to blow the front door off its hinges and shatter the shutters, glass and mosquito screens of several windows. Seconds later light-machine gun fire enfiladed the ground floor. The terrorists left the searchlights alone. Lee Swee Peng wanted to be able to see his enemy when it was driven out into the open.

Earlier in the day Laura had arrived back from Europe, flying in to Kuala Lumpur by regular service and then hiring a light plane to take her to Kuala Kelan, where Mike met her. She had cabled from Vienna that she would be in Malaya before her twenty-second birthday on May 25, but it wasn't until she telephoned from Bangkok that she knew her flight number to KL and her precise time and date of arrival in Kuala Kelan.

She had cleared Customs and Immigration at KL and, the last leg of her journey being an internal flight, there were no formalities at Kuala Kelan. She was in Mike's arms a few minutes after her plane touched down.

If he'd worried that her months away might have changed her feelings for him, he need not have done.

"I've missed you," she whispered, clinging to him, leaving him in no doubt that she meant it.

"And I've missed you. I thought you might come back with an Italian count in tow."

"No chance. My taste is definitely for slightly insecure Britishers who don't quite know their own minds."

"I do now."

"Sure?"

"Absolutely. I must have been mad to turn you down in the first place."

For security's sake on the road and also to handle the heavy baggage, Mike had brought with him one of the estate servants, who took the luggage to the waiting car while Mike and Laura followed.

"Can't we stop off somewhere?" She smiled up at him seductively, looking as fresh as paint in spite of what must have been a gruelling flight.

Mike indicated the servant.

"Not with him along."

"Why did you bring him? I've tried to keep up with what's been going on in Malaya from Europe, and I thought most of Paselabilan was 'white.'"

"Parts are, parts aren't. I sometimes drive into Kuala Kelan alone, but the roads are far from safe. I wasn't going to risk it with you aboard."

"Tonight then."

Mike sighed. There were few things that he wanted more, but his parents, together with Dan and Luke, had decided to throw her a celebration dinner at the bungalow ahead of her birthday.

"Couldn't you have talked them out of it?"

"Probably, but your father will want to see you almost as much as I did, and you might have wound up spending the evening with him and Luke at Mahal Rumah. This way at least I get to be with you."

"Point taken. How long will it go on for?"

"Who can tell? Your guess is as good as mine. Midnight. One o'clock."

"Okay," said Laura, resigned. She changed the subject. "How's Jeff making out? I was shocked to hear they couldn't do anything for him."

"We all were. He's facing up to it, as he has to. Being bloody brave about the whole business, too. Braver than I'd be under the same circumstances. He gets black moods, of course, mopes around the house or just sits there without saying anything, but that's only to be expected. The worst of it is, he can't go anywhere without someone taking him. He's got the geography of the bungalow well worked out now, and part of the gardens and lawn down as far as the summerhouse. He's also learning Braille, but it's a long, long process."

"What about a seeing-eye dog?"

"We've looked into that, but there are a grand total of two in the whole of southeast Asia. They have a pilot scheme going in Singapore but there's a chronic shortage of dogs suitable to train. Dad's pouring money into the school via the usual charities and we're waiting for the right dog to come along. However, Jeff is adamant that he won't jump the queue because of Dad's money or influence. He'll wait his turn."

During the afternoon Laura unpacked at Mahal Rumah. Luke sat with her, anxious to hear all about Europe.

Laura had bought gifts for everyone, a miscellany of tobacco, cigars, scent and silk. Luke received perfume from Paris and a silk square from Rome.

"I have the imagination of a tapeworm when it comes to buying things," admitted Laura.

"What about men?" asked Luke.

"Now listen," said Laura with mock severity, "you're my step-mother and I'm not sure you should be asking me questions like that. How would you like it if I started questioning you about your sex life with Pop?"

"What do you want to know?"

The two women grinned at one another.

"No affairs," said Laura finally. "Mind you, I came close once or twice—in Rome and London. Then I thought the hell with it long before I got anywhere near the wire. It's somehow easier when you're in love, but I guess I don't have to teach you that. To tell you the truth I got bored after a while. I've got the sort of brain that can only absorb so much culture before reaching for the martini jug. I thought of flying back several times, but then I decided against it. I stipulated six months or so before I left, to give Mike a chance to adjust to the new circumstances with Jeff and to see if he really missed me."

"He missed you, all right. Most of the time he was walking around like Bo Peep with no sheep. Whatever you set out to prove I reckon you proved it. When's the big day?"

"I'm going to tread softly softly on that one. We'll probably do it quietly, the way you and Pop did. I don't want him being reminded of what happened last time. How's the book coming?"

Luke pulled a face.

"Don't ask. I thought it would just be a question of slapping together some of my old articles and adding in a few of the better pictures. Not a bit of it. I got the message pretty fast from some of the publishers my agents approached that, while I'm probably a very saleable product—they talk like that, publishers—they're not interested in anything I cobbled together in, say, 1948, in a big hurry for a magazine piece. They want original stuff. They'd also like it spiced up. They don't just want to know about the Japanese family I lived with outside Hiroshima after the war; they're rather hoping I slept with a couple of two-star generals to get permission. If I slept with them both at the same time, a military sandwich, so much the better. They're also more than interested in that mad Irishman I married—or rather didn't marry because he already was. Makes good copy. I can see their point, but I don't want to rake over old ashes. Apart from all that it's a hard slog. Journalists, I've discovered, don't necessarily make good authors. Two thousand words and supporting pix are one thing, a whole book another. You need the stamina of a marathon runner and a liver like Hemingway's. Still, I'm not discouraged. It'll get finished sooner or later and the finances are in good shape. What are you wearing tonight?"

"Grab an eyeful of this."

From one of her bags Laura produced a celadon-green dress—slightly crumpled but the creases would iron out—she had bought in Paris. She held it up against her. The hem came just below her knees. With her complexion and hair it was exactly the right color, and she had bought shoes to match.

"Rat," said Luke enviously. "Well, if that's the competition I'd better start rooting through some of my old rags."

They had pre-dinner drinks in the library, just the two families. Although the table would be out of balance, Jeff had made it perfectly clear that he did not want anyone invited to partner him and make up the numbers. Jess accepted his decision without argument. There would come a time, perhaps, when he would change his mind. That time wasn't yet. The scars around his eyes had long since healed, but the scars in his mind were another matter. Even when only his parents and brother were around, he never removed his dark glasses except in bed. Nor did he go anywhere without his white cane, though there were practical reasons for that. It was asking the impossible for the servants to replace a chair or table in the same spot after cleaning a room.

Occasionally throughout dinner the wireless transceiver burst into life. There was no longer any need to have the loudspeaker switched on permanently. A sophisticated gadget picked up the signal and illuminated a lamp above the radio-room door if the caller was trying to reach the Camerons. Even so, the diners tensed noticeably and all eyes turned to the lamp moments after the first hum of static.

There were fewer calls across the whole network than there had been during the more dangerous years of the late Forties and early Fifties, but that didn't mean the Emergency was over. Far from it. With the exception of no longer locking up the servants in their compound at night unless the police advised of terrorist activity in the area, and the absence of the Malay Specials in the summerhouse bunker, all precautions were more or less as before. Sandbags still surrounded the bungalow, especially in front of the verandah balustrade; weapons were never far away, personal weapons as well as the Bren guns in the observatory and in the entrance hall, and were checked, fired and oiled regularly; shutters were closed and doors and windows bolted after dark, making the overhead fans work overtime; the searchlights were switched on at eight every evening and estate guards posted in the summerhouse bunker; flashlights were still next to the gun rack.

They had coffee and brandy at the table rather than decamp to the library, for Jeff's sake partly but also because Harry Cameron had always thought it incongruous, if dining in company and the conversation was stimulating, to spoil the atmosphere by moving from one room to another. Unless Jess instructed them otherwise, the servants left the bungalow at ten, as they had this evening. It was unfair to keep them awake to clean the table and wash up if the night was going to be a long one. The kitchen door, through which the servants exited, locked automatically.

At ten eighteen—he noticed the hour particularly because Laura, obviously tired from her flight and several time zones out of kilter, stifled a quick yawn and smiled apologetically— Mike left the table and returned with a box of cigars she had bought him. Fine Havanas not regularly available in Malaya. He selected one for himself before sliding the box toward his father, who was nearer to Jeff and would clip the end for him. Then the mortar bomb exploded and blew in the front door and several of the windows. Moments afterward machine gun bullets raked the front of the bungalow, thumping through the shutters and the mosquito screens and scattering lethal shards of razor-sharp glass that could take a man's arm off as easily as a surgeon's knife. The ferocity of the attack and the firepower behind it struck Harry and Dan simultaneously. This was not half a dozen terrorists raiding a target of opportunity. There had to be a score or more of them to create such sustained havoc.

Laura screamed.

Jesus, Jesus, thought Mike, remembering Diana and fearful for Laura's safety, not again. Dear God, not again.

He was the first to react, launching himself from his chair and dragging Laura to the floor where he lay on top of her, protecting her body with his own from the flying glass.

Dan and Luke followed him, unhurt, scrambling around among the dust and chaos while round after round whined above their heads and ricocheted off the walls, smashing ornaments and paintings.

Jeff remained immobile, unable to think or move, until Harry pushed him from his seat. He lost his cane and his glasses in the fall but felt surprisingly calm. So this is how it ends, he thought.

Although Jessica had not been called upon to perform her duties when under attack for over a year, second nature took control the moment the initial panic passed and she recovered her wits. On her hands and knees, crawling toward the radio room, she threw the master switch which instantly doused all internal lights except for the two dim bulbs, one in the hall, which could be seen from the dining-room, and one above the wireless. From the gun rack she collected a flashlight. Before she got any further, a second and third mortar bomb landed on the roof. Whether by accident or design one or both destroyed the aerial. When she reached the wireless the set was hissing with static. It still had power but no range. She could neither send a message out nor receive one. Using the flashlight to see her way she crawled over to the telephone. As she had suspected and feared, the line was dead. She shouted this information across to Harry but he didn't hear her above the bedlam. She repeated it as there was a momentary lull in the shooting, while the terrorists outside considered the effect of their first volleys and changed magazines. For a few seconds, twenty at the most, the bungalow was hit only by rifle fire.

Dan grabbed a second flashlight. "I'm going upstairs."

His post was in the observatory, manning the Bren gun there. If it was still in one piece. Christ knows what damage those mortars on the roof had done. He hesitated, wondering whether to take Luke with him or leave her where she was, where she could possibly hide behind furniture or an overturned table. She made up his mind for him. "I'm coming with you." He nodded, though he doubted if she saw him. She could handle a rifle and there were two, he recalled, next to the Bren as back-up weapons. She could also pass him fresh magazines and refill those he emptied. Mike would certainly take care of Laura as far as he was able. But who would look after Jeff?

"No grenades yet," he bawled as he took the stairs three at a time, with Luke, stumbling, just behind him.

Harry knew what his American friend meant. The mortars, machine guns and rifles were just a softening up process, intended to keep the defenders' heads down while the terrorists got closer to hurl grenades through the gaping holes the first attack had produced. They wouldn't have limitless ammunition and it had never been their style to fight battles of attrition. Quick kills, in and out. They hadn't thrown any grenades yet, which must mean they were still some distance from the bungalow. They mustn't get any nearer. If they did, that would be the end of the Camerons and the Holdens. He and Mike from the ground floor, from the outside, the verandah, possibly Laura too, and Dan from the observatory would have to hold the terrorists at bay until help arrived.

Except . . .

Where would help come from? The two Specials at the end of the drive had been outflanked—they could even be dead—and were only there anyhow to prevent the casual terrorist looking for suicidal glory stealing a vehicle, filling it with explosives, and driving it into the house. In any case, they didn't have wirelesses. His own wireless and phone were out of action. The phone in Mahal Rumah, an extension of the same line, would be out of action also. And if he were the commander of the attacking force he would have made sure that, with another mortar and a secondary action, the wireless there would be useless too. The terrorists couldn't have known that Dan and his wife would be spending the evening here. There would be no point in destroying one wireless aerial if another, just a few hundred yards away, was still functioning.

The two men in the summerhouse bunker, if they were still alive, were right in the middle of it all and would be able to do no more than defend themselves, and the rest of his tiny militia—European clerks as well as Malays, Indians and loyal Chinese—was a mile away. They were brave enough and he had trained them as well as he could, but they'd never been led to believe that they would be forced to fight more than a handful of terrorists. They might decide not to risk their necks. Or approach the problem cautiously.

There was a phone and a radio in the estate office if whoever was on duty tonight had the wit to use either. The jungle frequently muffled the odd gunshot, but it was D-Day out there.

He shook his head, annoyed with himself. The estate office phone too would be useless, the wireless maybe not. However, the nearest police were at Ruang. It would take them close on an hour to arrive, and in sixty minutes there might be no one left to care one way or the other.

Harry began cat-crawling toward the hall. A fierce and sustained fusillade forced him to take cover, pin himself against a wall. Behind him he heard Mike call, "Wait, Dad."

Mike levered himself off Laura. She was shaking uncontrollably. Hardly surprising considering she had never been under fire before. It was the noise as much as anything. They were in little danger from the bullets, which were hammering into the masonry five or six feet above their heads. Short of a lucky shot with a mortar they had no immediate worries.

He lay lengthwise next to her, scarcely able to see her face because of the choking dust. Her Paris dress, though, he noted abstractedly, was torn at the shoulder.

"Can you hear me?" She didn't answer and he was compelled to shake her roughly. "Can you hear me?"

"Yes."

Her voice was faint, a small child's awaking from a nightmare. Except this was real.

"I'm going to have to help Dad. We have to get out on the verandah and stop them getting any closer. Do you understand that?"

"Yes."

"Wait."

On his backside, pushing himself along like a baby, Mike headed for the gun rack. Why us, he thought. Why now? The bastards.

His mother, he saw, vaguely making out her silhouette, was crouched beside Jeff. Jessica had a revolver in her hand. She spun the chamber before locking it into place.

Reaching up, from the gun rack Mike took a Sten and several magazines of ammunition. He spilled a box of the same 9mm caliber on to the floor and filled his pockets with the shells he could reach. Stupid, he told himself, stupid. Takes ages to refill a Sten mag. He also removed a 12-bore shotgun and a box of cartridges. This achieved, he made his way back to Laura. A 12-bore had a hell of a kick for a woman, but Laura would have to manage. He'd taught her how to use his mother's 16-bore the previous summer, but not against birds or other live targets. She didn't approve of killing, Laura.

"You remember how to use one of these?" Another HE mortar landing somewhere overhead drowned her answer, if she made one. He had to repeat the question.

"Yes."

He broke the gun and loaded both chambers before handing Laura the weapon and the cartridges.

"We're going to need your help too. A shotgun's not much use"—he regretted his words as soon as they were uttered but couldn't take them back—"except at close quarters, but when you see an opportunity drag yourself over to one of the windows. Keep your head down, though. Don't take any chances unless you're sure. If anyone's close enough to hit, you'll know about it. Just pull the triggers. Are you all right? Do you understand what I'm saying?"

He sensed her relax, pull herself together.

"I'm fine, okay now. It's a bit different from Vienna, I'll tell you that."

He wasn't sure whether she was on the verge of hysteria or making a joke. He hoped the latter.

"We can't wait much longer," he heard his father call, from his position against the wall.

"With you, Dad."

Then Mike thought: Shit. The back of the house. Dan couldn't cover it. His mother would have to, but not with a revolver.

"Don't move yet," he said to Laura. "You'll have to leave Jeff," he added to his mother, a few seconds later, arriving at their side. "We've got to cover the rear." He handed his mother the Sten and the spare magazines, relieving her of the revolver.

"Jeff can't see," Jessica reminded her younger son.

"Under the circumstances Jeff can see better than the rest of us. Please, Mum." Impulsively, Mike kissed her on the cheek. "We need you out back. The kitchen's the easiest room to defend. They may not rush it at all. But if the shooting suddenly stops . . ."

"I know. I'll see you later," said Jessica, accepting the obvious.

She disappeared into the shadows.

"Can I have the revolver?" asked Jeff, stretching out an open palm.

Mike gave it to him.

"For Chrissake be careful."

"You know me."

"Give me your hand."

Both men on all fours, Mike led Jeff over to Laura. They could comfort and support each other. It would give Laura someone to look after and make Jeff feel as if he was contributing. Which he was. The frightened Jeff of a few years ago no longer existed, if Mike were any judge. Since the derailment and his loss of sight, his brother had become a different man.

"Good luck," said Mike.

On his way across to collect one of the other Stens, quite by accident Mike found himself looking at the luminous dial of his wristwatch. The time read ten twenty-two, which he could hardly credit. Only four minutes since he had last checked? Since he left the table for the cigars? Christ, he could use a cigar now. From a different war he remembered the American troops he had fought alongside. Most of them had a cigar somewhere available, and chewed on them, unlit, as a child chewed on a pacifier. Brave troops, all of them. A company, or even a platoon, he would give ten years of his life for now. If he had ten years to offer.

"Right, Dad," he shouted, in the same moment as one of Lee Swee Peng's converted incendiary mortars thundered on a low if perfect trajectory into the library and started a small fire. That none of the defenders as yet could see, or was aware of.

The front door was hanging off its hinges. Beyond it, across the verandah and away from the glow of the searchlights, Mike could see flashes of gunfire. There seemed to be no returning fire from the direction of the summerhouse. Presumably the occupants were already dead, or terrified.

Mike wondered why the terrorists did not attempt to shoot out the searchlights. That would make it easier for them to advance. However, they hadn't, were leaving them strictly alone, and he was grateful for that small mercy.

The hallway Bren, Harry saw, was undamaged though off its bipod and on its side. He grabbed it by its carrying handle. A magazine, as always, was in place. There were a dozen filled magazines close by, in several canvas satchels. He seized the nearest satchel. Jesus, it was heavy. Then he scrambled to his feet. There would never be a good time, a perfect time, to gain the verandah. A man could wait fifteen minutes and be shot the second after. He could wait fifteen seconds and miss death by an aeon.

Sixty-five, he thought in wonderment. I'm sixty-five and still fighting wars I started to fight before I met Jess.

Mike kept on remembering his own war as he tracked his father to the shattered front door. Men in trenches, foxholes, pill boxes, hedgerows. Normandy. The rest of France. Frog's legs. Saw enough of those, legs of Frenchmen and other nationalities. And torsos. And other bits. The most complex piece of machinery in the universe, Man, rendered into so much fertilizer by shrapnel or a chunk of metal weighing an ounce.

"About now, Dad. You go right, I'll go left."

They ran for it.

Reaching his position Mike kept his head below the level of the sandbags for the moment. The air was thick with bullets, much of the firepower coming from the jungle on his left, an arc stretching, in military jargon, from ten o'clock to eleven. Apart from the mortars. They seemed to be coming from out front, twelve o'clock to two. He winced involuntarily as an HE round whistled over his head. This was followed by another incendiary round.

He couldn't see the mortar teams. They were hidden somewhere beyond the searchlights. He tried to recall the range of a 2-inch mortar. Something under five hundred yards was the best he could do. Far outside the effective range of his own Sten, anyway. No point in shooting yet, therefore, giving away his position. His father, however, was already firing. The smell of cordite drifted along the verandah. Joined by another, more sinister odor.

He sniffed the air. Fire. Then he glanced over his shoulder. Through the partly smashed shutters he could see that the library was ablaze and that the flames had a firm hold and were spreading rapidly. That was why the terrorists had left the searchlights alone, why, doubtless, they did not seem interested in moving forward to hand grenade range. They were going to drive the defenders out into the open where they would be silhouetted against the lights and the burning house. Where a child of ten could locate a target and eliminate it.

There were lengths of hosepipe on reels attached to the water tower and an electric pump to provide pressure. But the tower was bathed in light. He had no means of reaching it without being cut down, and it had to be considered doubtful whether the flames could be put out manually from inside the house. There were buckets of sand outside every room for just such an emergency as this, but they were intended only to extinguish a fire in its early stages.

Could he get to the switch that doused the searchlights and the water tower light? Probably, but he couldn't see in the dark. The terrorists would be able to get within grenade-throwing range within seconds if the lights went out. His father and Dan had to be able to pick out their targets.

He prayed that Laura would realize that she and Jeff were in danger of being incinerated and do something about it. Except, what could she do? Leave by the back? Regardless of what he'd said to his mother a few minutes ago, he would now stake a lot of money that the terrorists' commander had posted men out there to forestall such an escape route. They wouldn't have to shoot yet. They'd simply have to wait.

He, however, could not. He had to do something about the blaze. For the moment, with his puny Sten, he was the only one who could be spared. Dan and Luke had to man the Bren in the observatory, where they would be roasted before long. His mother had to guard the rear. Laura must take care of Jeff, his father defend the front of the bungalow.

"Dad, we're on fire."

He had to shout the warning several times before his father heard him. Harry glanced up. From his angle he could see very little, a faint orange glow perhaps. So they were on fire. Maybe that would shake the militia and the buggers down at the estate office out of their lethargy. If the bungalow really caught, the blaze would be observable for miles.

"I'm going to try and put it out."

Rather than risk another dash across the verandah, Mike chose to go in through the nearest french window. Still keeping his head down he reversed the Sten and, with the butt, hammered at a broken shutter and mosquito screen until they splintered and fell apart. The blast from the incendiary mortar or gunfire had already removed most of the glass. Sitting on his hind quarters and buttressing himself against the balustrade, he kicked out as much as he could of what remained. Then he scrambled through, cutting his arms and legs in the process. The sudden inrush of air fanned the flames.

He dropped to the floor, recognizing that he would be silhouetted and a perfect target if he stood up. He inhaled a lungful of vile black smoke, and coughed.

Although the whole room was alight the worst of the fire was near the door to the sitting-room, which regrettably but naturally had been left open before they'd all trooped in to dinner. An hour and a half ago? A year? From there it would soon spread to the rest of the house—unless he could do something to prevent it. Fortunately the switch that extinguished the internal lights also turned off the overhead fans.

He soon realized that he was faced with a hopeless task. He removed his light cotton jacket and stripped off his shirt, which he tied as best he could across his face. Then he took hold of a rug and tried to beat out the fire. To no avail. A sofa and several armchairs were an inferno. So was a bookcase, at whose contents the flames were licking greedily. Worse, he couldn't get as far as the door, beyond which stood the buckets of sand. Though sand would be next to useless under the conditions.

Also beyond the door, in the dining-room if they hadn't moved, were Jeff and Laura, who must surely by now have fathomed what was happening and be about to take some action. For them it would have to be the back of the house, through the kitchen, or the right-hand side, through one of the french windows there. But then of course they would be in the open and probably shot.

Since there was no means of getting to the dining-room and other parts of the house via the library door, Mike retreated to the window by which he had entered. But a sharp-eyed terrorist saw his outline and opened up with a rifle. He must have informed his comrades for soon the entire window area was being peppered with rifle and machine gun rounds.

Mike quickly pressed himself against the wall, his back to it, sliding down until he was on his haunches. For the moment there was no escape that way either, and the flames were creeping ever closer, gobbling up wood and fabric and paper, reaching for the night air.

He would give it a minute. He peered at his watch. It appeared to have stopped. So much for Swiss workmanship and Kuala Kelan traders. He'd only had it a month.

If he kept still and didn't show himself the terrorists might believe they had hit him and turn their attention elsewhere. After a minute he would have to leave anyway. His eyes were watering so badly he could hardly see. He would probably lose consciousness through inhaling smoke if he left it longer than a minute.

Above Mike's head in the observatory Dan had hardly fired a shot. The terrorists had seemed to know that there was a Bren positioned in the upper storey and several machine guns, almost certainly Brens like his own, had hosed in magazine after magazine. Where on earth were they getting their ammunition? He reassessed his earlier estimate of a few more than a score of attackers.

A few more than a score couldn't carry that much ammo. There had to be forty or fifty of them.

There was precious little left of the huge picture windows on any side of the observatory. For most of the time since they had arrived, Dan and Luke had been compelled to cower behind the sandbagged parapet for fear of being injured by flying glass as much as bullets. Dan's major worry was mortars. This position was indefensible against such an attack. One well-placed barrage and it was goodbye. The last HE round had whistled somewhere over their heads and exploded harmlessly in the jungle behind the bungalow. Well, maybe not so harmlessly for that was where Harry's house servants had their quarters. They must be terrified by now. He felt unfamiliarly jittery himself. The odds were enormous. Eight or ten to one after Laura and Jeff were discounted.

The decision to quit the observatory was made for him. Luke smelled the smoke a minute or two after Mike. Then the floor beneath her feet started to get hot.

"We're burning. I think they've set the house on fire."

Luke's emotions were a combination of fear and frustration, with fear predominating. She didn't want to die and felt she might, but—*but*—she also wanted to report this event, get it down on paper. Now *that* wouldn't do her book sales any harm. Always provided she was alive to complete the damned book.

"We'd better get out of here," said Dan. "Leave the Bren mags to me. Bring a rifle."

As with the Bren in the hallway, the magazines were in canvas satchels. Dan slung one over his shoulder and picked up the weapon by its carrying handle. He tried to snap the bipod into place but it was jammed. Damn it, did Harry say these things were checked regularly? And where the hell was the estate militia? Christ, all they had to do was climb into the nearest truck.

The staircase didn't lead anywhere from the hallway except to a storage room and the observatory, which were each entered by a door. Dan didn't remember closing the one to the observatory, but it was shut. When he flung it open he saw tongues of flame leap across the hall from the sitting-room, heading for the open door of the dining-room and the main door, the one off its hinges. Seeking fresh oxygen and other combustible material. Flames also began to lick the foot of the staircase. There was no way he and Luke could gain the verandah without exposing themselves to severe burns at best or providing a sitting target for the gunmen at worst. They would have to make for the back of the house, through the kitchen and out. Or along the corridor that led to the bedrooms and bathrooms. But outside there must surely be other terrorists. Waiting.

"Jesus," he swore.

"Let's leave praying for another day, shall we?" said Luke.

It only took a few strides to reach the hall and turn right for the kitchen, but they felt the fierce heat from the flames and had their hair and eyebrows singed. The fire was out of control. Seconds after entering the kitchen, slamming the door behind them, they heard the sound of ammunition popping. The fire had got as far as the gun rack.

Jess was crouched by the sink. She whipped around as the newcomers burst in. Dan, she was to think afterward, was lucky he was so tall. There were few terrorists his height. Had he been six inches shorter there she might have squeezed the Sten's trigger.

Jessica shone the flashlight in their faces.

"Put that out, for Christ's sake," said Dan.

Jessica did so. She too knew the house was on fire.

"What's happening?" she asked. "Where are Jeff and Laura, Mike and Harry?" There was only a slight quaver in her voice.

Brave woman, thought Dan, recalling how he'd first encountered her on Luke's father's ship all those years ago. A quarter of a century ago, a generation. Meeting Luke too. Bloody strange how, to a large extent, all their lives had been governed by that one voyage, all inextricably intertwined.

He experienced a spasm of alarm. Why weren't Jeff and Laura with Jessica, he wanted to know?

"I left them in the dining-room," said Jessica. "Laura was to look after Jeff. How bad is the fire?"

"Very bad at that end of the house"—Dan gestured—"and spreading rapidly this way. We can't stay here."

Between the dining-room and the kitchen was a corridor that led to the bungalow's six bedrooms on the one side and a small drawing-room, rarely used, on the other. Beyond the drawing-room was an office that Harry occasionally occupied, using it as an auxiliary study. Beyond that there were only gardens and jungle. Intercommunicating doors linked the dining-room with the drawing-room and the drawing-room with the study, and each room could be entered from the corridor also. Dan fervently hoped Laura had kept her head and retreated to at least the drawing-room as soon as the ammunition started cooking-off.

"Take two of the bedrooms overlooking the rear," said Dan to Luke and Jessica. "If the worst comes to the worst, get out any way you can and make for the undergrowth. They'll have men out there for sure, but it's the best I can suggest. I'm going to find out what's happened to Laura and Jeff and then try to give Harry and Mike a hand."

"Hold it," said Luke. She could scarcely see her husband but she sensed where his face was and kissed him on the lips. "I love you, don't forget that."

Moments before the ammunition in the gun rack began exploding, followed shortly by whisky and gin bottles splintering in the heat, the contents feeding the conflagration, Laura had spotted through the open doorway the fire creeping toward them across the hall. Clouds of black smoke obscured everything else. She didn't need Jeff to tell her that they had to retreat ahead of the flames, though for several seconds she was paralyzed with fear, the result of the incessant rifle and machine gun fire as much as the inferno. Was it possible that she had been in Bangkok just a dozen hours ago, and in Europe a dozen hours before that?

With an effort she pulled herself together. They were not going to die, she and Jeff.

She realized she'd spoken aloud.

"Of course we're not," said Jeff confidently, "but I think we should move from here. I'm afraid you'll have to lead the way. Without my stick I'm useless."

Laura took one of Jeff's hands in one of her own and with the other kept a tight grip on the shotgun. They had reached the drawing-room and shut the door behind them before she found she had left the box of 12-bore ammunition behind. Well, she couldn't go back for it. She had no idea where she'd put it down. She had two cartridges in two barrels and they would have to do.

On her hands and knees she rolled up one of the drawing-room's rugs and placed it against the foot of the door as a smoke barrier. Then the corridor door opened and Dan appeared, calling his daughter's name.

"Pop!"

"Are you both all right?" He gave his daughter a swift hug and tapped Jeff reassuringly on the shoulder.

"Nothing wrong that a long cool beer wouldn't cure," said Laura. "What's happening? Can we expect any help?"

Dan told them as much as he knew, adding that they should retreat to the study if the fire breached the drawing-room door. Then he gave them the same advice he had given Luke and Jessica. Wait until the very last moment before leaving the bungalow, when being fried was the only alternative. Then run like hell for the nearest trees. He hesitated before using the word "run." Jeff would find that difficult. Jeff also correctly read the hesitation.

"Don't worry that I'll hold her up," he said, without any hint of irony. "I can sprint with the best of them if there's trouble at my backside."

No one mentioned the obvious, that they would probably be running into a wall of bullets. Out of the fire and into the frying-pan.

Dan recalled a time when he hadn't thought much of Jeff, but he had to admit the man had changed.

"Have you seen anything of Mike?" asked Laura anxiously.

"Not for a while. Keep your heads down. I'm going on to the verandah via this french window. Don't bother to close it. You'll get some illumination from the searchlights."

Dan took a chance by standing up to unfasten the catches of the mosquito screen, unlock the double windows and throw back the shutters. There was less shooting now from the outside, he noticed. Probably for a very good reason. Even fifty men would have limited ammunition and the terrorists would be able to see, as would anyone else with a clear view for about ten miles, that the bungalow was ablaze. They would be conserving what ammunition they had left for the moment the bungalow's occupants had to flee the flames.

With the shutters fully open Dan rolled out on to the verandah. Someone put a few rounds over his head, but they were much too high. Cradling the Bren in his arms and with the satchel of magazines still over his shoulder, he crawled toward Harry, calling his identity in case Harry became nervous and thought he was being attacked from behind. Not that Harry ever got nervous. Dan remembered that from the war. Angry maybe, pissed off. Never nervous.

To Dan's left the flames from the library and the sitting-room and the hall were licking up the outside of the house, toward the observatory and the store room. As well as trying to set the verandah at that end alight.

Harry was crouched on his haunches, the Bren on the balustrade. He'd used up quite a few magazines judging by the empty ones at his feet.

"There are a bunch of them out there," he announced casually, as though directing Dan's attention toward a herd of water buffalo. "Two o'clock. There's a mortar somewhere down there too, but it's been quiet for the last few minutes. What's going on inside and have you seen Mike? I haven't heard a damned thing from that end of the verandah for ages."

Between the verandah and the sandbagged parapet was a three-foot gap, designed like that, as a trench, so that someone, without being exposed, could vault the balustrade and run the length of the house. Except where the steps led up to the front door, there was cover all the way.

After Mike had counted off sixty seconds in his head when he realized he could not extinguish the fire in the library, he concluded that the trench was his last chance. Pausing only to slip on his shirt, he climbed out of the window, crossed the verandah bent double, and leaped over the balustrade. The Sten's sling snagged the woodwork and destroyed his momentum. Instead of making a clean jump he caught his foot and tumbled headlong, colliding with the sandbags and momentarily knocking himself cold. When he recovered consciousness he had no idea how long he had been out, but behind him the bungalow was blazing with demoniacal fury. There was no question about it, they'd better get some help soon. Otherwise they'd all be dead.

While running along the trench to where he could just about make out his father and another figure, probably Dan, he wondered who was out there, out beyond the searchlights. Waiting, waiting. So determined to kill them all. It could even be Hamid, about whom Mike had thought hardly at all for quite a number of years.

At the precise moment Mike was thinking about Hamid, the Eurasian had reached the fringes of the estate and could easily see the conflagration in the middle distance. He had chosen to approach by the drive where, just before he stepped off it and into the rubber trees to skirt the barbed-wire barricade, he could hear the Malay Special Constables chattering excitedly to one another in their sentry-box. He wondered why they were not trying to help the people they were paid to protect. But what could two men do against fifty? They would be hoping that assistance was on the way, which it might well be.

Since leaving Kampong Elok just after dawn Hamid had made excellent headway even though he had been exhausted then and was still exhausted now. He had known from the moment he made a rational estimation of the time it would take that he would not stand a chance of reaching the Camerons' bungalow, and therefore Lee Swee Peng, before the battle began if he was compelled to make the entire journey on foot. He had therefore asked Rihana's father for the use of a small boat or dug-out. There was no shortage of river craft, proas and sampans as well as smaller vessels, and no shortage of offers when it was understood what Hamid intended to do.

Lee Swee Peng had also considered taking his guerrillas by water, to save their legs, before rejecting the notion as too risky. His men would be carrying weapons and ammunition, and the security forces patrolled many stretches of the rivers and sungeis. One man alone, however, would attract little attention. Hamid reluctantly left behind the submachine gun he had taken from Abdullah, arming himself only with a parang.

Elok stood on a tributary of the River Pakelan, and the sungei rose from a spring on Bukit Lamir. The current would take Hamid downstream to the river and thereafter the river in the direction he wished to go. He proposed abandoning the dug-out a few hundred yards before the Pakelan flowed beneath the railway line and the main highway north of Kota Napek. He estimated it would be dark by then, impossible to travel the remaining distance through the jungle. Apart from leaving the road to bypass Kota Napek, he would therefore use the highway as far as the drive of the Cameron estate even though that would mean taking cover in the undergrowth every time a vehicle approached. He calculated he would be in the vicinity of the estate, perhaps even the bungalow, before the attack started. He was out by twenty minutes.

Leaving the sentry-box behind, Hamid rejoined the drive. He slipped the parang from its sheath and carried it in his right hand. He knew Lee Swee Peng's battle plan entailed the guerrillas assaulting the bungalow from the front, shooting and mortaring from the cover of the jungle. He had no idea where he would find the guerrilla leader. He would just have to keep looking and listening until he saw or heard him. One thing was certain: Lee Swee Peng would be somewhere in the vanguard when the moment came to make the final kill.

Hamid wasn't worried that he himself might be seen. In the darkness, he was just one more guerrilla, dressed as they were dressed. No one would be expecting him, and he would allow no one to see his face until he had done what he set out to do.

Rounding the final bend in the drive he saw that the bungalow was ablaze virtually from end to end. The incendiary mortars had done their work. Only the far side of the structure was undamaged and that would be on fire before long. Which was when the occupants would be forced to come out into the open. Which was what Lee Swee Peng was waiting for.

The sudden chatter of several machine guns over to his left made him jump. He mustn't get careless now, he reminded himself.

When the shooting stopped he heard several voices calling to one another from a few feet inside the jungle. Seconds later the searchlights flickered and died. Several came on again, but less than half as many as before. The blaze had evidently severed some of the cables.

Hamid slipped into position behind the guerrillas, far enough away to be invisible if they turned around but close enough to hear what they were saying. He was fluent in the Cantonese dialect they used. From bursts of conversation he understood them to be waiting for Lee Swee Peng to give an order by firing a flare, and that the guerrilla leader was among the trees on the far side of the lawn.

Hamid backtracked, moving on a diagonal behind the guerrillas until he reached the jungle fringes facing the lawn, with the bungalow now above him to his right. When he was outside the glare thrown by the searchlights, he ran across the lawn to the far side.

Harry cursed when the lights went out and heaved a sigh of relief when at least some of them were re-illuminated. But those few wouldn't last much longer if he were any judge. Nor would the bungalow.

He began to worry about Jessica. Perhaps it was poor strategy to leave his wife and Luke in the back bedrooms.

"Bloody searchlights are doing us more harm than good anyway," grunted Dan. "They're not going to come at us while they're on. At this rate we'll be hamburger before we get a decent shot in."

On Dan's left Mike rubbed his forehead where he had hit it against the sandbags. It didn't feel like much, just a small bump, but he'd clobbered himself hard enough to cause a ringing in his ears. Except it wasn't a ringing. It sounded more like a car horn.

A moment later he realized that that was exactly what it was, and no figment of his imagination. Above the intermittent gunfire and the crackle of the bungalow burning, he could definitely hear it. Maybe more than one, and coming from the direction of the drive.

"Listen!"

They listened. And saw.

Behind the trees that lined the drive, headlights were probing the night air.

"And about bloody time too," said Harry, thumping the balustrade with excitement. Whether it was his own militia or police or troops didn't matter. Someone was coming to help them and making a lot of noise to announce their arrival. A minute or two and they'd be here.

"They'll have heard it too," said Dan. "They'll throw in everything now."

As if to confirm his prediction a green flare suddenly rose in a gentle arc. From their right, two o'clock. Then came the whistle of mortars. One . . . two . . . three. . . . Close. Too damned close.

The mortars were high-explosive. Two went wide. Or rather overshot, landing in parts of the bungalow already in ruins. Perversely, the third fell short. Fragments of shrapnel blasted in the french windows of the study that overlooked the side of the house.

Laura and Jeff were in the study when the explosion happened.

Obeying her father to the letter, Laura had shepherded Jeff into the furthermost room when not only had the drawing-room caught fire but falling timber and masonry from the upper storey seemed likely to kill them before the flames and smoke did.

Doing her utmost to keep the panic from her voice, she discussed with Jeff the advisability of retreating to the back of the house, to the bedrooms where Luke and Jessica were and which might not, as yet, be ablaze. But the moment she put her hand on the corridor door, she had to snatch it away. The handle was red-hot. The corridor was on fire also.

Leaving Jeff crouched behind a table, Laura went across to the french windows. There were two sets in this room. One led out to the verandah, the other to the side of the bungalow. Through these would be safer.

They were locked but the bolts were on the inside. The heavy shutters, however, were fastened with a padlock and there was no sign of a key. Because this room was used only rarely, Harry took no chances on the shutters being left open by mistake.

Almost weeping with frustration Laura peered around her in the darkness for something heavy with which to smash open the shutters. Then she remembered the shotgun. She would shoot the padlock off—except she had put down the 12-bore when trying the corridor door and could not recall where she had left it.

She came away from the window.

"Is the shotgun . . . ?" she started to ask, which was when the mortar detonated.

The blast flung her across the room.

Hamid was upsides of the summerhouse, keeping in the shadows of the jungle but heading toward the bungalow, when he heard the distant wail of the klaxon. There were other guerrillas around him, some within touching distance, but none of them paid him the slightest attention. Most had stopped shooting and were talking anxiously among themselves. The significance of the klaxon and, now, the sight of headlights coming along the drive was apparent. Even as he stood there one or two groups were starting to withdraw deeper into the jungle. None of the voices he heard was that of Lee Swee Peng.

When the flare was fired the man with the pistol was some fifty yards in front of Hamid and making for the side of the bungalow, where the machine guns on the verandah would be unable to traverse and reach him but where he would be within grenade-throwing range. Hamid deduced that the figure was Lee Swee Peng or, if not, that he would be close by.

Then the mortars exploded and everyone ducked.

Behind Harry, Dan and Mike the drawing-room and part of the small study were on fire and the heat on their backs becoming unbearable. It was time to move and the only way was forward.

"Go out, damn you, go out," Mike heard his father muttering and thought he had become deranged until he understood that Harry was willing the last of the searchlights' cables to rupture.

"Into the trench," said Harry. "It'll give us another minute. And pour everything you've got at them."

Although he was fifteen years older than Dan and over thirty older than Mike, Harry was the first to straddle the balustrade and drop in behind the sandbags, tossing the Bren and the spare ammunition in ahead of him.

Jessica and Luke were in the same bedroom, crouched either side of the same window, which was wide open in spite of the potential dangers from a hand grenade because the room was rapidly filling with smoke.

They heard the racket being made by the klaxon, and saw the glare of headlights drawing closer. Then two figures emerged from the undergrowth, shortly joined by a third and fourth. They huddled together, arguing in high-pitched voices.

Luke raised the rifle to her shoulder, not entirely sure she could shoot another human being whatever the circumstances.

Jessica put her hand out and made Luke lower the muzzle.

"They can't know we're here," she murmured.

After a further urgent discussion the four men ran off. They were, it seemed, the only terrorists at the back of the house.

"But we'll give it a little longer," said Jessica. "We can afford another minute."

Luke found it impossible to stop her hands shaking.

"I think you just saved my soul," she said.

There was no doubt about it now. One of the figures in a group of half a dozen was Lee Swee Peng. Hamid could hear him calling almost hysterically for just one more effort, though the other five men seemed reluctant to press home the attack now that the headlights were less than a hundred yards away. More than one truck by the look of it.

The nearest guerrilla to Lee Swee Peng tried arguing the wisdom of staying any longer. Much of the attack had been a success. The Cameron house was destroyed. Why risk capture or death?

Lee Swee Peng shot him from close range. Amid the bedlam a few more bullets went unnoticed. The other guerrillas withdrew slowly, muttering mutinously among themselves and keeping their weapons trained on their leader. They were unwilling to kill him unless he tried to kill them, but they were also unwilling to die pointlessly for him. No doubt there would come a day of reckoning if Lee Swee Peng survived, but it seemed preferable to face that than almost certain annihilation.

Alone, Lee Swee Peng glared about him, perhaps also wondering, Hamid conjectured, whether he was being wise. Then he saw Hamid. Or rather, he saw someone who hadn't run with the others.

"You! Come here!"

Hamid obeyed, trotting forward as if eager to do his leader's bidding. He would have one chance and no more. Lee Swee Peng would not hesitate to use the submachine gun.

When close enough, Hamid launched himself at the Chinese. The blade of his parang flashed in the firelight. If the blow had connected, Lee Swee Peng would have been headless.

But the blow did not connect. Lee Swee Peng recognized his assailant at the last moment and raised the Sterling like a quarterstaff to ward off the attack. Metal clashed on metal and both men fell to the ground. Hamid emerged on top but without the parang, lost in the fall.

They struggled for possession of the Sterling, both pairs of hands gripping the stock and barrel. Lee Swee Peng was strong but Hamid had hate and revenge on his side. He straddled the guerrilla leader's chest and bore down on the submachine gun, desperately pushing it against Lee Swee Peng's throat, into the flesh, attempting to crack the windpipe.

The Chinese let go of the weapon and clawed for Hamid's eyes. Hamid leaned back, out of reach, and continued to press down with all the strength he could muster until he heard something break. And then the death rattle, a peculiar sound that was half gurgle, half sigh.

The body beneath him went limp but Hamid kept up the pressure. Lee Swee Peng had had it too easy. He should have suffered more.

Momentarily Hamid was insane.

Finally he rolled off the corpse and lay still, breathing heavily. The stench of bodily wastes pervaded his nostrils, and he was sick.

Afterward he looked around until he found his parang. On all sides now men were shouting and shots were being fired. It was hard to make out who was who, but dimly he perceived uniforms and knew he was in grave danger.

He made for the rear of the house. He knew this area well, better than most. He wouldn't escape via the immediate jungle as the others were doing. Six hundred yards further on lay Mahal Rumah. Beyond Mahal Rumah, at the end of a trail familiar to him since he was a boy, was the kampong he had grown up in. He would hide out until dawn and make for there. Someone might remember him and offer him aid. Even if they wouldn't he knew places where the finest fish were to be caught. He wouldn't go hungry. He would rest up for a day and a night and then return to Elok. Rihana's father had a right to know that his daughter had been avenged.

As he passed the study windows that had been destroyed by the third mortar, the last cable burned through and the remaining searchlights went out. But it was not that which caused Hamid to halt. From the blazing room he heard a man's voice. It was raised and anxious but not panicking.

"Can someone help us, please? I can't see. Is anyone there? Can someone help us, please?"

A few feet beyond the windows and silhouetted against the flames, the man who was speaking was carrying a woman in his arms. He was standing stock still as if paralyzed. What did he mean, he couldn't see? And why didn't he get out of the house, Hamid wondered, before understanding instinctively that the man was Jeff Cameron. Who was blind.

Self-preservation shrieked at Hamid to ignore the cry for help.

"Tuan Jeff," he said, the old-fashioned courtesy sounding strange in his ears after all the years that had passed.

"Who's that?"

"Hamid."

It took a moment to sink in. So it was Hamid who had destroyed the house, and who would no doubt destroy him.

"Don't be alarmed," said Hamid, stepping in through the shattered windows. The heat was unbelievable. "I won't harm you. Can the memsahib walk?"

"No. I don't think she's badly hurt but she's unconscious."

"Let me take her. You hold on to my shirt. Be careful here, there's a drop."

Carrying Laura, Hamid led Jeff away from the house, wondering how far would be safe. A few more feet. Just a few more feet. Over his shoulder a burning beam crashed into the study.

He lay Laura gently on the ground. She stirred. She would be all right, he thought.

A uniformed policeman ran around the corner of the bungalow and saw the trio.

"Halt!" he yelled in Cantonese and English.

Hamid heard a rifle bolt click.

"I must leave you now," he said to Jeff. "You're out of danger. Stay where you are and someone will soon be with you."

Hamid sprinted toward the back of the house. Fifty yards and he'd be out of the firelight. Fifty yards after that and no one would find him.

"Halt or I shoot!" Again the command was issued in Cantonese and English.

The first shot whistled over Hamid's head.

"Don't shoot, don't shoot!" he heard Tuan Jeff shout. "He's a friend. He helped us."

But the rifleman chose to pay no attention. The fleeing man was dressed like a terrorist.

He took greater care with his second shot. It hit Hamid between the shoulder blades and penetrated a lung, but his momentum carried him forward for a few more strides. Far enough, anyway, for a third shot to strike him in the neck. A lucky shot, although the rifleman would take credit for superior marksmanship when he made his report.

Hamid fell. He tried to crawl but found he couldn't. Dimly he heard Tuan Jeff shout again. "He's a friend."

Was a friend, he thought the moment before he died. Was.

22

The embers burned for days. Even after several torrential downpours, smoke still rose from the ruins.

Harry rewarded a young European clerk, Eric Jennings, and his Indian assistant, Irfan Ajeeb, with an extra month's paid leave, starting immediately, and air tickets to wherever they wanted to go. They were the two men on duty in the estate office the night of the attack and had contacted the police at Ruang and Kota Napek by wireless before rounding up the militia. To give the impression there were more of them than was the case, they had used three trucks. Fortuitously they met up with the Ruang convoy on the edge of the estate.

It had all taken far too long, Jennings apologized. They would try to do better next time. Harry told him not to worry but pray there would not be a next time.

Jennings took his leave in England. Cannily, Irfan Ajeeb cashed in his ticket and went nowhere, saving the money.

The estate casualties had been light. The house servants, though terrified in their quarters when the mortar barrage began, suffered none. Only the two guards in the summerhouse bunker had been killed, taken out by grenades early on before they could fire a shot. Although he recognized that it was inadequate, Harry awarded their families a pension.

"You're a lucky man," Bill Hyde's replacement told Harry.

Apart from minor burns, delayed shock, and the after-effects of inhaling smoke, none of the Europeans with the exception of Laura had been hurt. Dan's daughter had back injuries from flying glass, and other cuts and bruises. She was in Sandwood Lodge and would remain there a week.

She knew that it was Hamid who had probably saved her life and Jeff's at the cost of his own, and had been told, because now seemed the right time if she was to become a member of the family, the true story of Hamid's parentage. As had Luke. Harry left nothing out, including his killing of Hamid's father.

Luke winced when she realized she was sitting on one of the scoops of her career and would be unable to use it. But she accepted that. Some things were better left unsaid.

As well as Lee Swee Peng and Hamid, the security forces found six other bodies scattered around the estate, one of whom Lee Swee Peng had shot. They were puzzled at the manner of the guerrilla leader's death, but there was no one alive to tell them what actually happened. Besides, they had more important things to deal with. A major terrorist gang had been broken up, its members fleeing in all directions. They had to be hunted down.

Hamid's body had been taken away with the others. To the security forces he was a terrorist and would be interred as such. He might have saved a life, two lives, for reasons they did not understand, but there had been a price on his head since 1948.

Dan found it hard to rationalize his feelings concerning Hamid. He had killed Barbara but saved Laura's life. None of the Camerons knew what to think. Hamid was Jenny's flesh and blood and had led Jeff to safety; he was also a murderer and would be buried as one.

"He was a victim," Harry said eventually. "As much a victim of the times and of Malaya as any of us are."

The Camerons were staying at Mahal Rumah for the moment. Harry was unsure whether he wanted to rebuild. He had half a mind to quit, leave the country for good.

"You can't," said Jessica. "Your roots are here and you'd be miserable anywhere else. Dan's staying on, he and Luke. Laura's made it clear that she'll live wherever Mike wants to. And Mike wants to live here. There's also Jenny. She wouldn't run. Didn't."

"And I thought you were a hard-bitten old woman."

"You don't know me."

"We'll put it to a vote," said Harry.

"Rebuild," said Jessica.

"Rebuild," said Mike.

"Rebuild definitely," said Jeff.

"Okay," said Harry, "we'll rebuild. But this time we'll add on another storey. It's been a bungalow since my grandfather's days, and I've a hankering in my old age to climb a few stairs to go to bed."

Epilogue

August 31, 1957

It was the day of Merdeka, and a public holiday. In Kuala Lumpur the Head of State and the new Cabinet had been sworn in. Tonight there was to be a huge water pageant in the lake gardens.

The Duke of Gloucester, the Queen's representative, had said in a speech, referring to Malaya: "A jewel is beautiful in itself, but far more beautiful when it is set and mounted in gold."

Listening to the radio on the verandah of Mahal Rumah, Jessica rather agreed with that sentiment.

Further along the verandah Luke was discussing some aspect of the evening's menu with Laura. Independence could not be allowed to pass without a party, and the Holdens had invited twenty guests. Jess hoped her head was up to it.

Behind Laura, Mike was talking to Dan, but he had his arm around Laura's waist and every so often ran his fingers through her hair. Knowing Mike, thought Jess, they'd probably steal away and get married without so much as a word to anyone. Oh well, perhaps that was the way it had to be.

On the lawn Jeff was talking sternly to his seeing-eye dog, whose name was Billy. It didn't appear to be doing much good, for Billy, far from being chastened, jumped up and nuzzled Jeff's face. It was a policy of the establishment from which Billy came to allow the dog time at home with its future master before training was over, to get it accustomed to its new surroundings. Training would not be complete much before Christmas. Jeff was returning to Singapore on Monday with the dog. Harry was going with them and thereafter flying to Kuala Lumpur where he had a meeting with the new education ministry. He wanted permission to set up a number of primary schools on the estate, where rural Malays could get enough of an education to prepare them for secondary school.

Jessica wondered where her husband was. She hadn't seen him for an hour, but as it was almost dusk she thought she could guess.

After calling along the verandah, "I'll see you later," she drove, because it was so hot and she was feeling her years, the six hundred yards to where the new house was going up on the foundations of the old. They were working fast. About the time Jeff and his dog were fully partnered, the house should be ready.

Harry was where she had suspected he would be, at the foot of the flagstaff. As she watched he lowered the Union Jack for the last time. She remained motionless. This was a private moment. His.

After he had folded the flag and tucked it under his arm, he saw Jessica standing in the shadows. Wordlessly he went over to her. Then together they walked back to the car.